THE SONGBIRD

A WORLD WAR TWO NOVEL

STACY LYNN MILLER

SEVERN RIVER
PUBLISHING

Severn River Publishing
www.SevernRiverBooks.com

ISBN: 978-1-64875-612-2 (Paperback)

ALSO BY STACY LYNN MILLER

Hattie James WWII Novels

The Songbird

The Rio Affair

The Secret War

Lexi Mills Thrillers

Fuze

Proximity

Impact

Pressure

Remote

Flashpoint

To find out more about Stacy Lynn Miller and her books, visit severnriverbooks.com

To Leslie and Allison.
My daughters and keepers of my heart.
They teach me every day that love is unconditional and enduring.

1

Washington, DC, December 23, 1940

Karl James thought he had more time, but the sound of a door opening meant he had to hurry. The secure office suite at the State Department was typically unoccupied after midnight, except for the diehards like himself, who had no one to go home to and preferred solitude over companionship when he wasn't doting over his grandkids. He couldn't turn on another light without alerting whoever had come onto the floor, so he relied on the dim desk lamp to complete his task.

Glancing again at the sheet of paper on his desk, he ensured he'd gotten the spelling correct for the city associated with the last name on the lists from the classified folder. His German heritage and the four years he'd spent there on a diplomatic posting had done little to improve his spelling of German towns, yet he could remember the combination of dots and dashes that made up every letter, number, and symbol in Morse code. His mind worked oddly sometimes, but his penchant for numbers and patterns had served him well, especially tonight when time was short.

Karl placed the final dot within the musical staff of the last piece of sheet music and shoved the stack into his satchel. The sound of footsteps in the hallway meant he had seconds to cover his tracks, or else he would be caught with his hand where it wasn't supposed to be. He snatched the official folder containing the list of names and cities from his desk and dashed to the open high-security file safe. After returning the file to its precise home, he closed the drawer, spun the dial, and retraced his steps to his desk when the overhead lights turned on.

Karl stretched and yawned before turning off the lamp and glancing over his shoulder. The roaming security guard was making his rounds. "Evening, Simon."

"Working late on the floor tonight, Mr. James?"

"Just finishing up some paperwork and leaving it for my secretary."

"It's Christmas Eve tomorrow. Couldn't it wait until after the holiday?"

"You know diplomats, Simon. Nothing can wait." Karl threw on his winter coat and grabbed his satchel. "Walk out with me?"

"Sure thing, Mr. James."

They exited the office suite and took the elevator down, chatting about the expected foul weather for Christmas Day. "I hope to be at my daughter's place in Alexandria, drinking hot cocoa and watching my grandkids open presents," Karl said, stepping into the grand first-floor lobby adorned with shiny marble floors, classical stone accents formed into faux Greek columns, and limestone statuary he'd never cared to inspect in his three and a half decades with the Department. "How about you, Simon?"

"The morning shift here. Then hopefully ham and candied yams for dinner at home."

"That's a shame, working on Christmas." Karl approached the security guard at the exit and placed his bag on the inspection table.

The guard inspected the case and asked, "Sheet music?"

"It's a present for my daughter, the singer," Karl said, hoping the man wasn't a musician and didn't look too closely. But Karl had been careful, blending the series of dots and dashes into the staffs to make them appear to be printing imperfections. Only a trained eye by someone who had spent a lifetime studying music could note the difference.

The guard nodded, returning Karl's satchel. "Ahh, Hattie. Hope she enjoys it."

"I'm sure she will." Karl wished both guards a Merry Christmas and walked out, flipping up the collar of his wool coat to combat the night's wintery air. Instead of going straight to his car, he went to the corner phone booth, stepping carefully so as not to slip on the scraped remains of the afternoon's snow. He put in a dime after lifting the receiver. "Overland four-two-two-one-five."

"One moment, please," the operator said.

The professor was a sound sleeper and could sleep through a fire alarm, so Karl let the call ring ten times before he considered hanging up. He prepared to hang up on the eleventh but heard the call connect.

"What the hell time is it?" the woman groused.

"Late, Professor. It's Karl."

"Why on earth are you calling in the middle of the night?" she asked, sounding more awake and agreeable.

"It's too hot, so I'm leaving the package with Songbird." Karl checked his surroundings and hid his face when a set of headlights drove by, illuminating the phone booth.

"When?"

"Tomorrow."

"Be careful, Karl." Emotion cut through her voice. She had taken him under her wing years ago, teaching him everything she knew about this business, and a close bond had developed between them. "Trust no one."

"I hate doing this." He sighed, feeling the crush of the vise. Rogue elements from both sides were closing in, and it was only a matter of time before he was caught.

"Until you can find the mole, you need to survive. This is your insurance."

He paused, thinking of how many people he trusted blindly in this world besides his children and could only name one. "I'm grateful you're in my corner, Professor."

"Gratitude is not only the greatest of virtues but the parent of all the others."

"You are the only person I know who can find a Cicero quote for any occasion," he said.

"His wisdom is timeless," she said.

"I can't disagree. I just hope I can get through this." Karl had gotten in deep and, at times, thought he was in over his head. However, things were already in motion and could not be stopped.

"Do I have to remind you about Cicero's take on facing challenges?"

Karl sighed. "I remember. The greater the difficulty, the greater the glory." However, he wasn't doing this for the glory. All he knew was that his country needed him to find the traitor in the War Department. He hung up, hoping he was doing the right thing.

New York City, the following day

Karl stepped away from his meeting, pondering the same question he'd asked himself for years: Who was the real enemy? After everything he'd done and sacrificed for his country, he had plenty of candidates to choose from, some more obvious than others. However, tonight, he considered himself his own worst enemy. Who in his right mind would agree to a meeting on Christmas Eve? His consolation was knowing the lists would soon be in safe hands and he'd be ringing in the holiday with the daughter he adored and whose love and respect he valued most.

Hailing a cab two blocks from the consulate while standing in the frigid New York City night air, he cursed under his breath for needing to coddle a demanding British diplomat's well-developed sense of self-importance when they both should have been sipping eggnog with family. He longed for his simple and innocent early days with the State Department when all he did was process visas. Tonight, he loathed his current duties as the senior cleanup man for every diplomat's son or wife who couldn't hold their liquor. But as he was instructed, Karl would see that this man's son, picked up for drunk driving and assaulting a police officer two days ago, could stay in the country to graduate from high school and start Harvard next fall. However, he'd be damned before lifting a finger the next time the entitled brat landed in a holding cell.

"Where to, Mac?" the stubble-faced cabby asked as Karl slid into the back seat of his well-kept taxi. The sweet smell of his cigar filled the compartment.

"Ten East Sixtieth Street." Karl leaned back, adjusting his wool overcoat across his lap and placing his satchel on the bench seat beside him for the mile drive.

The cabby maneuvered in the thick holiday traffic, filled with businessmen in hats and long wool coats, picking up last-minute gifts and rushing home to their families. The taxi stopped at the canopy-covered entrance. A doorman dressed in a light-gray uniform and matching Pershing hat opened the passenger door, inviting him onto the welcoming red carpet. Karl smiled with fatherly pride, reading the A-frame sign near the building's entrance, announcing the night's performance: The Copacabana Club Presents Hattie James.

He paid for his fare, slipping his driver an extra five-spot and wishing him well through the holidays. The cabby's eyes danced with surprise. "And a very merry Christmas to you, mista." Any man who worked late on Christmas Eve deserved a tip large enough to compensate for not being home when his kids went to bed.

As the taxi drove away, a second uniformed club employee greeted Karl with a warm smile and opened the heavy wood door. "Welcome to the Copacabana. Enjoy your evening, sir."

"I'm sure I will."

Karl descended the stairs to the basement. The thumping sound of drums and a muffled voice coming through the loudspeakers drew him in. Once at the bottom, the room's ambiance instantly transported him to a dimly lit Brazilian paradise. Pillars in the large, packed club were decorated in white plaster to resemble palm tree trunks with fronds sprouting from them to cover the ceiling in a tropical canopy. The sea of tables flowed onto the dance floor, full of patrons drinking, eating, smoking, and focusing on the performance.

Hattie's mesmerizing voice drew Karl's attention to the ample stage, and his eyes misted with love and pride. The full band behind her kept the beat as she stood center on the elevated platform, caressing the microphone. Karl hated to think it, but it was as if she were making love to it to seduce every man in the room. Her mother did the same thing, which he supposed was why they were both so popular. He scanned the room of patrons. Most men had their eyes glued to her as if hoping to take her home for the night, and Karl would have broken a few bones if they tried.

The head server asked him if it would be a table for one, to which Karl gave an affirming nod. A tuxedo-clad twenty-something escorted him through the dining room, passing several scantily clad women in matching tropical-themed outfits, selling cigarettes and cigars from a tray strapped around their necks.

They stopped at a small table barely large enough for a cocktail glass and dinner plate near a palm tree pillar. "Sorry, sir," his escort said. "Pickings are slim this time of night."

"No worries." Karl slipped the man a dollar before he scurried off. He then removed his overcoat and placed his satchel under the table.

This seat was perfect. It offered a full view of the stage but was far enough away so Hattie wouldn't see him with the spotlights in her eyes. He long suspected she held back when he was in the audience, and he wanted to watch his daughter in her natural environment, lost in the music, not worried about what her father might think of her seductive performance.

Song after song, Hattie played to the crowd, emphasizing her exceptional looks and perfect shape with a tight dress that revealed a little too much leg for Karl's comfort when she crossed the stage. However, he liked the curls she'd added to her long, dark-blond hair. She reminded him so much of her mother when Eva was thirty-one. Their singing careers had taken off at the same age, though Hattie's was on an even higher trajectory. The whistles, hoots, and applause supported what he already knew—she was a star in her own right, not merely the daughter of Eva Machado.

When she finally left the stage to a standing ovation following two encore songs, Karl left cash for his drinks, grabbed his coat and satchel, and weaved through the tables to the stage side entrance, where a muscular man guarded the door and put up a stopping hand. "Sorry, Mac. Employees only."

Karl reached into the breast pocket of his jacket and handed him a business card with his name and title at the State Department. "Can you tell Hattie her father is here and would like to see her?"

The man narrowed his eyes at him before disappearing behind the door. He returned minutes later and pointed down the brightly lit, tiled corridor. "Last dressing room on the left."

"Thank you." Karl adjusted his overcoat draped over his right arm and gripped his satchel tighter in his left hand. He dodged several pieces of stage equipment and band members lounging in upright chairs with cigarettes and refreshments. One he recognized as Hattie's piano player from his previous visit locked eyes with him and fixed his stare until Karl passed and reached the door. Though temporary, the sign with Hattie's name over a glittered star made him smile.

Karl knocked and waited for the muffled invitation before entering.

Hattie beamed at his reflection in her dressing mirror. "Father." She bounced from her chair, spun around, and hugged him, wrapping both arms around his neck.

He tightened his right arm around her. "Sweetheart."

"I didn't know you were in the city."

"More babysitting." Karl loosened his hold and dropped his things, draping his coat over the arm of the small sofa and setting his satchel on the floor against the side of it.

"On Christmas Eve? I thought you would be in Virginia with Liv and the kids."

"You know how it goes. Diplomats think they're more important than my spending the holiday with the grandkids." He turned around to find she'd formed fists and placed them on her hips, arms akimbo—her fighting-mad stance.

"Don't they all?" Hattie rightly rolled her eyes.

He snickered, holding her at arm's length. "And that will never change." He'd spent most of her life complaining about the common trait among diplomats assigned to the United States—a strong sense of entitlement. "Since I was in town, I thought I'd take my favorite girl out for a bite before asking to flop in your guest room for the night. Every hotel I called was booked solid."

Her soft grin said she would like nothing better. "Give me a few minutes to change."

"Of course." He kissed her on the cheek, grabbed his things, and waited in the hallway. The piano player who had eyed him earlier resumed his territory-marking stare, but Karl stifled a laugh, donning his winter coat and keeping to himself.

Minutes later, Hattie emerged from her dressing room, wearing a long blue-green wool overcoat with the curls brushed out of her hair. "Ready?"

"You look beautiful, sweetheart." Karl offered his arm and escorted her down the corridor until the intrusive piano player stepped into his path, forcing him to stop.

"Father, this is David Townsend. He's my . . . We're . . ."

"Dating." Karl finished her sentence and extended his hand. "Karl James. I'm Hattie's father."

"Pleased to finally meet you, sir." David shook his hand with an extra-firm grip. Karl understood the need to make a good first impression, but this was over the top, as if he were compensating for something. Karl's first positive impression of his skills as a musician didn't extend to his opinion of him as a self-assured man.

"I'm sure." Karl patted Hattie's hand folded over his arm, keeping his stare squarely on David. "I hope I didn't dash your evening plans, but I'm staying the night with Hattie."

Hattie squeezed her arm against him, signaling him to behave. "I'm sorry, David, but I have to cancel tonight. Father came to town unexpectedly."

"Of course." David kissed Hattie on the cheek. "I'll check in with you after the holiday."

Karl ushered her down the hallway, waving a hand over his head. "Good man."

Hours later, following a late-night meal at a twenty-four-hour café, Hattie let Karl into her Lennox Hill third-floor brownstone apartment. It hadn't changed since his previous visit over the summer, a promising sign that David hadn't made himself at home. It was tasteful with some signs of splurging, but nothing too lavish. He was glad to see her spoiling herself with her hard-earned money, even a little.

After he removed his coat, Hattie hung it on the stand next to the door. He placed his satchel next to her couch and plopped down, tired from the trip and wine from dinner. "So, you and David. He doesn't seem your type."

She dropped on the cushion beside him, appearing as tired as he felt. "Oh? What *is* my type?"

David was of average height and had unremarkable looks and could easily be lost in a crowd. The only thing going for him was his superior piano skills. Karl had to admit that even his ex-wife, who now taught music, would have been impressed.

"I don't know," Karl said. "I picture you with someone a bit more athletic or fair-haired, but especially someone more self-assured, like that Roger fellow you dated two summers ago."

"You mean like you." Hattie laughed. "I hate to disappoint you, Father, but I do not possess a feminine Oedipus attitude toward you."

"The way you and your mother compete against one another, it's a natural conclusion."

"I do not compete with her."

He bellowed a full, hearty laugh.

"I use her as motivation."

"One and the same in my estimation."

"There's a big difference, Father." Hattie sighed, pushed up from the couch, signaling he'd pushed one of her buttons, and went to the kitchen. He knew she could only stomach her mother once a year during her summer visits. When Eva wasn't trying to make nice with Hattie, she relived the highlights of her decades-long stardom as a singer.

When she didn't return immediately, Karl followed, finding her leaning against the sink with both palms. "I'm sorry, sweetheart. I know you don't like talking about your mother."

"After what she did to you, I wanted nothing to do with her and still don't."

Karl leaned a shoulder against the doorframe, worried she would never find it in herself to forgive Eva. "That was almost twelve years ago. It's time to let the past be."

"You weren't the one to catch her in bed with another man. Other than singing, I never want to be anything like her. She cares only for herself."

Seeing her this angry for this long broke his heart. Yes, he was upset when he learned of Eva's infidelity, but he also blamed himself. He wasn't the same man when he married her, and his job had pulled him away from home for long periods. It was only a matter of time before one of them strayed. She merely had the first opportunity.

"To be fair," he said, "Eva was never cut out to be a housewife. She thrived in the limelight. She was, though, an exceptional mother, teaching you and Olivia how to be strong, independent women and never be satisfied with the status quo. I will always be grateful for her giving me two incredible daughters." He approached her and placed a hand on her shoulder. "Let's not ruin the holiday by arguing. I have to catch the morning train to DC from Penn Station."

Hattie wiped her eyes and turned. "You're right. I have a present for you." She gestured for him to follow her to the living room. She disappeared to the back of the apartment for a moment, returning with a potted plant. "I was going to bring it with me on the train for my visit on Sunday, but since you're here, you might as well enjoy it on Christmas."

Karl inspected the plant and smiled. "Edelweiss. My favorite. But I thought it wouldn't grow in DC."

"The florist said as long as you're a few miles from the Potomac, it should be fine. Since you moved to Alexandria to be closer to Olivia, I thought this was the perfect gift."

"It is perfect, sweetheart. Thank you." After kissing her cheek, Karl placed the plant on the coffee table and opened his satchel. From beneath his change of clothing and toiletries, he fished out a package wrapped in holiday paper. "I have something for you as well."

"Thank you, Father."

As she opened the gift and leafed through the collection of old and contemporary sheet music, he hoped she would not notice the alterations he'd made to them last night. "Each of these songs holds special meaning to me." He explained how they brought back childhood memories from his youth in Germany or a recollection of something significant or whimsical he recently experienced. "I want you to never sell them or throw them away. Can you promise that?"

"Of course, Father. I'll treasure them."

The next morning, on Christmas Day, Hattie said goodbye to her father at the train station. Karl placed his cherished Edelweiss plant on the seat beside him and leaned back for the four-hour ride home, thinking again about the question that had plagued him for years. Who was the real enemy? In his other job, not the one at the State Department, he'd learned to trust no one, especially his superiors. One of them was a mole, and his task was to surface him or her. He had only his instincts to rely on and hoped he had done the right thing by giving Hattie the sheet music. If anyone knew what he'd hidden in the staffs, she would be in mortal danger, but considering what was at stake, he had to take the risk.

2

New York City, January 1941, twenty-four days later

The smell of sweat and stale cigarette smoke overpowered the RCA recording studio. The band members were on the far side of the room, warming up by tuning their instruments and stretching their muscles in advance of a long session. Hattie was at the microphone, reviewing the new sheet music that had arrived from the printer hours earlier. She was elated over the slate of songs for her next record, scheduled for release in early May—a duet with the incredible Maggie Moore. Two sound engineers, a producer, and a handful of looky-loos packed the booth on the other side of the glass wall. One of those onlookers was Hattie's agent, who appeared angry—his default state. As long as he didn't extend that look to Hattie, she appreciated the intimidation tactics he used to get her better contracts and singing gigs.

David finished running his chords on the piano and joined Hattie near the microphone. "She's late."

"She'll be here. Maggie is waiting to make a dramatic entrance."

"I know you trust her"—David shook his head while rubbing the back of his neck; he was worried—"but word around the studio among the musicians is that she's a true diva and puts everyone behind schedule."

"Don't worry, I'll handle her." Hattie was raised by a diva and was accustomed to playing off their vanity to get what she wanted, but Maggie was a piker compared to her mother.

He kissed her on the cheek. "I hope you know what you're doing."

So did Hattie. Maggie Moore was wild and loved her liquor. Collaborating with her would test Hattie's sobriety, but she had no choice. Once an RCA executive saw a picture of Hattie and Maggie together at the Copacabana opening, he insisted on pairing up his top two female recording artists for a duet record and promoting it with joint performances at the club. Maggie was already a household name, and Hattie's hit song this summer had put her on the same track.

Hattie would have to summon every bit of strength while working with Maggie. She didn't like the person she'd become when she was drinking heavily, especially after heartbreak. Her tendency to avoid conflict by walking away became prominent in her teen years from living with her mother, and booze had become the ultimate avoidance crutch as an adult. She could forget everything wrong in her life for the night, but then came the horrible hangovers. Just when she started making a name for herself, they made her forgetful, zapped her energy, and made her voice croaky for hours. Giving up drinking was her only hope of making it big. And her father was right. She needed to prove to herself that she was better than her mother, which meant staying sober.

Maggie Moore entered the recording studio only five minutes late with her agent and personal assistant in tow. She went directly to Hattie, kissing her on the cheek, their customary greeting. "Sorry I'm late, darling, but my hair wouldn't cooperate today."

If she'd stop bleaching it regularly, perhaps her hair would be more amenable to her schedule. But Hattie liked Maggie as a blond, not a natural redhead. The lighter color suited her hazel eyes and pale complexion.

"No worries. You're here now and look gorgeous. I'd say it was time well spent."

A smile crept onto Maggie's lips as she fluffed her hair. "Well then. We better get to it."

"Before I forget," Hattie said. "The club manager asked us to extend the show tonight by fifteen minutes to accommodate a late-arriving VIP."

"He better spend a bundle in the club, then."

"Do you have any ideas for songs?" Hattie asked.

"I've always wanted to sing 'Cheek to Cheek' with you." Maggie added a wink. "Other than that, surprise me. I'll fake it."

Hattie took in a rattled breath. If Maggie only knew how attractive Hattie found her and how distracted she would be on stage, she might reconsider, but Hattie was all in. She turned to David. "Do you have sheet music for it?"

David scratched his jawline. "No, but I think I saw it in the stack your father gave you for Christmas."

"That's right." Hattie snapped her fingers. "I'll bring the collection. We can go with only piano for that song."

In two hours, they'd practiced and recorded three songs, a long one for the A side and two shorter ones for the B side. Each had a unique melody and hook in the chorus to make them guaranteed hits on the radio. The producer and their agents appeared happy from behind the glass, and the RCA executive patted them on the back for a job well done.

Later that night at the Copacabana, Hattie and Maggie sang to a packed house of patrons thirsty to see RCA's two most prominent female recording artists on one stage. The VIP had arrived halfway through the set of songs Hattie had arranged. When Gerald Reed, a New York Stock Exchange seat holder and one of the city's most influential men, and his guests sat at his reserved table in the front row, Hattie froze at seeing his petite blond daughter with him. Helen Reed was the ultimate heartbreak, with her perfect curves, sexy walk, alluring eyes, and inability to remain monogamous.

Flashes of passion-filled nights between Hattie and Helen kept Hattie glued in place until Maggie moved side by side with her and elbowed her in the ribs. Maggie's concerned look knocked Hattie from her daze, and they finished the song as choreographed. Hattie kept her eye on Helen for the rest of the show, enduring her smiles and subtle flirtations with the young man on her left—the decoration for her father's sake—and put on the performance of her life to show Helen what she had given up. When she performed "Cheek to Cheek" with Maggie, standing cheek to cheek on the stage, a glint of lust filled Helen's eyes. That was when Hattie knew she had succeeded, making her wonder if she would take Helen back if given a chance.

The applause was deafening when Hattie and Maggie left the stage. They giggled arm in arm down the private corridor to the dressing rooms. Hattie opened the door to her room, and they stumbled inside, still high on the adrenaline. "That was incredible." She plopped onto the small sofa.

"I haven't had this much fun on stage in years," Maggie said, landing beside her, shoulder to shoulder. "And that's saying something." Maggie Moore had a reputation for putting on energetic shows, leaving the house begging for more, which explained her skyrocketing record sales. "By the way, who was the tall, dark, and handsome cut of meat in the first row? You couldn't take your eyes off him."

"Was I staring? I hadn't realized." Hattie bounced from her seat, snatched a towel from her dresser, and wiped the sweat from her face, thinking she had hidden her distraction well if Maggie thought she had been drooling over the hunk all evening.

"Oh, honey, you were undressing him with your eyes."

A knock on the door came at no better time.

If she only knew the truth, Hattie thought before yelling, "Come in."

The bouncer from the stage door popped his head in. "Miss James. Miss Moore. Mr. Reed has asked you to join him at his table for drinks."

The thought of sitting at the same table with the woman who had broken her heart sounded like torture. Before Hattie could answer, David appeared, carrying his portfolio of sheet music, including the gift from Hattie's father that had come in handy tonight. She silently thanked her father for putting together the thoughtful collection.

David pushed past the man and kissed Hattie on the cheek. "That was an incredible performance."

"What should I tell Mr. Reed?" the bouncer asked.

"The man's buying. Tell him we'll be right out after we change," Maggie said, waving her hand dismissively, making Hattie cringe.

The bouncer acknowledged with a two-finger salute and closed the door behind him.

"Well then." Maggie pushed herself up from the sofa. "We better change. I'll see you at the table in, say, fifteen?"

"Sure." Hattie put on her biggest smile for Maggie before she left for her dressing room, thinking about two things: Helen and booze. Why was liquor always front and center when she was around?

Once the door closed, David turned to Hattie with a concerned look. "Did you know Helen would be here?"

"No." Hattie let out a long breath, dreading having to make an appearance at Mr. Reed's table. "If I had, I would have bowed out."

"Do you want to slip out the back door? I can make your apologies."

"Thank you, but this is part of the job." She grazed a finger down his clean-shaven cheek, thinking he made an excellent cover but was an even better friend. "Now, what about you? Did you see any prospects in the audience tonight?"

"One."

"You should go out there. Perhaps you can catch his attention."

"I have plans later tonight." He shrugged, giving in to his bashful side.

"Are you holding out on me, David Townsend?" She playfully swatted him on the shoulder.

"It's nothing, really, but I'm more concerned about you. I'd hate seeing you take a step back."

"From what?" Hattie took a swig of water from the glass on her dresser, suspecting where this was going.

"Oh, come on, Hattie. You're about to walk back into the lion's den with Helen. Throw Maggie and her booze into the mix, and you're asking for trouble."

She thumped her bottom against the dresser, thinking how right David was. She had opened her heart to two women in her life—her mother and Helen Reed. Both turned out to be selfish cheaters with no remorse. Neither considered the impact of their infidelity, caring more about gratification than the people who loved them. And both had driven her to drink to forget their betrayal.

"You need to forget the past," David said softly, "and focus on the present."

But how could she? Once a heart breaks, it can't heal without scars.

After changing in their respective dressing rooms, Hattie and Maggie returned to the dining room. Hattie felt Helen's stare before locking eyes with her, making her heart thump harder, not at the memories of the passion they once shared but at the bucket full of heartache that came with seeing her again.

"I hope you'll excuse our tardiness," Mr. Reed said, rising when Hattie and Maggie joined them, "but it couldn't be helped."

"No worries, Mr. Reed," Hattie said, glancing at Helen before taking a seat with Maggie. It was hard to pin down the woman's emotional state, but she appeared intrigued by Hattie. "It gave us the chance to perform some different songs. I hope you enjoyed it."

"I did, as I have with all your performances." He briefly glanced at his table partners. "I believe you already know my daughter, Helen, and this is her escort for the evening, Russel Madison."

"Of course." Hattie nodded politely, holding in her instinct to scream at the woman for breaking her heart. "It's a pleasure seeing you again, Miss Reed. Mr. Madison. May I introduce Maggie Moore?"

Helen's eyes lingered on Hattie, drifting between her face and bustline. She then grazed Russel's hand with a light, seductive touch before focusing on Maggie. "You're quite the lively one on stage," Helen said.

"In my world, it's the only way worth performing." Maggie grinned at her response.

Hattie kicked Maggie's shin under the table, hoping she would behave the rest of the evening. She glanced to her left. David remained near the stage door, but his protective stare was omnipresent.

"May I buy you a drink, ladies?" Mr. Reed asked, waving over a server.

"Champagne," Maggie said. "Tonight is worthy of celebrating."

"Coffee," Hattie said, hoping the choice didn't insult Mr. Reed after his kind gesture.

"If I had coffee this late, I would be up all night," Russel said, nursing his amber-colored cocktail.

Helen smiled with her eyes. "Make it two coffees." The flirtation was tempting.

~

David was quiet, climbing the stairs to Hattie's apartment. He was often hard to read but was more withdrawn during the drive to her building tonight. Seeing her to her door after a show or long day in the recording studio was part of their dating ruse, but it had become a ritual Hattie looked forward to. They'd started it to further the perception they were dating, but it had transformed into their personal time, cementing their friendship.

At the top of the stairs, David said, "I'm proud of you for not falling into Helen's trap again."

"I can't afford to go back there," Hattie said, slipping the key into her lock and opening the door for David to follow her inside. Flipping on the light switch, she gasped. "What the hell?"

The living and dining rooms appeared ransacked. Every drawer was open, and contents were strewn about the floor. The couch cushions were across the room, lying haphazardly against the wall. Her coats from the hallway closet were piled on the floor, and the pictures were off the wall.

David ushered her back to the doorway, giving her his music satchel. "Stay here."

He peeked in the kitchen before heading down the short hallway to the bedrooms and bathroom, returning moments later. "It's safe. No one is here, but the other rooms look the same."

Hattie felt violated. Someone had broken into her home—the one place she felt truly safe to be herself—and gone through her things. She shuddered at the thought of some street criminal pawing through her underwear and toiletries, thinking she would have to wash and sanitize everything.

As she walked through her apartment to assess the chaos, nothing appeared broken or missing, only rifled through. “I don’t think I’ve been robbed.”

“What do you think they were looking for?” David returned the cushions to the couch.

“I don’t know.”

“Should I call the police?” he asked.

“And tell them what? Nothing is missing, so this wasn’t a burglary.” Hattie went to the apartment door and inspected the lock. “It’s not broken.”

“So, either you forgot to lock it, or someone picked it.”

“I *was* in a hurry leaving this morning, so I probably forgot. I bet some kids from the building got in here and had a little fun, that’s all.” Hattie slumped on the couch with the freshly replaced cushions. “I’m such an idiot.”

David joined her on the couch. “You’re not an idiot. We all forget to lock up sometimes.” He patted her leg. “How about we clean up this mess?”

“I thought you had plans.”

“Oh, that. I was supposed to meet the guys in the band for drinks, but this is more important.”

She squeezed his hand. “I hope you find someone soon.”

“Me too.” David stood and picked up things, returning them to their proper places.

And Hattie hoped the same for herself.

3

The phone ringing on her nightstand woke Hattie from a restless sleep. Memories of intimate encounters with Helen had kept her tossing and turning most of the night. Fumbling her hand in the dark, she knocked the phone off its hook. "Dammit." She blinked to clear the fog in her head, sat up, and shuttled the curly cord hand over hand until the receiver appeared. She placed it against her ear. "Hello?"

"Hattie?"

"Who is this? What time is it?"

"Oh, Hattie." The familiar voice cracked with emotion, instantly shaking out the cobwebs of sleep.

"Liv?" Hattie opened her eyes wider, her heart racing. She flung her legs over the edge of the mattress, dreading why her sister might be calling in the middle of the night. "What's wrong?"

"It's Father. He's been arrested!"

Hattie shook her head to make sure she had heard her sister correctly. "Arrested? What on earth for?"

"The FBI has him. They say he's been giving secrets to the Nazis."

"That's preposterous. He's been with the State Department for thirty-five years. Why would they think he's giving away secrets?"

"I don't know. An agent has arranged for us to see him this afternoon. Can you take the train down?"

Hattie glanced at the wind-up alarm clock next to the phone. It was nearly five o'clock. If memory served her, two southbound trains departed Penn Station on Saturday mornings, and she could make her way to DC by midafternoon. "I could be there around three or four."

"Thank goodness. We'll pick you up at Union Station."

"I'll be there. Hug Frank and the kids for me." When Olivia sobbed, Hattie added, "I love you, Liv. We'll figure this out."

"I love you too, Hattie. See you soon."

Hattie hung up the phone and buried her face in her hands. Her father always managed things of consequence when Hattie or her sister faced them. He instinctively knew what needed doing and made things happen with a few phone calls. Now, he needed her help, and other than getting a lawyer, she had no clue what to do.

After getting dressed, Hattie called her agent, explaining she had a family emergency and needed to cancel her appearance at the Copacabana that night. Thankfully, she had nothing else scheduled until later in the week. She then called David, telling him what had happened and that she needed to go to Washington, DC, that morning.

"I'm coming with you," he said.

"Oh, that's not necessary."

"Yes, it is. Your father thinks we're dating, and thanks to him, so does your sister. They'll ask questions if I'm not there."

"You have a point," Hattie said.

"Pack your bags," David said. "I'll pick you up in thirty minutes."

"Thank you, David. You are a good friend."

David would make the perfect husband. He was kind and attentive and put her needs above his. As a cover, the idea didn't sound absurd. Musicians and singers were often drawn to one another based on their shared love of music. If they married, they could live together but be free to pursue the men and women who interested them in private. Maybe if she were different . . . if he were different . . . she might consider marrying him for real.

Four hours on a southbound train gave Hattie time to consider the allegations against her father. He was born in Germany to an American diplomat and a German school teacher, but he didn't return until the State Department sent him there on assignment. Yes, he hosted several German diplomats at their home after his post in Germany, but those social gatherings were well-attended by other senior State Department officials. She witnessed nothing out of the ordinary and could not think of a reason the FBI would suspect him of giving the Nazis secrets. This must have been a giant misunderstanding, or her father had been framed as the scapegoat. She choked back her fear that he could go to prison for something he didn't do.

David had been quiet, offering to get her something from the snack car twice, but all she wanted were sips of water, preferring to watch the winter scenery outside her window while lost in thought. Her stomach had been in knots since her sister's call, and she feared eating anything substantial would do more harm than good. Instead, he held her hand occasionally and gave her reassuring winks. Hattie was sure she would have been a nervous wreck without him.

When the train pulled into Union Station, David tipped the porter to gather their bags and position them on the crowded platform. The cold winter air nipped at Hattie's face as she scanned the people in both directions up and down the train, looking for her sister and brother-in-law.

Someone called her name. She turned, finding her sister weaving through the crowd. "Hattie!" Olivia repeated. Frank, a head taller, was right behind her. As she got closer, the bags under her eyes suggested she hadn't slept and had spent her waking hours worrying.

"Liv," Hattie whispered, pulling her into a tight embrace and gripping at her gray wool coat. Quiet, shaky sobs passed between the sisters until Frank cleared his throat.

"We should get going. They're expecting us at four thirty."

Hattie pulled back and introduced David as her boyfriend, who offered, "It's nice to meet you finally. I'm sorry it was under these circumstances."

Frank shook his hand, and Olivia greeted him with a hearty hug, the type that had "welcome to the family" written all over it.

Frank and David collected their bags and walked the ladies through Union Station. Passing a flower shop, Hattie stopped after spotting a display of her father's favorite flower. They were out of season, so they must have come from a local grower with a greenhouse, like the plant she had given him for Christmas. The FBI likely wouldn't allow him to have an entire bouquet, but they might overlook a single edelweiss stem. She picked one in partial bloom from the container and approached the vendor.

"How much for a single?" Hattie asked.

She received a bright smile of recognition. "On the house, Miss James."

"That's very sweet of you. Thank you."

David dug through his pocket, left a quarter on the counter, and tipped his fedora politely. "For your trouble, sir."

David helped stow the luggage in the trunk of Frank's black four-door Dodge, and everyone boarded with the men in the front seat and the women in the back. The sedan was old and rusty but big enough for the family on trips. Frank and her sister could not afford much more on his government salary.

Olivia gestured toward the flower Hattie was holding. "For Father?"

"I hope the FBI lets him keep it. It should cheer him up until his release." Hattie inspected the delicate lance-shaped white leaves surrounding the clumps of white-and-green floret pods that were not yet fully developed. Once in full bloom, it should last another week or more. Hopefully, by the time the leaves wilted, her father would be back home with these ridiculous charges dropped.

They rode silently for the short drive through the heart of the Federal Triangle. Frank let the others off in front of the limestone-faced Department of Justice Building so he could park the car and be the only one dashing through the wet, wintry mix. David held the main door open for the ladies, revealing a magnificent lobby void of people except at the reception desk—not an unexpected sight for a Saturday. Hattie and Olivia checked in and were told to wait there.

David and Frank soon joined the women, waiting for the escort to arrive. The men engaged in small talk, getting to know one another, while the women remained silent. Hattie felt her sister's nervous energy and linked their arms. She studied the building's opulent interior while they waited. Its design had Art Deco and Greek influences, creating a unique blend of modern and classical architecture in white limestone with copper tin accents.

"So, this is where my tax dollars go," Hattie harrumphed to break the uncomfortable silence.

Olivia playfully swatted her sister. "Stop the subtle brag."

Hattie wasn't rich like the Carnegies or Mellons, but she made more than most, more than both her parents combined. It was a goal she hadn't considered until reaching it unexpectedly with six record releases last year and this summer's massive hit. Money wasn't a priority, but it was proof she was damn good at her job. Still, she considered it criminal that the federal government took a third of her earnings on top of what the state grabbed, which was why she lived modestly. She kept a small apartment she lived in for only half the year, spending the other half on the road at singing gigs or visiting her sister and father in Virginia.

"Our government needs buildings, not palaces. This is over the top."

"It also put thousands of men and women to work for years when decent-paying jobs were few." Olivia had a way of putting things into perspective and Hattie in her place simultaneously, a trait Hattie wished she possessed.

Hattie patted her sister's arm. "You're right."

A man in his forties dressed in a dark suit appeared from a corridor behind the welcome desk. "James family?" he asked, approaching their group.

"Yes," Frank said, extending his hand first. "This is my wife, Olivia, her sister, Hattie, and Hattie's companion, David Townsend. Olivia and Hattie are Karl's daughters."

"I'm Special Agent Sam Knight. Please follow me." Without bothering to shake hands with the rest of the group, he turned on his heel and walked briskly down the empty, tiled corridor.

The sound of clicking oxfords and ladies' heels echoed off the walls. Hattie expected bright lights leading their way, but the deeper they went into the building's bowels, the darker their surroundings became, giving her a chill. If this was intended to intimidate, it was working.

Instead of going to the upper floors, Agent Knight led them down the stairs to a second-level basement, where the lighting got duskier. The shadows cast downward from the overhead lights created the impression that on the other side of a door, the FBI likely had her father chained to a wall in a dank, mildewy dungeon.

Agent Knight opened a door near the end of the hallway and held it open for the others to enter. Two men in suits were seated at a table and turned to watch their group enter but quickly returned to reviewing the files before them.

"Only family can go in," Knight said. "Ladies, I'll need you to leave your jackets and handbags here."

"Of course." Hattie laid her purse on a nearby desk and draped her coat over a chair. Her sister did the same. Hattie picked up the flower by the stem. "May I give this to my father? It's a sign of our love."

Knight inspected the flower, cocking his head to one side. "Sure. You have five minutes." He looked the sisters over once more before opening a secondary door.

Her father was seated at a small table with his hands cuffed together. He looked strange in dungarees and a lighter denim button-down long-sleeve shirt, not one of his trademark double-breasted suits—the mark of a statesman.

"Father." Olivia rushed to him first, wrapping her arms around him in a long embrace. "Are they treating you well?"

"Yes, sweetheart. They have been cordial hosts." He turned to Hattie and gestured her over. "Let me see my little songbird." He held her at arm's length with his chained hands before she hugged him. When she pulled back, he glanced at the flower in her hand. "What is this? I'm surprised they let you bring it in."

"It's rather hard to sneak a metal file in it, I suppose." Hattie forced a chuckle, snapped off all but three inches of the stem, and tucked the flower into his jail uniform shirt pocket. "I thought this would remind you how much we love you." She patted his chest lightly before they took their seats.

"What's going on, Father?" Olivia asked. "Why do they think you've been spying?"

Karl glanced to his right, and Hattie followed his stare. The mirror there was obviously two-way, and she suspected agents were on the other side, listening and waiting for her father to give them any information they could twist and use against him.

"This is all a misunderstanding, sweetheart." He reached across the table and clutched Olivia's hand briefly. "I'm sure we'll clear this up."

"Is there anyone we can speak to? Anything we can do to resolve this sooner?" Hattie asked.

Karl shook his head. "I'm afraid not. My supervisors can untangle this, but they're unavailable until Monday."

"Monday?" Olivia said. She sounded as surprised as Hattie. "That's horrible. How long can they keep you here?"

"Days, I suspect. They mentioned transferring me overnight to another facility for some hearing on Monday."

"Have you called Albert?" Hattie asked. "Is he representing you?" She wasn't sure if her father's college chum, who represented him during the divorce, also practiced criminal law.

"I have, but he's sending another lawyer to speak with me tomorrow."

"Good, good." Hattie patted his hand. "Can we get you anything? Do you have your reading glasses?"

"Yes, back in my cell. I don't suppose they'll let me have anything else, but with any luck, I'll be released on Monday."

"Does Mother know you've been arrested?" Olivia asked. "Shall we call her?"

Her father's eyes turned sad. "No, and I don't want her to know. She has her own life now."

"But, Father—" Olivia started.

"No buts. This is the way I want it. The way it must be."

Olivia started to cry. She was only twelve when their parents divorced and didn't fully understand why they broke up and their mother moved back to Brazil. Despite Hattie telling her it was useless, Olivia had tried to bring them back together for years. She only gave up at her wedding five years ago when it had become apparent their mother had moved on. The disdain Eva held for their father was unsurmountable, something Hattie never understood since her mother was the one who cheated.

"Just leave her out of this, Liv," Hattie said. "That's the way he wants it."

A knock on the door meant their time was up.

Hattie turned to her father. "We'll call Albert tonight to find out more about this lawyer. If we're not satisfied, I'll hire you the best in town."

"I'm sure Albert wouldn't steer me wrong, sweetheart. Keep your money."

The door opened, and Agent Knight appeared. "Time's up."

Olivia gave Karl another long, drawn-out hug. "I love you, Father. You'll beat whatever this is."

"I love you too." Karl turned to Agent Knight. "May I have one moment alone with Hattie?"

Knight eyed him carefully. "Sure." Hattie was certain he only agreed in order to give him another opportunity to slip up. Olivia appeared miffed as the agent escorted her out the door.

Hattie turned. "You still love Mother, don't you?"

"Whether I do is of no consequence. She no longer loves me. I want you to make sure your sister doesn't contact her. This is a family matter, and I no longer consider her family."

"I'll speak with her, Father. She's worried and always leans on Mother for support."

"Please make sure that doesn't happen. A man has his pride."

"I will." She hugged him and whispered, "I love you. I know you didn't do this."

He looked at her with sad eyes and caressed her cheek. "I love you." He leaned closer and whispered into her ear, "I did what I had to in order to keep you safe. Remember what you promised me at Christmas."

David and Frank lugged their bags into the first-floor guest room of Olivia's two-story Alexandria home and returned to the living room. It was getting late, and Hattie was tired and finally hungry.

While Frank got the kids from the neighbor, the others prepared dinner. Soon, four-year-old Matthew ran in, followed by his two-year-old sister, Sarah, each grabbing one of Hattie's legs.

"Auntie Hattie," both squealed.

"There are my munchkins." She picked each up individually, giving them giant hugs and big raspberry kisses.

"What did you bring us?" Matthew asked with expectant eyes.

"I'm so sorry, but I didn't bring anything on this trip. I promise to bring you two things the next time I'm in town." She crossed her heart. His sad puppy dog eyes nearly broke her heart. "But, if your mom says it's okay, I'll take you and your sister out for ice cream before I leave."

"Ooohhh, I want chocolate." He jumped up and down, clapping his hands, and his sister did the same. She likely didn't understand why she was clapping, but she always got excited when her brother did.

"And you shall have it." She tapped him on the nose.

They had dinner, and Hattie helped bathe the kids and put them to bed. Frank poured brandy for himself and David while Olivia and Hattie sipped coffee in the living room. While the men chatted about sports and things uninteresting to the sisters, Olivia withdrew into her thoughts, as did Hattie. She mulled over her father's earlier cryptic message about keeping her safe and the sheet music, but it mystified her.

Olivia finally asked, "Do you think he's been transferred yet?"

"I'm not sure," Hattie said. "He said it would be sometime overnight."

David patted his pockets. "Hattie, I'm out of smokes. Do you mind if I run out and get some?"

"Of course not." Hattie gave up smoking when she gave up drinking years ago and didn't care for it when David smoked. But, like with alcohol, she couldn't expect those who partook to give them up because of her. David, however, had the decency to not smoke or drink in front of her unless cornered like tonight.

"Let me drive you," Frank offered, forcing back a yawn. "There's a late-night drugstore not far from here."

"I don't want to force you out this late. I saw the store on the way over. If you toss me the keys, I can drive myself."

"Appreciate that. I didn't get much sleep last night."

Once David left and Frank went to bed, Hattie retrieved the old family photo albums on the bookshelf beside the fireplace, thinking a stroll down memory lane might help her sister. She flipped through the first album with pictures of her and Olivia as little girls in their Washington, DC, brownstone. She laughed when she came to the photo of them dressed in Halloween costumes—Hattie as a witch and Olivia as a clown.

Olivia leaned forward and laughed. "You were terrifying in that costume."

"At least you could take off your mask and bob for apples. I had that horrible crooked nose glued to my face. It was like having a pencil stuck to it."

Hattie turned the page to a collection of pictures around Christmastime. Their parents had hosted several holiday parties over the years, inviting music friends of their mother, various State Department officials, and diplomats their father had worked with.

"Mother always had the best decorations," Olivia said.

"She overdid most holidays." Hattie flipped through the photographs of the parties her parents hosted and those her father continued to hold after the divorce and her mother returned to Brazil. Several of the men appeared in pictures of multiple parties. She remembered being introduced to some from the British, Swiss, and German embassies. She thought nothing of those parties then, but considering the allegations against her father, she pondered how it must have looked to the FBI to have German diplomats in his home. He was born in Germany, so she could see how the agents would think he had a deeper connection to his birth country.

David returned, and he and Hattie went to the guest room for bed and shut the door. "I'll take the floor," David said.

"You're being silly. We can share the bed. One below the sheet and the other above."

They changed with their backs to each other and crawled into bed with their respective covers up to their chests. "How long do you think we'll stay?" David asked.

"At least through Monday. My father thinks this can all be wrapped up once his superiors open the office." Hattie thought about her father lying on a jail cot. He was a proud man who rubbed elbows with some of Washington's most powerful men. He had put on a good front in that small room today, but she could tell this ordeal had shaken him. It had rattled all of them.

They lay in the dark, side by side, for several moments until David broke the silence. "Hey, Hattie."

"Yeah."

"Don't take this wrong, but sometimes I wish I didn't have to pretend."

"Me too, David. Me too." Lying to her sister was never easy, but at a time like this, with their family in turmoil, it made her feel more distant . . . more cut off. Hattie missed the days when they were kids and told each other everything, but as she got older, she learned some secrets should never be told. Before falling asleep, she wondered what secrets her father had yet to tell.

4

A thunderous pounding startled Hattie awake. Her heart pulsed wildly, instantly shedding the fog of sleep. David shot up beside her in the bed, turning his head toward the door. The pounding came again. "Someone is at the front door," he said. He flipped back the covers, put on the trousers he'd worn yesterday, and lifted his suspenders over his white undershirt. "Stay here. I'll see what's going on."

Hattie got up and removed her nightgown without caring whether David saw her body. After he shut the bedroom door behind him, she heard thumping on the stairs—likely Frank descending to investigate—and a muffled voice.

She rushed to put on a blouse and a pair of loose slacks. Slipping on a pair of flats, she heard a commotion in the living room with men yelling, "Get down." Whatever was happening out there, it was chaotic. She grabbed a sweater to counter the overnight chill in the house and hide that she didn't have a bra on. Creeping the door open, she was immediately met by a man in a black wool overcoat pointing a pistol at her. Once Hattie focused on the steel end of the barrel, she saw nothing else. This was the first time she'd experienced the business end of a gun up close, and having it aimed at her was terrifying.

"Hands up!" he shouted.

She heard the words but barely processed their meaning, frozen in place. But when he waved the pistol slightly and stepped closer, on instinct, she raised her hands.

The man lowered his weapon, grabbed Hattie by the arm, and forced her down the short hallway to the living room. Two men with guns ran upstairs while two others held Frank and David face down on the floor at gunpoint. Three others were there, totaling seven. One man, whom she recognized as FBI Agent Knight, stood in the room's center, surveying the area.

"Don't frighten my children!" Frank yelled with his fingers laced together and pressed against the back of his head. He struggled to raise his head enough to observe the stairs.

"What's going on?" Hattie shook at the fear and anger in Frank's voice.

"Who else is in the house?" Knight asked Frank, pressing a foot against the small of his back over his robe.

"Just my wife and kids. So help me. If you hurt them, I'll—"

Knight pressed his foot down harder. "You'll what?"

A sense of helplessness filled the house when the children screamed from somewhere upstairs. Frank squirmed and issued more threats, earning him a pair of handcuffs with his hands behind his back.

Olivia appeared at the top of the stairs, looking terrified while holding Sarah in her right arm against her hip and Matthew's hand in her left. Both children were crying. An eighth agent appeared behind her, thankfully without his gun drawn.

While they descended the stairs, a ninth agent appeared on the top landing. "This is it."

Olivia sat on the couch, holding Sarah tightly. Hattie joined her, bringing Matthew into her lap and letting him bury his face on her chest. He shivered with fear.

Two agents pulled David and Frank up and sat them on their bottoms.

"Will someone tell me what is going on?" Frank asked in a firm voice.

"We have a warrant to search the premises," Knight said, holding up a folded piece of paper.

"For what?" Frank asked.

"All in good time. First, we need to take all of you in for questioning."

"What about my children?" Olivia asked, pressing Sarah's head more firmly against her shoulder. The children had never looked more terrified, refusing to look at the activity in the room or loosen their hold on their aunt and mother.

"I'll have the police pick them up," Knight said.

"God, no." Olivia shuddered. "Can I wake my neighbor? She can watch them."

Knight gestured for an agent to string the phone on an end table over to her. Olivia spoke to Marge, apologizing for the early morning call, and asked her to get the children straight away because of an emergency. Hanging up the phone, she blew out a long breath. "She'll be right over. May I pack some clothes for them?"

Knight gestured to the agent still on the stairs. "Grab some clothes and shoes for both kids and bring them down."

The agent reappeared moments later, carrying a stuffed pillowcase. This was cruel for the mother and the children by any stretch. Olivia sifted through the case and pulled out some clothes. Hattie dressed Matthew while Olivia focused on Sarah and stuffed their pajamas into the sack. Both children were sniffling with fear.

"Where are we going, Mommy?" Matthew asked.

"We need to go with these men, so Mrs. Baker is coming to get you. You can go back to sleep and stay in bed as long as you want."

"But it's Sunday. What about church?" Matthew asked in a darling little boy's voice.

"We can go next week, honey." Olivia pulled a sweater over his head. "Today, I need you to be a good boy, watch over your sister, and do as Mrs. Baker says. Can you do that for me?"

"Yes, Mommy."

The doorbell rang, and an agent opened the front door. A woman's voice came from the stoop. "I'm Marge Baker. I'm here to fetch the children."

"Let her in," Knight said.

Hattie recognized the last name, sending her stomach into knots. She'd met the Bakers during a previous visit and remembered the husband as a reporter for the *Washington Post*. She hoped Mr. Baker put being a gracious neighbor above a newsworthy scoop. Otherwise, all this mess might end up on the front page.

Marge stepped inside and looked around. “What on earth?”

“This is an FBI matter, ma’am,” Knight said. “Please take the children.”

When Marge approached the couch, Olivia stood and handed her Sarah. “Thank you for coming. They haven’t had breakfast.”

“I wouldn’t suppose so at this early hour,” Marge said. “Where are their coats? It’s freezing outside.”

“In the hall closet.”

Knight snapped his fingers. An agent pulled the coats from the closet and searched them before handing them over. While the women helped the children don their jackets, Olivia explained she had to go downtown and wasn’t sure when she would return.

“Don’t worry about a thing. They’ll be fine. Our kids would love having playmates today.”

Olivia walked them to the door and kissed her children goodbye.

“Get dressed. You’re coming with us,” Knight ordered.

While agents escorted both couples to their rooms, others rifled through the house. Hattie simply put on a pair of warm socks, and David put on the rest of his clothes while the agent watched and glanced at Hattie occasionally. He appeared anxious but not completely thrown as Hattie was. She appreciated his calm, drawing strength from it.

When they returned to the living room, every drawer and cabinet was open, and their contents were strewn about the floor, reminiscent of the condition Hattie and David discovered in her apartment Friday night. This was no coincidence. Hattie now suspected the FBI was behind the search of her home, not hooligans.

Hattie grabbed her purse, which the agent snatched from her hands. He combed through it, making her feel as violated as she’d felt Friday at her apartment. Once he handed it back to her, he grabbed her by the arm, directing her toward the door.

“Let go of her,” David demanded, forcing the agent’s hand away.

The agent released Hattie, shoved David, and a scuffle ensued.

Hattie stepped aside and cried, “David, stop.”

Another agent rushed in and punched David in the kidney, doubling him over. The agents threw him in handcuffs. Hattie followed, fearing for his safety.

"You are a feisty one," Knight said, leaning in to look David in the eye.

"You need to control your agents. There's no need to manhandle the women. They pose no threat." David shrugged his shoulder violently, loosening the agents' hold on him.

"If you don't behave, I'll arrest you for obstructing justice," Knight said.

"Justice, my ass. This is intimidation, pure and simple. When can we call a lawyer?" David's tone and stance were defiant and protective. The latter was a side she'd recently thought might become a problem with his constant reminders of being cautious, and tonight showed her concern was warranted because David was only making things worse.

Knight waved a hand and said, "Take them. I'll be there after the search."

Four agents each grabbed an occupant by the arm, collecting and inspecting their jackets as they passed the closet. Once outside, Hattie blinked. It was still dark, but a crowd of neighbors had gathered around the parade of government sedans parked haphazardly in front of Olivia's house.

A flurry of camera flashes blinded Hattie as the FBI agents placed her and David in the back of one car and Frank and Olivia in another. Any hope of keeping this matter quiet was moot.

Hattie and David weren't allowed to speak during the drive. Once at the Department of Justice Building, FBI agents led them into different interrogation rooms, and Hattie assumed the same was true for Olivia and Frank. No one had cared to explain to her why she was hauled in or why agents tore apart Olivia's home. The agents had to be looking for something related to her father's arrest, but pounding on their door before dawn made no sense when she and the others were in this building yesterday. If the agents had questions, they should have asked them then.

Hattie had been sitting in this stale room on a rigid steel chair for hours, and no one had popped inside to see if she needed anything. A glass of water would have been nice. Her mind drifted to the possibilities of what may have prompted such harsh treatment, but besides intimidation, as David had called it, she was stumped.

Finally, the door opened, and Agent Knight entered. He sat in the chair across from her at the small table and laid out a manila folder. "After you left here yesterday, where did you go?"

Under normal circumstances, Hattie would have been polite and answered any question from a law enforcement official. However, she wouldn't make it easy for Knight after how he and his men roughed up David and Frank and treated the children. "Tell me why I'm here, and I'll consider answering your questions."

"All right, Miss James." He closed the folder. Everything from his stiff posture to his cold, steely stare said he suspected her of something. "Two FBI agents were shot and killed while transporting your father to another facility last night."

Hattie gasped, throwing a hand over her mouth. "Was my father hurt? May I see him?"

Knight leaned forward. "I ask you again. After you left here yesterday, where did you go?"

Hattie's mind swirled at the revelation . . . and implication. Her father might have been lying dead in a morgue, and the FBI suspected she or someone in her family was responsible for the murder of two federal agents. This was as bad as it could get. "I'm not answering any questions without my lawyer."

"That seems to be a family theme." Knight shifted uncomfortably in his chair, his stare becoming more suspicious.

"What do you expect? You invade my sister's home without explanation, frighten her children, haul us out like criminals, and virtually accuse us of murder."

"We can do this one of two ways. The easy way is where you answer our questions and lead us to your father. The hard way is where you wait for that lawyer, and we make your life a living hell until you tell us what we want to know."

Hattie slumped in relief. The fact that the FBI was looking for him meant her father was alive, but then she reassessed the situation—it wasn't as positive as she first thought. Her father was missing and possibly injured, and Knight was out for blood to avenge the two fallen agents. Anything she said would be twisted to fit any narrative the FBI wanted to paint. Hattie needed help. Considering how long she had been waiting, Olivia had likely been questioned before her.

"I'm sure my sister asked for Albert Wright. If he's here, I want to see him." Hattie would not say another word. She folded her arms across her chest and leaned back in her chair, fearing for David's and Frank's safety the most.

"Then I guess it's the hard way." Knight shook his head, an evil smile forecasting he was about to enjoy the challenge of getting what he wanted.

Moments later, the door opened, and Albert Wright stepped inside, holding a briefcase in one hand. "My client is leaving," he said, encouraging Hattie to stand. "If you have further questions, please contact my office to arrange a time for an appropriate interview."

"This isn't over." Knight stood and snatched the folder from the table. "Brace yourself for a living hell, Miss James."

Hattie grabbed her bag as Albert placed a hand on the small of her back and left that awful, small room without looking back. When he led her toward the corridor, other agents eyed her as if she was their primary suspect for killing two of their brethren. It was a terrible feeling.

Once out of earshot of the agents, Hattie asked, "What about Olivia, Frank, and my friend David?"

"They're waiting in the lobby. Say nothing until we're in the car."

Hattie slipped on her wool coat and walked silently in her soft flats. The rhythm of Albert's oxfords clicking loudly against the sleek white tiles matched her nervous, shallow breathing. The light filtered through the lobby windows, and a clock on the wall read two o'clock. The FBI had questioned them for ten hours.

The others were huddled together near the exit. They greeted each other with hugs and soft eyes but remained quiet on the way to Albert's Cadillac parked two blocks away.

David sat in the front seat, with Albert at the wheel. Frank and Olivia slid into the back seat, with Hattie getting in last, seated behind David. Once Albert pulled out, navigating the sparse late Sunday morning traffic in the District, Hattie asked, "Does anyone know if Father is okay?"

"We'll talk at the house," Albert said. Thick, silent tension filled the car to the driveway of Olivia's Alexandria home. "Get the kids later. We need to talk first."

After stowing their winter coats and preparing coffee, the group sat in the living room, staring anxiously at Albert for answers. Olivia had turned pale from the ordeal, and Frank had an arm around her shoulder for comfort. David sat close to Hattie, with their thighs pressed together and him clutching Hattie's nervously clasped hands in her lap.

Albert sipped his coffee before speaking. "Your father is missing. He escaped with help."

"So he *is* alive." Hattie lowered her head in relief. "Why would he escape? Was he hurt?"

"A witness said your father was whisked into a waiting sedan and appeared uninjured."

Hattie threw a hand to her chest. "Who took him? Was he forced?"

"That's unknown. Based on the number and types of bullets found at the scene, the FBI suspects at least two accomplices ambushed the transport vehicle."

Olivia sobbed, but Hattie held her emotion. One of them had to remain strong.

"Every law enforcement officer within a hundred miles is looking for him," Albert said. "Also, FBI agents found several State Department documents in this house."

"What documents?" Hattie asked.

"Unclassified but sensitive schedules of several foreign diplomats."

"I told them Matthew took the folder from Father's briefcase and hid it when he was here last week, but the FBI didn't believe me," Olivia said. "They think Frank and I might be involved with giving secrets to the Nazis."

Hattie jerked her head back. "That's ridiculous. What do we do now?"

"Nothing," Albert said. "The FBI is about to tear your lives apart, looking for anything that will lead them to your father. We will cooperate by appearing when asked, but I want you to say nothing."

"But we had nothing to do with it," Frank said, shoring up his arm around Olivia.

"It makes no difference," Albert said. "Two of their own are dead. They are looking for any morsel to twist. It is against the law to provide a false claim to a federal agent, and that is precisely what they are hoping for. They want to trip you up to hold it over you and squeeze you for information." He shook his head. "No. You say nothing. Exercise your right to remain silent."

"What's the next step?" Hattie asked.

"We wait. At this point, the FBI is grasping at straws. We do nothing to help them. I'll talk to the senior partners in my firm and have a criminal lawyer standing by to represent you. If the FBI harasses you, I want you to call me right away."

"This is insane," Hattie said. The FBI arrested her father for spying, and twenty-four hours later, two agents were dead, her father escaped and was missing, and her sister and brother-in-law were suspects. The possibility that her father might have gone willingly made her think the FBI's allegations had merit, but she could not bring herself to believe he was anything but a good man. No matter the case, she was convinced whoever was behind this had a long, powerful reach.

5

New York City, two days later

Hattie fluttered her eyes open to start another day without a sign of her father. Albert told her yesterday that the FBI's investigation into Karl's disappearance had stalled with no more leads to follow.

Morning light shone through the window, painting the room in a soft orange tone. The silence in the room meant the city had yet to come to life. She eased out of bed, grabbed the robe draped over the chair, and padded quietly down the hall to the bathroom. After starting the coffee in the percolator and bread in the toaster, she opened the front door and grabbed the morning *Times* from the hallway floor.

The door across the hall opened, and her neighbor stepped out and froze.

"Good morning, Mrs. Donnelly."

The woman turned her nose up, harrumphed, and slammed the door without saying a word, which was odd. Mrs. Donnelly was always friendly and greeted her with a smile and polite conversation.

"Okay." Hattie shook off the strange behavior.

Walking inside, she heard the toaster pop up, one of the few luxuries she indulged in. She placed the newspaper on the table without unfurling it from its rubber band and went to the kitchen to finish getting her breakfast together. Once at the small dining table, she added sugar and a splash of milk to her coffee, chiding herself for forgetting to hit the market for cream.

Opening the newspaper, she gasped, her mouth falling open. "What the hell?"

A photo of David in handcuffs and Hattie being taken from Olivia's home by the FBI filled the front page directly below the headline, "Singer Hattie James Questioned." The picture made it appear that they were under arrest. Heat flushed Hattie's body as she remembered that night and Matthew's and Sarah's screams. Every muscle tensed.

"That jerk," Hattie mumbled. Agent Knight had promised to make her life a living hell if she didn't help them find her father, and this headline proved he was a man of his word. She read the byline for the article, gritting her teeth. Hattie wasn't sure of the neighbor's first name, but she was confident the author was the same Baker who lived next to Olivia and watched the children the night of the raid.

She calmed herself enough to read the article headline to the right: "Karl James: Arrested for Spilling Secrets to Nazi Germany Now Missing. Two FBI Agents Dead." The details said that her father had access to highly classified state and national secrets, some of which had already made it into the hands of the Nazis, but she knew it couldn't be true. He had been a loyal diplomat for thirty-five years and would never hurt a fly.

The phone rang.

Hattie picked up the receiver in the living room. "Hello."

"Hattie." Olivia's voice sounded harried. "Did you read the paper?"

"Yes, Liv. I read it."

"This is a nightmare. As far as the country knows, Father is a traitor, and you are part of it. It could not get any worse."

"Don't tempt fate. Every time I have that thought, something else happens."

"This is no time to be joking, Hattie."

"Would you rather I be in hysterics?"

"Of course not," Olivia said. "I have a call into Albert Wright. His office said he'll call me tomorrow. Hopefully, he'll have some course of action for us for a libel case."

"I read the article, Liv. It's factual. Baker carefully poses questions without outright accusing us. I doubt we'll have grounds to sue."

"Maybe not, but we sure as heck won't let our kids play together again. The Bakers are now persona non grata." Olivia must have been furious. That was the closest she'd come to cursing in years.

"I figured as much. Let me know what Albert says tomorrow." Once Hattie finished the call and returned the handset to its cradle, someone knocked on the door. She opened it. David stood there, holding a newspaper with worry on his face.

"I take it you read the headline," Hattie said.

"What can we do about this?" David asked.

"Nothing, I'm afraid. Come in." Hattie opened the door further and let him in.

David pelted her with questions about the article and the FBI as she closed the door behind him, but she had no answers. She was equally upset and confused.

"The byline attributes the story and photograph to Tom Baker of the *Washington Post*. Aren't Olivia's neighbors the Bakers?" David asked.

Hattie felt her anger build again. "Yes, I believe that's him. Agent Knight likely fed him the story."

"How can we fight back? We did nothing wrong, but this story sounds like we were involved."

"I bet my agent can help. He's dealt with bad press before." Hattie walked to her telephone and had the operator connect her call. "Hello, Howard. This is Hattie."

"Yes, Hattie. I was about to call you. Have you read this morning's paper?"

"That's why I'm calling. It's all a twist of the facts. I was not arrested, only questioned following my father's disappearance."

"Why didn't you tell me about your father? We could have gotten ahead of this."

"I wasn't sure what to say." Actually, she hoped it would never have seen the light of day.

"Well, I don't like being blindsided, nor does RCA. David Sarnoff wants to see you tomorrow at nine."

This could not be good. The president of RCA rarely met with the talent. She had a sinking feeling the meeting would not end well. "Will you be there?"

"I'm your agent. I'll be there."

~

The top floor of the RCA Building was as ornate with gold finishings and as spacious as Hattie expected, with rich woods with brass and gold trim fitting for the company president with a reputation for enjoying his late-in-life riches. She'd heard stories about Mr. Sarnoff's humble roots and his demand for hard work and excellence from his employees. If they didn't perform to expectations, he sent them packing. He gave no second chances, which was precisely what Hattie needed, but she predicted she would meet the same fate.

Her agent gestured for Hattie to sit in a guest chair while he greeted the receptionist. "Mr. Howard Price and Miss Hattie James to see Mr. Sarnoff."

Before Hattie could sit, the woman stood, replying to Howard, "Please follow me. Mr. Sarnoff is waiting for you."

The hair on Hattie's arms prickled. Judgment was awaiting her. Howard waited for her to enter and followed her inside. Two men dressed in crisp dark suits were in guest chairs facing the door in the room's center. The company president was seated behind a substantial mahogany desk. The wall of windows behind him revealed the most magnificent view of Central Park Hattie had seen, and the scenery was worth more than all the gold finishings prominent throughout the floor.

The men rose when Hattie entered.

"Welcome, Miss James. Mr. Price." Mr. Sarnoff gestured for her and Howard to sit opposite the other men. "This is head counsel for RCA, Troy Metcalf, and vice president of public relations, Christian Allen." They greeted Hattie and Howard with polite nods, not handshakes. "Please have a seat."

"I'd prefer to stand, Mr. Sarnoff," Hattie said. "I assure you the story in the *Times* is an exaggeration and full of assumptions."

"Whether it is has no bearing on this meeting, Miss James. My primary concern is the publicity surrounding the daughter of an accused traitor and Nazi collaborator."

"I understand your concern, but Mr. Townsend and I were not arrested. The FBI harassed us and brought us in for questioning following my father's disappearance. We had nothing to do with what he was accused of or his escape."

"That's good to hear, but my concerns rest solely on the impact to this company. Considering the political climate, I cannot expose RCA to the backlash, so I am terminating your contract. Any unreleased records will be scrapped."

"On what grounds?" Howard asked. "You're still obligated to record six more records."

"For violation of the morals clause," Mr. Metcalf said. "Her failure to report her detention by law enforcement within twenty-four hours violates the clause."

"But I wasn't detained. I was questioned," Hattie objected.

"The use of handcuffs on Mr. Townsend arguably constitutes detention," Metcalf said. "If you disagree, you are within your rights to file suit for breach of contract, but I wish you luck in finding a judge in the state who will side with you. None are fans of Hitler."

"Neither am I, Mr. Metcalf." Hattie's anger threatened to boil over. "My father is only accused of spying. In any case, the sins of the father should not be visited upon the children."

"That's good in theory," Christian Allen said, "but in practice, radio stations won't play records of the daughter of a traitor, nor will housewives buy them. In short, you have become toxic, Miss James. We need to cut you loose."

Hattie glanced at Howard, but he said nothing, nervously rubbing his chin.

"You'll hear from my lawyer." She raised her head in righteous defiance, spun on her heel, and left, suspecting the worst was yet to come.

She marched down the corridor and pressed the elevator call button, stewing in anger. How could she fight against the stink of being deemed guilty by association? She understood being cautious, but RCA folded without putting up a defense. No public relations campaign to tell her fans she had nothing to do with her father and was appalled at how the circumstances of his arrest unfolded. Nothing. Hattie was easier to dump than to fight for, making her madder than hell. She felt like ripping the plush curtains from the walls and screaming obscenities at the top of her lungs, but she needed to be bigger than their small minds. She folded her arms across her chest to keep herself from losing it for all to see and preserve her chance of still working in the music business.

Howard caught up to her when the elevator door opened. They stepped inside, and he instructed the attendant to take them to the lobby.

"Don't pick up any more passengers." Hattie remained silent for the downward trip, clenching her fists so hard she broke a few nails. Though they were the only guests in the car, she could not air what had transpired inside that office in front of the attendant. The last thing she needed was another story in the *Times*, spotlighting her tantrum in the aftermath of her father's escape.

By the time she stepped into the busy lobby, her chest heaved with outrage. She walked toward the glass door exit, but Howard stopped her, pulling her by the arm. "We need to talk," he said.

"Unless the conversation starts with finding me another recording contract, can it wait until I calm down?"

"No, it can't." He looked at the people around him and guided her to a more secluded part of the lobby. "Mr. Allen was right. This story about you and your father is toxic. You need to lie low until it blows over and the country forgets you're the daughter of a traitor."

"What are you saying?"

"I'm saying I took four cancelations this morning, including the Copacabana. I'm sure I'll have more when I return to the office. No one wants you stepping foot in their club."

Hattie's breathing labored. She struggled to control it. "Well, find someone who will. That's why I'm paying you."

"I'm afraid that won't happen because I quit. I can't chance this blowing back on the rest of my clients."

Hattie cocked her head back. "You too, Howard? You're gutless. No wonder you're single."

"Let's not make this personal, Hattie."

"It already is personal. My livelihood is at stake."

"You'll have to find another way to pay the bills. I suggest you start looking."

~

The cab ride home did little to bring Hattie back from the edge. She'd lost her recording contract, performance bookings, and agent in less than an hour. The only day worse than this was when her mother returned to Brazil, leaving her father and sister brokenhearted.

She trudged up the stairs, discovering the one person who could make this day even worse standing at her doorstep. "Not now, Agent Knight."

"Have you had enough yet?" He pushed himself from the wall.

"I despise you."

"We're even, then. I despise everything about your father. Our government trusted him with its highest secrets, and he handed them to the Fatherland."

"What secrets? He was a diplomat who babysat foreign diplomats in the States."

"That was his cover job. You really don't know what he did for the State Department, do you?"

"What are you talking about?"

"He helped run the Black Chamber for years."

Hattie squinted in confusion. "The Cipher Bureau that accessed everyone's private telegrams to find secrets being traded? I read about that. You're saying my father was part of that? He said it was time they shut that thing down."

"Yes, he was. Once it closed, he was reassigned as the State Department liaison to the War Department's Signal Intelligence Corps. He had access to our nation's highest military secrets, including lists of overseas facilities we're targeting for intelligence gathering."

Hattie struggled to wrap her head around the actual work her father had done for the government, but it explained why the FBI had searched her and her sister's homes. "What makes you believe he gave information to the Nazis?"

"He was seen with this man." Knight showed him a picture of a blond man dressed in a German military uniform. He looked familiar, resembling the man in the family holiday photos she looked at with her sister the other night.

"What about him?" Hattie's stomach knotted as the pieces fell into place.

"He's assigned to the German Embassy. We captured him with the list, and he gave up your father as the one who gave it to him, but we were too late. He'd already sent a copy to Germany in a diplomatic pouch. Three facilities have since been abandoned, and our intelligence gathering has been set back years."

Hattie's knees went weak. Her head spun at the double life her father led and the supposed evidence against him. "I have to go." Her hand shook as she inserted the key into the lock.

"One day, we'll catch your father," Knight said. "Would you rather we take him in alive or dead?"

Hattie slammed the door in his face. Knight had her doubting the man she'd loved and trusted all her life. Had her thinking her father might have been a traitorous spy. She felt sick, knowing her life would never be the same.

6

A month later

The Playhouse was packed and reflected the poverty, criminal element, and squalor common in the Five Points neighborhood in which it was located. Cigarette and cigar smoke rose, adding to the thick cloud hanging stubbornly at the ceiling. A fistfight broke out at the far end of the bar, which the rest of the raucous Friday night crowd dismissed as commonplace. After last night's debacle, Hattie tapped the microphone at center stage to ensure it was operational before starting to sing. David gave her an apologetic smile before tinkling the keys on the dilapidated piano.

This was what had become of Hattie's career in the weeks following the sensational news of her father's arrest and violent escape from federal custody. The duet record with Maggie Moore was scrapped, but she still had royalty money coming in. Though she expected that to dry up like decent singing gigs had. The Playhouse only took her on after their regular performer caught the flu. She was told to wear her hair differently to avoid being recognized, so she cut her signature long, wavy hair and curled it to hit right below the collar. The owner introduced her under the stage name Jamie Thetas, an anagram of her name.

Last night marked her first job since the FBI turned her life upside down and, by extension, also David's. RCA refused to keep him even as a studio musician, so he moved from his boarding house to her guest room until he could afford a room again. Hattie lived modestly and could survive on her savings for years, but sulking in her apartment, as she'd done most nights since returning to New York City, was no way to live. Sadly, neither was this.

Hattie kept her set to the required length and not a second more, to be off stage before another fight broke out. After her final song, she sidled up to the bar.

The bartender approached her, placing both palms atop the counter. "What will it be?"

She seriously considered ordering a vodka gimlet on the rocks, thinking if there was ever a valid reason to fall off the wagon, this was it. There was still no word about her father, yet somehow, the story of his disappearance and his connection to Hattie kept cropping up in the papers.

When Hattie was about to answer the bartender, David sat beside her on the neighboring barstool with his satchel of sheet music and said, "Two coffees, please."

He had stopped her from succumbing to temptation several times since her career took a nosedive, bringing her coffee and keeping her company when she felt low. He'd become her constant companion and acted more and more like her boyfriend each day. If he hadn't confessed his interest in both men and women and proclaimed she wasn't his type, Hattie would have thought he was in love with her, not merely a loving friend.

When the bartender brought their hot drinks, David threw down two quarters, more than the swill's worth. At least it was strong. Really strong. "You did great tonight. Just like old times."

Hattie surveyed her surroundings. Peeling paint, a broken bar mirror, and the stench of stale beer were anything but old times. However, until the news storm passed, she could not hope for anything more. She lifted her coffee mug and clinked it against David's, forcing a smile. "Just like old times," she said with an edge to her tone.

"Hey." He rubbed her arm. "It's a weeklong gig. Things will pick up."

"Will they?" Hattie envisioned performing in dives like the Playhouse for eternity. She hadn't played in places like this since arriving in New York City nearly ten years ago to make a name for herself.

"Not if I have anything to do with it," a man behind Hattie said.

She turned, finding the last face on earth she wanted to see. "Agent Knight, I suppose you're behind my continued misery."

"You suppose correctly." Knight grinned, narrowing his eyes. "And it will continue until you help us find your father."

"Then I suppose I'm destined to be miserable." Hattie sipped her coffee, keeping her stare on Knight in the broken mirror behind the bar. Her dislike for the man was as strong as the coffee.

"I think you may change your mind once you hear what I have to say."

"And why would I listen to anything you say?" She narrowed her eyes at him in the mirror. "You've made my life a living hell for a month."

Knight smirked. "You have no idea what hell is, sweetie."

David bounced from his stool, grabbed Knight by the lapel with both hands, and snarled, "Watch your mouth."

"Your boyfriend must love it in handcuffs." Knight glanced at David's grip on him and sneered. "He has five seconds to let go. Otherwise, I'll arrest him for assaulting a federal officer."

"David, please." Hattie pleaded with her eyes.

David released his hold, but not before giving Knight an extra shove. "Watch your manners." He looked at the nearby patrons and the attention he stirred up, which wasn't much. The bartender showed interest but quickly turned away. This place really was a dive. If David had done that at the Copacabana club, he would have been escorted out and told never to return.

"Is there someplace we can talk?" Knight asked.

"Go to hell," Hattie said. If Knight was with other agents, they would have stepped in when David showed aggression, but no one did. Hattie guessed he was alone, preferring not to have witnesses for what he was about to do.

Knight leaned in so only Hattie could hear. "Unless you want me to arrest your sister and her husband, you'll take me somewhere so we can talk."

Could this man sink any lower? *Probably*, she thought. But experience told her his threats were not empty and demanded she consider them a promise. "In the back, but David is coming with me."

He winked at David. "I wouldn't have it any other way."

Hattie took a long sip of coffee, thanked the bartender, and led Knight through a door behind the stage. The area didn't have a traditional dressing room like the Copacabana or every other club she'd performed in, but the janitor's closet off the dank back corridor provided some privacy.

She opened the door, turned on the overhead light, and stepped inside. David closed the door behind them. The room was large enough for the three but not much more.

"Nice office," Knight quipped. The smell of his Aqua Velva was strong and offending.

"Don't waste my time, Knight. What do you want?" Hattie said.

"A man fitting your father's description was seen departing a cargo ship two nights ago in Rio de Janeiro."

The mention of Rio caught Hattie's attention. It was the city where her mother and father first met and where her mother retreated after their divorce.

"I thought that would interest you," Knight said. "Your sister sent a telegram to your mother in Rio, telling her Karl was missing and asked if she had seen him. Your mother then made an overseas call to her the same day your father was seen at the docks there. That's too coincidental. Combine that with the State Department documents we found in your sister's house the night your father escaped, and we have enough to arrest her and her husband for aiding a fugitive."

Dammit, Liv, Hattie thought. Before returning to New York, she reminded her sister to not discuss anything about their father with anyone, including their mother. She should have predicted Olivia couldn't hold out since that woman always looked to their mother for comfort.

"What do you want me to do?"

David snapped his head toward Hattie. "You can't be serious. You want to help this creep?"

"It's not a matter of wanting to," she said. "Frank and Olivia will go to jail if I don't do as he says. Then what would happen to Matthew and

Sarah? I'm their only living relative in the country, but I'm sure Agent Knight would make sure the court considered me unfit to take them in."

"You're a smart girl," Knight said.

"I hate you, Knight." David balled his fists. "Really hate you."

"Then I'm doing my job." Knight turned to Hattie. "We suspect your father will contact your mother if he hasn't already. We want you to go to Rio and flush him out."

"When would I have to leave?"

"As soon as possible." He handed her a business card with his phone number on it.

"I'll let you know by morning."

~

David inserted the key into the lock of Hattie's apartment. Since the night they returned from the Copacabana and found her place ransacked, he insisted on opening the door and going in first. He eased the door open, slid his hand inside, and turned on the wall switch.

"Geez." He glanced over his shoulder at Hattie. "Stay here. Your place is a wreck again."

"This is ridiculous." She pushed past him, finding her belongings strewn about the floor like they were a month ago, similar to the condition the FBI had left Olivia's house in after hauling everyone in for questioning. "Knight had a party here before coming to see us tonight."

"What do you think he was looking for this time?" David asked.

"Does it matter?" Hattie calmly put her handbag on the entry table.

David placed his music satchel next to Hattie's bag. "Are you still serious about going to Brazil?"

"What choice do I have? Knight won't stop until he gets what he wants. Either I go, or my niece and nephew end up in foster care because their parents are in jail." She started putting things away, thinking Knight's personal mission perhaps meant the evidence against her father wasn't as strong as he claimed, bolstering her belief that her father was innocent.

"Then I'm going with you. Whoever broke your father out of custody is dangerous. They've already killed two men," David said.

Hattie had yet to share with him what Knight had told her about Karl's actual job with the State Department the day he showed up at her apartment and doubted she ever would. She hadn't even shared the information with her sister. Verifying Knight's story was impossible without speaking to her father. Until she could, the fewer people who knew the seriousness of the allegations against her father, the better.

Hattie hugged David for a long moment before saying, "Thank you." The idea of going to Rio without him was daunting. At least with him there, she knew he would watch her back. "I better call Knight." She picked up the phone handset and had the operator connect her to the number on Knight's business card.

He answered on the first ring as if he were expecting her call. "Hello, Hattie."

"I'll go, but if anything happens to my sister and brother-in-law, the deal is off. Oh, and David is coming with me."

"I figured as much. Your passports will be ready on Monday. You fly out that night."

Hattie hung up the phone, thinking Knight had leveraged the perfect weapon against her—her love for her family. Though she resented her father for putting her in this position and still believed in his innocence, she would do anything to protect the people she loved.

7

After twenty-four hours of shuttling between continents in a Boeing 314 Clipper—starting at Pan Am's Marine Air Terminal at LaGuardia Airport, where the Clipper was moored on the water, and flying to the Azores Islands, Lisbon, Portugal, and Natal, Brazil—Hattie understood why her mother only traveled to the United States via ship. It was a leisurely twelve days on the water, whereas this was a constant "get on the plane, get off the plane." At least the plane had a dining room for the fifty or so passengers to take their meals. The trip had been exhausting, and it wasn't over yet. She and David were finally on the last leg of the journey to Rio de Janeiro.

She found only two positive aspects of the trip. The FBI had footed the bill for their tickets, a first-class passage she otherwise would never have sprung for. Then there were the stewardesses. All were young and pretty, and their uniforms were delicious. Each wore a blue Chesterfield jacket with a tuxedo-front blouse in white cotton, a matching flared camisole skirt that reached above the knee, and a pair of low-heel shoes in black leather. The outfit conveyed elegance and sophistication. However, the pillbox hat with the Pan Am logo was a bit much.

With her destination finally in reach, Hattie allowed herself to consider the predicament Agent Knight had skillfully thrust upon her. He'd presented her with the worst imaginable scenario: turn in her father to save her sister and her family. Sacrificing one family member for another was not a choice. It was coercion. Despite Knight's claim of having justice in his corner, anyone who would leverage the life of a two-year-old was morally bankrupt.

Her mind drifted to her father, and she envisioned coming face-to-face with him. Her breathing shallowed as she imagined the look of betrayal in his eyes when Knight or one of his men emerged from the shadows to hold him at gunpoint. Before the bloody escape, she would have forecasted her father's surrender without a fight. However, considering how long he'd been on the run, she wasn't sure how he would react. He might resist, provoking the FBI to fire—a predictable, bloody consequence Hattie could not live with, no matter what it might cost Olivia and her family.

David placed his hand on hers. "Are you okay? You're crying."

"I'll be fine." She squeezed his hand, thinking she had to devise a compromise between handing her father over and protecting Olivia.

"I hate this too." He looked at her with sad, consoling eyes.

A stewardess came through their compartment, asking the passengers to put away their personal items for landing. The look of contempt reappeared on the faces of the American couple across the aisle when the attendant approached Hattie's seat. The stain of being the daughter of an accused traitor and Nazi collaborator had followed her five thousand miles to another continent.

The next few minutes would mark Hattie's fourth water landing in the Clipper. She expected another bumpy ride and held on to her chair's cushioned arm to prevent being jostled like the last time. Once the plane landed and they were safely on the dock, David collected their luggage with the help of a porter. Unsure how long her assignment would take, Hattie and David had packed every piece of clothing they owned and a handful of belongings into a steamer trunk and several suitcases. She also prepaid her rent and utilities for six months and told her landlady she would be out of town for some time.

The afternoon taxi ride into town was chaotic. The last day of Carnival was in full swing, with revelers filling the streets. Their driver bypassed the throngs by traveling on side streets, but Hattie got brief glimpses of the parade with dancers and performers of all types dressed in bright, festive outfits. Musicians played their instruments to the beat of a lively samba, and revelers cheered and clapped as the parade strolled along. The scene was a wild party Hattie could never have imagined.

People moved in large groups, men and women alike, wearing the same vibrant red, yellow, orange, green, or aqua blue, transforming the boulevard into a river of flowing colors. Hattie focused on the women in daring outfits that showed more leg and skin at the waist than she would ever dare on the stage. Though she loved their layers of beaded necklaces and bracelets and hats. My, those hats. Nearly every woman had on some type of head covering, ranging from simple handkerchiefs wrapped around their heads to elaborate wide-brimmed straw sun hats decorated in bright colors to match their outfits.

The cabbie took them to one of the few hotels with a vacancy off the parade route in a quieter part of Rio. The Novo Sol was newer and pricier than most established hotels in town but not as expensive as the Palace or anything on the beaches. Nevertheless, she couldn't stay there long and maintain the ruse that the government had frozen her assets. Otherwise, her mother would see right through Hattie accepting her help.

While David and the driver tended to the luggage, Hattie entered the lobby teeming with people. While the staff were all dressed in matching white uniforms, guests were a mix of business attire or bright carnival clothing. She wasn't surprised the desk clerk spoke perfect English. Rio had become South America's leading tourist destination, and English was the common language among most international travelers. Thankfully, it appeared that during her stay in Rio, Hattie would not have to rely on the Portuguese her mother had taught her, a second language she never thought she would use and likely could not do efficiently.

The clerk was polite and eager to please, clearly not recognizing her as the notorious Hattie James. She checked in as Mr. and Mrs. Townsend, paying cash for the first two nights as part of the ruse, and had to trust the desk clerk wasn't taking her for a ride with the incredible amount of Brazilian reals he said she owed. She then asked for a bellhop to bring their luggage to their second-floor room. After David tipped the man, Hattie flopped on the bed and let out a loud breath. She was no stranger to traveling and being on the road for long stretches, but this trip was as mentally taxing as it was physically.

David joined her on the bed, lying next to her. "You hungry? I saw a café down the street and can pick up something."

She was more thirsty than hungry, but the dresser across the room with a pitcher of fresh water seemed too far to walk. "Not yet, but I could use a drink of water."

"Me too." David rolled over, propped himself on one side, and kissed Hattie on the cheek, letting it linger longer than he ever had before. She didn't know what to think of it other than exhaustion may have played a factor.

He poured two glasses, offering one to Hattie. "What's the plan?"

"Knight said to wait. Someone would contact me." She sipped her drink, half hoping the FBI had already returned her father to custody so she wouldn't have to do their dirty work.

Following a brief rest, she and David unpacked a few things, leaving the steamer trunk untouched. If things worked out, they would return to the United States without cracking it open and diving into the rest of their wardrobe.

Soon, a knock on the room door drew their attention. "Housekeeping." The muffled voice came from the other side.

Hattie was cautious. The room was spotless, the bathroom had plenty of towels, and it was too early for turndown service, though she doubted this hotel was of high enough quality to pamper their guests in such a way. She squinted her confusion, prompting David to rush to the door.

"We're fine," he said. "Come back in the morning."

"I brought extra towels. Management thought you might need some after your long trip," a woman said through the door. Her English was suspicious. It made sense for the clerks and porter to be conversant in English, but not the cleaning staff.

Maybe it was exhaustion or perhaps instinct, but something told Hattie she might be Knight's contact. "Open the door."

David looked at her with questioning eyes, but Hattie repeated her instructions. He let in a petite brunette. She appeared to be a local of Portuguese descent, wore a maid's uniform, and had her hand hidden beneath a set of hotel towels. Before her father's escape, Hattie would have thought nothing about the maid's hand. However, after staring down at the barrel of a gun in her sister's home in the middle of the night, she saw danger lurking in every corner.

Once the door closed and the maid walked further inside, David picked up a heavy glass ashtray from the entry table, raised it chest-high, and followed steps behind her.

"Hello, Miss James," the maid said, stopping a few feet from Hattie.

Hattie's pulse picked up as she focused on the towels draped over the woman's hand. "How can I help you?" she asked in a shaky voice.

David closed in.

Then.

The maid placed the towels on the dresser, exposing an empty hand. "Agent Knight sent me."

Hattie blinked her relief and waved David off. He backed away and returned the ashtray to its proper spot.

"Have you contacted your mother yet?" the woman asked.

"Not yet."

"We have eyes on her home and music studio and want you to get inside both. If your father is there, you need to signal us immediately. Otherwise, look for any sign he's been in either place."

"How do I reach you?"

The woman handed her a business card to Cohen Dry Cleaners with a phone number and an address in Rio. "Ask for Nala."

"Are you an agent, Nala?"

"I'm an asset like you. We expect you to keep us informed of any changes. We'll also be watching you, so don't think of leaving before we find your father." Nala's haughty expression made Hattie think she was also a pawn and wonder if the FBI was also holding something over her head. Had they threatened her family to get her to cooperate? Or was she simply paid well to help make Hattie's life miserable?

"As if I have a choice."

"The sooner you contact your mother, the sooner we can wrap this up. I suggest you start today. Oh, and get a job to further your cover."

"What kind of job?"

"Anything that pays. Otherwise, your mother will question your staying here."

After Nala left, Hattie paced her hotel room, gathering the courage to make that call. With Nala or someone else with the FBI watching her every move, she feared the call would set something in motion over which she would have no control.

After all these years, the twelve-year-old image of her mother being mounted by another man in her parents' bedroom still turned Hattie's stomach. Eva's annual summer visits to Olivia's had tested Hattie's patience, but Hattie had always put on a pleasant exterior to avoid ruining the family reunion for her sister's sake. She simply needed to draw on that strength to make it through the next few hours, days, and perhaps weeks.

Hattie took a deep breath and grabbed her handbag. "We better make that call." Once in the lobby, she sat in a far corner with David, away from other guests, and arranged for an outside line on a house phone. Considering the holiday, she had the operator connect her to her mother's house for the first time . . . ever . . . and took several long, calming breaths. That woman had a way of making every conversation about her before anyone could explain why they called.

The call connected. "Olá."

"Hello, Mother."

"Hattie? Is that you? Is something wrong with Olivia and the kids?"

"No, Mother, Liv and the kids are fine."

"Then you must be calling about your father. Your sister sent me a telegram asking about him. Of course, I had to arrange a radio call to learn what happened. She told me about his arrest and escape and how RCA dropped your contract. I'm so glad the news has yet to reach here. If anyone knew my ex-husband was working with the Nazis, parents might stop bringing in their children for singing and music lessons."

"Accused, Mother. He's only been accused."

"Assumed innocent and all. I understand the American system of justice, but—"

"No buts, Mother." Hattie took another calming breath to get through this. "I'm calling because I'm in Rio."

"Rio?" her mother squealed. "What on earth has brought you here?"

"Could we meet today? We can discuss things in person."

"Oh, sweetheart. This is wonderful. Of course we can meet. Where are you staying?"

"At the Nova Sol. There's an outdoor café at the end of the block. We could meet there."

"I'll be there in thirty minutes. Oh, Hattie, this makes me so happy. I'll see you soon."

Hattie hung up the phone, fearing what she had set in motion. And dreading it.

~

The street their hotel was on was not on the parade route nor part of the traditional Carnival celebration, so pedestrian traffic was light to the corner café. They arrived between the lunch and dinner crowd, the hottest part of the day, and had the pick of the outdoor tables. The waiter instructed them to sit anywhere and said he would be right there.

They took a table closest to the restaurant windows which was still in the afternoon shade and furthest from the street to avoid sucking in gas fumes once traffic picked up. The morning edition of the *Jornal Do Brasil* had been left on the table, so Hattie picked it up. Her Portuguese was rusty —really rusty—but the photographs helped to discern the headline story centered on Carnival, the most significant holiday celebration in the country.

The waiter dropped off the water and menus. He spoke broken English but well enough to work in a restaurant in the heart of the capital's tourist sector. After he took their orders, Hattie resumed her scan of the newspaper on page two. A collection of photographs of eight women caught her eye. The accompanying story was hard to read, but she discerned the women had gone missing in the last month, sometimes two in one night. She studied the photographs, assessing most of the women were young and pretty.

Their food came, and Hattie started in, hoping to be done while she still had an appetite before her mother arrived. But that wasn't to be.

"Sweetheart." The voice behind Hattie was unmistakable. Even while issuing a simple greeting, Eva Machado used the trademark sultry voice that once made thousands swoon over her.

Hattie steeled herself, putting on her brightest smile before standing and turning. "Mother." She hugged her, trying to keep it brief, but her mother sustained her hold tight, clearly making a point.

"I've missed you, sweetheart." Eva finally pulled back. "Let me look at you. Beautiful as always."

"Same with you."

At fifty-five, Eva appeared forty. Her warm, light brown skin tone made her look perpetually sun-kissed. Her long brown hair was still full and wavy, styled like a movie star. She had put on ten pounds since her performing days when she starved herself regularly to look attractive on stage, but Hattie preferred a little curve on her mother. It meant she ate when she was hungry, not to avoid fainting.

Eva glanced across the table. "And who do we have here?"

"Mother, I'd like you to meet my fiancé, David Townsend."

Eva's eyes widened with joy.

"David, this is my mother, Eva Machado."

"It's a pleasure to meet you, Miss Machado." David extended his hand.

"Please, call me Eva." She waved off his hand and pulled him into a hug. "Fiancé, huh? I never thought anyone could capture my little songbird."

"I wouldn't call her captured," David said. "More like safeguarded."

Eva grinned. "I like him, Hattie. He knows Machado women can never be tamed."

Hattie harrumphed, returning to her seat while David politely held her chair. "Then explain Olivia."

"She's her father's daughter, through and through, always a follower. But you and I are never happy with the beaten path. We find our own way." Eva sat next to Hattie, and David scooted her in.

David laughed, reclaiming his seat across from Hattie. "No truer words."

As much as Hattie wanted to deny it, she and her mother were much alike. They were independent, determined, and strongheaded, but there was one big difference between them. Hattie put the needs of her family above her own.

Eva squeezed Hattie's hand briefly. "So, what brings you to Rio?"

"Work. Olivia told you only half of it. My agent dropped me, and my singing engagements have dried up."

"So, you come to Mother. You have no idea how happy this makes me."

Hattie sucked in her frustration. Eva had made this about her in record time. "I need to kick-start my career again. I thought if you could do it here twice, I could too."

"I'm sure I can help. I'll reach out to my friends and call in a favor to get you in at the Palace."

"No, Mother." Hattie's age-old battle with her mother had already raised its head. Eva was never happy with letting Hattie's career unfold on its own. She had to help it along at every turn. "No string pulling."

"A little push won't hurt."

"I said no, Mother. I need to do this on my own." Hattie dug deep to not lose her temper. "I'll make the rounds and audition like everyone else. I only need you to point me in the right direction."

"A Machado doesn't audition." Eva turned her nose up.

"This one does."

Eva harrumphed, another tic she and Hattie had in common. "I suppose there's no talking you out of it." After rattling off the names of several downtown nightclubs, she turned to David. "Tell me how you met my daughter. How did you propose?"

"Don't pepper him with questions, Mother." Hattie rolled her eyes.

"It's all right, Hattie." David chuckled, turning to Eva. "I'm her piano player."

"Ahhh, a musical romance." Eva patted his arm. "Every performer's dream."

Hattie remained silent. Her mother had focused the conversation on her in the stealthiest way. Of course, a musical romance was her dream, though drummers were more her style—at least the one Hattie had discovered in Eva's bed.

"Yes, I suppose," David said. "We've been engaged for a month."

"Any wedding plans?"

"None yet," he said. "We need to see how Rio plays out."

Hattie bit her tongue. There would be no wedding. She only needed to find her father and get back home.

"Ahh, practical." Eva nodded. "Have you looked for a place to live?"

"We just arrived today, Mother."

"I can recommend several nice neighborhoods. Until you find something suitable, I have a perfectly good guest room with a private bath. You're welcome to stay for as long as you need."

"The last thing I want is to live in my mother's house with my fiancé." However, the offer was exactly what Hattie needed. Nala had told her to get inside her mother's house, but Hattie couldn't accept it too quickly. Considering the years of animosity between them, Eva wouldn't buy it. "Let us get settled, and I'll let you know."

"That's all I can ask." Eva squeezed her daughter's hand again. "This is wonderful, Hattie. I predict incredible things for us."

8

The following day

Hattie stood on the balcony of her hotel room, sipping her first coffee of the day, the exhaustion of twenty-four hours of traveling still wreaking havoc on her body clock. The sun was high, and a sticky heat had already set in. Despite the late morning hour, the city was quiet, still hungover from three days of celebration.

Rio reminded her of Miami's mix of old and new architecture and tropical climate. She could see why her parents loved it here and why her mother retreated here after the divorce. This modern paradise was a place Hattie could get used to. No more winter coats, only summer dresses and bathing suits.

The sliding glass door opened, and David stepped outside, clutching the morning newspaper's classified section. "I had the porter circle all the rentals close to downtown."

"Good. That should make it believable," Hattie said. With eyes watching her, she needed to ensure her cover story of looking for work and a place to live was believable. The prop should advance the ruse that she and David had difficulty finding affordable housing prospects when they met up with Eva. Her mother was no fool and could spot a fake as easily as a glass diamond. "Then we should be going." Hattie kissed him on the cheek before downing the rest of her coffee.

After exchanging a thousand dollars in American currency for Brazilian reals at a nearby bank, they taxied to her mother's music studio in the Lapa district. Its location wasn't surprising. Eva thrived on the nightlife, and according to the hotel clerk, that part of town came to life after sunset.

Hattie stepped from the cab and read the ornate sign above the door: Eva Machado, Professor de Música. Her mother had taken to teaching music two years ago. Despite her continued popularity, she hadn't recorded a song in five years, and, other than short-term appearances, her performances were too few to pay the bills. Her mother must have swallowed every ounce of her pride to open the studio. Hattie knew the feeling. She was about to do the same by entering her mother's studio.

David held the door open. Before Hattie walked inside, she looked up and down the street. Traffic was picking up, a sign this part of town was slowly coming to life. Two businesses down, at the corner, a man in casual attire was leaning against the building, reading a newspaper. He was the only pedestrian on the street, making Hattie think he might have been one set of eyes assigned to watch her.

"Coming, Hattie?" David asked.

"Yes." She stepped inside.

The reception area was elegantly decorated in purple velvet and gold trim, her mother's favorite colors. The walls were adorned with framed photographs of Eva on stage, in the recording studio, and with several American and Brazilian celebrities. No one was at the desk. The muffled sound of a piano and a young girl singing somewhere in the back were the only signs of activity. The girl was quite good.

A hand-painted sign said to ring the bell for service, but Hattie didn't want to interrupt the girl's performance. Instead, she snooped, looking for a sign her father might have been there. An appointment calendar was centered on the desktop, displaying the current week. Names filled many time slots, suggesting her mother had a busy schedule. A wooden box near the telephone on the desk corner contained index cards with alphabet dividers sticking out prominently. Hattie thumbed to the *J* and flipped through the cards, finding only students' names, but she didn't expect to locate her father's name. Hell would have to have frozen before her mother kept her ex-husband's number at her office.

Pulling open the drawers, she found only office supplies and blank forms for new clients. *This is silly*, she thought. Eva hated Hattie's father, which had perplexed Hattie for years. Her mother would not keep information about him here.

The music and singing stopped, and Hattie returned to David's side near the studio entrance. Moments later, a secondary door to the back opened, and Eva stepped out, escorting a young girl about ten years old and giving her words of encouragement. The girl nodded and smiled, clearly bathing in the ego boost of Eva Machado praising her singing ability.

Eva slowed and smiled when she glimpsed Hattie but continued toward the entrance with her hand on the girl's shoulder. "Quero que você pratique por uma hora todos os dias. Uma voz deve ser exercida para que seja boa."

Hattie's Portuguese was coming back to her, and she remembered her mother's daily instructions after her voice lessons as a child. "Practice for an hour every day. A voice must be exercised if it's to be any good," her mother used to say. It was a lesson Hattie carried with her to this day.

The girl left, and Eva turned. "Sweetheart, it's good to see you. What brings you here?"

Hattie glanced out the glass windows at the busy street traffic to start the ruse. When the man from the corner walked past, the eyes on her made her uncomfortable. "Can we talk somewhere more private?"

"Of course." Eva led Hattie and David through the back door to the studio. The grand piano in front of the small stage looked familiar.

Hattie stopped. "Is that the Steinway that was in our home in Washington?"

"Yes. It's the one I bought after making my first record. I couldn't bear to part with it."

Interesting, Hattie thought. While the State Department must have paid to send the piano to the United States after her parents married, it must have cost her father a small fortune to ship it back to Brazil, further proof he still loved her. Why else would he accommodate a cheating wife?

Eva continued to an office at the far end of the studio. She sat at the desk and invited Hattie and David to the guest chairs. The office was decorated smartly, like the reception area, and contained more pictures of Eva at the height of her career. An oscillating fan stirred the humid air, making the stuffy space sufferable.

Eva poured a glass of water from a pitcher sitting on a credenza behind her desk. "Water, anyone?"

"Yes, please," David said. The sweat streaking his face said he was unaccustomed to the humid weather.

"I'm fine, thank you," Hattie said, still scanning the office. She focused on a photograph of her mother seated at her piano with a young Hattie on her lap, pressing her fingers against the keys. A tug of emotion hit her when she realized the piano in the photo was the same one in the next room. "Sometimes I wish I would have taken to the piano."

"It's not for everyone," Eva said. "Think of it as a blessing. If you had, you wouldn't have met young David."

Hattie glanced at him and patted his hand. "Yes, a blessing."

"So, what brings you here today?" Eva asked.

"This is embarrassing." Hattie shifted uncomfortably in her chair to sell the lie. "The FBI has frozen my accounts back in the States until all this mess with Father is sorted out. All we have is what we brought on the trip." She grabbed the classified section of the paper from David's hand. "We've been looking for a place, but everyone wants advance money, which would drain us. I need to find a singing gig right now."

"I made some inquiries last night." Eva offered an impish smile, but it spun into a frown. "Only one showed interest. Everyone is booked solid because of Carnival. I'm afraid it's not the level of the Palace, but—"

"I'll take anything I can get. Where is it?"

"The Halo Club. It's here in the Lapa." Eva jotted down some information on a sheet of paper. "The club is under new management since June, but they haven't done much with the place yet."

"It doesn't matter." Hattie glanced at the paper with the club address and the owner's last name.

"I doubt they can pay much." Eva circled her desk and took Hattie's hand into hers. "Until you find something that pays commensurate with your talent, please stay with me. I would love having you both there."

"Let me speak with the owner and see what they offer." Hattie studied her mother. She never doubted her motherly love, and her concern sounded genuine, but if the past had taught her anything, Hattie was sure her mother would use the opportunity of her moving in to steer her career in the direction that mirrored hers.

"I can call—"

"Mother, please. You've already inquired. The rest is up to me. I'll call the owner today and arrange a meeting." Hattie stood and pulled her mother into a hug. This one felt more genuine than their first yesterday, and strangely, it felt good. "Thank you."

"I love you, Hattie." Eva pulled back. "We're family. No thanks are necessary."

"I'll let you know how it goes."

Eva led them back through the studio to the reception area when the front door opened. A tall man dressed in a crisp white suit stepped inside. His cropped blond hair and light skin weren't typical in this part of town unless they were tourists, and he carried himself with distinction, reminiscent of her father.

The man eyed both women but spent more time scrutinizing Hattie. The extra attention was familiar and made her uneasy. Every time Hattie performed at a nightclub, she encountered at least one man who stared at her like she was something to acquire . . . a possession he wanted no matter what it took to get her. This man's stare gave her the same feeling, though it didn't come across as sexual. It was something more primal, and that frightened her.

David stepped forward, positioning himself between Hattie and the man. He was marking his territory, and Hattie was never more grateful for his protective side.

"Olá. Você fala inglês?" he asked, using a funny accent.

"Yes, I speak English," Eva said. "How may I help you?"

"I'm looking for Eva Machado." He spoke with a German accent.

"You have her."

"My name is Heinz Baumann." He extended his hand. "I run a coffee plantation not far from town. My daughter turned thirteen recently, and I'd like you to give her singing lessons for an upcoming church recital."

"I'd be happy to teach her." Eva went to the desk and pulled a form from the bottom drawer. "Please fill this out, and I'll call you with available studio times."

"You misunderstand, Miss Machado. I need you to teach her in my home."

"I'm sorry, Mr. Baumann, but my schedule is too full to accommodate home lessons. However, I'm happy to move my schedule around to make it more convenient for you."

"That won't do, I'm afraid," Baumann said. "I need someone to come to the plantation."

"I simply don't have the time. Perhaps my daughter might be interested." Eva gestured toward her.

"I couldn't." Hattie waved her off. "I have no way of getting out there."

"You could borrow my car," Eva said.

Hattie gave her the side eye. The man made her uncomfortable as he stared at her again. He seemed to appreciate her appearance, but his dismissive smirk was insulting.

"I came here because you are considered the best vocal instructor in the country. I only want the best for my child."

"And you would get the same with my daughter. If you listened to American music, you would know Hattie James is an icon who has recorded with RCA and performed at the opening of the Copacabana club in New York City."

Hearing Eva sing her praises left Hattie dumbfounded. When her mother visited, she waffled between being proud and critical of Hattie's choices, comparing Hattie's accomplishments to hers. She didn't know what to make of it but wanted to believe her sentiments were genuine. This turn of events was refreshing and long overdue.

Baumann looked at Hattie again, this time with a glimmer of respect. "Perhaps it's something to consider. But why are you here, Miss James? Why are you in Rio?"

"Umm . . ." Hattie mumbled. Neither the truth about the FBI nor the story she gave her mother about being ostracized from the music business would work.

"She came to Rio at my request," Eva said. "Sometimes a mother simply needs her daughter." Her mother's fabricated yet believable story left Hattie speechless. It helped her out of an awkward position and proved how quickly her mother could come up with a lie, a disturbing realization.

"I see," he said, turning to Hattie. "I would be honored if you would offer my daughter singing lessons at our home."

"May I think about it? My fiancé and I only arrived yesterday."

"Of course." Baumann reached into his interior breast pocket and handed Hattie a business card. "Please call if you're interested." He walked out, giving Hattie one more long, penetrating look.

His stare left her feeling exposed. It had a sinister quality, yet he was polite and had an air of sophistication. Even more disturbing was that he reminded her of her father, which would have been ridiculous a month ago. During her childhood, he never once raised his voice or a hand to her, and before the night of his escape, she never considered him capable of wrongdoing. However, after a month of him not coming forward to clear his name, anything seemed possible, even the similarities to a man who frightened her.

"You're not seriously entertaining his offer?" David asked.

Hattie focused on the door and turned to David when he touched her arm. She had seen him worried many times, but the look on his face was not concern. It was pure anger. Her earlier assessment of Baumann's stare being primal was prophetic. He had brought out a primal instinct in David to protect her. It was a natural extension of how their friendship started—provide each other a cover and have the other's back because they both had much to lose if their sexual orientations were made public.

Hattie handed Eva the man's business card. "Not particularly," she said, covering his hand with hers to reassure him. "I want to sing to a crowd, not teach it."

9

The following afternoon, Hattie and David taxied through the Lapa district after a brief summer downpour. Their driver was the same gentleman—a timid fellow in his thirties who spoke broken English—who drove them to Eva's studio yesterday. It could have been a coincidence, but Hattie was suspicious of everything and everyone in Rio. She kept quiet in the back seat until the driver pulled in front of the Halo Club.

David paid the fare and held the cab door open.

Hattie stepped onto the sidewalk into the blistering heat and instantly understood her mother's concern. While the Halo Club had an ideal location near the waterfront, the building was an eyesore. The design had many classic architectural elements, but half the arches were boarded up, and the dirt-stained limestone façade stuck out among the other refurbished buildings on the street. A bright neon sign on the rounded portico above the corner entrance was the only evidence of improvement. The large pink letters spelling the club's name were modern and attracted people from blocks away. A good scrubbing and new window glass could easily make the place attractive.

This place was more than a step down from the Copacabana club, but Hattie had performed at worse places when she started her career—and last week. And since no one in New York would hire her anytime soon, the

Halo Club would be her proving ground. No one in Rio considered her the daughter of a traitor except for the FBI agents. If she could make her mark here based only on her talent, she would know she had what it took to remake herself anywhere.

"Are you sure you want to work here?" David asked, surveying his surroundings.

"I'm positive." Hattie was determined to rebuild her career and reputation after her father unwittingly stole that from her when he escaped custody. The bottom was the perfect place to start over.

She straightened the skirt she'd chosen for the way it showed off her figure. It was tight but not too tight. She'd decided on her blouse for the same reason. Hattie had learned from her mother that it wasn't enough to have a pitch-perfect voice. She had to be an entertainer to make it in the singing business, which meant selling herself as much as her talent.

David held the club door open, and Hattie entered. Recorded music played in the background. She stopped to listen and chuckled silently at the Maggie Moore song playing. She walked deeper inside, which wasn't much of an improvement from the outside. It was worn and dated but clean, a step up from the Playhouse she performed in a week ago. The room smelled of cigarette smoke. Only smoke. The absence of stale beer and urine odors meant the management took pride in the establishment. She already liked the place. It reminded her of her humble beginnings. And if the new management had plans to make changes, she would love to see the transformation.

According to the sign on the front door, the club had opened minutes ago for the day. The center dining area had seating for about two hundred, and the bar area had room for another fifty. A handful of patrons were seated at the tables, each nursing a cocktail or beer glass.

Two women were behind the bar. One with short hair was making a drink in front of an Anglo customer, and the other with long hair was stocking glasses. The Anglo customer said something to earn the ire of the bartender, and she gave him a shot of seltzer water to the face. He reached across the bar, grabbed her by the arm, and yanked her forward. "You like it rough?" he bellowed in English in a lewd way.

The long-haired woman rushed to the other one's aid. She bent the man's thumb back, forcing him to grimace and loosen his hold. Pushing his hand to the bar top, she leaned in and spoke in a Portuguese accent. "That's no way to treat a lady."

"Lady? She sprayed my face," he said, seltzer dripping from his hair onto the bar.

"I heard what you said to her. It wasn't very gentlemanly. I believe you owe her an apology."

"Apology?" He struggled against her hold but couldn't break free.

"Yes, an apology." She bent his thumb back farther. "Or would you prefer two months in a cast?"

He grunted through the pain. "I'm . . . sorry."

"Now, give the lady a nice tip." Once he reached into his pocket and threw some money on the bar, she released her hold. "There. That wasn't so hard. If you're rude again, that's it. You're out."

He rubbed his thumb, and the two men with him snickered.

Hattie was impressed. Strong, independent women who could manage themselves always caught her eye. Helen was a prime example. Neither her ex-lover nor this woman took an ounce of guff from anyone, especially a man.

She waited until the woman returned to stacking the glasses before approaching. "Excuse me. I'm looking for the owner."

"Who's asking?" The woman continued her work without looking up.

"Hattie James. I called last night about singing here. The woman I spoke to said to come today when the club opened and speak to the owner."

The woman stopped her task and looked at Hattie. "You're going to wear that to perform?"

Hattie inspected her clothes. They were clean, pressed, and all the fashion in New York. "What's wrong with my outfit?"

"Nothing if you're going to church. People in Rio expect a little splash from their performers." The woman grinned in amusement. It was a cute smile.

Hattie felt out of her depth. She was half Brazilian-Portuguese but had no sense of the culture and only a basic grasp of the language. Then she remembered more of her mother's advice when she first considered a singing career. She'd said to never show doubt. No one wants to hire an entertainer unsure of her own talent.

"Then I'll need to go shopping after the owner offers me the gig."

"You're pretty sure you're talented enough to sing here." The woman folded her arms across her chest while eyeing Hattie more closely.

"I'll let the owner be the judge."

"Well then, we better get to it." The woman emerged from the bar, wiping her hands on a towel. She extended her hand. "I'm Maya Reyes. My sister and I own the place." She gestured toward the bartender.

They shook hands.

"Pleased to meet you, Miss Reyes." Hattie gestured behind her. "This is David Townsend, my piano player. Shall we set up?"

Maya glanced over her shoulder and spoke in Portuguese. "Anna, can you finish up here?"

The woman behind the bar looked up. "Yes, go."

"Follow me," Maya said, switching to English. She led Hattie and David around the club's perimeter, following the wall to the far end. Her strides were long and fluid, the sign of a confident woman.

The elevated stage's ample size had enough room for her regular band, so Hattie could perform her songs as she had choreographed them. Maya ascended the stairs and set up the microphone at center stage. She turned it on, and feedback echoed from the speakers, but it settled once she adjusted the settings. "It's all yours."

"How many songs would you like?" Hattie asked.

"Enough to show me what you got."

"Okay." Hattie had no clue how many that meant, but she was prepared to perform a complete set to get the job. She had set up the audition to further her cover story and justify being in Rio, but she hadn't realized until now how much she needed the affirmation.

They passed on the narrow stairs, brushing lightly against one another. Hattie took the contact as a challenge to impress Maya enough to hire her.

David sat at the piano, opened his satchel, and removed his sheet music. "How many, Hattie?"

"Let's give her five." She rattled off the songs she wanted, three up-tempo and two slower ones to showcase her vocal and performance range.

"Perfect." David smiled. He warmed up by playing a few scales to test how in tune the piano was. It sounded flawless.

After Hattie sang her scales to warm up her voice, David asked, "Ready?"

"Let's do it." Hattie scanned the crowd. Several more patrons had arrived, but they still totaled less than twenty. It would be the smallest audience Hattie had performed for. Ever.

David started playing. Hattie stepped up to the microphone and imagined herself at a packed Copacabana club, where she knew she belonged. Note by note, she chipped away at the stifling chaos that had turned her life upside down and swept her into a foreign land. She harnessed that high of feeling powerful again and put every ounce of that energy into her performance. Finally, she felt some control again.

During her final song, she glanced at Maya sitting at a table for more inspiration and discovered her staring. Her fixed gaze went well beyond assessing Hattie's talent and was reminiscent of the mesmerized patrons who would undress her with their eyes. That primal attention typically made her uncomfortable, especially from men, but she welcomed Maya's fascination.

When she finished, the wild applause and wolf whistles meant she had made an impression on the clientele. David offered his arm and escorted Hattie from the stage and to Maya's table. Maya's eyes followed them . . . well . . . followed Hattie. He pulled out a chair for her before sitting next to her.

Hattie removed a handkerchief from her handbag and wiped the sweat from her brow before asking, "So, do I go wardrobe shopping or not?"

Maya shook her head as if coming out of a daze. "Huh?"

"Do I get the job?"

A smile slowly appeared on Maya's lips. Then she cocked her head. "First, why does Eva Machado's daughter want to perform in a place like this?"

"I see you've done your homework."

"I wouldn't be a good club manager if I didn't. I still want to know why you're auditioning here and not for the Golden Room at the Palace."

"I won't buy my way into the Brazilian market on her name. Either I do it on my own, or I don't do it at all."

Maya considered Hattie for several silent moments . . . searching . . . penetrating . . . and Hattie swore it was *the look*. The sign of interest beyond business or friendship. Having her heart broken had taught Hattie one crucial lesson about her attractions—she was drawn to a particular type of woman in terms of character, not appearance. Maya Reyes fit the mold—confident and charismatic—but looked nothing like Helen. She was more athletic than her past interests.

Funny, Hattie thought. Except for the dark hair and her sex, she was precisely like someone her father had envisioned for her, and Hattie was beginning to believe he could not have been more right. She returned the probing look and felt a tension give birth, if only for a brief second before Maya blinked.

The moment was gone.

"When can you start?"

"That depends on how much you're paying." Hattie cocked her head and locked eyes with Maya, trying to recapture that elusive force, but the woman turned all business and threw out a weekly amount in Brazilian reals.

"I'll need you to perform four nights a week, with Monday, Tuesday, and Wednesday off. Payday is Monday. I'll throw in dinner for you two every night you perform."

"How much is that in American dollars?" The moment slipped further away, drowned by numbers and schedules, making Hattie think it was simply a mirage, a hopeful fantasy.

"I'm not sure?" Maya said.

"Twenty-five at yesterday's exchange rate," David said.

The number shook Hattie out of her head. Twenty-five dollars a week would have been an insult last month, but from what she had seen of the prices for things in Rio, it was a fair offer. However, it wasn't enough for her and David to continue living in a hotel. She would have to take her mother up on the offer of her guest room, which wasn't ideal for Hattie's sanity, but the arrangement would make the FBI happy. "We'll take it. I know I'm not properly dressed, but since it's Friday, we'd be happy to put on a full show tonight."

"That would be great. Your shows start at eight and eleven. We close at one. If word spreads tonight, we could pack the house tomorrow." Maya looked Hattie up and down again in more of an assessing manner, not a "can't take my eyes off you" way, which was, as silly as it might seem, disappointing. "I have something in my office that might fit you." She turned to David. "Mind if I borrow your girl for a minute?"

"By all means," David said.

"Order dinner on the house. Anything you want . . . within reason." She laughed.

Maya led Hattie through the kitchen, where the staff was preparing meals. Hattie noticed a trend between the bartender, servers, bussers, and cooks and asked, "Do any men work here?"

"Only your piano player. I trust women more than men."

"I get that." The music business in the States was controlled by men, and a man was behind every setback Hattie encountered. She trusted few but included the one with her tonight among them. "Though, David is a good man and an even better friend. I trust him."

"I hope he works out."

Hattie pulled Maya to a stop. "What do you mean you hope? If he doesn't play, I don't sing. That's the deal. Take it or leave it."

Maya folded her arms across her chest again as a slight grin formed. "He must be pretty special."

"He is," Hattie said without hesitation. Since the day David walked into the RCA recording studio two years ago to play piano for her and saw how he eyed the drummer, she knew he was just like her. They'd had each other's back since. He had protected her more times than she could count, and with the FBI watching her, she wanted him around.

Maya stared at her for several beats as if sizing her up again but without the piercing, hopeful stare. "All right, then. We better get you that stage dress."

She took Hattie into her office, opened a small closet, and pulled out a festive dress made from bright red, yellow, and orange fabrics and accented with puffy sleeves and a ruffled hem. "I wore this for Carnival. It should fit you." She drew closer to Hattie and held the dress up, pressing her hands slightly against the ends of her shoulders.

The subtle touch stirred the hopeful fantasy again, making her oblivious to whatever Maya said until the contact was broken. Hattie shook her head. "I'm sorry. What were you saying?"

"You're a bit taller than me, so it hits about an inch above the knee. Is that okay?"

"Oh, sure, sure. I don't have a problem with showing a little skin. Where can I change?"

"There's a dressing room behind the stage." For a brief second, *the look* returned, but then commotion in the kitchen drew Maya's attention. She sighed, lowering her head. "I'd show you, but I better see what's going on before the place burns down."

And the moment was lost again.

~

At eight o'clock, she and David started the full-length set she had performed at the Copacabana club before her bookings dried up. During her performance, more patrons filled the seats to half capacity, and Maya was more occupied with the customers. Hattie recognized one latecomer as the plantation owner who had come into her mother's studio yesterday, asking for a music teacher for his daughter. She considered saying hello after her set, but he and his table companions were gone when she finished.

At the night's end, she and David met with Maya near the bar, who broke away from restocking the glasses. "That was great, Hattie," her new boss said. "Mix it up tomorrow night if you have enough material. That should entice some regulars to stay for the second show."

"There's a lot more where that came from." David threw an arm around Hattie's shoulder. "My girl is a seasoned professional."

Maya pinched her expression as if David's affection bothered her. "That was clear to everyone in the room."

"Thank you for trusting me with your club, Miss Reyes," Hattie said.

"Call me Maya. We're all family here."

"Yes, a server told me that, and I got the same impression tonight." Hattie paused at Maya's blushing smile. "If we want to practice, is there a time we can come in before the club opens?"

"We open at four, but my sister and I get here by two."

"That will work," Hattie said. "We're heading out. We'll see you tomorrow."

Hattie and David turned to walk out when a server called out, "Hattie, a customer left something for you." The woman looked behind the bar and handed her a flower. "You already have a fan."

Hattie accepted the flower, inspected it, and gasped at the single stem of edelweiss. She scanned the room, looking desperately for the only person who would have left her this gift. She walked the room's width at a brisk pace, hoping to find him. Reaching the end, she realized he was not there and snapped her stare back at the server. "Where is the man who gave you this?"

"He left with the man who Anna left with."

Maya's eyes narrowed. "She left with a customer again? She told me she wasn't feeling well." She shook her head. "How many times do I have to remind everyone? No flirting with the customers."

The server had a confused look before walking away.

"We have to go," Hattie said without further explanation, pulling David out to the street. She showed him the flower. "My father was at the club tonight."

"Did you see him?"

"No, but who else would have given me a single stem of edelweiss?" The bigger question was how her father got the fresh flower in Brazil since it didn't grow in a tropical climate.

"Are you going to tell the FBI?"

"I don't know." That was the ultimate question. Could Hattie give up her father to save her sister? She considered the question for the entire ride to the Novo Sol but was still torn when they entered the hotel lobby.

Her father's last words to her ran in her head on a loop. He'd said, *"I did what I had to in order to keep you safe. Remember what you promised me at Christmas."* Maybe her initial reaction after her father's escape was spot on, that what the FBI had accused him of had merit and it wasn't merely Agent

Knight's vendetta. Perhaps he did share secrets with the Nazis, but only to protect her from some threat. But the promise she'd made to him still had her perplexed. He'd asked her to never sell or throw away the sheet music he'd gifted her. Why would he mention that at their final meeting? She felt the mystery surrounding her father would clear if she figured out the answer.

David unlocked the door of their room and flipped on the overhead light. They stood in the doorway, staring at yet another invasion. Their room had been scoured through and left a mess, more proof the FBI didn't trust her. They would continue harassing her until she did what they wanted.

"Not again," David said, resting his hands on his hips. "The FBI certainly is persistent."

"Well, that does it for me." Hattie started folding her clothes and returning them to her suitcase. "We better call my mother and tell her we're moving in. They won't dare search her place. Doing so would make her suspicious."

"What about your father?" David asked.

"I'm not telling the FBI a thing until I come face-to-face with him." The more the FBI pushed, the more Hattie felt cornered, and if she were honest, the more she feared her father might be guilty. Eventually, they would leave her without wiggle room and get exactly what they wanted—her father handed to them on a platter, guilty or not. Until then, she would do what she had to in order to keep him safe.

10

Hattie and David packed their things and sat at the room's small dining table, sipping coffee while waiting for the bellhop to fetch their luggage. Moving into her mother's home might drive Hattie crazy, but it had the advantage of placating the FBI until she could decipher her father's last message and speak to him.

Hattie thought again about the last thing her father had told her. She then pulled from David's satchel the collection of sheet music he had gifted her and looked over each piece critically. She wasn't as good at reading music as David, and David wasn't as proficient as her mother, so it was no surprise she couldn't spot anything odd or something that should not have been there.

David gathered their empty coffee cups, placed them on the dresser, and peered over Hattie's shoulder. "What are you looking for?"

She could tell him the truth, but something told her to keep that information to herself. Her father had entrusted the gift to her and no one else. That she let him carry the music in his satchel was enough of a betrayal. "Nothing. This was the last present my father gave me, and I was admiring it." She flipped to another page. "Have you noticed anything odd about the music?"

"No. Why would I?"

"Some of them are quite old. I was curious."

"Your mother could look at them. She teaches music."

"Absolutely not. She hates my father. There's no telling what she might do if she found out why we're here."

"Why *are* we here, Hattie? If you're not willing to turn your father in, we should go home."

The thought of going home had crossed her mind. It would have been easy to call the FBI's bluff and see what they would do to Olivia and her husband if Hattie refused to cooperate. The evidence against them for supposedly abetting their father—a telegram to Eva asking if she had seen their father, a phone call between Olivia and Eva the day her father was seen arriving in Rio, and a few sensitive State Department documents found in Olivia's house—was circumstantial at best. However, she wasn't prepared to take that chance. She had to stall until she found a better way out. "We're buying time. I hope I can save my sister without turning on my father."

"That may not be possible."

"Thankfully, I don't have to make that choice today."

Hattie returned the sheet music to David's satchel when there was a knock on the door.

The bellhop gathered their luggage onto a cart, and David and Hattie followed him down on the elevator, carrying their personal bags. Hattie checked out at the front desk while David followed the bellhop to the waiting taxi. When she exited the hotel, the luggage was already loaded into the trunk, and David was giving the staff member a sizeable tip.

The driver was different this morning, putting her somewhat at ease. Perhaps she had been a little paranoid around their previous driver, and the hotel was simply on the man's late afternoon route. He took them deeper into Rio, where the terrain was hillier and the roads were narrow and paved in brick. Homes on the hills were built close to the street behind high stone walls, making it impossible to glimpse the passing properties.

Hattie thought a man standing on a street corner resembled her father, but they zoomed by too quickly for her to be sure.

After reaching a flat plateau, the driver turned up a private access road, which ended at a courtyard with terra-cotta pavers. He stopped at the two-car garage, a few yards from a polished wood entry gate, and helped David unload the luggage while Hattie rang the bell at the gate. An eight-foot-tall solid wall hid the house, but the tiled roof line peeked out between towering tropical trees.

The door opened, and Eva stepped out, pulling Hattie into a brief hug. "You made it." She glanced at the pile of luggage and spoke to the cab driver in Portuguese, telling him where to take the largest piece. He gestured for David to pick up one end of the steamer trunk while lifting the other. They disappeared inside the gated area.

"I appreciate you taking us in, Mother," Hattie said.

"Of course. We're family." Eva picked up two smaller bags, as did Hattie, and led her through the door to a lush, immaculate garden about thirty feet wide and twenty feet deep. A concrete path meandered to the one-story house. Its red clay roof tiles contrasted against the modern white exterior. The building appeared modest, smaller than Olivia's Virginia home.

"This is beautiful, Mother."

"I love taking care of my little oasis. It reminds me of my childhood home when we lived on the city's outskirts." Eva rarely spoke of her beginnings. Her family was poor and struggled until they moved to Rio, where her father got work at the docks. All Hattie knew about her grandparents was that her grandmother was a skilled cook and her grandfather was strict and hated Eva pursuing a singing career.

"Well, it shows."

They entered the house. It was much cooler inside with two ceiling fans swirling the air. The living room was fresh and modern, minimally decorated with sleek teak furniture, gray fabrics, and glass accents. The sliding glass doors were closed but revealed a covered patio and another garden with a small grass area in the backyard.

"I have you in the guest room with a private bathroom and entrance to the back garden. That way, you can come and go as you please."

"That's very thoughtful."

Once all the luggage was inside and David tipped the cabby, Eva toured Hattie around the house. It was the image of her mother—trendy and elegant. The small sunroom filled with various non-native flowers Eva kept extra cool with multiple fans and a window air conditioner caught Hattie's attention the most. "An air conditioner? How on earth did you get one in Brazil?"

"I didn't." Eva laughed. "I had it shipped from the States last year, and for a pretty penny, I might add. The handyman who installed it had a heck of a time mounting it, but now I get to enjoy my favorite flowers all year."

Hattie spotted a small planter in the center containing four white flowering plants. "Edelweiss? How do you get it to grow here?"

"A lot of trial and error. I have to keep this room extra cool in the summer like now, but it's worth the cost."

"Interesting," Hattie said. This was where her father got the edelweiss, but how he got it remained unanswered. Did he take it, or did Eva give it to him? No matter the case, this was evidence he had been here, but Hattie was hesitant to ask, considering the bad blood between her parents, so she let the issue go for now.

Eva ended the tour at the guest suite, where they found David unpacking their things. Once her mother left, Hattie plopped on the bed. She hated everything about the mission the FBI had coerced her into. It endangered her sister and father, interfered with her career, and forced an awkward reunion with a mother she'd despised for years for breaking up their family. In other words, her task pressed every one of her buttons.

After a while, Hattie heard the telephone ring somewhere in the house but continued putting her things away.

"Hattie," her mother called from the hallway.

"We're in the bathroom setting up."

Eva appeared at the bathroom door. "Sorry to bother you, but Cohen Dry Cleaners called. They said the rush job you put on an outfit is ready for pickup."

Hattie pinched her expression. She hadn't dropped off any dry cleaning but remembered the business card Nala gave her on her and David's first day in town. "Yes, my dry cleaning. I'll pick it up before we go to the club."

"They suggested you come right over because they're closing early today. You can borrow one of my cars. Would you like the Ford Coupe or the Deluxe?"

Hattie threw her head back. Her mother had resisted learning to drive when she lived in the United States, saying it wasn't ladylike. Now, she had two cars and a luxurious house, all from the money she earned. "I can't believe you drive."

"Quite well. The streets around here are tricky. Do you drive?"

"I do, but it's been a while."

"I'll drive," David said. "Which car do you prefer, Eva?"

"The Coupe, but—"

"Then we'll take the Deluxe."

Eva handed him a set of keys. "The clutch sticks a little going from second to third."

"I can look at it if you'd like. My uncle runs a garage, and I used to help him after school and on weekends."

Eva beamed widely. "You *are* a keeper."

Armed with the directions Eva had jotted down, David navigated the streets of Rio to the central part of town. On Hattie's recommendation, he parked around the block in case they were followed. The street was busy with pedestrians, so they blended into the flow until they reached Cohen Dry Cleaners and slipped inside.

The interior resembled the reception area of any dry cleaner store in New York City, with a welcome counter, a cash register, and a rotating rack with hundreds of laundered garments wrapped in transparent plastic bags hanging from it.

A young woman was at the cash register. She smiled and said, "Posso te ajudar?"

Hattie understood enough Portuguese to know the woman was asking how she could help. Hattie handed her the business card and said, "Nala, por favor."

"Me siga," the woman said, gesturing for Hattie and David to follow. She led them behind the rack of clothes and through an office door. "Espere aqui," she said before leaving the way she came and closing the door behind her.

The office was cluttered with a desk, file cabinets, and various calendars, photos, and newspaper clippings on the walls. Moments later, a section of the wall swung open. It was a hidden door. Nala appeared at the entrance and said, "Come in, please."

They entered, discovering an office of the same size. This one was clean and organized. A man seated at a long table in front of a sizeable two-way radio had headphones on and jotted down something on a piece of paper. Seconds later, he pulled the headphones off and turned around.

Nala remained silent in the corner.

"Hello, Miss James. Mr. Townsend. I apologize for the wait." He stood and offered his hand. "I'm Special Agent John Butler."

Hattie refused his gesture. "The next time you search our things, I'd appreciate it if you would put them back where they belong."

He narrowed his eyes. "When was your room searched?"

"Last night, but you already know that."

"I assure you that wasn't us." A look of concern swept over his face, which made Hattie uneasy. Someone else knew who she was and was looking for her father. Butler grabbed a photograph from a manila folder on the desk and showed it to Hattie. "What was this man doing in your mother's music shop on Thursday?"

Hattie studied the picture. "He said his name was Baumann. He was looking for a voice coach to come to his home to give lessons to his teenage daughter. Why are you asking?"

"He is Heinz Baumann. We suspect he's the local leader of the SS Security Service, the intelligence arm of the Nazi Party."

"What are Nazis doing in Rio?"

"Gathering and forwarding intelligence on the Atlantic shipping lanes. The British and French blockaded Germany last year, restricting the import of materials that could help their war effort," Butler said. "With the Suez Canal blocked, Germany was forced to import goods from Asia and ship them around the Cape through the Atlantic. Their ships have been slipping through the lines with the help of U-boats using Brazil as refueling and resupply points."

"Why Brazil?" Hattie asked.

"Brazil saw a mass migration from Germany in the last twenty years," Butler said. "Many of the newcomers are sympathetic to the Nazi Party, and we believe they are helping them."

"What does that have to do with me?" If Hattie were honest, she would say she already knew the answer. Her father had been lying to her for years. In the last few weeks, she had figured out she was surrounded by spies all her life. The men her father brought to their house under the auspice of a party for diplomats were likely Nazi officers, and he likely knew. Now, Hattie didn't know who or what to believe, which was the most unsettling aspect of this entire ordeal.

"Baumann came into your mother's store when you were there. Considering your father's history, we don't think Baumann's visit was a coincidence."

A chill raced through Hattie as the feeling of being stalked took root. "You think he was trying to discover why I'm in Rio. And from the look on your face, he was the one who searched our room last night."

"That's a possibility," Butler said. "He knows you're here and will probably continue to watch you. We can turn his curiosity against him. We believe he has a radio station in the hills of this plantation that sends coded messages to the offshore U-boats. You need to find the location of that radio or the codebook he uses."

"How do you suppose I do that?"

"You said he invited you to teach his daughter to sing at his house. He's likely fishing for information about your father. Turn it around and get information on him by taking pictures of his compound. We've tried infiltrating, but the plantation is walled off and well-guarded. If you agreed to give her lessons, Baumann would invite you."

"That's too dangerous, Hattie," David said. "You don't know what he's capable of."

Butler waved off David's concern. "It would only be dangerous if you were to go there without anyone knowing. Baumann wouldn't risk bringing the police there if you went missing. Your mother knows, so you'll be fine. We think he could lead us to your father, so you could go home sooner than you thought possible."

Hattie knew it was dangerous, but she had to see this through. She had to know if Butler was right about Baumann's association with her father. However, she still wasn't sure if she could turn on him. "All right, Agent Butler. I'll accept Mr. Baumann's offer."

"You can't be serious." David tossed his hands in frustration.

"I have no choice."

"Then I'm going with you. You'll need someone to play piano."

Hattie gave David a thankful nod before returning her attention to Butler. "How am I supposed to take pictures? I can't walk around with my Kodak, taking pictures willy-nilly."

Butler opened a cabinet, rummaged through a wooden crate, and handed Hattie a metal device about three inches long, one inch wide, and a half inch tall with two dials on one side.

"What is it?" she asked.

"A Minox camera." Butler slid it open and demonstrated how it functioned. His focus drifted briefly to Hattie's chest. "Hide it"—he gestured awkwardly—"in your brassiere. The camera doesn't have a flash, but it's designed to take pictures in low light. Any light is better than none."

Hattie slipped it into her bra between her breasts, adjusting it until it felt comfortable. "Fits perfect. I'll make arrangements soon."

As Hattie and David drove back to Eva's home in the hills, an uneasy feeling settled in that she was in over her head. She was in a foreign country where she spoke little of the language and was about to enter what Butler described as a hotbed of Nazi spies.

11

The dinner rush at the Halo Club on Saturday night was in full swing, with three-quarters of the tables occupied—an improvement from yesterday. Recorded music played in the background while the servers bounced between tables, bringing drinks and dinner plates to the patrons. Hattie and David had ordered two modest meals so they wouldn't perform on a full stomach. The head server told them to eat at a small table nearest the kitchen with the heaviest foot traffic in the dining room to keep the more desirable seating available for paying guests. The feijoada, a black bean and pork stew her mother used to make frequently when she and Olivia were children, was particularly delicious.

During the meal, Hattie kept an eye out for her father and occasionally touched the stem of edelweiss she'd tucked into the buttonhole of her blouse. After a while, she noticed Maya working behind the bar. She found it odd that her sister, Anna, wasn't in the club on what should be the busiest night of the week. Maya filled glass after glass, wiping sweat from her brow between pours. The fast pace would have overwhelmed anyone, but Maya didn't skip a beat. However, they locked eyes once, and the bright look Hattie had seen in them last night was gone.

Hattie and David walked their plates to the kitchen when they finished. A mixture of pleasing scents hit her, reminding her of how her house smelled when she was a child. Steam and smoke rose from stovetops and grills, and cooks and bussers shouted things to each other in Portuguese across the chaotic room.

After placing their plates in the bucket for dirty dishes, they returned to the dining room.

"I'm going to set up and test the sound equipment," David said.

"Go ahead. I'll be right behind you. I want to have a word with Maya."

David gave her a look of warning, which she likely deserved. Perhaps she had read too much into last night, letting hopefulness taint her perception of reality. She had the signals down in New York. A silent, piercing, lingering look. A slight hitch of breath or lick of the lips when locking stares. A grazing touch. Instead of complimenting her shoes, complimenting how well she made the shoes look. But Hattie had no experience with the underground lesbian culture in Rio and was unfamiliar with the social cues. She had no way of telling whether last night's stares were *the look* or something innocent. However, the subtle touch in her office stoked her hopeful side.

Hattie approached the end of the bar, deciding to limit her curiosity to business. She waited to wave her over until Maya had finished talking to a customer and glanced her way. A slight smile would have been another sign in the positive column, but Maya offered nothing beyond a nod. If anything, she looked annoyed.

"Hi, Hattie," Maya said in her slight accent. "All set for tonight?"

"David is setting up right now. You look busy tonight. Do you need an extra hand?"

"Have you tended bar before?"

"No, but I'm a quick study."

"Thanks, but this isn't the night to train someone."

"Where's Anna?"

"I don't know, and I'm worried." Maya pinched her expression. "She never came home last night."

"Is that unlike her?"

"No, she occasionally spends the night with a man, but she's never been this late for work."

"She likely found love and can't pry herself away," Hattie said.

Maya laughed. "Anna? She's not the type to fall smitten. It's the other way around." She dropped her smile and placed both hands on the bar, elbows straight. "Besides, we have an agreement to never let a romantic interest interfere with operating the club. Sisters stick together."

On instinct, Hattie clutched Maya's hand. "I suppose she'll come waltzing in any time, wearing the same clothes she wore yesterday."

Maya locked stares with Hattie and squeezed her hand before letting go. "I hope you're right."

There. *The look* again. Hattie didn't imagine things last night. *Please give me another sign*, she begged silently. *Hitch your breath or lick your lips, and I'll know*. But a sigh wasn't the reaction she'd hoped for, though she understood it.

"All right then." Hattie also sighed, worry building for the missing Anna.

She went to the dressing room and changed into the stage dress she had brought from her collection for the night's performance. While touching up her makeup in the mirror, she reminded herself of the reason she came to Rio and what hung in the balance, ultimately cautioning herself about keeping distractions at bay. Especially the attractive ones.

She and David performed a long set, adding three encore songs, the unreleased tunes she recorded with Maggie Moore. If RCA wouldn't publish them, Hattie figured she should get some mileage out of them. During the show, she thought a man in the audience resembled her father, but she realized it wasn't him when he turned to face the stage. She shook her head, thinking she would see her father everywhere in every tall blond man until she found him.

The audience roared at the end, whistling and applauding louder than any American crowd Hattie had sung to. Their energy was electrifying, reminding her how much she'd missed performing. Her love of being on stage wasn't about being in the spotlight but was based on the connection she felt between the music and the audience. It was like nothing else she'd experienced.

The second show was equally exhilarating, with Hattie performing longer than she had planned. By the time she changed and freshened up, the front door was locked, the staff was gone, and Maya had flipped a few chairs upside down atop the dining tables.

"I'm going to help her close," Hattie told David.

He patted his pockets. "I forgot my smokes in the car. I'll be right back to help."

That was his way of giving her time alone to test the waters. She glanced at Maya, noting the same troubled look she had most of the night. "Take your time."

"Remember why we're here," he said, giving her the same look as he did after dinner and a kiss on the cheek. It was a well-deserved caution.

"How can I forget?" Once David left, Hattie approached Maya, flipped a chair at the table she was preparing, and placed it on top. "Is it usually this busy on a Saturday night?"

"Except for Carnival, not in months. Word must be getting around." Maya positioned another chair and locked stares with Hattie for much longer. "I should order posters to advertise your shows."

"I brought some headshots I had done last month in New York. You can use them if you'd like."

"I'd like." Maya's lips spread slightly. Hattie willed her to lick them and give her another sign, but to her disappointment, Maya returned to her work. Perhaps that was the signal here, and Hattie had missed a host of advances. Unfortunately, showing interest in another woman, especially her employer, was risky. She had to be absolutely sure before taking the leap.

They finished stacking the chairs and returned to the bar. Maya went behind it, performing more cleanup while Hattie sat on a stool.

Hattie asked, "I didn't see Anna tonight. Did you ever hear from her?"

"No, and I'm worried. It's not like her to miss a day of work and not call me." The lines at the bridge of Maya's nose became more prominent, highlighting her concern.

"You said she didn't come home. Does that mean you live with her?"

"Yes, and it's a daily challenge to not rip her hair out. She's an excellent bartender and keeps a clean work area, but that woman can't clean a dish at home to save her life."

Hattie laughed, drawing out a slight grin from Maya. Smiles suited her more than the worried frowns she'd worn most of the night. "She sounds a lot like David."

Maya averted her stare and continued her work. "I take it you and David are a couple. Based on how he looks at you, I can tell the man adores you." The comment suggested that Hattie had blown it by bringing up David and needed clearing up.

"Our relationship is . . . colorful." If Maya were a New York underground lesbian, that would have instantly clued her in that Hattie and David were in a lavender relationship. That he was her cover, and she was his.

But Maya squinted. "Colorful?"

More disappointment crushed Hattie's hope. "Call it complicated."

12

An epiphany hit Hattie when she fluttered her eyes open after a rough night's sleep. She hadn't woken up in the same home as her mother in eleven years. Eva visited the States each summer but stayed with Olivia in Virginia while Hattie stayed with her father. Yesterday's talk during the tour of her house marked the longest conversation they'd shared since her mother returned to Brazil. Their limited contact wasn't because of Eva's lack of trying but rather Hattie's resistance. She never took betrayal well, and since Helen's, she squashed every attempt by her mother to repair their fractured relationship.

The sound of shower water stopped, accompanied by the creaking of closing faucets. Minutes later, David emerged from the bathroom with his hair slicked back and a towel wrapped around his trim waist. "Good morning," he said. "You tossed most of the night. Why don't you sleep in for a while?"

Hattie sat up, drawing the covers over her chest and night clothes. "I smell cooking." A mix of sweet and savory notes, with hints of butter, honey, and cornmeal, had drifted into the room, reminding her of Sunday mornings when her mother would cook before church. "I need to get Baumann's business card before my mother heads to mass."

"Then I'll get out of your hair in five minutes so you can shower and get dressed." He grabbed a change of clothing from the dresser and returned to the bathroom without another word or his typical morning chipper banter.

Hattie flopped back on the mattress, splaying her arms. He was still upset about her agreeing to spy on Baumann, and she couldn't blame him. She felt like a puppet, and Agents Butler and Knight were the puppeteers, making her do their bidding. And until she found her father, she saw no end to their manipulation.

Half an hour later, Hattie entered the kitchen. David was at the table, sipping coffee, and her mother was in her element at the stove, swaying her hips to the lively samba beat of "Aquarela do Brasi" on the radio. She pulled a Brazilian cornmeal cake from the oven and placed the round pan on the island atop a hot plate. She looked up. "Good morning, sweetheart. Perfect timing. I just popped out the bolo de fuba."

"Good morning." Hattie scanned the countertop and saw slices of bread and other ingredients out. "The cornbread smells great. Are you planning to make misto quente?"

"Yes, I know it's your favorite. I also sliced papaya earlier."

"What's misto quente?" David asked.

"Essentially a fried ham and cheese sandwich," Hattie said.

"That sounds great, thank you," he said.

Once Eva made the sandwiches and Hattie retrieved the fruit and sliced the cornbread, they sat at the table with David and chatted during the meal. Eva had dozens of ideas for their wedding. "If you're not up for a church wedding, we can have the ceremony in my courtyard. I'm sure we can fit fifty guests easily."

"Fifty? We only know a few people at the Halo Club," Hattie said, shaking her head. Her mother was doing it again. She had turned her sister into a blubbering mess in the weeks leading up to her wedding with her many helpful ideas . . . whether Olivia agreed or not.

"We'll fly in Olivia and her family. And, of course, the governor, foreign minister, and chief of police must receive invitations."

"Stop, Mother. I won't let you turn this into a circus like you did with Olivia's wedding." Hattie took a deep, calming breath. Her job was to stay close to her mother and watch for her father. An argument might release the pent-up anger she harbored for years but would not get her closer to her goal. She softened her expression and tone. "Let David and I consider a date before you mail out the invitations."

Eva laughed. "Of course, sweetheart. It's just that I'm happy my baby girl is getting married. When you become a mother, you'll understand. You won't be able to help yourself either."

Hattie's stomach churned on the papaya and cornbread. She had known two other lavender couples in New York that got married to further their cover, and it worked for them. However, she hadn't considered the pressure from her mother and perhaps David's mother to give them grandchildren. That was a topic she wasn't willing to dodge in perpetuity, but this wasn't the time to come clean, especially about her sexual preference. Her mother would never approve, nor would her sister, she imagined. Her father, though, might come around, given time. Nevertheless, as much as she dreaded the idea and hated doing this to a man who had been nothing but kind to her, she and David would have to fake a breakup and part ways when this ordeal was over.

"Having children is a long way off." Hattie needed to change the subject. And quickly. "I was thinking, Mother. My job at the club doesn't pay a lot. Perhaps I should accept that man's offer to teach his daughter." Though she was only taking the job to counter Baumann's ruse and find out what she could about her father. "Do you still have his card?"

A broad smile grew on Eva. "That's a grand idea." She stood from her chair and padded to the corkboard on the wall beside the refrigerator. "I put his card up here in case you changed your mind."

"He mentioned I would have to go out to his home. Would you mind lending us a car until we find something affordable?"

"We?"

"You know I haven't kept up on my piano, so I'll need David to accompany me." *And protect me*, she wanted to add.

"I think it's sweet you're doing everything together." Eva returned to the table and handed Hattie the card. "Use the Deluxe for as long as you need."

"Thank you. May I use the phone to call him?"

"Please do." She gestured toward the wall phone next to the corkboard. "Just pick up and ask to be connected."

Hattie spoke to the operator, who connected her to the number on the card. A woman answered after several rings. "Plantação de Lobo."

"Você fala inglês?" Hattie asked.

"Yes, I speak English. How may I help you?" the woman said in a German accent.

"My name is Hattie James. Mr. Baumann gave me this number when he came to my mother's music studio earlier this week, looking for a voice coach for his daughter. May I speak with him?"

"One moment, please," the woman said.

Moments later, a man answered. He spoke in a German accent. "Miss James, this is Heinz Baumann. Does this mean you've changed your mind about teaching my daughter to sing?"

"Yes, Mr. Baumann. I'm interested in the teaching job."

"That's wonderful. What are your rates? I can pay in reals or American dollars if you prefer."

Hattie wasn't sure what the going rate was in Rio, but she knew what her time was worth in dollars. "Considering the distance I would have to drive, I couldn't do it for less than twenty American dollars per lesson."

Her mother spat her morning coffee, making Hattie think the number was too high.

"That's a bit more than I'd expected, but after seeing you sing at the Halo Club Friday night, I know you would be an excellent teacher for my daughter."

"I'm so glad you saw me sing. I hope you were entertained."

"Yes. It was quite good. Then again, any artist with RCA Records must be talented." Hattie blushed, thankful RCA had kept her departure from the recording label quiet and simply pulled her records from distribution. Baumann continued. "Elsa has a church recital at the end of April. What would it take to prepare her?"

"I'd have to assess her skill level first, but if she works hard, we should have plenty of time to prepare her for her recital. If you'd like, I can come to your plantation today to meet your daughter and start my assessment."

"I'm afraid that's not possible. We have a special event on the grounds tonight. Preparations are already underway. Can you make it out here tomorrow, say around nine?"

"Nine would be perfect."

"Are you singing at the Halo Club again tonight?" he asked.

"Yes. Two performances, at eight and eleven."

"Perhaps I might slip away if things go well here."

"Hope to see you there." Hattie hung up the phone and returned to the table. David had a big grin, and Eva's mouth was agape. "What?" she asked.

"Twenty dollars a lesson? Perhaps I should give home lessons." Eva shook her head, making Hattie laugh.

The phone rang.

Eva walked over and answered. "Olá . . . Oh, sweetheart." Eva spoke more loudly. "It's so good to hear from you . . . Yes, I heard . . . She is staying in my guest room . . . She's right here. Hold on." Eva gestured for Hattie to take the call and mouthed, "It's your sister."

Hattie muttered under her breath. She'd sent Olivia a telegram, telling her about her travel plans to restart her career to avoid the interrogation that was about to unfold. She had also said she would send another telegram when she arrived in Rio. "Can I take it in the other room?"

"Yes, of course." Eva frowned, perhaps wondering why Hattie needed privacy to talk to her sister.

Hattie hurried to the living room and picked up the other receiver. "I have it, Mother." She waited for the click, signaling Eva wasn't eavesdropping. "Hi, Liv. I'm sorry I forgot to send you another telegram." She spoke loudly to make her voice clear over the static.

"I'm glad you're safe, but why go to Rio to restart your career? You haven't talked to Mother in years." Olivia's voice sounded monotone through the static.

Hattie raked her hand across her face. Having to yell on the phone with Eva in the next room made it impossible to tell Olivia the truth. "That hit piece in the *Times*. I need to start my career over. I thought with Mother's connections, Rio was as good of a place as any."

"Toledo is a new start, not moving in with the woman you've despised for years. You could wait tables or become a secretary and use your full name."

Hattie hated the name Harriet. Yes, she was named after her paternal grandmother, but the name was too formal for the stage, and the mean kids at school used to call her Hairy. They had teased her so much she'd taken to wearing hats to school every day, and her new nickname, Hattie, was born.

"My picture was in all the major papers, and I've sold over a million records with my photo on the covers. People will recognize me, and I'm not moving to someplace in the middle of nowhere to get by. I'm a talented singer, Liv. I won't wait tables while I still have a good voice and figure. I already have a job singing at a nightclub and accepted a job teaching a rich man's daughter to sing."

Olivia went quiet, leaving only static from her end and suggesting Hattie was getting through to her.

"Are you still there, Liv?"

"Yes, I'm here, Hattie. I'm worried about you, considering everything going on. What about David?"

"RCA dropped him too, so his job prospects are also in the gutter. He came with me and plays piano at the club for my performances."

"So Mother knows you're dating?"

Hattie sighed. The connection sounded clearer, so she lowered her voice. "I told her we're engaged, which was a big mistake since we're only dating. Now she wants to have the wedding in her courtyard and invite the governor."

Olivia laughed. "That sounds like Mother."

"Now you know why I called her Smother when we were little."

"She means well."

"Surprisingly, she insisted on us staying in the same room." If Hattie were honest, she would have preferred separate rooms. David was her best friend, but spending twenty-four hours a day together pushed the limits of friendship.

"You're kidding?" Olivia sounded shocked. "She really has loosened up in her old age."

"I wouldn't call fifty-five old, but she does seem happier here."

The pause was telling. Hattie could hear Olivia's smile through the static. "I've been telling you that for years. It's great you're finally seeing it for yourself."

"Hey, Liv. I gotta go. I need to decide on an outfit before my next show tonight."

"All right, Hattie, but don't do anything like this again without calling me."

"I won't. Love you, Liv. I'll call you soon."

After completing the call, Hattie returned to the kitchen, where David and Eva had nearly finished cleaning the breakfast dishes. "Sorry I wasn't here to help," she said.

"No worries." Eva was at the sink and glanced over her shoulder. "How is your sister?"

"Fine. She was checking up on me."

Eva harrumphed.

Hattie rolled her eyes. It had been a while since she'd been around her mother long enough to catch her subtle cues, but the loud harrumph was her signature reaction to something that didn't sound right. "All right, Mother. I'll bite. What did I do wrong now?"

Eva turned around, draping a damp dish towel over her shoulder. "Why didn't you call to tell Livvy you were coming here? Sending a telegram was thoughtless."

"I know, but being unable to find work isn't exactly something I'm proud of. She'd either offer me money or a place to stay. I can't have my little sister supporting me."

"But it's okay for me to?"

"You're my mother. That's different." Hattie shifted on her heels. The topic had made her uncomfortable when only half of it was true. She had access to the thousands she'd saved but had told her mother the federal government had frozen her accounts. "Can we table this? I need to do some shopping. My employer said my dresses might need a little local flair."

"Nonsense." Eva waved Hattie off, eyeing her figure up and down. "I have closets full of Brazilian stage dresses. I'm a little thicker now, but you're about the same size I was when I was performing. We can piece together some outfits and accessories that will make your wardrobe sing as well as you."

Eva threw an arm over her daughter's shoulder and guided her to the primary suite. The walk-in closet was massive, larger than most New York

City apartment bedrooms, and filled with dresses, outfits, and shoes from floor to ceiling.

After an hour of sorting, trying on various outfits, and pairing them with shoes, Hattie had eight new outfits for the stage and extra jewelry and scarves to add local flair to her dresses, as Maya had suggested. "Thank you, Mother. This is incredibly kind of you."

"It's nothing, really," Eva said, wiping a stray tear from her cheek. "I'm happy these old things are getting good use again."

Hattie sensed an emotional moment for her mother but resisted the urge to comfort her. Yes, the woman loved her daughters, but a motherly bond failed to erase her infidelity. The pain and betrayal Hattie felt when she abandoned her and Olivia to come here still ran deep. Perhaps it was irreparable.

13

The dress Hattie wore on stage later that night fit her like a glove and was sexy as hell, but it was Eva's. The thought of men objectifying her mother in the same outfit, fantasizing about taking her to bed, made her uncomfortable. Eva had been a sex symbol in Brazil for decades, even throughout the periods she lived in the United States as the performing wife of an American diplomat. As a child, Hattie had recognized the adoration from fans but hadn't connected the sexual aspect of being a celebrity until she experienced it in her own career. It made meeting women easier, but the audacity of some men who equated their looks and suaveness to Clark Gable was bothersome and, at times, troubling. Hattie imagined the same happening to her mother, and the thought nauseated her.

Halfway through her first set, Baumann appeared, wearing another crisp white suit, and sat at the same table he had occupied two nights ago. Two other men had come with him, but only one joined him at the table. The other stood by the mouth of the corridor leading to the restrooms and an emergency side street exit, giving the impression he was a bodyguard. Baumann came across as a rich man but not so wealthy to need personal security. Perhaps Agent Butler was right, and Baumann was a Nazi SS officer running an intelligence operation, which would make the two men with him Nazis as well. She kept an eye on them.

When her first show was over and the recorded mix of local and American music took over, she and David went to the bar and asked Maya for two glasses of water. Returning with the drinks, Maya placed them down and was about to leave without a word or even a stare when Hattie grabbed her wrist and said, "Any word from Anna?" The look of dread in Maya's eyes told her the answer. "I assume you've contacted her friends."

"No one has seen her." Maya squeezed Hattie's hand before pulling back. The subtle touch expressed a mountain of gratitude, but the strain in her voice said she was more than troubled.

"Have you reported her missing?" Hattie supposed a person had to be missing for a certain period before the police could get involved like they did in New York.

A man shouted for service from the end of the bar, drawing Maya's attention. She gestured she would be right there. "I will after we close." She ran her fingers roughly through her hair, explaining how it had become so unkempt.

"Is there anything I can do to help?"

"I'm not sure if I can get to the kitchen before closing. Can you pass the word for everyone to stay? The police might have questions."

"Of course."

Maya gave her a long, thankful look before stepping away to help the loud customer. Hattie watched her for a moment, and her heart broke for the woman. When they first met, Maya was full of confidence and determination and clearly loved running the business. Tonight, she appeared harried and pushed to her limits. Hattie had to help. Women, after all, had to stick together, but first, she needed to satisfy the FBI.

Hattie turned to David. "I'm going to speak to Mr. Baumann and make sure we're still on for tomorrow before passing the word around."

He took a swig of water. "I'll go with you."

"I won't be long. Stay here." He gave her a questioning look. "Look, David. Considering how you marked your territory at my mother's studio, I think it best to keep you two apart." Hattie rose to leave, but David grabbed her arm.

"It could be dangerous, Hattie."

"He won't do anything in the middle of a crowded nightclub. I'll be fine." She leaned closer and spoke in a whisper. "He might know where my father is. He'll be more talkative without you staring him down. Okay?"

"Okay, but don't take any chances. I'll be right here. Tug on your ear if you need me to come over."

"You're the best, David." Hattie kissed him on the cheek.

A lively samba played in the background while she weaved through the tables to the back. Baumann's eyes lit up when she approached. He and his tablemate stood. Baumann pulled out a chair for her. "Miss James, please join me. Can I get you a drink?"

"Thank you, Mr. Baumann. Only water or hot tea between shows." Hattie sat. "Did you enjoy the set?"

"Very much. May I introduce Aren Beck, my plantation manager?"

Beck offered a polite nod before retaking his seat.

"Pleasure," Hattie said.

"Did your mother teach you to perform?" Baumann asked.

"My mother taught me to sing. Years on stages like this one taught me to perform."

"Your experience shows." Baumann studied her intently for several beats, making Hattie uncomfortable. "I hope you can impart some of your expertise to Elsa."

"I'll do my best."

Baumann pulled a folded piece of paper from his breast pocket and handed it to Hattie. "I jotted down directions to make your trip to my plantation easier."

"Thank you. Do you have a piano? I prefer live music when teaching."

"We have a baby grand. Will that do?"

"Yes. I'm a bit rusty, so I'll bring my piano player, the young man you saw in my mother's studio. I hope you don't mind."

"Whatever you need is fine, Miss James."

"Thank you. David and I have never been to a coffee plantation. It should be interesting."

The conversation was so businesslike Hattie almost forgot he was likely a Nazi SS officer, but his air of sophistication reminded her he wasn't merely a local plantation owner and father. He was likely the enemy and may have ordered those FBI agents killed to get to her father, so the danger was very real.

"Ah." Baumann nodded. "I'll have Mr. Beck give you two a tour of the facilities."

"Wonderful." Hattie shook off her thoughts of doom and smiled, realizing she would get to look around and snap some photographs. She pushed up from her chair. "I should change for my next show."

The men also stood.

"I'm afraid we must also be going," Baumann said, "but I look forward to seeing you tomorrow."

Before changing in her dressing room, Hattie went to each employee and passed along Maya's message. Hattie glanced at Maya behind the bar, and she still appeared beleaguered, crushing her a little more.

~

She performed her second show to a smaller crowd, put on the clothes she arrived in, and returned to the dining room to wait with the staff for the police to come. While others huddled in groups, she and David sat silently at a small table with a server who had arrived during the second show. She was the same server who had passed along the stem of edelweiss. The staff's murmuring generated a low, tense-filled hum until two uniformed officers walked in with two men dressed in dark suits.

The room went silent.

The older man in a suit spoke. "Onde está Maya Reyes?"

Maya emerged from behind the bar. "Aqui." She asked him to speak in English to accommodate Hattie and David.

"I'm Chief Inspector Silva." His English was good, but he spoke with a thick accent. He gestured toward his partner. "This is Investigator Vargas. You reported your sister missing?"

"Yes." Maya explained further that she and Anna lived together and co-owned the club. "A server saw her leave the club Friday night with two men. No one has seen her since."

"Can you describe these men?"

"Nessa." Maya waved up the woman sitting next to Hattie. "Please tell the inspector what you told me."

"Anna left around ten with a tall, blond Anglo. Another Anglo was with them, but she was definitely with the first man. The second man left a flower for our singer that night."

Hattie gasped. Her father might have been the one who left the flower and was involved in Anna's disappearance. She whispered so not even David could hear, "What have you gotten yourself into, Father?"

"Who was your singer?" Silva asked.

"That would be Hattie James." Maya gestured toward her table.

He looked at Hattie. "Who was this man?"

"I don't know." Her heart thumped faster at the thought of being questioned again about something her father might have done. "By the time I received the flower, he was gone. I assumed he enjoyed the performance and wanted to show his appreciation." If Hattie explained the flower's significance and her suspicion that it might have come from her father, he would ask many uncomfortable questions that could jeopardize her finding him.

"So, other than the men were Anglo, no one can describe them," Silva said. "Has she gone off with men before?"

"Yes, but she's never been gone this long," Maya said. "She always came home in the morning and never missed work."

"It appears she may have found someone who interests her for more than one night." His tone showed contempt. So did the rise of his nose.

"She isn't like that." Maya spat her words, throwing contempt back in his face.

"We'll make a report based on the information you provided when you called the station, but a hundred people disappear in Brazil every day. My guess is she'll return when she and the Anglo tire of each other."

"That's it?" Maya raised a photograph of Anna she'd been holding. "You didn't even ask for a picture of her."

Silva gestured for Vargas to take the photo and handed Maya a business card. "We'll add it to the report. Let us know when she returns so we can take it off the books."

Silva left, taking the other officers with him and infuriating everyone in the room. Hattie understood about half their shouts in Portuguese, but the anger behind them all was clear. Their employer was missing, and the police showed enough interest in making a report but not enough to investigate.

Hattie had only met Anna once, but the effect her absence had on Maya struck Hattie to the core. Maya broke down in tears, something the staff should not see. As the club owner, she presented herself as a tough and unemotional woman capable of competing in a man's world. She could not let her people see Silva had turned her into a quivering mess.

Hattie wrapped her arm around her and led her to the dressing room. David followed. She sat Maya in the only chair, snatched a handful of tissues from the box on the vanity, and kneeled in front of her.

"Here. Take these," Hattie said.

"Thank you," Maya said through her sobs. "Unless we line their pockets, the police never listen. They don't care what happens to us." Her anger slowed her weeping.

"Trust me. It's universal in big cities." Hattie caressed Maya's arms. "Have you considered hiring a private investigator to look for her?"

"If I had the money for a private investigator, I'd line Silva's pocket to entice him to do his job."

"You can use my pay. Would that be enough to help?"

"It would only earn a laugh." Maya shook her head. "I would need everyone's pay this week to get him to look into the case. I'm afraid no one can help." She cried.

Hattie wished she could offer more right then. The lie she had told her mother about her assets had boxed her in. She could not draw on those accounts without upending the story she had told to cover up the real reason she was in Rio unless she was smart about it so Eva would not find out. Hattie glanced at David, who stood quietly near the door. "Could you get her a glass of water?"

"I'll be right back," he said.

When the door closed behind him, Hattie focused on Maya again, who was quietly crying. Hattie leaned closer to comfort her, and Maya fell to the floor on her knees. She threw her arms around Hattie's neck and buried her face against Hattie's shoulder. Hattie wrapped her arms around her, tugging her into a tight embrace.

Maya wept more, her body shaking against Hattie. No woman had ever let Hattie comfort her like this, especially not Helen. That woman was wealthy, sexy, and an incredible lover but never showed weakness. "Emotionally distant" was her best description.

Maya was different. She'd shown her interest in Hattie—or so Hattie had hoped—yet wasn't afraid to reveal her vulnerability. Perhaps she'd misread the looks, and Maya was still figuring out why a singer of Hattie's stature was performing in the Halo Club. Whatever the case, Hattie felt close to her, a true first. She knew what it felt like to open her heart to a woman, but no one had done so for her. If this was what feeling needed was like, Hattie liked it. A lot.

Maya quieted and pulled back, giving Hattie the long, silent look again. It was like she understood what that moment meant to Hattie, and Hattie hoped it meant the same to her. She gently brushed a few strands of hair from Maya's face and cupped her cheek, sensing the pain in her eyes. "We'll find her."

The door opened, and the two separated.

David walked in, clearing his throat. "I have your water, Maya. How are you feeling?"

Maya accepted the glass and returned to the chair. "Thank you. Much better. Is the staff still out there?"

"They left after putting the chairs up. We're the only ones here," he said.

"They're so good to me." Maya took a few sips, placed the glass on the vanity, and focused on Hattie. "Thank you for staying and calming me down."

"You're welcome, Maya." Hattie reached for her handbag. "We should be going."

"Then I'll see you two on Thursday."

"If you're ready to leave, we'll walk you out," David said.

"I have to check the safe first and grab my bag."

"We'll meet you at the door." David offered Hattie his arm and led her through the dining room. At the door, he whispered, "You have to be careful, Hattie. What if someone else had walked in?"

"Haven't you figured it out?"

"Figured out what?"

"Maya hires only women." Hattie had discounted the stares by some servers and kitchen staff Friday night, but tonight, it had become obvious that they were interested in her, not her performance.

"Yeah? So what?"

"Half the ladies working here are like me, and I would venture to say the other half don't care."

"You can't be too sure. Do you really want to give the FBI another thing to hold over your head?"

Hattie sighed. "You're right. I'll be more careful."

"You don't get it." David clutched her elbow, emphasizing his point. "They have eyes everywhere. Don't give them anything to see."

"I hear you."

"But do you really understand? Whatever happens to you also happens to me. We're in this together, remember?"

Hattie rubbed his arm. "I remember. I'll try to keep my distance." She turned her head slightly when Maya approached, and couldn't stop the incessant smile. Keeping her distance would be nearly impossible.

David elbowed her in the side and laughed. "Sure you will." Once Maya locked up, he offered her his arm. "May we walk you to your car?"

"That's very kind." Maya accepted his arm. "I'm two blocks from here in the public lot."

"So are we," David said.

Hattie walked side by side with Maya during the walk, so they were three abreast. At that early morning hour, the streets in the Lapa district were mainly empty, so Hattie felt comfortable brushing her arm against Maya's as they walked. Maya didn't flinch or brush her off, making Hattie's stomach flutter a little. She still wanted Hattie to comfort her but was likely holding back because David was with them. Hattie wanted to scream she didn't have to show restraint, that David understood and would even encourage it. But with her sister still missing, this was not the time, and Hattie walked without speaking.

Maya thanked David with a handshake at her car and Hattie with a genuine smile and a one-arm hug she let linger for a few extra beats.

Pulling back, she grazed Hattie's cheek with her own and whispered, "Thank you." She then turned to David. "Thanks for the escort. I'll see you two on Thursday."

But Thursday was too far away.

"I have to give a music lesson tomorrow," Hattie said, "but I'd like to check on you if that's all right. See if there's news."

"I appreciate the concern, but it's not necessary."

"Nonsense." Hattie caressed Maya's arm. "I won't get a wink of sleep until I know Anna is okay."

"Then I'd like that."

14

The house was dark when Hattie and David returned home, so they used the private entrance through the back courtyard to avoid waking Eva. If memory served Hattie, there were chairs and chaise longues under the patio cover. However, the waxing crescent moon provided scant light, making it difficult to see their placement. Her toe caught the leg of something, and she stumbled, landing a palm in a chair. The sound of metal scraping against concrete and Hattie's cursing created a ruckus and woke several neighborhood dogs.

David snickered quietly.

"That will probably leave a bruise," she groaned in a whisper.

He helped her up, snorting.

"I'll remember this the next time you stub your toe against the bed."

Once inside, Hattie changed into a light nightgown, and David stripped to his boxers and sleeveless T-shirt. While brushing their teeth in the bathroom, David held his stare on Hattie in the mirror.

She spat the toothpaste into the sink. "What?"

He did the same. "What what?"

"You were quiet all the way home. Why are you angry at me?"

He sighed. "Between Baumann and Maya, you're taking too many chances."

Hattie rinsed and returned her toothbrush to its holder. "I know you're upset, probably as much as I am. I hate how Butler uses me, but I have little choice."

"Then why are you adding to the chaos by taking on Maya's troubles?"

"Because she needs me." Hattie turned, pressing her bottom against the counter and burying her face in her hands. "I've never had that before."

David put his toothbrush down and wrapped an arm around Hattie's shoulder. "That's because you've sworn to never do what Helen did to you. And the best way of not breaking a person's heart, including your own, is to let no one in. I can see she needs a shoulder to cry on, but your plate is already full. There are eyes everywhere." David shook his head. "I gotta tell you, Hattie. This business with your father and Baumann gives me the shivers. Maya will only complicate things."

Hattie shrugged off his arm. "She has no one else. I won't abandon her."

"You're being unreasonable."

"Unreasonable?" She marched into the bedroom, and David followed. "If you're getting cold feet, feel free to leave." Hattie raised her voice, probably too much, so she lowered it. "And don't worry about the money. I'll pay your passage home."

"It's not the money. I'm not leaving you here alone."

"Then I guess we have something in common, but the difference between Maya and me is that I'm not alone." She placed her hands on her hips. "I have my mother."

He threw his hands in the air in frustration. "A week ago, you couldn't stand her."

"I still don't like what she did to our family, but being here has been . . . I don't know . . . revealing. It's like I'm finally getting to know who she is."

"But you can't trust her. You can't tell her why we're really here."

"I know I can't. That's the problem. I can't tell anyone the truth." Hattie's dander was up. Everything surrounding this situation, from her father to Butler to Baumann to her mother to Maya, frustrated her. She was living so many lies. Lied to David about the sheet music. Lied to Butler about the edelweiss. Lied to Baumann about why she wanted to teach his daughter. Lied to her sister and mother about why she was in Rio. Lied to the world about who she preferred in her bed.

"Sometimes . . ." Hattie stopped and slammed her eyes shut.

"Sometimes what?"

Hattie gritted her teeth. "Sometimes, I question the sanity of the life I've chosen." She had no control over who she was attracted to, but she decided long ago to hide it publicly and pursue it privately. "I would be better off abandoning a satisfying sex life for a life of conformity."

"Don't say that. You're just stressed, Hattie."

"That's an understatement. I need some fresh air." She rushed to put on a robe before storming out their private entrance to the back courtyard, slowing when she reached the area where she had tripped minutes earlier. She felt her way to a chair at the small outdoor dining table. As her eyes slowly adjusted to the darkness, items on the table came into focus—a glass ashtray, a pack of cigarettes, and a lighter.

She used to smoke to calm her nerves and drink to forget she was nervous, but she had given both up on the same day years ago. The first few weeks were hell. Every minor setback amplified and compounded, testing her resolve to straighten out her life. Her current predicament was not that different. The lies had piled up so high that she doubted her ability to recognize the truth.

She picked up the lighter, flipped open the lid, and sparked it to life. The flame danced in the heavy, humid air, fighting to stay alive. Her mind drifted to Anna and why she might have been missing for two days. Hattie didn't say it to Maya, but she feared her disappearance might have been related to the eight missing women in the newspaper article she read on her first day in Rio and feared Anna was fighting for her life.

The sliding glass door to the living room opened. Eva stepped outside. "Sweetheart? Are you okay? I heard you and David arguing."

Hattie cringed, not realizing how easily their voices traveled late at night. "I'm fine, Mother. It was nothing. Sorry we woke you."

Eva stepped closer and handed Hattie one of the glasses she was holding. "I thought you could use a sip to take the edge off."

"Thank you." Hattie sniffed its contents—red wine. Every fiber in her body wanted to guzzle every drop and extend the glass out for more. It would have been easy to give in . . . give up the battle. She would tell herself it would be only this one time to avoid an awkward conversation, but she knew herself too well. After the second time, she would lie to herself again and say it would be only until she could escape the mess the FBI had forced her into. Yes, that would have been the easy way out, but Hattie had fought too long and hard to keep herself centered. One drink, she was certain, would flip her world upside down like Agent Knight had.

The choice was obvious but required more strength than she possessed. Her hand shook as an internal battle raged. She forced herself to recall the night that had prompted her to give up booze four years ago. Helen had admitted her infidelity, but instead of begging for forgiveness, she had excused it by saying she was not the girlfriend type. That she loved who she loved. She loved Hattie, but she also loved lots of women. Her callousness had triggered a weeklong bender that ended in Hattie falling off her apartment building roof. If not for the fire escape breaking her fall, she would have died. She imagined herself atop another rooftop and discovered another well of untapped strength.

"But I don't drink." She placed the glass on the table and slid it toward Eva.

"Oh. Is that something new?"

"Not particularly."

"I remember you drinking like a fish at Livvy's wedding." Eva laughed at some memory. "My, you were the life of the party. What changed?"

Hattie considered saying nothing more, but she'd had enough of lies. She might not tell the whole truth, but at least an ample portion would be known. "My heart was broken."

"I'm so sorry, sweetheart. What happened?"

"Infidelity."

"Oh." Eva lowered her head. It was hard to be sure in the dark, but her expression turned sheepish.

"You broke my heart first, and I guess it never healed. When it broke again, it destroyed me, and I spiraled for months. You were there at the start of it, so you didn't see the worst. But I stopped before I did myself any permanent damage."

"I'm sorry I hurt you, but I was doing my best."

"I'm sure." Hattie's reply came out sharper than she intended.

"I don't want to fight with you, sweetheart. I've always wanted you to be happy." Eva's voice was soft like a caress, conveying her remorse. "Does David make you happy?"

"No one can make me happy. Only I can."

"You've grown into a sage woman. I wish I'd learned that lesson earlier. Then again, I wouldn't have had you and Livvy." Eva's deep sigh was very telling, making Hattie believe there was more behind her infidelity than she realized.

"You're saying Father didn't make you happy, and that's why you cheated on him?"

"I'm saying he changed."

"Everyone changes, Mother. That's how we grow."

"This wasn't growth. It was an obsession." Eva cleared her throat. "But let's not talk about the past. I heard you and David arguing about a woman, Maya. Isn't she the owner of the Halo Club? Did she do something inappropriate?"

"I wouldn't call it inappropriate." It was the opposite, Hattie thought. It was appropriate, wanted, and reciprocated.

"But—" Eva started.

"It was all my fault." David appeared through the private door. "When Maya hugged me, she misunderstood."

"I'm confused," Eva said, glancing at Hattie. "If she hugged him, why wasn't it inappropriate?"

"She was upset," Hattie said. "Her sister has been missing for two days, and the police aren't interested in looking for her."

"That's not surprising," Eva said. "People go missing all the time, and the police rarely show interest, especially when women are involved. I have a neighbor who went missing last month. So did two mothers of my students."

"That's horrible. I read an article about eight missing women," Hattie said.

"That was the editor pressuring the police to finally do something, but they are too corrupt to be swayed by anything other than money or a gun to their head."

"We should get to bed," David said. "We have an early day."

"You're right." Hattie pushed out of the chair and tapped the table next to the glass of wine. "Thanks for the gesture."

"I should get back to bed, too." Eva stood. "Teaching with bags under my eyes is a sin in my book."

They laughed and went their separate ways.

With her eyes adjusted to the dark, Hattie navigated easily back to the private door. Passing the window to her and David's bedroom, she spotted something protruding from between the slats of the outside window frame. It was a flower stem. She studied it in the dark, discerning the white star-shaped flower with a yellow center before plucking it from its resting place. It looked like it had come from Eva's greenhouse room, but why would her mother leave a single stem of edelweiss on her window?

The neighborhood dogs barked again, alerting her that someone or something should not have been there. Hattie scanned the courtyard, half expecting to find her father lurking in the shadows, but saw only bushes and trees.

15

Baumann's Plantation, later that night

Karl pulled up slowly to the main entrance, dousing his headlights so as not to blind the night guard and cranking his window down. The guard approached with caution with his Luger pistol holstered at the waist and his MP 40 submachine gun strapped over his shoulder at the ready. The stock was folded for quick reaction. The guards typically kept the heavy weapons out of sight beneath their light jackets so as not to draw attention, but this one was apparently skittish working the gate overnight.

Karl recognized the man, and though he was rusty at it, he spoke German, "Good evening, Max."

This guard always kept to himself in the compound and was leery about everyone and everything, so Karl held his hands on the steering wheel where they could be seen. Max said nothing while he inspected the empty passenger seat and truck bed. Returning to the open window, he said in German, "Out late?"

"A woman in town," Karl said. The woman was Hattie, and he hoped she got the message that he was watching over her when he left another stem of edelweiss he'd sneaked out of Eva's plant room.

Max pressed a button inside the guard shack and waved him through.

After parking in the vehicle barn, Karl crossed the compound, entered his assigned cabin, and walked lightly down the center corridor so as not to wake the others. He went into his room, closed the door, and undressed down to his T-shirt and boxers. While this place was run with military precision, with guards on the perimeter and morning briefings to receive assignments, the barracks-like sleeping accommodations provided more privacy than he expected, with private rooms for each man. Like any soldier, Karl trusted the next man to perform their duties but not with his money, so he hid it.

He kneeled beside his bed, removed the section of baseboard covering the compartment he'd cut into the drywall, and pulled out the leather trifold document case he'd hidden there. After fishing out the rest of his unspent pay from his pocket, he slid it into the case next to the pistol he'd lifted from the man with whom he had shared a cabin room aboard the freighter before tossing his body into the ocean—the same man who had helped break him out of FBI custody so Berlin could get their hands on the lists he'd safeguarded with Hattie.

His original plan was to work here another month to save enough money for a new passport and set of identity papers to replace the ones he'd also taken from his overboard rescuer and another two for passage back to the United States. However, his plans changed after seeing his daughter a few nights ago and noticing she was being followed, likely by the FBI. He needed to stay in Rio to ensure she and the lists were safe while avoiding FBI and SS detection. If he failed, everything he'd sacrificed for the last fifteen years, including his marriage to the love of his life, would have been for nothing.

A knock on the door drew his attention. He hurried to return his money and documents to their hiding place before calling out in German, "Yes?"

The man answered in German. "It's Beck."

Karl rose and opened the door. "Yes, Herr Beck."

Beck was dressed in traditional plantation attire—dark linen pants and a light button-down white shirt with the sleeves rolled to his elbows. "A man is sick. I have a job for you, Herr Fuller."

Karl's German was still a little rusty, and he had difficulty understanding the rest of what Beck said, but he gathered he was to do a job in fifteen minutes in the compound. He stood at attention in his underwear and said in German, "Yes, sir."

Beck left without further explanation.

Karl had observed men going out to work late last Sunday night, but this was the first time he was ordered to be part of it. He put on clothes, dressing similarly to Beck. Despite the tepid, humid air, he opted to wear a light jacket in case it rained, which was commonplace this time of year. Unsure of the task ahead of him, he grabbed his utility belt and snapped on a small flashlight, buck knife in its sheath, and a canteen full of fresh water he filled himself. He then combed his hair back in the fashion of Joseph Fuller, whose identity he'd assumed since stepping off the Brazilian freighter two weeks ago, the SS officer who was supposed to report to Heinz Baumann after sending Karl off to Berlin for interrogation. After double-checking the baseboard to his hidden compartment, he grabbed his fedora, exited the cabin, and followed the other men toward the compound.

Karl stood alone while four others murmured about a hunt. He heard one say the word *Wolf*, the plantation name and nickname the men had given Heinz Baumann.

Beck soon arrived and announced the hunt was on for the night. He instructed everyone to set out the torches first, then for Jacobs and Fuller to collect the animals while the rest prepared the horses and weapons. Beck returned to the main house without further explanation, making Karl curious about the hunt's target.

He had lived in Rio off and on for eight years during his diplomatic career and was familiar with Brazilian wildlife. The plantation was called Plantação de Lobo, so he assumed the maned wolf ran wild in the coffee fields at night. He also knew jaguars and pumas were prevalent in the hills, as were capybaras, the world's largest rodents. Capybaras were plant eaters and weren't dangerous like the wolves and wild cats, but they were rapid breeders and could ravage a crop if not kept in check. But mentioning animals for prey suggested the hunt involved a killer, not herbivores.

Karl followed the group of men into the large barn, where they loaded four barrels of pre-made torches and a bucket of kerosene onto a truck bed. A man hopped in the cab, and the others, including Karl, jumped in the back, holding down the cargo while the driver took them across the compound and slowly down the fifty-yard-long access road to the vegetation line marking the edge of the coffee fields.

After the truck turned around to face the compound and stopped, two men remained on the bed while the others got out. The ones in the truck bed dipped the torches into the kerosene and handed them to the men on the ground one by one. The men worked in teams, placing each torch into a pre-positioned metal holder sunk into the soft dirt on either side of the twenty-yard-wide access road. When they finished, the driver parked the truck in the compound near the beginning of the road. Three men went to tend to the horses and weapons.

"Follow me to the pen," Jacobs said. Karl knew little about this man other than he was an SS officer like the rest of the men there to collect intelligence for the Fatherland and perform whatever duties Baumann assigned.

Karl expected Jacobs to take him to another barn to fetch rabbits or deer as prey. Instead, he led them to the main house's back entrance and descended the stairs. Karl had been in the basement several times, retrieving and storing equipment, but Jacobs opened a steel door to a remote section Karl had never explored. Experience had taught him he would be told and shown only those things he was allowed, so he did not ask questions.

They went down another level and through a second padlocked metal door. The area resembled a dungeon. Once he rounded the corner to a dank corridor lit only by three overhead lightbulbs, a sinking feeling settled in his stomach. Six cells fronted by steel bar doors lined the passageway, three on each side. His early assessment was confirmed. This was not a pen for animals but for people, and he imagined what kind of sadistic hunts transpired on this plantation. Was the prey shot from afar? Or tortured into a slow, agonizing death?

Further inside, he felt his stomach turn sour when he realized six women occupied the cells. They recoiled to their respective back walls when Jacobs walked past and grabbed a skeleton key hanging at the end of the center aisle out of reach of the last cell.

What kind of sick bastard hunts women? Karl thought, but he had no choice but to play along.

"Eu já vi você antes," one woman said in Portuguese when Karl came even with her cell. She repeated in English, "I've seen you before."

Karl turned toward the voice. He recognized the woman from the Halo Club Friday night. She was the bartender Baumann had his eye on and had taken home that night. He ignored her and studied the other women. He'd seen one other before when Baumann had returned to the plantation late one night in this woman's company. Karl had assumed she was his nightly conquest, not a would-be prisoner, as he did with the bartender.

"Why is he holding us here? I told him I know nothing about the American diplomat."

That caught Karl's attention, but he could not question her for more information in front of Jacobs without raising suspicion.

Jacobs unlocked two cells opposite the side of the woman who had recognized Karl. When Jacobs entered a cell, Karl went into the other one and dragged the woman out. She screamed and flailed her arms, but as much as it pained him to do so, Karl slapped her across the face, dazing her. He lifted her by the waist when she fell limp, carried her into the corridor, and joined Jacobs and his capture.

Both men dragged the women barefoot, retracing their steps outside to the compound. Beck had returned. The three other men who had helped with the torches stood nearby, armed with rifles. Three German shepherds were leashed, sitting near their feet. The dogs barked at the commotion, but their handlers quickly quieted them by letting them sniff their prey. Five horses were saddled and waiting for their riders. The torches had been lit, setting the access road aglow like a runway in the night. At the end, there was a dark abyss of the coffee fields, where Karl surmised these women would meet their fate.

Jacobs and Karl loosened their holds. The women clung to each other, terrified in their tattered clothing, and scanned the area rapidly, focusing primarily on the men with the guns and the line of torches.

Jacobs tossed leather sandals at the women's feet and said, "Put these on. You'll need them."

The women trembled while putting on the sandals. They were a size or two too large for their feet and would make walking clumsy. "Please let us go," one begged in English. "We won't tell anyone about this place."

Jacobs laughed.

Moments later, Baumann arrived on horseback, dressed in what Karl would describe as safari clothing, minus the silly hat. He had a Luger attached to a belt around his waist and a sniper's rifle with a scope slipped tightly into a leather holster strapped to the saddle.

Baumann was the hunter. *He* was the wolf. El Lobo.

The men fell silent. The only noises were the hoots of spectacled owls, the croaks of the toucans nesting in the taller coffee trees in the distance, and the clopping hooves of Baumann's horse as he circled the women, sizing up the night's prey.

Baumann pulled the reins. The horse snorted and shuffled its feet, resisting briefly until it finally stopped. "For the last time, tell me about the American diplomat from the ship."

"Why are you doing this?" one woman asked in a shaky voice, speaking English. "We know nothing about him."

Karl's stomach twisted harder when he realized Baumann was looking for him, but he could not give himself up to save them, not while Hattie and the lists might be in danger. It sickened him to think that these women were about to die because of him.

"If you let us go, we won't tell anyone about this place," the woman said to Baumann.

"We both know this is not the case, so I offer you the hunt," Baumann said in English so the woman could understand. Except for a thick accent, it was quite good. "I will give you a fifteen-minute head start. If you can stay alive until sunrise, I will give you a choice."

"What choice is that?" the same woman asked.

"A gun with a single bullet, or I sell you to the highest bidder." Being sold into sexual slavery or committing suicide was not a choice. It was a life sentence either way.

These women had no chance of surviving until dawn. They were on foot with ill-fitting sandals and appeared weak from their captivity. Plenty of water sources were in the fields, but even if they could evade men on horses, the plantation perimeter was a solid ten-foot wall. They would be pressed to scale it by working together, but it would be impossible if they were alone. The only way off the plantation was through the guarded gate or in a body bag.

"It is time," Baumann said in German. He pulled his Luger from his holster and raised it toward the night sky. Meanwhile, the armed men moved into position, one near the women and the other three forming a gauntlet toward the access road. "Let the hunt begin," he said in German and fired a single shot, marking the start of his sadistic game.

The women flinched.

The dogs barked.

An armed man pushed the women toward the starting line of glowing torches.

The women ran for their lives, clopping down the lit pathway. They disappeared into the darkness, but their fate was sealed. The Wolf would find them.

16

The men laughed—a first for Karl to witness. These SS officers did their work day in and day out and returned to cabins at night in solitude. Some assignments were on the plantation, but most took them into town or on boats to gather intelligence on the shipping activity and enemy diplomats in Rio. No one complained. And no one laughed. Tonight, Karl finally understood why there were no gatherings at night for entertainment. The hunt was their amusement.

"Fuller," Beck bellowed.

Karl stepped toward him. "Ja, Herr Beck."

"You're riding tonight," Beck said in German.

Again, Karl did not ask questions, responding only with a firm nod. He would be told what to do when the time came. However, he was suspicious about why he was invited to fill in for the night's hunt, not one of the other men, and why tonight. The timing made him think one of the captive women, either from this group or those still in the basement, had some information about his true identity. He would have to watch his back the entire night.

Karl approached the three dogs after their handlers released their leashes and ordered them to stay. He had grown fond of them during his two weeks on the plantation. Two were quite playful, and the alpha was overly protective of her pack, but they all obeyed impeccably. Karl presented the back of his hand to the alpha, letting her smell and recognize he was not a threat. The other two remained back, waiting for the alpha to signal it was safe. Once she wagged her tail, the others came over, sniffed, and received several pets. He had sympathy for these incredible creatures. They were well-trained and loyal and should have been performing their duty as sentinels, not this.

When the other men climbed on their horses, Karl inspected the last one available. His saddle was equipped with a long rifle, a rope, and a filled canteen he would not touch. Unsure what might be in the container besides water—a drug perhaps—he would only drink from his personal supply or what he could forage himself. He inspected the cinches, ensuring they were tight, and opened the saddlebag on each side. The contents perplexed him—two large sacks and extra rope. Satisfied the mare was free of booby traps, Karl climbed on top.

Beck remained on foot, approached the men on horses, and spoke in German. Karl was to guard Baumann and ensure he encountered no surprises, human or animal. Under no circumstance was he to shoot the prey. That honor was left to Baumann. Karl answered with another firm nod. The rest were to serve as wranglers and keep the animals, meaning the women, away from the perimeter.

"Ja, ja," the men mumbled and laughed again. The hunt was apparently the highlight of their week.

Karl eased his horse over and struggled to keep it still next to Baumann's steed, which stood statuesque except for a flick of his tail. The other horses, though, were restless like Karl's. Like their riders, they were eager to start, and so were the dogs.

Karl studied Baumann. His rank in the SS was Standartenführer, which was the equivalent of a colonel in the American Army. Karl had worked with several senior American officers. Many carried themselves with poise and grace like Baumann, but an air of mystery followed him. Karl knew four things about the man: he ran the plantation to pay his men, somehow relayed the information he gathered about enemy activity to Germany, had a teenage daughter in the house, and his men feared him. That was enough to know to keep his head down and follow his training until he could figure out who he could trust. Besides Hattie, he had yet to come across anyone in Rio who fit the bill, not even his ex-wife.

Baumann checked a watch from his lower front shirt pocket and returned it to its hiding place. He turned his head toward Karl and studied him briefly before speaking in English, "I understand you spent several years in the United States, Herr Fuller. Your English must be good."

"Yes," Karl said.

"I admire a man of few words."

"Silence is one of the great arts of conversation," Karl said.

"Nothing is more noble, nothing more venerable than fidelity," Baumann said.

"Loyalty binds me." Karl tilted his head and offered a single nod. His assessment of Baumann had just taken a turn. The man knew his Cicero, which meant he was educated enough to veil it in a threat. Karl didn't doubt Baumann would reward loyalty and punish treachery, which made tonight's hunt as dangerous for him as the women.

Baumann rechecked his watch, stuffed it back into his pocket, and thundered in German, "Wranglers, it's time. Herd them."

A man whistled. The dogs took off running. The men hollered as they galloped between the torches. In seconds, they disappeared into the dark coffee fields. When they quieted, the toucans and owls took over.

Baumann turned to Karl and asked in German. "Do you know your role, Herr Fuller?"

"Dich beschützen." Karl's job was to protect him tonight.

Baumann offered a rare smile. "Die Jagt beginnt."

The hunt was on.

Baumann had snatched those poor women, thinking they might lead them to Karl, but now he would hunt them down because they knew nothing and too much at the same time. Other than the one from the nightclub, none of the women had ever seen Karl, but now they knew too much about Baumann and his operation, so they had to die. Karl feared the guilt about what was about to transpire would haunt him for many years.

Karl pulled out his rifle and held it in his right hand on his lap for a quick reaction. When he twisted the reins in his left, he glanced at his wristwatch, estimating the sun would peek over the eastern horizon in three hours. The wranglers and Baumann had plenty of time to search the fields and jungle inside the perimeter on horseback.

Baumann took off at a trot between the torches.

Karl followed, protecting Baumann from behind. He swiveled his head left and right, scanning one hundred eighty degrees for threats. The waxing crescent moon made his job difficult, but he'd been trained to look for the slightest movement and objects glistening in moonlight. Focus was key. He pushed all thoughts of danger from his mind and concentrated on navigating the terrain while probing his surroundings.

Baumann slowed his horse to a walk at the far end of the first coffee field a few yards short of the clearing. Karl imagined experience had likely taught him this was where the fun began. Where his victims typically escaped to the jungle to better their chances of hiding and evading their predators. Baumann turned slowly and fixed his stare on Karl. His blue eyes were piercing in the near darkness. A sinisterness was behind them.

They spoke in German.

"Tell me, Herr Fuller. When you first arrived at my compound, you said Mr. James had transferred to the U-boat."

This was the confrontation Karl had been expecting. His answer tonight had better match what he had told Baumann his first night on the plantation. Otherwise, his cover would be blown, and everything he'd done to stay alive long enough to ferret out the mole would have been for nothing. He slid his finger over the trigger of his rifle, ready to shoot his way out if this conversation went the wrong way. "No, Herr Baumann. That is not what I reported."

"Refresh my memory."

"I said I had given him a compass and lowered him into the dinghy when the freighter slowed. Then I instructed him to row a hundred meters due east and wait for the U-boat to surface." At least those were the instructions the real Fuller had given Karl.

"Did you see him get picked up?"

"No. It was too dark."

He studied Karl for several beats. "Aren't you curious why I'm asking you these questions?" The question proved he knew Karl wasn't about to take his bait.

"Yes, but if you wanted me to know why, you would tell me."

Baumann tilted his head in curiosity. "You are either a very complex man or the simplest one on earth."

"I shall leave that for you to decide."

Dogs barked in the distance, thankfully drawing Baumann's attention.

A woman screamed. It was the sound of terror from being chased, not of agony from being attacked. The men and dogs were herding her into Baumann's kill zone. Now he understood why his nickname was the Wolf. He hunted in packs, encircling his prey before going in for the kill.

"Another time, perhaps." Baumann tugged on the reins, and his horse came to a gentle stop in the clearing at the entrance of the only worn trail into that part of the jungle. He pulled out his rifle, leveled it down the path, nuzzled his cheek against the cherry butt, and pressed his right eye against the scope. Light was at a premium, which should have made moving shadows easier to see but not objects. Taking a shot under these conditions was tantamount to firing while blindfolded, but Baumann seemed the type to thrive on the challenge.

A branch cracked to Karl's left. He snapped his stare toward the noise, bringing his rifle level simultaneously. Two small orbs glistened in the underbrush of the smaller coffee trees. The animal growled and lunged toward the horses. Karl fired without being sure of the target, but it was likely a wolf. The animal whined in pain and scurried off into the dark.

Baumann glanced over his shoulder and said, "Guter Schuss."

"Danke," Karl said. It was a good shot. He likely only winged the beast, but it was enough to impress the man who could have been onto Karl's true identity.

The barking got louder, but the screams had stopped, replaced by rustling in the underbrush and panicked grunts. Karl moved even with Baumann and focused on the left side of his face.

Baumann adjusted a dial on the scope. He was calm, patient, and formed a slight grin, taking pleasure that his prey was in his sights. Then he released a partial breath, held it, and squeezed the trigger, sending the shot toward his target in the jungle. He still controlled his breath and kept his stare fixed downrange.

Held it. Held it. Held it.

He finally exhaled with a gasp. His body quivered a fraction in what resembled a sexual climax. Karl had spent four years on a diplomatic mission in Germany, meeting several SS officers. Most had a sadistic streak, but Baumann was in a different league. He loved watching his victim die.

Baumann returned his rifle to its pouch and nudged his horse forward. Karl followed. Thirty yards into the wooded area, a woman lay still on the ground. Karl dismounted and checked for a pulse, but she was lifeless, with signs a bullet had gone directly through her throat. He indeed hunted like a wolf, who killed medium-sized prey by biting them around the neck until they were dead.

Karl shook his head to Baumann, indicating she was gone.

"Bag her," he said in German. "Bring her with you."

Karl opened his saddlebag and pulled out a large sack and rope. He paused for a moment to gather himself. He'd seen enough death that bodies no longer bothered him, but this was senseless and sadistic. It was one thing to kill the enemy on the battlefield or for survival, but this girl posed no threat. The enjoyment Baumann took in the kill was the mark of a twisted man. Karl shook off his discomfort and, with some effort, slipped the woman into the bag, tossed her over his horse's back end, and tied her to the saddle.

The second woman proved evasive. The first ribbon of purple appeared in the eastern sky. Sunrise was minutes away. Baumann was agitated, shouting commands and directing his wranglers to area after area without success. With any luck, the second woman had escaped over the north wall, where it was slightly shorter.

The sun peeked over the hill, tipping the scale in Baumann's favor of finding the last woman and earning her a choice of life over death. Daylight would make it easier to spot the last prey. An hour later, one of the men blew a whistle continuously until Baumann and Karl reached him. The man pointed up a tree.

The woman who was vocal about the insanity of the hunt before its start had climbed up it and was soaking wet. She must have dipped into a nearby stream to dampen her scent, thereby throwing off the dogs, and ascended high enough to be out of their range. Her tactic was brilliant.

Baumann laughed. "Creative," he said in English, gesturing for two men to climb up and retrieve her. She struggled, but they overpowered her and brought her to the ground. She fought against their hold, but they were too strong.

Baumann dismounted his steed and approached the woman. "You proved resourceful." He grabbed her by the chin, inspecting her. "Young. Strong. Attractive. You will fetch a high price. I think I might send you directly to the selling block."

"You promised me a choice." She shook his hold loose. "I've earned it."

Baumann laughed again. "That you have." He unholstered his Luger. His men all took aim at the woman. "One bullet. Choose wisely," he said, handing it to her with the barrel facing downward.

If she chose to fire at Baumann, his men would shoot, and she would be dead before pulling the trigger. If she put the gun down, she would live a life of untold misery and abuse. Her stance and eyes were defiant as she accepted the weapon. "Rot in hell," she said, spitting her words. She raised the gun to her head and fired, blood and brain matter spraying a wrangler beside her. She fell to his feet.

"Hergott!" the man said, wiping the material from his face. He picked up Baumann's sidearm and returned it to him.

"Wise choice," Baumann said in German and turned to Karl. "Bag the body. Herr Beck will show you how to dispose of them."

"Yes, Herr Baumann."

The men and Baumann took off through the jungle toward the compound. Karl stood over the second body, admiring the woman's feistiness. She died courageously. Life as a slave would have been no life at all.

He bagged her, placed her beside the other woman atop his saddle, and walked back to the compound, noting the torches had been taken down. He now understood why the field workers had Mondays off for a three-day weekend. No one would be around to see the bodies being brought back on horseback. He tied his mount to a hitching post inside the horse barn to keep the bodies out of sight.

While Karl tightened the ropes securing the bodies to the saddle, Beck greeted him. They spoke in German. "Herr Baumann tells me you did well against the wolf."

"I did as I was told," Karl said, tightening the last rope.

"Well, you've earned a day off. Take them to the milling barn and toss them into the old roasting kiln."

"I will, thank you."

Karl led the horse across the compound at a leisurely pace so as not to draw attention. The kiln was already lit and roaring, waiting to engulf Baumann's victims. He tossed in the bodies one by one, despising every minute since Beck knocked on his door last night. However, he had to do as he was told to maintain his cover, no matter how depraved the order was, to keep his daughter and the lists safe. Baumann had seen Hattie on stage. He knew her name and who she was, and eventually, he would try to leverage her as he did with tonight's prey. And if Baumann tried, Karl would ensure everyone involved met a worse death than these poor women.

After returning the horse to the barn and turning her over to the hand, he showered off the blood from dealing with the bodies, changed, and checked the time. If he hurried, he could make it for the breakfast service with the other men before it closed. He crossed the compound toward the canteen. Three men caught up with him, and they walked in silence. Beck approached their group, stopped them, and asked the others to help load a truck with some equipment before breakfast.

"Mr. Beck," Baumann called out from behind Karl and the other men. Addressing Beck by Mister and not Herr gave Karl pause. He didn't turn with the others. "I need you to tour Miss James and her friend around the facilities."

Miss James? Karl froze at the name and Baumann's use of English. Dear God. Hattie had entered the wolf's den. Baumann had already killed two women in search of Karl James, and there was no telling what he might do to Hattie. Karl scolded himself for being unprepared. Other than his knife, Karl was unarmed and unable to defend Hattie against Baumann and the dozen SS agents in the compound. Baumann's next move would decide whether everyone lived or died.

17

Fifteen minutes earlier

Eva had suggested allowing an hour for the drive to the plantation, but Hattie tacked on an extra thirty minutes to ensure she and David were not late for her first music lesson . . . and had enough time to tour the grounds and take pictures.

The drive north through the coffee farms brought back flashes from her childhood. Hattie lived in Rio for three years as a toddler after her father was reassigned here but had no clear memories of that time except for a handful of images. She vaguely remembered sitting in the family car, staring out the window, and seeing row after row of lush green trees and bushes. The scenery had mesmerized her, as it did today, and the memory stirred a warm feeling of family and carefree days. She recollected other family trips while living in the States before the divorce. Between her father's work trips and her mother's singing appearances, those family moments were few but had left a lasting impression on Hattie.

David turned off the highway while Hattie watched the rows of farmland. Soon, a ten-foot-tall stone wall appeared, blocking the coffee trees from view—the wall Agent Butler had mentioned. They had reached the outer perimeter of Baumann's plantation. David slowed, pulled over to the side of the road, and looked Hattie in the eye. "I don't want you going anywhere without me, understand?"

She patted his leg. "We'll be fine."

Moments later, he pulled up to the gate and rolled down the window of Eva's Ford to speak to the guard. "Hattie James and David Townsend to see Mr. Baumann. We're here to give a singing lesson to his daughter."

The man approached with his palm on the butt of the holstered sidearm attached to his belt. The weapon bolstered Butler's claim that this was a well-guarded compound full of intelligence-gathering SS officers. After checking the back seat, he focused on Hattie, staring at her long enough to give her the shivers.

"Is there a problem?" David asked in a sharp tone.

"No." He reached inside the guard shack, pressed a button, and spoke again with a thick German accent. "Park in front of the main house."

David drove through the gate and stayed on the paved road, passing rows of coffee trees on both sides. A sizeable two-story house appeared after a half mile, and an odd fact became apparent. For a large plantation, no one was working the fields on a traditional workday.

Hattie felt her blouse between her breasts, where she had hidden the micro-camera Agent Butler had given her. She pressed it further down to ensure its outline could not be seen.

A woman greeted them at the door and escorted them to the music room. The space was lined with built-in teak shelves filled with books and small statues. Two chairs and an end table formed a seating area along one wall. The lack of windows would provide excellent acoustics.

"Mr. Baumann will be right in," the woman said in a German accent, leaving them with a pitcher of fresh coconut water.

David sat and unpacked his satchel of sheet music at the piano in the room's center.

Hattie poured a glass, but David called out. "Don't." He walked closer and whispered. "We don't know if it's spiked. Stick to the water we brought in our pack."

Hattie thought he was paranoid, but this was not the place or time to argue, so she responded with a nod.

David returned to the piano. "What do you want to start with?"

"'Over the Rainbow' in Ab major," Hattie said. "She should know it, and it has a range of an octave and a quarter."

"Good choice for a young girl." He pulled out the sheet music and began his warmup routine.

The door opened, and Mr. Baumann entered. He smiled and shook their hands. "You're early."

"We weren't sure how long the trip would take, so we allowed extra time," Hattie said.

"I'm afraid Elsa is in the middle of her history lesson. Would you like a tour of the farm while you wait for her to finish?"

"We would." Hattie glanced at David, who gave a confirming nod. They were on their way to fulfilling Agent Butler's task—getting pictures of the compound from inside the walls.

"I brought a camera," David said. "Would it be okay to take some pictures?"

"Yes, of course. Bring it," Baumann said. "But not in the milling barn. We have some new equipment there. It's experimental, and we don't want photos reaching our competitors."

David pulled out Hattie's Kodak camera from their knapsack with their water thermos and shouldered the bag. "Ready."

Baumann escorted them through the house. Ample windows, ceiling fans, teak and bamboo accents, and various white fabrics gave each room a tropical feel. While they walked, Hattie removed the camera from her cleavage and held it in her clasped hands with her clutch bag. She could get pictures of the milling barn, and David could cover everything else.

Baumann led them out a back door. A dozen buildings came into view—three large barns, three medium-sized buildings, and a row of six small white huts. The rooflines appeared normal, without an antenna that might tell her where the radio Butler had mentioned might be kept. Mr. Beck, the man with Baumann at the Halo Club last night, was speaking to four other men dressed in long khaki pants and sleeveless undershirts in the middle of the compound. The men had their backs to Hattie.

"Mr. Beck," Baumann shouted. "I need you to tour Miss James and her friend around the facilities."

"I'll be right there." Beck acknowledged with a wave of his hand. He finished with the men and hurried over. "It's good to see you again, Miss James."

Hattie introduced David as her piano player. "We'd love a quick tour before today's lesson."

"It would be my pleasure," Beck said.

After Baumann returned to the house, Beck walked Hattie and David to the edge of the compound at the mouth of an access road. Rows of coffee trees lined the gently sloping hill on both sides. The jungle was beyond.

"How large is your farm?" Hattie asked.

"About two hundred fifty square hectares of farmland and nearly double that of jungle," Beck said.

"I'm sure it's beautiful when it blooms," Hattie said.

"Yes. For a week or two in October, the hills are a sea of white flowers."

"That's like the cherry trees around the Tidal Basin in Washington, DC, in March or April. They form an incredible ring of pink-and-white flowers."

Beck seemed uninterested in the American reference and walked them to an area beside a large barn with several dozen wood tables topped with bamboo mats. "Once the fruit grows, we harvest the cherries between May and September."

"Cherries?" Hattie asked.

"Yes, the coffee fruit is called a cherry. We pick, sort, and lay them on these raised beds to dry for three to six weeks."

"Interesting," David said, taking more pictures.

This place was an operational coffee plantation run by Germans. Either Agent Butler was utterly wrong about Baumann, or this place was the perfect cover and base for an elaborate Nazi clandestine operation.

Beck walked them inside the barn. It was unusually warm. "No picture taking in here." Thousands of stacked bulging burlap bags filled half the space. An oversized furnace was in the corner. Three of the men in sleeveless undershirts Hattie had seen earlier were loading crates into the back of a truck. One man was missing. She watched them for several moments, noting each had a similar marking on their armpit.

Beck ushered her and David to a row of three machines. "Once the cherries are dry, they are called beans. We send them through a milling machine to remove the parchment skin. Then we bag and export them for roasting."

"You don't roast them here?" David asked.

"When the operation was quite smaller, we did, but we've outgrown our old kiln," Beck said.

Hattie's heart thumped harder. This was possibly her only opportunity to get a picture of what Agent Butler wanted, but four of Baumann's men were there. Either of them could glance at her at the wrong time and catch her taking pictures secretly with a camera so small to make anyone assume she was spying on them. The risk was high, but the safety of her sister, niece, and nephew hung in the balance.

She stepped back. Her hands shook, but she took a deep breath to calm her nerves and silently told herself, *You can do this.*

Hattie kept the camera at hip level and positioned it with the lens out. Turning as if surveying the room with awe, she snapped several pictures, capturing the entire facility, including the men and the crates they were loading. Completing her turn, she hid the micro-camera against her handbag again. "I never knew the coffee process was so complicated."

"Coffee has been around for centuries," Beck said. "We've had hundreds of years to perfect the process. The new milling machines should speed that step dramatically."

"I see," Hattie said. She was relieved that no one noticed the camera, but her hands shook. "We should get back to the house."

"Of course," Beck said, gesturing toward the entrance.

When they returned to the compound, Hattie asked, "What are the other buildings?"

Beck pointed toward the barns. "More storage for the beans and a stable for the horses we use in the fields."

"And those?" Hattie gestured toward the row of six smaller white buildings. When Beck turned, she snapped more pictures of the structures.

"Housing for the laborers who can't afford a place in town. We can accommodate thirty-six. We also run a canteen for them so they don't have to worry about meals."

"That's very efficient."

"We think so." Beck returned Hattie and David to the main house, and they thanked him for the tour.

The woman who had greeted them at the door returned them to the music room, where a young blond girl in a pretty white dress was at the piano, struggling to play "The Celebrated Chop Waltz." Her father was sitting in a nearby chair in the corner and focused on Hattie. She expected him to stand and greet her, but he remained seated, keeping his stare on her. She was accustomed to constant attention on the stage, but this made her as uncomfortable as the first time she met him at Eva's studio. It was like he knew she had taken photos of the milling barn and was contemplating how to deal with her.

Hattie froze at the thought, expecting Baumann's men from the compound to come rushing in and haul off her and David for torture and interrogation.

David sat beside the girl on the bench and played without missing a note. When they finished, he smiled and said, "Do you speak English?"

"Yes." Elsa nodded. "I speak English and German, and I'm learning Portuguese."

"Wonderful," David said. "Your playing is good. How long have you been playing?"

"A year," she said, "but I can't get the hang of it."

"It took me years before I got really good. Keep at it," he said, offering his hand. "Hi, I'm David."

The girl shook his hand. "I'm Elsa."

Hattie enjoyed this touching scene, thinking David would make a great father one day.

David pointed to the girl's right. "And that's Hattie. She plays too. Can you keep a secret?"

Elsa nodded.

"She's good, but not as good as me because she never practices. Playing the piano is like running. If you don't do it every day, it takes time to get back in shape. Understand?"

"That's what Papa says. Practice daily if you want to get better."

"Good advice." David winked.

When Baumann laughed, Hattie walked over and shook Elsa's hand. "Pleased to meet you, Elsa. I'm Hattie. Can you keep another secret?"

Elsa nodded.

"He can sing but not in tune at all." Hattie winked. "I hear you have a nice voice. I was told the same thing when I was your age, so I practiced every day. Now, I sing professionally. Would you like me to teach you?"

Elsa smiled broadly. "Yes, I would, Miss James. Papa played one of your records for me. I want to sing just like you."

"Please, call me Hattie." She turned to Baumann. He was relaxed with his legs crossed, still with his eyes on Hattie, and appeared prepared to stay. "Mr. Baumann, I find it easier for students if the parents aren't hovering."

"I understand." He crossed the room and kissed Elsa on the forehead. "Enjoy your lesson, Spatzi."

Hattie recognized the term of endearment. Her father called her Spatzi when she was little. He had said it meant little sparrow, but once she started to sing, he gave her a more mature nickname, calling her his little songbird.

"Please tell the housekeeper when you're done, Miss James, so we can discuss your assessment."

"Of course," Hattie said.

After ninety minutes of assessment and instruction, Hattie sat with Elsa in the chairs. "Your father tells me you have a recital at the end of the month. Do you have the list of songs you're supposed to perform?"

Elsa frowned. "The pastor told me to pick three songs that aren't bla . . . bla . . ."

"Blasphemous?" Hattie laughed. "Then I think we can find you three appropriate songs. I'll talk to your father, but I'd like to see you twice a week. You'd have to practice every day, though. Can you do that?"

"Yes, I can sing every day, but please don't make me play the piano."

Hattie made the cross sign on her chest, hitting the micro-camera she'd hidden there. "Promise."

After saying goodbye to Elsa, Hattie alerted the housekeeper that the lesson was over, and Baumann joined her and David in the entry room minutes later.

"Well, how did Elsa do?" Baumann asked.

"She has a pleasant voice and understands the musical scales. With training, she could be quite good. With lessons twice a week and daily practice, she will knock them dead at the recital."

Baumann laughed. "I don't think that's the goal of a church recital, but I understand your meaning."

"I can come out here again on Wednesday. That's my last day off."

"Wednesday won't do. I have business to tend to. Could you come on Thursday?"

"I suppose if it's early, like today. I have to perform that evening."

After paying her for today's lesson, Baumann shook Hattie's hand. "You're hired, Miss James."

18

As Hattie and David entered Rio's city limits, the parade of cars behind them on the highway since leaving Baumann's coffee plantation peeled off onto other roads, relieving Hattie of the feeling they had been followed. David gave her a confirming glance and drove toward the town's center. He parked two blocks before the dry cleaner's shop again, and they walked the rest of the way on foot.

As they entered, the bell above the door announced their arrival. They waited until Nala Cohen finished helping a woman at the counter—the only customer in the store. Once the woman left with a stack of freshly cleaned garments, Cohen gestured her chin toward the back, directing Hattie and David to follow. She led them through the office to the secret room, where Agent Butler was waiting.

"How did it go? Did you get in?" Butler asked.

"Yes, we got in." Hattie handed him her Kodak and the micro-camera he had issued her. "We took pictures of the facilities and some men working there. They seemed protective of the milling barn, claiming they had some new machine they didn't want to get into the hands of their competitors."

Butler handed the cameras to Cohen. "Develop these."

"Right away," she said.

Assuming they had a dark room in the building for such needs, Hattie told Nala, "I noticed some of the men had similar markings on their armpits, but I was too far away to make them out. If I was lucky enough to capture one, can you enlarge it?"

"I'll check," Nala said before scurrying off.

"Those markings are likely the mark of an SS officer," Butler said. "They traditionally have their blood type tattooed on their left armpit in case they are injured on the battlefield and separated from their identification tags."

Hattie nodded her understanding. Butler was right. Baumann was running a Nazi spy ring from the plantation, gathering information on who knew what. She feared her father's coming to Rio wasn't only because he was familiar with the city but because he was associated with Baumann, as Butler suspected. Her father was just like her, keeping so many secrets from the world.

Butler sat in his chair and spun to face Hattie. "Tell me about Maya Reyes. You two seem . . . close."

Hattie didn't like the question or the way he phrased it. She felt he was invading her privacy and perhaps knew more about her personal life than she would want. "You told me to get a job. She owns the Halo Club and offered me a singing gig."

"The police came to the club last night. Why?"

"She reported her sister missing. Anna hasn't been seen since Friday."

"Interesting," Butler said.

"What aren't you telling me?" Hattie suspected more behind his benign reply.

"Nothing. Let the police conduct their investigation and steer clear of them."

Hattie could tell he was holding something back, but pressing him on the matter would only yield more lies. "The police took a report but aren't interested in investigating a missing woman when no money is involved."

"Then that should tell you to stay out of local police business. Do your job. Nothing more."

Half an hour later, Nala Cohen returned with the developed photographs and cameras. "You were right about those arm markings."

Butler inspected the pictures with a magnifying glass. "We were right about the plantation. They are definitely SS officers." He turned to Hattie. "How many were there?"

"Besides Baumann, I saw six others, including the guard at the gate."

"There were only three in the photographs."

"They were the men Beck talked to before touring us around the facilities. Beck is the plantation manager."

"What about the row of white buildings? They look like cabins."

"Beck said they're for laborers who couldn't afford housing and could hold thirty-six."

"Thirty-six? That's more than we estimated." Butler looked up at Hattie. "Can you get in that milling barn again? It sounds like they're hiding something there."

"I doubt it. My lessons are limited to the main house."

"Did you see an antenna on any of the buildings? Anything that might tell us where the radio station is?"

"Sorry, nothing." Hattie shook her head.

"Then it must be camouflaged. When are you going back?"

"Thursday." Hattie didn't like where this was going.

"Good. That means you can get us more pictures from inside the house. We're looking for the information his men gather and the code they use to transmit it."

"Whoa." David raised his hand in a stopping motion. "You wanted pictures of the compound. We got them. Her job is to get her father, not some Nazi spy ring. You've put her in enough danger."

Butler turned to him with sharp eyes. "She'll do exactly what we tell her to do. You both know the consequences if she doesn't."

Hattie disliked being manipulated into doing things, but exploring more of the house and plantation might give her answers about her father, none of which she planned to share with Butler and the FBI. "He's right, David. I need to go back." She turned to Butler. "I'll get your pictures." But that was all she would give him.

Butler gave her both cameras. "Come back when you get the photos."

Back in the car, David twisted the wood steering wheel. "I don't like this one bit, Hattie. They're asking too much of you."

"I can't disagree, but I don't have a way out. At least not yet." Until she did, she would do what she thought was right for her family. She glanced at her watch. It was nearly two o'clock, so Maya should be at work soon to prep for the day. "I'd like to stop at the club."

"Talk about dangerous." David shook his head and drove through town, stopping at the parking lot two blocks from the Halo Club. "Let's not be too long. Remember, they're watching."

"In and out, I promise." Hattie entered the club with David. The dining room was lit, silent, and unoccupied, but she heard noises in the kitchen. She glanced over her shoulder and said, with pleading eyes, "Stay here."

David gave her an affirming nod. "I'll be at the bar."

Hattie pushed through to the kitchen, discovering Maya stocking the walk-in refrigerator with meat and fresh produce. She was the only one there. "Hey, you."

Maya stopped her work and turned. The dark spots under her eyes suggested she had gotten little sleep. Her long, sad expression telegraphed that her sister still hadn't reappeared.

"No news?" Hattie asked.

Maya shook her head. "Nothing." She raked both hands down her face. "I don't know what else to do."

Hattie reached into her handbag and pulled out an envelope she'd stuffed into it before leaving for the plantation earlier that morning. She handed it to Maya. "You said you needed everyone's pay for the week. Five hundred dollars should be close to two weeks. I wish it were more, but it's everything I brought from the States." It was a reasonable lie.

Maya's mouth fell agape. "I can't take your money, Hattie."

"Yes, you can. I live with my mother, so I don't need the money. I want you to use it to find your sister. If that means bribing Inspector Silva, so be it."

Maya shoved the envelope back into Hattie's hands. "I can't. It's not right."

"Then consider it an investment. You said business was up after I started singing here. Anna is an important part of the club. We must get her back to tend bar and free you up." Hattie slapped the money into Maya's palm. "Take it. I'll expect a ten percent return on my investment by the end of the year."

Tears filled Maya's eyes. "Thank you. No one has ever helped me like this."

Hattie wiped away a tear with her thumb, caressing Maya's cheek with the same hand. "Get used to it. I want to help you." For a brief second, she closed her eyes to take in the feel of Maya's soft skin against her fingertips. Hattie had touched several women like this as a prelude to intimacy, but none were ever intimate with her beyond the physical. Even in this momentary touch, Hattie felt her vulnerability.

Maya locked eyes with her in another silent stare. Then her breath hitched—the long-awaited second sign. Butler's cryptic warning and David's caution played in her head. Common sense told her to back away and not give the FBI more to hold over her head, but Hattie didn't build her career or carry on with her love life by always doing what was expected. She had learned through experience that sometimes life required giant leaps of faith.

"You're driving me crazy with the long looks." Hattie struggled to keep her breathing in check.

"I . . ." Maya drifted her stare to Hattie's lips and licked her own. Yet another sign.

Hattie's instincts were right. Her body warmed with anticipation when Maya moved closer without breaking her focus. She leaned in until their lips were an inch apart. Maya's breathing labored, mixing the warm air between them.

The situation was crystal clear. They both wanted this kiss. But then Maya clutched Hattie's hand, held it against her chest, and looked at her with questioning eyes. "Tell me about David."

"He's a friend."

"But you seem close."

Hattie took a weighty breath. "We are, but it's complicated."

"That's the second time you said that. I don't understand."

"It means he's okay with this." Hattie squeezed Maya's hand to stress her point.

Maya narrowed her brow and pushed back. "I'm not into that sort of thing. I won't let him watch or join us."

"You misunderstand." Hattie was going about this wrong. A lesbian in

New York would have understood, but Maya wasn't familiar with their code. A little forthrightness was called for . . . but not too specific. "We each do what we want . . . separately. Understand?"

"I'm not sure, but I think it's a good thing." Maya formed a slight grin.

"Yes, very good." Hattie matched her smile, focusing on Maya's lips. They were plump and moist from just having been licked and begged to be kissed. She leaned closer, and Maya did as well. Their breaths mixed in steamy exhales and heads continued a slow march until their lips grazed.

Then.

Noise in the dining room forced them to step apart to a respectable distance. A look of lust, longing, and frustration filled Maya's eyes. She clutched the envelope when a cook entered the kitchen. "Thank you for this, Hattie. I'll walk to the police station tomorrow. It's not far from my home. Maybe this can convince Silva to do his job."

Hattie squeezed Maya's hand when the cook's back was to them. "I'm coming with you."

19

The following morning

David turned the corner in Eva's Ford. The three-story police station in central Rio had many of the same classical architectural features as the Halo Club, but unlike the club Maya was restoring, this building had been pristinely maintained by the state government. Official vehicles were parked in a lot across the street, and a half dozen uniformed officers were lined up at the corner coffee stand.

"There she is," Hattie said, glimpsing Maya in line for coffee. Her head felt lighter with Maya in her sight again. That near kiss—or maybe it technically was a kiss since their lips touched for a fraction of a second—had fueled several heat-producing fantasies before falling asleep last night. Her head told her those fantasies were best in check until this business with the FBI was over. Still, her lips tingled at the inevitability of that kiss becoming a reality.

David circled the block, parked along the station's side, and walked with Hattie around the corner. They waited near the entrance until Maya approached.

Maya smiled, offering Hattie the second drink. "Good morning.

Coffee?" She turned to David. "If I'd known you were coming, I would have gotten three."

He waved her off. "That's fine. I had some before leaving the house."

"Thank you." Hattie reached for the hot drink, and their pinkies grazed ever so slightly. Their hands remained on the paper cup for a beat longer than necessary, and at that moment, they locked gazes, and each released a breathy exhale. "Do you have an appointment?" she asked, sipping her coffee while keeping her eyes on Maya.

"No, but I'm sure he'll see me." Maya patted her purse and extended her arm toward the main entrance. "Shall we?"

They went inside the lobby. Dozens of people were seated in chairs along the wall nearest the entrance. Several were queued in a line, waiting to speak to the desk officer. Multiple conversations created a low hum while the squeak of ceiling fans spinning overhead dominated the room.

David found a seat against the wall while Hattie and Maya joined the line. They stood quietly, sipping coffee, with their arms pressed together. The touch was subtle enough to avoid being noticed and delicate enough to reawaken last night's fantasies.

Maya stepped forward when it was their turn in line, and Hattie stood beside her, a step back. Maya spoke in Portuguese to the officer, sliding a thin envelope across the desk. He opened it, nodded, and summoned another officer over. The two whispered back and forth before the second officer scurried off. The first officer told them to wait, so Hattie and Maya joined David at the chairs.

"Well?" David asked.

"They're getting someone," Maya said.

Hattie leaned in and whispered to Maya, "How much did you give him?"

"Twenty American dollars. It's enough to grab his attention."

If Maya had to grease every palm at every level before talking to the inspector, Hattie's money wouldn't last long.

Twenty minutes passed before the second officer returned. He told them to follow him, but when David stood, the officer put up his hand to stop him. "Somente as mulheres."

David looked at Maya for translation.

"I'm sorry, but you have to wait here."

David nodded his understanding, but his piercing stare at the officer communicated his dissatisfaction.

"We'll be fine." Hattie touched his arm.

She and Maya followed the officer to the elevator, dumping their paper cups in a nearby trash can. Once on the third floor, they navigated a maze of corridors and entered an office suite. The writing on the frosted glass on the door indicated the office was home to some type of investigators. The large squad room housed eight desks and twice as many filing cabinets. Ceiling fans stirred the summer air, cooling the investigators as they talked and typed at their desks.

Two walls were littered with bulletins, wanted posters, and clipboards, but the wall with the blackboard caught Hattie's attention. It contained photos of nine women. Eight looked like they were the pictures from the newspaper article detailing the rash of women who had recently gone missing in Rio. The ninth made her gasp. It was the picture of Anna that Maya had given the investigator Sunday night.

Maya clutched Hattie's hand. The gentle squeeze of their hands conveyed a mutual understanding that Maya had also seen it, as well as Hattie's support.

The officer knocked on a secondary door and stuck his head inside. A moment later, he opened the door farther and gestured for the women to enter. They walked inside. Chief Inspector Silva was behind the desk, and Investigator Vargas stood near the far wall.

"Entre, por favor," Silva said, gesturing for them to sit in the two guest chairs.

The officer left, closing the door behind him.

Hattie and Maya sat.

"May we speak in English, Inspector? Miss James is American."

Hattie nodded her thanks, thinking she'd never let on that she had a basic knowledge of Portuguese, which could be an advantage someday.

"Yes, of course," he said.

"Thank you for seeing us, Inspector Silva," Maya said. "First, is there any news on my sister? I see you added her picture to the board in the other room."

"I take it you haven't heard from her," Silva said.

"No, I haven't."

"Then we'll file our report by Friday. You can request a copy next week."

"If you've added her to the board, then you must think her disappearance is linked to the other missing women."

"It means she is among the missing, nothing more."

"Do you have any leads on the others? Any suspects?" Maya asked.

"I cannot discuss the broader investigation with you. We will contact you if we have any news about your sister."

"You have no interest in looking for her, do you?" Maya's tone contained an accusatory sharpness.

"Like I told you the other night, women go missing all the time. Give it time. We had more pictures on that board, but several showed up unharmed a week after a failed romance. Your sister will do the same." Silva's dismissive tone was infuriating.

Hattie felt her anger grow, but Maya remained calm and slid a thicker envelope across his desk. "Perhaps this will convince you to look for her."

"Bribery is a crime. I'd arrest you if not for my sympathy for your circumstance." He slid the envelope back without looking inside. "Go home, Miss Reyes."

Maya laughed, jerking her head back. Clearly stunned as much as Hattie, she snatched the envelope. "Then I'll find her myself." She marched from the office with Hattie steps behind. Both gave the board with the women's photos a long look. "I'll find you, Anna, and when I do, hopefully, I'll find the others." She spun on her heel and strode down the tiled corridor.

Hattie struggled to keep up. "Slow down, Maya." But Maya didn't listen. She continued with a full head of steam. Hattie picked up her pace and grabbed Maya's shirt sleeve when her arm swung back, bringing her to a stop. "I know you are angry. I am, too."

"The arrogance of that man. He doesn't care about Anna or any of those women."

"Then let's find someone who does. We can use the money to hire a private detective."

"You're right, but we've wasted so much time on the polícia. The chance of her still being alive shrinks every day."

"Then let's go now." Hattie squeezed her hands with both of hers. The gentle touch seemed to calm her.

Maya nodded and walked to the elevator. After pressing the call button, they boarded. Hattie started to close the door, but someone shouted, "Segure o elevador, por favor."

She paused to allow the person on. Investigator Vargas stepped inside. Maya gave him a death stare.

"Thanks." He closed the door behind him. Once the cab was between floors, he said, "Can we talk?"

Maya cocked her head to one side, sizing him up. "Why?"

The elevator reached the bottom floor, and he said, "I want to help, but not here."

Hattie had no reason to trust him, but she was desperate to help Maya find Anna and would grasp at virtually anything resembling a life raft. "I have a car around the corner," Hattie said. "A white Ford Deluxe. Meet us there."

"Five minutes." Vargas opened the door, letting the women off first. He exited and turned down a hallway.

Hattie and Maya crossed the reception area and met up with David. He asked, "How did it go?"

"Not well," Hattie said. "Let's go." Once outside, she turned toward where they had parked their car. "We're around the corner," she told Maya.

Once at the car, David and Hattie hopped in the front while Maya jumped in the back on Hattie's side. He asked, "Where to?"

"Wait here," Hattie said.

"Why?" he asked.

Hattie spotted Investigator Vargas walking toward their car. "Him."

"The gumshoe?" he asked. "I thought it didn't go well."

"He wants to help." Maya slid across the seat to David's side.

Vargas slipped into the back with Maya. "Thank you for waiting. Inspector Silva is right about most women returning after a few days. It happens every week, but he's wrong about the ones on the board." He handed Maya a folded sheet of paper. "Their friends and family say they weren't dating or looking. I believe they're all linked, but Silva refuses to let us investigate."

"That article in the newspaper about the missing girls," Hattie said. "That was you. You leaked the photos and information." If a junior detective had to resort to leaking news to the press, someone clearly didn't want those women found. Hattie and Maya were Anna's only hope.

Vargas shrugged. "Silva scared off the families, so they won't talk to the police anymore."

"What is Silva covering up?" Maya asked. "Who is he protecting?"

"I don't know." Vargas pointed to the slip of paper Maya was holding. "But that list might help you find out."

"What is this?" Maya unfolded the paper and studied its contents.

"It's the names and addresses of the missing women and their next of kin. They won't talk to me but might talk to you."

"Would they talk to a private investigator?" Maya asked.

"I doubt anyone would take the case. Most are former police who check with headquarters first."

Maya touched his arm. "Thank you, but why are you doing this? Couldn't you lose your job?"

"We're supposed to work for the people, not for only those who can pay."

"Then why wouldn't he take my money?"

"My guess is someone is paying him not to." Vargas handed her a business card. "If you find out anything, let me know. I'll do what I can." He exited the car and hovered at the open door. "Good luck, Miss Reyes. I hope you find your sister." He shut the door and disappeared inside police headquarters.

Maya studied the list again, and her lips trembled. "This isn't right. All these women. I have to find them."

"We'll help you," Hattie said. Her heart went out to the woman. Their circumstances weren't the same, but both their lives were suddenly turned upside down when someone they loved went missing. Hattie knew precisely what Maya was going through, and a nagging thought picked at her conscience. She hated to think it because she always believed her father to be a good man, but the more she looked into this, the more she thought he might have been involved in Anna's disappearance, and that hurt more than anything. Hattie could not live with being betrayed by him.

Maya was too upset to walk home, so David offered to drive her. Hattie walked her to the door, brushing her hand lightly so no one could see. "Would you like me to stay?"

Pain was behind Maya's eyes. "I don't think we should. I have to open the club soon."

"Do you plan to speak to those people on the list?" Hattie asked.

"I have to. Anna is counting on me." Maya wiped a tear that had fallen down her cheek.

"Then we're going with you," Hattie said. "We'll pick you up early."

"You're a good friend, Hattie James."

20

The following morning

David was sullen during the drive to Maya's home. He had barely spoken to Hattie since she confessed last night to telling Maya their relationship wasn't as it seemed. If he kept this up, Eva might ask questions, so she turned to him and asked, "Why are you so upset this time? I've told several women about us. It's the heart of our arrangement."

"It's not that you told a potential lover about us, but what do you know about her, Hattie? You're betting your sister's and her kids' lives on Maya's goodwill."

"I trust her, David. I wish you could, too."

He shook his head. "And this helping her find her sister. You're asking for trouble. Butler told you to stay away from the investigation."

"I know I'm taking a chance, but I won't abandon her. She has no one else."

He pulled up to her house and parked. "I still think you're crazy for doing this."

"This entire situation is crazy." Hattie exited the car, holding the door open. "What's a little more?" She slammed the car door, walked up the concrete pathway to the house, and knocked. Staying away from this woman was impossible at this point, but as long as the three of them were always together in public, the FBI would have nothing more to throw at her.

The door opened. Maya had added loose curls to her long hair and let it hang past her shoulders. She wore a formfitting white blouse and a red skirt with an asymmetric shape cut higher on her right leg than her left. The skirt screamed sexy, but her white sneakers said she was ready for walking.

Hattie was speechless.

Maya grinned, smoothing her skirt . . . slowly . . . seductively. "Like what you see?"

"Very much so," Hattie said. "You look great."

"If men answer the door, we want them to ask us in."

"That outfit would work on anyone." Hattie suddenly remembered she was in public and stopped her leering.

Maya stepped out, locking the door behind her. "We better get started. I've mapped out the addresses to make our route easier."

Once in the car, Hattie asked to see the list Vargas had given Maya yesterday. "My mother's neighbor and two mothers of her students are among the missing. I wonder which ones are them?"

"Three women live in rich neighborhoods. I bet those are the ones your mother knew. Did the police ever talk to her?"

"No." Hattie returned the list. "Which tells me Silva has been stonewalling the investigation from the beginning."

"Interesting." Maya made notes on the list. "We should leave those three for last. The other missing women all live in favelas by the harbor. My guess is that they work near the docks."

"Would that be close to where the cargo freighters come in?" Hattie asked.

"Yes, why?"

"Just asking." As much as she trusted Maya, Hattie couldn't explain further without revealing information about her father, and that was a step she wasn't prepared to take. If pressured, Maya might give up information about Hattie's father to find her sister. However, David gave her a knowing look, clearly making the connection that Karl had arrived in Rio via a cargo ship weeks ago.

Maya leaned closer to the front seat and directed David to the first address. He parked on the outskirts of the working-class neighborhood, and they went on foot down the narrow roads and pathways. The street markings were informal, and house numbers were hand-painted, but they added a semblance of organization to the neighborhood. The area resembled the Hoovervilles that popped up on the alleys, parks, and vacant lots at the height of the Depression. Central Park's Great Lawn had become the city's largest, with temporary wood and tin huts lining the pathways. This neighborhood had the same construction, but the structures were painted bright colors, mostly faded from the sun and tropical climate.

Children played in the streets with a worn, grimy soccer ball. A pack of mangy dogs feasted at the collection of garbage cans. Otherwise, the area was free of loose trash.

A group of men eyed them as they walked past, making Hattie grateful David had insisted on coming. One man whistled, and another grabbed Maya's arm. In two seconds, the touchy one learned he had made a colossal mistake. Maya twisted his wrist and thumb back like she had done to the handsy customer at the Halo Club, bringing the man to his knees.

"Isso não foi educado. Na próxima vez, eu quebro. Entender?"

The man nodded, and Maya loosened her hold.

"Procuramos a Rua Esperanza."

Hattie snickered, understanding most of the exchange.

"A próxima rua." The man pointed with the other hand before nursing the injured one.

"Obrigado."

Their group continued down the street, and David asked, "What did you tell him?"

"I told him he wasn't polite, and I would break his thumb the next time," Maya said with a grin. "He was kind enough to tell me Esperanza is the next street over." Her confident stride was sexy as hell.

They found house number sixteen. Hattie and David remained across the dirt road in view of the door while Maya knocked on the doorframe. An older woman in her fifties or sixties answered. Maya spoke to her in Portuguese, and the woman answered a few questions, but Hattie was too far away to hear most of what they said. Soon, the woman's posture stiffened, morphing into dramatic hand gestures. Her reaction smacked of fear, and the woman retreated inside and slammed the door closed.

Maya rejoined the others, and Hattie asked, "What did she say?"

"She's the mother of one of the missing girls and said her daughter worked at a cantina near the dock. She said her daughter wasn't dating and had a rule of never going out with the customers. When I asked her about the police, she shut down. It was clear the police had threatened them or paid them off."

"That's not much to go on," David said.

"It's more than we knew yesterday," Maya said.

The next stops with family members and neighbors, including several at an adjacent favela, yielded the same results, but before slamming the door in Maya's face, one family member said something about having to pay back the money if he talked to her. Soon, a pattern emerged from what little information they had gleaned. The five women from the favelas worked in restaurants around the docks, and all had gone missing within days of the three women loosely connected to Eva.

Maya checked her watch. "I have time for another stop. Then I have to go to the club." She reviewed the remaining names on the list and pointed out one closest to her home to shorten the driving time.

David drove to the address, stopping in an upper-class neighborhood similar to Eva's—the polar opposite of the areas they had spent the morning scouring for information. The walled-off properties were large and pristinely manicured without a single stray weed. Dogs were on leashes, and no children ran loose in the streets.

David drove up the access road and parked in the courtyard. The house was hidden behind a whitewashed stone wall, but the property projected wealth like her mother's home. They gathered at the exterior gate, and Maya rang the bell.

Minutes later, the gate opened. A man in his forties appeared, looking worn down from heartbreak and worry. "Sim? Como posso ajudá-lo?"

"Você fala inglês?" Maya asked.

"A little," he said. "How may I help you?"

"My name is Maya Reyes. I'm looking for Tobin Moyer."

"I'm Tobin."

"I understand your wife went missing a few weeks ago."

He started to close the gate. "I'm not speaking to press."

Maya raised her hand, stopping the gate before he could close it. "Não sou da imprensa, Sr. Moyer. Minha irmã desapareceu há cinco dias."

Her plea that she wasn't from the press but the sister of a woman who disappeared five days ago earned her a look of sympathy from the man.

Maya continued. "We think their disappearances might be connected. Can you answer a few questions?"

"What do you want to know?"

"May we come in?" Maya asked.

His posture stiffened, making him appear suspicious. He started to close the gate again.

"Mr. Moyer," Hattie said. "I believe you know my mother, Eva Machado. Your son takes piano and singing lessons from her."

He squinted at her. "You're Eva's daughter? Which one?"

"Hattie."

"The singer. Why are you here?" he asked.

"I perform at the club Maya and her sister operate, and I wanted to help. Please, may we come in and ask you a few questions?"

His posture relaxed. He invited them in and led them through the lush courtyard to the house. Once seated in the living room, he offered them something to drink, which they declined. "What questions do you have?"

After questioning a dozen neighbors and family members today, they learned to avoid mentioning the police until the end. Maya opened with a benign question. "Does your wife work?"

"No, she cared for our son."

"Do you know where your wife was the day she went missing?"

"I worked late that day." He struggled to find the right words in English but spoke in Portuguese.

Maya translated. "He came home to find their twelve-year-old son asleep in bed. He said Marta had gotten dressed up and gone out but didn't know where. She never came home." Maya then asked, "Was there a ransom request?"

"No, nothing."

More of Hattie's Portuguese was returning, and she understood most of the conversation without translation.

Maya shifted uncomfortably in her chair and asked in Portuguese, "I hate to ask, but the police think my sister is off with some man and will return any time. Is there a chance—"

"Stop right there." Moyer raised his voice in Portuguese. "I'll tell you what I told them. My wife is not having an affair. She would not leave our son."

"I know the question is upsetting, Mr. Moyer. I felt the same way, but I had to be sure. Do you have any leads? Any suspects?"

"Nothing," he said, and Maya translated as he spoke. "The police haven't been helpful. They took the report and said they would sweep the favelas for her but have yet to tell me a thing. I stopped going in when one told me to stop asking questions. That they would contact me if they had news."

"Did you consider what they said to you a threat?" Hattie asked. Though the other neighbors and family members hadn't said as much, she suspected the police had intimidated them into silence.

"I took it as a testament to their incompetence, and my questions made them look bad."

"Did they offer you money to go away?" Maya asked.

Moyer turned to her. "No. I would have thrown it in their face if they had."

"One last question, Mr. Moyer," Maya said. "Who told you to stop asking questions?"

"Chief Inspector Silva." He shook his head in disgust and mumbled something else in Portuguese that Hattie didn't understand.

"He told me the same thing, but he's anything but an empty suit," Maya said. "I think he's corrupt and dangerous. Since he won't investigate, I am."

Moyer raked a hand down his face. "If I didn't have my son to think about, I would join you."

Maya stood. "Thank you for your time. May I call you if I have more questions?"

"Please do." He jotted down his phone number, and Maya did the same.

After leaving the Moyer home, David drove to Maya's house, and Hattie walked her to the door. "When do you plan to speak to the family of the last two names on the list," Hattie asked.

"Tomorrow morning."

"I have a singing lesson to give. Otherwise, David and I would go with you."

"Don't worry. I can take care of myself."

"I don't doubt that."

They stood silently for several beats, staring into each other's eyes and letting their connection build. They were getting closer to finding Anna and closer to giving in to the attraction.

Hattie lowered her gaze briefly, resisting the urge to give Maya an appropriate goodbye. "I'm having dinner with my mother tonight, so I'll see you tomorrow before my show."

"Tomorrow, then."

After Maya disappeared inside, Hattie returned to the car. David glanced at her before starting the engine. "We better get home. Your mother is taking us out tonight."

Hattie acknowledged with a nod, soaking in the pattern of the victims they'd uncovered today.

David squeezed her hand. "Are you thinking what I'm thinking about the docks?"

Between the timing of the abductions and the connection to her mother and the docks, Hattie couldn't help but come to the same conclusion. "Yes. This is somehow linked to my father." A chill coursed through her at the thought her father might be behind all the abductions and quickly morphed into anger. She likely never knew the man she trusted and loved all her life. The diplomat was likely a Nazi spy, and the loving father was likely a killer. The confusion almost brought her to tears, making a drink sound ever so tempting right then.

21

Later that evening

Sitting in a car with Eva behind the wheel was a novel experience for Hattie. During her childhood, her father did all the driving, and when Hattie was older, her mother would catch a taxi anywhere she needed to go in DC or New York. Hattie glanced at her from the passenger seat. She seemed stronger, more independent, happier, and more accessible. This was the version of her mother Hattie wished she had all these years instead of the self-absorbed woman who had raised her and become bitter toward her father. Eva had changed, and it might have been time for Hattie to let go of her resentment toward her.

Eva drove into the paved curved entrance, stopping under the portico at the welcoming red carpet. A young man dressed in a sophisticated black-and-white uniform and a hat with the hotel logo jogged up to the driver's side and opened the door. "Boa noite, Senhorita Machado."

"Good evening, Thomas. English, please." Eva patted his hand. "I have my daughter with me tonight."

"Ah, how nice for you." Thomas smiled. "A cause for celebration along with the governor's birthday."

"Indeed," Eva said, stepping out.

Another valet opened the passenger side doors, letting David and Hattie out. "Welcome to the Copacabana Palace Hotel."

"Thank you," David said, offering Hattie his arm.

They joined Eva at the entrance, pausing to take in the view across the street. The hotel faced the world-renowned crescent-shaped Copacabana Beach of white sand and a stunning view of the surrounding mountains. Its ideal location made it the premiere getaway for the rich and famous from around the world. While the last slivers of light cast the sky above the ocean in beautiful stripes of purple and gold, tourists still dotted the beach. The lights lining the boardwalk of concrete and cobblestone had come on, providing the perfect setting for a romantic sunset stroll.

They walked inside.

Glistening marble floors invited them into the grand lobby. Guests and staff bustled beneath the elaborate chandeliers and around the imposing white pillars. Eva flowed gracefully through the area, drawing whispers and glints of recognition, but she paid them no attention and continued past indoor shops and a café without breaking stride. Hattie and David kept pace and slowed when they approached the nightclub entrance.

The head waiter greeted them with open arms. "Senhorita Machado."

"English, please, William." Eva gestured to her left. "May I introduce my daughter, Hattie James, and her fiancé, David Townsend?"

"It's a pleasure." William snapped to attention and bowed a fraction, acknowledging both. "Miss James, your reputation precedes you. We're honored to have you dine at the Golden Room."

"Thank you," Hattie said, shaking his extended hand.

"Your table is waiting." William guided them through the dozens of tables, stopping at the center of the music hall, second row from the stage—a location of prominence, especially tonight, to honor the governor's birthday.

The room was two-tiered and trimmed in brass and gold finishings. The three-foot raised section started past the ornate bar and ringed the room on three sides. It was divided by a polished wood railing, giving those elevated tables an unobstructed view of the stage. But the room's center was the coveted location. Men in tuxedos and women in elegant evening gowns occupied the tables surrounding them. Hattie suddenly felt underdressed in her best dress next to her mother in her sophisticated dark blue floor-length gown. At least David wore appropriate attire. A dark suit with a proper tie could befit any occasion.

"I'd heard talk of the Golden Room by other singers, but this is magnificent, Mother," Hattie said.

"Isn't it?" Eva sat in her chair while William scooted it closer for her. She thanked him as he laid out her menu. "Maurice Chevalier inaugurated the venue and set the bar high. It's only been open for three years but has already become the pearl of high society."

"I understand you've performed here," David said to Eva, scooting in Hattie's chair before taking his seat.

The waiter placed menus in front of them.

"Yes, several times," Eva said with more than a hint of pride.

"She is our hometown star attraction," William said, stroking Eva's ego. "The house is always packed when she appears." He leaned closer to Eva. "The governor asked if you would stop by his table tonight."

Eva blushed. "I can't deny a man his birthday wish. Please tell him to expect me after we order."

William explained the night's specials before returning to his station.

Soon, a waiter took their orders and brought drinks and salads while Eva visited with the new governor, but Hattie and David waited to eat. Hattie watched her mother. Eva laughed and focused on the governor's tablemates, giving each one equal attention. She was in her element, rubbing elbows with high society and political elite, and always had. Hattie remembered her mother mingling with influential politicians and diplomats between performing at the piano at their house during her father's many parties. She was a natural and seemed to thrive on it.

The governor stroked the exposed skin of Eva's back in a way that would have had Maya twisting back his thumb. Eva shifted, appearing uncomfortable at the contact. She smiled, nodded her head slightly, and returned to their table.

"He's a friendly one," Hattie said.

"He's a handsy flirt," Eva said.

"Why do you put up with it?"

"I typically don't, but this is not the place to make a scene."

"Well, I don't like it." Hattie glanced at the governor, who was laughing with a cocktail glass in one hand and a cigar in the other. He was the picture of an entitled pig.

"Let's not beat this into the ground." Eva squeezed Hattie's hand. "Tell me. Has Miss Reyes heard any news about her missing sister?"

"Nothing. The police are uninterested," Hattie said, "but we spoke to many of the neighbors and family members of the other women who had gone missing recently, including Mr. Tobin."

Eva threw a hand to her chest and sighed. "His wife's disappearance is so sad. Marta is a lovely woman and an excellent mother. Did you learn anything that might help find her?"

"Nothing yet." Hattie couldn't mention the connection she suspected between her father and those women, but there was no harm in telling her what they unearthed. "Several of the women worked at restaurants near the docks."

Eva nodded. "All sorts of merchant sailors come through the docks every day. It doesn't surprise me."

"Can you tell me anything more about Mrs. Moyer?" Hattie asked. "When did you last see her?"

"Here, actually. She came to see me perform about two weeks ago at my invitation, and I stopped by her table before the show to thank her for coming. While I was on stage, a man joined her at the table, but she was gone when I returned after my performance. Apparently, she never made it home." Eva wiped a tear with her cloth napkin.

Hattie squeezed her mother's hand. "I'm sorry this has upset you."

"Enough of sadness." Eva waved over their waiter. "Champagne and sparkling cider," she told him, and he scurried off. "We need to celebrate your coming nuptial."

Minutes later, a server filled three glasses at their table, two with champagne and one with cider for Hattie, and placed the bottles in metal ice buckets on stands beside David. Eva lifted her glass. "To Hattie and David. May your marriage be long, happy, and fruitful."

David and Hattie raised their glasses and smiled at Eva's kind but misguided toast. They drank, knowing the marriage would never happen. Their fake breakup after all of this was over would disappoint her mother, and surprisingly, doing so would disappoint Hattie. She never thought she would think this, but she enjoyed seeing her mother happy.

A woman in a black-and-white dress—the hotel uniform—approached their table with a camera slung over her neck. "Good evening, Miss Machado. I understand you are celebrating tonight. Would you like your picture taken?"

"Grand idea." Eva motioned for Hattie and David to scoot closer before the woman snapped three pictures.

"They'll be ready after the show." The woman handed Eva a claim check, smiled, and went to the next table.

"Do you know who's performing tonight?" Hattie asked.

"Yes, a special performance for the governor and his guests. I think you'll like the surprise."

A man from the governor's table approached Hattie's group.

He touched her mother's shoulder. "Excuse me."

Eva turned and smiled. She beamed, actually. "Frederick. It was a pleasure seeing you earlier." She gestured toward Hattie. "This is my daughter, Hattie James, and her fiancé, David Townsend." Eva turned to Hattie. "This is Frederick Ziegler. He's the new Swiss ambassador."

The man tilted his head in a polite bow. "It's a pleasure meeting you again, Miss James."

Hattie squinted. The man looked familiar, but she could not place where she had seen him before. He was tall and broad-shouldered with fair hair and distinctive thick glasses. "Have we met?"

"You were a child when I attended your father's parties in Washington."

That was it. Hattie remembered the eyeglasses. Ziegler was a regular guest of her father, but he never stayed long. "Yes, of course."

"I understand you're staying with your mother and that you've already found work singing," Ziegler said.

"Yes, that's right," Hattie said.

"Hopefully, we'll see more of each other." Ziegler turned to her mother. "Shall I send a car for you on Friday since I'll be working late?"

"Don't be silly." Eva waved him off. "I'll meet you right here at seven."

Ziegler kissed Eva's hand, excused himself, and returned to the governor's table.

Hattie smirked. "Frederick, huh?"

"Hush." Eva grinned and spread a napkin across her lap.

Their food came, and they ate, discussing Eva's career since her return to Brazil and David's fictional plans to buy a house in Long Island once he and Hattie were married. After the staff cleared the plates and brought a second bottle of champagne, the room lights lowered. Tendrils of cigar and cigarette smoke floating toward the ceiling filtered through the stage's spotlights. A male voice came over the speaker system and spoke Portuguese and English. He ended with, ". . . proud to present Miss Maggie Moore."

The room broke out into applause.

"Maggie!" Hattie's stomach fluttered with giddiness. "Oh my gosh."

David threw an arm around the back of Hattie's chair and asked over the clapping crescendo, "Did she mention she was coming here?"

Hattie shook her head, unable to take her eyes off the stage. "No. It never came up."

Maggie strutted onto the stage in her signature flamboyant fashion, playing up to the hoots and whistles. Reaching the microphone, she broke into her first song—the piece she and Hattie had opened with in New York. Halfway through, she crossed the stage during a short piano solo and spotted Hattie in the audience. She pointed, smiled, and mouthed her name before returning to the microphone.

After finishing the song, Maggie waited for the applause to die before speaking. "It's a pleasure to be at the Golden Room. Thank you, Governor Azevedo, for inviting me to sing on your birthday." She stretched a hand across her brow to shield the blinding stage lights, searching the tables. "We have a special guest in the audience tonight."

No, no, no, no, no, no, no, no, no, no, no, no, no, Hattie thought. *Please don't say my name.*

"Maybe with a little encouragement," Maggie continued, "we can convince her to join me on stage." She extended her arm. "Hattie?"

Hattie waved her off, mouthing no. The last thing she wanted was to perform in front of her mother. The show she and Maggie had put together in New York was more risqué than a mother should witness her daughter performing, but the crowd applauded when the spotlight hit her.

"Ladies and gentlemen, I give you Hattie James." Maggie waved her up. "Come on, Hattie. Sing with me like we did at the other Copacabana."

Eva pulled Hattie up from her chair. "Go, sweetheart. Show them how it's done."

The crowd got louder. David looked at her with sympathetic eyes and shrugged. Hattie was cornered and out of options. She smiled, waved to the audience, and walked to the stage stairs. A band member offered his hand and helped her up. A stagehand brought up a second microphone.

The applause continued until Hattie reached Maggie, and they hugged. She covered the microphone with her hand and whispered, "You owe me for this."

"Don't be a pill." Maggie laughed and hugged her again. "It's great seeing you."

"Great to see you, too. Same set as last time?" Hattie was glad she didn't go for the pasta tonight. Unlike the chicken, it would have sat like a rock in her stomach over the next hour.

"You got it." Maggie winked. "I'll split my pay."

An hour later, Hattie and Maggie ended their performance with the three unreleased songs they had recorded with RCA to a standing ovation. They hugged once more, marking the show's end, and walked off the stage sweaty, arm in arm.

"I have to have a drink with the governor tonight," Maggie said. "It's part of the contract."

Hattie glanced at the governor. He was eyeing her and Maggie like they were prime cuts of beef. "Watch yourself. He's handsy. My mother already got the treatment."

"I thought that was Eva at your table. I'll cut it short. Please don't leave before we can talk."

"I won't." Hattie returned to their table, receiving a hug from David.

"You two were incredible," he said.

Hattie turned to her mother, who pulled her into a tight embrace. "You brought the house down," Eva said, releasing her hold. "Positively spectacular. You must be exhausted."

David pulled out her chair. "I had our waiter bring ice water and warm tea with honey."

"Perfect." Hattie sat and drank a substantial portion of the water.

Eva returned to her seat. "David explained that you and Maggie had performed that set at the Copacabana club not long ago."

"It was my last live performance at an A club until tonight." The Halo Club had reminded Hattie how much she missed performing at a place where fellatio wasn't being conducted under the tables. But tonight, once she stepped onto the stage with Maggie, looked at the sea of tuxedos and formal gowns, and heard the music fill the room with a rich sound, she knew her true worth. She was worthy of the Palace. However, the experience also reminded her of what she had lost, which made her angry enough to flip the table upside down.

Eva reached across and squeezed Hattie's hand. "I know this has been hard on you, sweetheart."

"I'll be fine, Mother. You always say Machado women can bounce back from anything."

"Yes, we can. We're both proof."

Hattie could see that in her mother now. She had rebuilt her career twice, once after moving from Brazil to the States and again after she returned to Rio. It gave Hattie hope that if she put in the hard work, she would be back on top again.

Maggie kept her word by cutting her visit short with the governor and joining Hattie at their table. Following introductions, she whispered, "You were right about the governor. He's going to be a little sore tonight."

Hattie laughed. "Good for you."

The four chatted about the music business, and soon Eva excused herself to visit the ladies' room. Maggie then lowered her voice to Hattie. "I want you to know that I think it stunk how RCA dropped you and scrapped our record. I don't believe for one minute you had anything to do with what your father was involved in."

"Thank you, Maggie. Your support means a lot."

"You should know that I've instructed my lawyer to secure the rights to our duets from RCA. If I'm successful, I want to record those songs with you under my own label. We'll split the royalties fifty-fifty. Are you game?"

"I don't know what to say, Maggie." Hattie fought back tears. After all that had happened, after everything she had lost to protect her sister and her family, Maggie laid this at her feet.

"Say yes," Maggie said, clutching Hattie's hand.

"Of course, yes." Hattie lost her fight. Tears fell down her cheeks in relief. "You're a good friend, Maggie Moore."

"You've kept me in check more times than I can count, Hattie James. We're friends for life."

Hattie wiped her tears when Eva approached, to avoid having to explain. "How long are you in town for?" she asked Maggie.

"I wish we had time to turn some heads on the beach, but my flight is in the morning. Please stay in touch."

"I will." Hattie jotted down her mother's address and phone number. "This is where I'm staying. I'm not sure how long I'll be in Rio, but I'll let you know if my situation changes."

After Maggie left, Eva, Hattie, and David gathered their things. Guests stopped Hattie several times in the aisle, asking for an autograph or picture with them. Once in the lobby, Eva reminded Hattie that she needed to visit the coat check desk for the photos taken of them at their table. She went with her.

The clerk recognized them instantly and gushed over Hattie when Eva handed her the ticket. At the third compliment, Eva broke in. "That's nice, dear, but can you find our photos and put them on my account?"

"Of course, Miss Machado. I almost forgot." The clerk snapped her fingers and handed Hattie a folded slip of paper. "Someone left you a message, Miss James."

Hattie read the note. *Urgent dry cleaning ready for pick up tonight.* She stuffed it in her pocket, remembering the FBI was always watching.

"What is it?" Eva asked.

"A fan." Hattie watched the clerk sift through hundreds of pictures. Each was labeled with today's date and a number, likely the table identifier. She was quite organized, considering the room had a hundred tables.

"Here we are." The woman placed the photos in an embossed hotel portfolio and handed it to Eva. "Wonderful picture of your group."

"Thank you," Eva said, letting Hattie look at them. People from neighboring tables were clearly visible in the background.

An idea about the pictures popped into Hattie's head. "Excuse me. How long do you keep unclaimed photos?"

"Thirty days," the woman said.

"Mother, which day did you say you last saw Mrs. Moyer?"

"Friday, February twenty-first. Why?"

"Perhaps her picture was taken that night."

"Splendid idea." Eva turned to the woman. "She was sitting on the upper tier near the bar."

"That would be section B-eight. On the twenty-first, you say?" The clerk looked beneath the counter, retrieved another box, and pulled out a dozen photos. "These should be from that night."

Eva flipped through the photos but said none were of her friend.

"Look more closely, Mother. She might be in the background."

Eva re-scanned the pictures and showed one to Hattie. "There's Marta."

Hattie examined the photo, noting a man was sitting with her. He was partially obscured, but he looked familiar. "Mother, do you recognize the man sitting with her?"

Eva looked again, bringing the photo closer to her eyes. "I'm not sure, but he looks like the man who came into my studio last week when you were there. The one whose daughter you're giving singing lessons."

Hattie focused on the man's hair and face and gasped. "Heinz Baumann," she whispered. Hattie had been looking at this all wrong. A wave of relief weakened her knees when she realized the worst she'd thought of her father wasn't true. He did not kidnap these women. Baumann did and had to be searching for her father since every missing woman had a loose connection to him by working at the docks or having contact with Eva when he arrived in Rio. The realization made her wonder when Baumann would become desperate enough to abduct her.

Hattie turned to Eva. "May I keep these? They might be of some help."

"Of course," Eva said. She told the clerk to put them on her account.

"It's such a beautiful night, Mother. Would you mind if David and I walked along the beach? We can catch a taxi home."

Eva smiled. "You two lovebirds go. This night is too romantic to pass up."

Romance wasn't in the plan, but a midnight run to her FBI contact was.

22

A cab dropped Hattie and David at the corner at close to midnight. They walked the half block to the dry cleaners along the dark, quiet street. When the taxi drove away, Hattie realized it was the only moving vehicle in the neighborhood and worried about how they would get back to Eva's. David tried the knob, discovering the front door unlocked. They walked in, finding the store was unoccupied. When the door closed, something clicked, and David checked the knob. "We're locked in." Someone had eyes on them, so they continued to the back office and waited.

Moments later, the hidden door beside the filing cabinet opened. They entered, the door shutting behind them. Agent Butler was at the worktable, but Cohen was absent. He closed the file in front of him and turned to Hattie. "Will you mind waiting in the outer office, Mr. Townsend?"

"I *would* mind." David folded his arms across his chest.

"Then I'll have to report you two as uncooperative, and you know how that will end."

Hattie matched Butler's posture, crossing her arms. "It's okay, David. Agent Butler and I have to talk."

"Are you sure?" David snapped his gaze toward her. "I don't trust him."

"I don't either, but he and I must come to an understanding."

David gave Hattie a piercing stare, telegraphing his uneasiness with the situation before leaving.

Butler spun on his chair when the door closed and pulled the other one up for Hattie. "Sit."

She did. "I hope you enjoyed the show."

"I did. We need more of that, building your cover for being here, not traipsing through the favelas, stirring the pot."

"Pot stirring is precisely what this town needs. Nine women are missing, and no one in a position of authority who is supposed to care does. I can't turn my back on that, but I think we can kill two birds with one stone." Perhaps a taste of what she was onto might get him off her back. Hattie placed the Copacabana Palace folio on the table and opened it, exposing the photograph from last month. "The woman sitting against the wall is one of the missing. This picture was taken at the Golden Room the night she disappeared. See who is sitting with her?"

Butler squinted, inspecting the photo closely. "Is that Baumann?"

"I believe so. This woman met with my mother at the club the night after you say my father was seen departing a cargo ship. Two other women who brought their children to my mother's music studio also went missing days later. Five more women who worked at restaurants near the docks where my father was supposedly seen also have gone missing. The night I showed up at the Halo Club and talked to her, Anna Reyes disappeared."

"You think Baumann is looking for your father. But why?"

"I don't know, but that should tell you Baumann doesn't know where he is. If my father was working for the Nazis, wouldn't he have contacted Baumann as soon as he got off the ship?"

"Not if he didn't trust Baumann. He would lie low until he found someone he could." Butler's reasoning was sound and made Hattie think the edelweiss at the Halo Club and her bedroom window was her father's way of reaching out to see if he could trust her.

"We both have our theories about Baumann. I'll get you pictures from inside the house because they might lead me to those missing women."

"If you screw this up, you know who will pay the price," Butler said.

"You really know how to make friends."

"As long as we understand each other. We need to find that radio or codebook."

"We understand one another quite well," Hattie said. "Do you have another camera we can take? I'm going to the plantation tomorrow."

"Yes." Butler handed her a second micro-camera from a storage bin. "It's my last one, so don't lose it."

"I'll be careful not to stir too many pots." Now that Hattie had a suspect other than her father, she would only stir Baumann's pot.

23

The following day

This was how Hattie imagined a working coffee farm. Baumann's plantation teemed with workers late Thursday morning. Many were in the fields, tending to the soil by clearing it of weeds and undergrowth to promote a greater yield. Others carted away the brush and burned it in piles in the compound. More loaded bags of milled coffee beans into trucks for transport to the roasting merchant.

After enduring the silent scrutiny of the gate guard, David parked near the main house again. He grabbed his music satchel and followed Hattie to the front door. The servant led them to the music room. Refreshments, finger sandwiches, and fresh fruit were on trays on the coffee table in the seating area, but David warned against eating or drinking anything they weren't sure of.

Hattie heeded his sound advice and kept to the thermos they brought while waiting for Elsa to come down from her school lesson. While David warmed up, she looked around the room, surveying the bookshelves more closely. The books weren't much different from what her father once kept at the family house. In fact, many of the titles were in her father's collection, which sent a chill through her. Baumann and her father were much alike.

Too much. Her father may have had nothing to do with the missing women, but Hattie had become acutely aware that he kept a side hidden from those who loved him, and that was disturbing. She hoped he had a reasonable explanation for all of it.

Elsa soon appeared at the door. She rushed to Hattie, giving her a hug around the waist. "You came back."

"Of course I did." Hattie loosened her hold, feeling a tinge of guilt. She would not have returned if she didn't want to get the goods on the girl's father. "Why would you think I wouldn't?"

"Papa told me not to get my hopes up."

"Well, I'm here." Hattie was curious why Baumann would think she wouldn't return, renewing her fear he was onto her. "Will your father join us today?"

"I don't think so. He had to travel yesterday and isn't back yet."

"All right. We better get started. Have you thought about what songs you would like to sing?"

"'Over the Rainbow' for sure."

"Good choice. What about the other two?"

Elsa shrugged. "The ones the pastor suggested were all for little kids." She seemed taken by Hattie, unwilling to appear childish in front of her.

Hattie smiled, removing a folded paper from her skirt pocket. "I made a list of five songs I thought you might like. How about we try them out, and you can choose?"

"I'd like that very much, Hattie."

Over the next hour, they sang and narrowed the list, and Hattie gave her more instruction on breath control and the difference between her head and chest voice. Elsa picked up the concepts quickly and demonstrated each on command. She was a quick learner when motivated, but Hattie also believed a little idol worship was at play.

Confident she had gained the girl's trust at the end of the lesson, Hattie felt terrible about her next question, but she needed a ruse to explore more of the house. "I meant to ask, Elsa. How big is the room where you'll be singing?"

"The recital will be in the church, so it's huge."

Hattie placed her hands on her hips and spun on her heel, inspecting the room. "Then this room won't do. We should find a place where your voice will echo so you'll know how it will sound in church and not startle you. Can we look in your kitchen?"

"While you two are scouting, I need to use the bathroom," David said. He had the second micro-camera and would have to watch out for the servant while snapping pictures.

"Do you remember where it's at?" Elsa asked.

"I think so. It's right off the entry room, right?"

"Right." Elsa grabbed Hattie's hand. "Let's go, Hattie." She led them from the music room down the hallway.

The other doors were closed, providing no opportunity to snoop. David peeled off left at the end of the corridor while Elsa and Hattie went right. Hattie cupped her micro-camera in her free hand, ready to snap a picture. They first entered the dining room. It was ornate with rich wood and an intricate chandelier but likely didn't house a secret radio or codebook. Baumann's office or a workshop were likely locations, but getting there was challenging with Elsa attached to her hip. Hopefully, David would have better luck.

Elsa stopped in the kitchen. It was large, but the many cabinets and decorations softened the sound, preventing an echo. However, Hattie needed to stall to give David more time to explore. "Let's give it a try," she said before belting out the first verse of one of her songs.

Elsa was mesmerized. "That was wonderful," she said after Hattie stopped.

"Thank you, but the room doesn't provide the right acoustics." Hattie rubbed her chin, pretending to think. "How about the basement? The block walls usually make a perfect echo chamber."

Elsa shook her head. "I'm not supposed to go down there."

"Okay." Hattie shrugged. "But I still think you should practice in the right environment several times. Perhaps your father can take you down there."

Elsa darted her gaze—the reaction Hattie had hoped for. She hated manipulating a young girl, but this was the only way to get downstairs if David couldn't find the entrance.

"Maybe if we're quick." Elsa glanced at the kitchen entrance leading deeper into the house as if checking for anyone who might have caught her doing something wrong. She stepped past the breakfast table and opened a secondary door, revealing steps going down.

After Elsa flipped on a light switch, they descended the wooden stairs. Halfway down, the walls changed from wood to cinder blocks. The bottom revealed a narrow corridor with a wood slat floor and wood beams supporting the subfloor from the first story above their heads. Several crates and barrels with symbols Hattie did not recognize were stacked against the walls. She snapped pictures secretly.

"How about here?" Elsa asked.

Considering the house's footprint above ground, the basement likely went on for a considerable distance. "It's a little narrow. Is there a wider section?" Hattie asked.

"Maybe. I've only been down here once and got into trouble."

"I don't want to get you into trouble, Elsa."

"It should be up ahead," Elsa said, pressing forward. She turned a corner that opened to a broader section—a crossroads of three corridors and two steel doors. "How is this?"

"Much better," Hattie said, snapping several pictures without Elsa seeing. "Try singing 'Over the Rainbow' while I see if there's a better location."

Elsa sang.

Hattie peeked down each corridor, snapping pictures, and tried the metal doors as the girl's voice resonated in the chamber, but they were locked. When she returned her attention to Elsa, a door creaked open, turning Hattie's stomach into a giant knot.

"What the heck?" The voice sounded familiar.

Hattie gasped and turned slowly, disbelieving what she had heard. She had traveled thousands of miles under FBI threats to flush out her father. She was supposed to act as bait and lure him out with nothing to go on. But now, in a damp, dingy basement on a coffee plantation in the hills north of Rio, she found him.

Her father stopped mid-stride, holding the steel door open. His dazed look confirmed he was as shocked as Hattie. Neither moved. Neither spoke. Neither took their eyes off the other. He combed his hair differently and had let stubble grow on his face. Otherwise, he looked healthy and fit in his work clothes. Perhaps more in shape than when he disappeared.

"Bitte sag Papa nicht, dass ich hier unten war, Herr Fuller."

Fuller? Hattie was confused. Why would she call him Fuller?

"Frau Baumann," he said.

"Elsa?" Heinz Baumann entered behind Hattie's father.

Dread swept through Hattie. She'd been caught in a place where she wasn't supposed to be, carrying a micro-camera she wasn't supposed to have. She envisioned Baumann's men upstairs, pummeling David to a bloody mess before dragging her somewhere for a similar beating or worse. Baumann would have their car set on fire before rolling it off a mountain road to make it appear she and David had perished in a fiery accident. Her father might put up a fight, but if he did, he would find the same fate.

Baumann spoke to Elsa in German. His voice was threatening but not menacing. He controlled his anger well.

Elsa burst into tears and cried something, ending with, "Papa."

Hattie had to say something for the girl and herself. "It's my fault, Mr. Baumann. I wanted to show her how her voice would sound in the church hall so she would know how to sing through the echo. I suggested the kitchen or basement."

Baumann's voice remained stern while speaking to Elsa, but his eyes became dark and steely. They were terrifying when he turned them on Hattie. He shifted to Hattie's father once Elsa ran down the corridor and spoke German to him.

"I was doing chores when I heard singing and came to investigate," Karl said in English, presumably so Hattie would understand what was being said and how to react.

"I see." Baumann shifted his attention to Hattie. "This place is off limits. She should have told you."

"Please don't punish her, Mr. Baumann. I made it sound important, and it is, but I should have recognized the hero worship in her before I asked her to take us to a suitable practice room. It really is my fault."

"I will deal with her later, Miss James, but I think it better for you and Mr. Townsend to return to the city."

"Of course," Hattie said. "I hope you accept my apology and continue Elsa's lessons. She really is quite talented."

"I'll be in touch." Baumann gestured for Hattie to come with him through the door.

She glanced over her shoulder at her father as he trailed behind her while going up the stairs, still dumbfounded by his presence. A thousand questions filled her head. Why was he going by the name Fuller? What type of work did he do on the plantation? Did he know anything about the missing women? And how could she get him alone to talk to him?

Hattie and Baumann emerged in the compound at the back of the house. Her father was steps behind but peeled off toward the milling barn before she could motion to him. While her head was still reeling, Baumann walked her around and entered through the front door, where David sat chatting with the servant in the living room. They both stood. On the outside, David acted normally, but his set eyes and fractionally faster breathing suggested he was panicked on the inside.

"Hattie," David said. "I was concerned when Elsa went running upstairs in tears. Is everything okay?"

Baumann stepped closer to David, giving him the same steely-eyed stare. "Hilda, do you have anything to report?"

David gave Hattie an unreadable headshake. Her stomach twisted again into a jumbled mess. She had narrowly escaped being discovered in the basement, but if the servant had caught David snooping with the camera, they would never leave this plantation alive.

Hilda clasped her hands at her abdomen in a relaxed fashion. "All is fine, Herr Baumann. Mr. Townsend and I were discussing Miss James's performance last night at the Golden Room with Maggie Moore. It is the talk of Rio today."

Baumann turned, giving Hattie a respectful nod. "I'm impressed. Wasn't the governor in attendance? I didn't realize you were on the schedule." His comment came across more as an insult than a compliment, making Hattie uncomfortable enough that she felt she had to defend herself.

"Yes, he was. Maggie and I have been friends for years, and we've performed together several times. It was all very impromptu, but I had a splendid time."

"Does this mean you're no longer performing at the Halo Club?"

"No. Last night's show was a one-time thing. Besides, I gave the owner my word."

Hattie and David gathered their things and were back on the road within minutes. Once outside the gate, David snapped his stare toward her. "What the hell happened? Where did you go?"

"I had Elsa take me to the basement and got some pictures. Then—"

"Baumann walks in?"

Hattie started to correct David but stopped before telling him she had encountered her father downstairs. David had fought her at every turn since stepping off the plane eight days ago. He didn't like her performing at the Halo Club. Thought she was crazy for helping Maya locate her sister. It all made her unsure how he would react if he knew her father was there. He might even tell Agent Butler, to bring this ordeal to an end, and Hattie wasn't prepared to turn her father in. At least not before she talked to him.

Hattie glanced at David. "Yes, Baumann walked in, but Elsa and I explained about needing to practice there. He was upset but bought the story. How about you? Did you find anything?"

"Nothing. Hilda caught me in the hallway, so I told her I was admiring the pictures. Then we started talking about the Golden Room when you and Baumann walked in." He turned onto the main highway and merged into traffic. "That was a close call, Hattie. Too close. We need to tell the FBI you're no longer in the spy game."

"I can't do that, David."

"Why can't you?"

Too much was at stake for Hattie to turn tail. Too many lives hung in the balance—her father's, her sister's family, Anna's, and those of the other eight missing women. Hattie had to go through with this.

"Because too much is at stake. I won't let any of this be my legacy."

24

Later that night

The Halo Club crowd was standing room only since word got out about Hattie James performing at the Golden Room. Shouts from the audience during her first show begged Maggie Moore to appear magically on stage for a repeat of last night. Hattie paused between songs to explain that Maggie had already left the country. Afterward, some patrons left, but she took the insult in stride. Just as she had taken David's pouting and refusing to make eye contact with her during the show.

The room was still more packed than during her previous performances. The server Maya shifted to tend bar handled the thick crowd through the mad rush with only a little help. Maya had remained behind the bar, keeping the glasses, ice, and garnishes flowing. They were so busy that Hattie hadn't the chance to speak with her before the first show to explain what she had discovered about Mrs. Moyer and Baumann.

Finishing her final song, Hattie descended the stage to whistles and loud applause, trying to make it to the bar. Three steps in, two fans cornered her, asking for autographs and to take pictures with her. Then another two, and another two. She realized this was a bad idea and slipped through the stage door with David.

Once in their dressing room, David threw his suit jacket off and sucked down a glass of water without offering one to Hattie. The slight didn't go unnoticed. She poured herself a glass and drank slowly to coat her vocal cords, but they still felt strained.

"Would you mind getting a cup of hot tea and honey? I don't think I'll make it through the gauntlet of fans."

"Sure. Why not? Is there anything else you'd like me to fetch?" he said in a snide tone.

"Stop it, David. You're acting childish. You pouted through the entire show."

"What do you expect? You won't listen to reason. This has gone too far. It's time to call the FBI's bluff and use the media against them if they try to go after your sister."

"They aren't bluffing, David. They've already ruined both our careers."

"Once we tell the newspapers what they've been up to, it would make national headlines. I don't think the American people would take kindly to coercing an innocent woman and using children as pawns."

"That might be true, but it won't help the missing women. I'm seeing this through. If you want out, I'll pay for your passage home."

"I'm not leaving you here to fend for yourself."

"I'm sorry this impacts you, but I need to do this. Please stop your whining and get me the tea, or I'll do it myself."

"Fine." David slammed the door on his way out.

Hattie sipped her water and wiped her perspiration with a towel from the vanity, thinking about her father. She had to get a message to him but didn't know how. Her only access to the plantation was up in the air until Baumann decided to continue Elsa's singing lessons.

She sat at the vanity, running through the information she had derived about her father since her arrival. She had proven Agent Butler's conjecture that her father might have connected with Baumann, though not as he had thought. Her father was using an alias, and Baumann didn't know he was right under his thumb. However, Hattie had yet to figure out why Baumann was looking for him. Why was he so important? The first sign of his presence in the city was the edelweiss left at the club and then again on her bedroom window. Rio had a tropical climate, so the flower could not grow in the area unless planted in a controlled environment like Eva's sunroom. Hers was likely the only supply of European edelweiss in the country, so how did her father get it? Did he break in and steal it? Or did her mother give it to him?

A knock on the door broke her concentration. "Come in."

The door opened, and Maya stepped inside, holding a mug. "David said you needed hot tea and honey."

"Yes, thank you." If this was David's way of apologizing, it was pretty damn thoughtful. "Did David send you?"

"Sort of." Maya handed Hattie the tea. "He ordered it along with a double scotch. He was on his second round by the time the water heated, so I brought it back."

"Oh." Hattie sipped, letting the warm liquid and honey coat and soothe her throat. His drinking meant he was more upset than she had first thought.

"Are you two okay? He seemed angry."

"It's nothing I can't handle, but I have something I need to tell you." Hattie invited her to sit in the other chair and laid out the photo from the Golden Room. "I found a lead to Mrs. Moyer's disappearance."

Maya perked up and leaned in. "What did you find?"

Hattie pointed out the man and woman in the photo and explained it was taken the night she disappeared. "This is Heinz Baumann. I'm giving his daughter singing lessons at his plantation north of town, and he was also here the night your sister went missing. I remember seeing him in the audience."

Maya breathed deeper with excitement. "We need to take this to the police."

"Do you really think they're going to look into him?"

"Not Silva, but Vargas might help. I'll call him first thing in the morning."

"I'd like to come with you." Hattie fought the urge to tell her more. Tell her about her father and the FBI. Tell her how she cried herself to sleep most nights since arriving in Rio because she feared failing the people who depended on her success. Tell her that, for the first time in years, she welcomed feeling as vulnerable as Maya had done with her.

"I'd like that." Maya's lips turned upward moments before she shifted her stare to Hattie's mouth. She wanted to be kissed, and Hattie was ready to oblige.

Three days had passed since their almost kiss when their lips touched for a fleeting second. It wasn't magical like in fairytales or electric like in romance novels, but it had felt right. It had made her feel more than desired, more than wanted . . . but needed. That was the most powerful feeling in the world and was perhaps why she was comfortable putting herself at greater risk.

Hattie lifted Maya's chin with her hand and slowly eased it closer, watching Maya's lips part ever so slightly. She considered diving right in to complete what they had danced around for days, but she wanted to savor the anticipation. She would only get one chance at a first kiss, but after scanning her surroundings, she realized this dressing room was not the place for it.

Hattie released her hold and pulled back, earning a confused look from the woman whose lips still begged to be kissed.

Maya asked. "Did I do something wrong?"

"No," Hattie said slowly during a breathy exhale. "I don't want our first kiss to be here. I want to let it breathe, not suffocate in the possibility of being caught."

Maya smiled. "That was the sexiest thing anyone has said to me."

"I want to do this right," Hattie said.

Maya let out a long, frustrated breath. "I do too." She sat back in her chair. "Tell me more about Baumann."

Hattie told her about meeting him at her mother's music studio and how he made her uneasy whenever he stared like she was a fine cut of meat. The vulnerability of sharing her feelings was empowering.

"It sounds like he might make you his next victim," Maya said. "All the more reason to get Investigator Vargas involved. Until then, I'll show Nessa the photo to see if she recognizes Baumann."

The door flew open, and David appeared, holding a cocktail glass. "It figures," he said, slamming the door behind him. His three steps in were enough for Hattie to realize he was drunk.

"How much have you had to drink?" Hattie asked.

"Not enough."

Hattie snatched the glass from his hand. "You've had more than enough. We need to sober you up for the next show."

"I'll get some coffee." Maya gave Hattie a sympathetic look before closing the door, leaving her with a mess to deal with.

David flopped in the chair, reaching for the glass of whatever had put him in a stupor.

"Oh no, you don't." Hattie plucked it from his grasp and poured it into the garbage can. "You have less than an hour to sober up."

"Who are you kidding, Hattie? Playing here is a joke. Last night proved it. You should sing at the Golden Room, not this dump. The only reason you're still here is to get into Maya's knickers."

"I'm not discussing her when you're like this."

David grunted. "It wasn't supposed to be like this. I should have listened. They warned me not to get too close." His head shook vigorously as if clearing the alcohol haze.

Hattie grew concerned and wondered who "they" were, but this was not the time to pepper him with questions. She knew his interests included both men and women, but he had sworn she wasn't his type. Perhaps attributing his attentive and protective nature around her as part of their arrangement was naïve. "David," she whispered, reaching to caress his face, but he pushed her hand away.

"Don't. I don't want your pity."

"It's not pity. I genuinely care for you."

He laughed. "Do you? You care about what I can do for you, playing piano and playing your boyfriend when it suits you."

"I know this is the alcohol talking." Hattie looked up when Maya walked through the door carrying a mug from the bar. "Let's get some coffee in you and talk about this at home later."

"I'll be fine. I've played half-drunk for years." David pushed past Maya in the doorway, walking with a slight wobble.

Once the door closed, Maya said that Nessa confirmed Baumann was the man in the photo, corroborating Hattie's suspicion. She then wagged her thumb toward the door. "Is he going to be okay to play tonight? I'm not sure if my old piano player is still available."

"I'll make sure he's fine."

But David wasn't fine. He continued to drink, and his playing during the second show was sloppy. The audience likely did not notice, but Hattie did and sang through it like a professional. She drove them back in Eva's car and kept her distance while he stumbled from the garage through the breezeway to their private entrance into the house.

After removing his shoes and suit jacket, he plopped face down on the bed and began snoring.

Hattie changed into loungewear and readied herself for bed in the bathroom but couldn't bring herself to sleep anywhere near David in his condition. He reeked of scotch all the way home, and the smell dredged up old memories she preferred to keep buried. Too many nights she stank of stale booze after trying to drown her pain. It never worked and only brought her more misery.

She put on a pair of flats, grabbed a blanket from the closet, poured a glass of water into one of the bathroom cups, and settled into a chaise longue on the back patio. Pulling the blanket over her torso, she scanned the night sky. A half-moon was out, and she remembered her father's lessons about the stars. They were upside down in the southern hemisphere, and she struggled to recollect what he had said about determining which direction was south. Then she remembered five stars made up the Southern Cross. She found them in the sky and drew an imaginary line to the horizon. She then located the bright stars—Alpha and Beta Centauri—drew another line, estimated where those two lines intersected, and followed it to the horizon. There. She had found true south.

The neighborhood dogs barked, disrupting her moment of silence. She sat up, sensing whatever had disturbed them was close. Movement in the shadows near the garage caught her attention, elevating her pulse rate. She grabbed the glass, figuring holding something in her hand was better than nothing, and called out in a soft voice, "Who's there?"

"Songbird?" a man said in the darkness.

Hattie had heard that voice all her life and would have recognized it anywhere. She squinted as the shadowy figure moved closer. Her heart pounded harder as she said his name. "Father?"

He stepped into the moonlight. "Yes, sweetheart. It's me."

"What are you doing here? The FBI is looking for you."

"They're watching the house and your work. Everyone is," he said.

She stood silent, unsure of what to say or do. Everything she'd experienced in the last eight days suggested he might be what the FBI suspected—a Nazi spy who killed his way out of custody. Even so, he was her father. He was the man who gave her piggyback rides before bedtime while singing "Camptown Races." The man who held her in the shower when she developed croup until her cough was under control.

"Oh, Father." Hattie threw her arms around his neck, tears soaking his shirt. Grateful he was alive, she trembled, but now was the time for the truth. She pulled back. "What happened in DC? How did you get here?"

"Two men ambushed the FBI when they were transporting me to the courthouse jail. They threw me in a car, drove to Baltimore, and ushered me onto a freighter. A month later, we docked in Rio."

"So you didn't kill those agents. What men? Who were they?"

"No, I didn't. They were Germans. I'd seen them before as part of my work."

"Why would they break you out of custody and bring you here?"

"I don't know, but before we docked, I overpowered the man who came with me and held me hostage and threw him overboard."

"You killed him?"

"I had to. We looked somewhat alike, so I took his identity papers."

"Is that why they called you Fuller today?"

"Yes. His name was Fuller."

"I have to ask, Father. Did you do what Agent Knight accused you of? Did you spy for the Nazis?"

"It's a long story."

"But you're working for Baumann. Isn't he a Nazi?"

"Yes, but so was Fuller. He was expected to report to Baumann, so I took his place. I thought it would be a safe place to hide until I could figure out what to do. Then, one night, when I was in town, you showed up on stage at the Halo Club."

"So, the edelweiss? That *was* you." She sensed he was holding back, particularly about knowing why the real Fuller had brought him to Rio, but doubted he would be forthright, at least not yet.

"Yes, that was me. I left it to let you know I was there. But what are you doing in Rio?"

"When news about your arrest and escape hit the papers, RCA dropped me, and so did offers to perform. I needed to restart my career." The partial truth was the safest route until Hattie fully assessed her father's story.

"But in Rio?" His question came across as suspicious. She would be too. Since the first intrusion by the FBI, she had been wary of everything.

"I'm not proud, but I'm playing off being Eva Machado's daughter."

"You must be desperate. Otherwise, you wouldn't have swallowed your pride for her."

"It hasn't been that bad."

"I'm glad to hear that, sweetheart," Eva said, stepping through the screen door. She turned her attention to Karl. "I told you to never come here again."

Hattie snapped her head toward Eva. "Wait. You knew he was in Rio and said nothing?"

"He came around before you arrived in town looking for help. I knew what he'd done, so I sent him packing. I didn't see the point in telling you." Eva turned to him. "How did you get in?"

"Through the side gate connected to your neighbor. No one is watching their property."

Eva harrumphed. "I'll have to change the locks."

"He's only been accused, Mother," Hattie said. "I believe him when he says he's innocent."

Eva laughed. "You have no idea what he's capable of."

Feeling her ire up, Hattie raised her voice. "Then tell me, Mother. What is he capable of? I know precisely what you're capable of."

Eva turned to Karl, folding her arms across her chest—her angry stance. "Tell her, or I will."

"Tell me what?" Hattie glanced between her mother and father, waiting for someone to speak.

Karl lowered his head.

"Fine," Eva said. "I'll say it. Your father is a filthy Nazi. He came back from his post in Germany in 1927 a changed man, believing the rantings of that lunatic Hitler and his gibberish about the master race."

"I don't believe you," Hattie said, her head spinning between the image she had of her father and what her mother and the FBI would have her believe.

"I shielded you from the truth because I didn't want you to know what he had turned into," Eva said. "My father has Jewish blood, and so do I, you, Olivia, and her children. According to the man he worships, we have no right to exist."

Hattie turned to Karl, questions swirling in her head. "Father?"

"Not everything is as it seems, sweetheart."

"What does that mean?"

"It means there's more here at play." Karl clutched her arm softly. "Things I can't talk about."

"So it's true?" Hattie recoiled, throwing off his grip. "You gave secrets to the Nazis, and they broke you out, protecting their own."

"It may seem that way," he said with pleading eyes. "But I am not a Nazi."

"It's exactly what it seems," Eva said. "Ask him about the tattoo under his arm."

Hattie gasped, recalling what Butler had told her about the SS officer markings. She turned to Eva. "Is it a letter?"

"Yes, A for his blood type. When I asked someone at the State Department what it meant, he said it was the mark of a Nazi SS officer. I'd had enough and couldn't stay married to someone who believed we had no right to exist. I'm sorry I didn't tell you, sweetheart, but I didn't want you to be disillusioned at a young age." Eva cleared her throat. "I stayed as long as I could."

"Then I made it impossible to stay," Hattie said as guilt washed through her. Pieces fell into place. The parade of German diplomats through their home over the years. The distance that had developed between her parents following his return from Germany. Her mother's drinking and sullenness until the divorce and her return to Rio. It all made sense when looking at it through the lens of Eva's revelation.

Hattie turned to her father, seeing the real him for the first time. "Tell me this is a mistake. That you can explain."

Karl rubbed his temple. "All I can say is that it's only part of the truth. I need you to trust me."

Hattie's stomach churned what was left of dinner. "I'm feeling sick." Tears fell at the realization that everything she thought she knew about her parents and her childhood was a lie.

"You upset her." Eva threw an arm around Hattie. "It's time for you to leave, Karl."

"All right. I'll leave." He turned to Hattie. "Don't go back to the plantation, sweetheart. It's not safe."

"I said go," Eva said, "or I'll call the police this time."

"Remember everything I told you, especially when I last saw you in DC, Hattie. Trust in me." Karl kissed her forehead and disappeared into the night.

"Thank goodness he left," Eva said.

Hattie dropped to the chaise longue, burying her face in her hands. Her world had turned upside down, and she didn't know what to believe. Her mother painted a horrible picture of her father, to which he offered little defense.

"I despise that man," Eva added.

"Not now, Mother." Hattie could no longer listen to Eva's tainted opinions of her father, nor could she stay there. Never had the urge to drink again hit her so hard, and with a fully stocked bar a few feet away, she didn't trust herself. "I need to leave."

"At this time of night?"

"I'll be fine," Hattie said, despite knowing she would not.

"Where are you going?"

"Somewhere I can think."

25

Driving the streets in the dark was more challenging than Hattie had expected. The street signs were not lit well, and her memory wasn't reliable as she replayed what her parents had said in Eva's backyard. She kept losing her way. However, when she found herself approaching the police station, she knew she was close. Turning onto the side street where they had parked Tuesday, she retraced the short route they had taken that day.

Four blocks and four turns later, the familiar house came into view. She circled the block once to make sure the set of headlights she saw two blocks back wasn't following her. After parking around the corner, she knocked on the door and waited, wringing her hands and debating whether this was a good idea. Showing up at Maya's doorstep at this time of night would lead to one thing, and Hattie had no desire to resist it any longer.

Every time she and Maya found themselves alone, they inched closer to this inevitability, though she didn't envision it happening so soon, not while they were both emotionally raw from Anna's disappearance and her father's reappearance. Maybe it would have been better to wait until—

The door opened. The interior was dark, but Hattie registered Maya standing there, wearing a floral silk robe gathered at the waist. Her hair was slightly mussed. "Hattie? It's three o'clock in the morning."

"I know it's late." Hattie nervously clutched her blouse, pressing her arms against her chest.

Maya stuck her head out the door, looking left and right. "Is David here?"

"No, he's passed out at home." Hattie had been on this doorstep twice before when Maya was troubled, and both times, she resisted the urge to comfort her. But tonight, the tables had turned, and Hattie needed comforting. She had no right to ask, but . . .

"May I come in?"

"Yes, please." Maya stepped aside.

Hattie took three steps inside and stopped. The only light came from the dim moonlight shining through the windows and open door, and when Maya closed it, she cast the hallway into near darkness.

Two hands eased her gently against the wall, and Hattie didn't resist. Instead, she welcomed it. Maya inched closer, placing her mouth close to Hattie's ear. "Is this what you expected?"

Coherent thought beyond recognizing overwhelming physical sensations evaded Hattie, making it impossible to answer. She responded by untying Maya's robe and sliding her hands against the skin of her waist. She raked them up Maya's smooth back and shuddered, finding no clothing.

"I need to be properly kissed first." Maya pulled back, eyes glistening with want and expectation of what would transpire.

"That I can do." Hattie changed position, spinning Maya against the wall. She brushed her lips lightly against Maya's in a gentle, languid caress. They were soft as she expected and moist as if having been just licked. She pulled back. "My, you're ready."

Maya's chest heaved. Expectant. Impatient. "For days."

Hattie grinned. She had kissed many women, but never was she so glad to have waited for a first kiss. These were the conditions she wanted, alone and safe, where she would be unrushed and could savor every moment, every aspect.

She pressed their bodies together as a prelude to what would follow, but it almost worked against her. The sensation made her dizzy, requiring more focus. She didn't trust herself to not go slowly, so she started at Maya's neck, kissing and licking up to the spot below her ear. Maya's first moan confirmed she was on the right track. The second meant her strategy was working.

Moving to the other side, she felt Maya's rapid pulse throb in her neck, signaling she could not wait much longer. Neither could Hattie. She shifted until their mouths were even. Maya's lips parted, releasing one steamy breath after another. Hattie captured them, absorbing another moan in a long, sensual kiss.

Maya hooked a leg around the back of Hattie's thigh, rocking it up and down in a slow, distracting rhythm. Hattie forced herself to concentrate on the kiss but failed when a palm caressed her left breast. The heat rising in her center was boiling over. She reminded herself that this was a first kiss, a memory maker, and ripped their mouths apart, earning a desperate, confused look from Maya.

"I don't think we got that right," Hattie said.

Maya smiled. "You didn't leave much room for improvement."

"We can always try."

~

Soon, Maya lay naked face down in bed with the sheets askew, covering half her body. Hattie sat against the headboard, admiring every curve and tracing a line down Maya's spine with a fingertip.

Maya turned her head and asked. "What time is it?"

Hattie glanced at the windup alarm clock on the nightstand. "Almost five."

"The sun will be up soon." Maya rolled over and joined Hattie at the headboard. "You should think about leaving. Your mother might wonder where you've been."

"That boat has sailed, and frankly, I don't care. I'll come up with something."

Maya clutched Hattie's hand, lacing their fingers together. "You looked upset when you arrived. What happened?"

"Everything I thought was true about my life was turned upside down last night. I didn't know where else to turn."

"I'm glad you came." Maya gave Hattie's hand a brief squeeze. "Can you tell me what happened?"

"Someday." Hattie drew Maya's head closer by the chin and kissed her. "I'm glad I came, too."

Holding back the truth was harder than Hattie expected. Becoming lovers muddied things, but it wasn't the driving factor. She had come to Maya when she felt her lowest, and Maya had done the same with her. The trust each showed in the other was rare and deserved more respect than Hattie could show. Searching for the missing women was risky enough, but telling Maya about her father and the FBI would only put her in more danger—something Hattie could not do.

"I suppose Vargas should be in his office in a few hours. Can I make you breakfast?" Maya asked.

"How about we make it together? I make a mean misto quente."

Maya smiled. "Look at you. You've been in Brazil a week and have already mastered local cuisine."

"I should. I've been eating it for nearly thirty years."

"Ah, that's right. Your mother."

"She's a great cook. I guess more of her talents rubbed off on me than vocal ones."

After showering and dressing, Hattie met Maya in the kitchen. "If you don't mind me asking, what's up with the tables and trays in the other bedroom?"

"It's my darkroom where I develop film."

"You're a photographer?" Hattie asked.

"My father was before he died. I guess I picked up his passion for it." Maya turned on the radio to a station playing upbeat Brazilian music.

"You have many passions." Hattie pecked Maya on the lips and winked.

They divided the duties, preparing the fruit and breakfast sandwiches while swaying to the music. They brushed against one another while reaching for a plate or a knife and, at times, for no reason other than it felt good. It was the most sensual thing Hattie had done in years. Eating was equally playful, but they were all business for the cleanup, finishing at half past eight.

After drying her hands, Maya slung the dish towel over the hook on the cabinet and appeared uncertain about something. “I know you must be tired, but I was hoping you might come with me to the police station to speak with Investigator Vargas.”

Hattie stepped closer and caressed Maya’s cheek. “There’s nowhere else I’d rather be.”

26

Armed with the Golden Room photo, Hattie and Maya walked the four blocks to police headquarters, hoping to make headway in the women's disappearances, particularly Anna's. She didn't care whether the FBI saw her. Finding Anna and the other missing women was more important than her career. Each stride closer should have brought more confidence and optimism, but they carried Hattie the opposite. Despite Investigator Vargas's disillusionment with his superior and unofficial help, Hattie had little confidence he or anyone else in the police department would provide more. However, Maya's fast pace signaled she was undeterred.

They passed the coffee stand and a dozen officers waiting for their morning brew and ascended the stairs to the headquarters building. After checking in with the desk officer, Maya asked to speak with Vargas and was told to wait with the dozen other people in the lobby. Soon, an officer escorted them up the stairs. Once on the third floor, they navigated the corridors.

The elevator door opened as they were about to pass, and Inspector Silva—the last person they wanted to see—stepped out. It was like parents catching Hattie and Maya sneaking into the house after curfew. Silva flicked his gaze upward and spoke in English. "What are you doing here? I said we would call if we had new information."

Maya stopped and adjusted the strap of the handbag over her shoulder. "It's been three days, Inspector. You said you would file a report by today. I'm here to make sure you do your job."

"You can request a copy next week." Silva narrowed his eyes at Maya. "We received calls about you. I understand you've been speaking to the family members of the missing women."

"I didn't know talking to people was against the law." Maya placed her hands on her hips, assuming a defensive posture.

"It is when you interfere with an ongoing investigation."

"From what I can tell, there's no investigating going on."

"I suggest you steer clear of police business. Otherwise, I will arrest you." Silva turned his attention to their escort. "Take them downstairs and make sure they leave the building."

The officer gestured for Hattie and Maya to follow, retraced their steps to the lobby, and opened the main door. He mumbled something, and Maya squawked back, making it clear she wasn't happy with how they were treated. As they descended the stairs, Maya cursed in Portuguese, her message equally animated by her hands and tone. She drew the attention of people waiting in line for coffee before turning the corner.

Once out of sight of prying eyes and ears, Hattie pulled Maya to a stop along the street. "You're sexy as hell when you're mad. Unless you want me to make a bigger scene by kissing you right here, you better hold that temper until we're alone."

Maya narrowed her eyes in confusion before forming a broad smile. "That's the best hand slapping I've received in a long time."

Hattie smiled back. "The one thing you never tell a woman is to calm down. We only dig in deeper. I find it better to distract."

"Well—"

A car pulled up beside them at the curb. The driver leaned toward the passenger window that was rolled down and said, "Get in." It was Investigator Vargas.

Hattie was hesitant to get into a car with a man they had met only once, even though he was a police officer. Perhaps she was more uncertain because of his profession in this town despite his previous help.

Maya appeared desperate, willing to take any chance to find her sister. She opened the front passenger door, gesturing to Hattie. "It's okay. Get in."

Vargas drove off in the late morning traffic and glanced at Maya in the front seat. "You should have called first."

"I did. You weren't in your office," Maya said. "I didn't think leaving a message was a good idea."

"You're lucky Silva didn't arrest you," he said. "What was so important that you risked coming to the station?"

Maya opened her purse and showed Vargas the Golden Room photograph, explaining its significance and where it was taken. She pointed to the man in the background. "This is Heinz Baumann. He was also in the Halo Club the night my sister went missing."

"I know Baumann, and this doesn't surprise me. He owns a coffee farm north of town and is rich and very connected. I can follow up, but I'm sure Silva will block me at every turn. People like Baumann pay those in charge to look the other way and bury evidence."

Hattie expected as much but remained silent.

Maya pursed her lips. "So there's nothing you can do."

"Nothing officially." He shrugged.

"How about unofficially?" Maya asked.

"From what I know of his farm, it's fenced off and guarded well against animals, thieves, and other farmers who have resorted to destroying competitors' crops. Without evidence of a crime, there's no way we can get in to search his plantation."

"I've been out there," Hattie said. "I give his daughter singing lessons, or at least I did."

"What can you tell me about it?" Vargas glanced back and continued to drive.

Hattie explained what she could without giving away her real purpose for being there, detailing the house, barns, and worker huts. "Baumann didn't want me poking around the milling barn, saying he had some curious competitors. But the main house has a vast basement with sealed-off rooms and corridors. My gut tells me the women could be there."

"You could be right, but we're back to getting evidence that they're there," Vargas said. "I'm not about to ask you to endanger yourself by going down there. You would be alone with no one to protect you."

Hattie smirked. The FBI had no problem putting her in danger and riskier situations as long as they got what they wanted.

"What if we found another way to give you a reason to search his place?" Maya asked.

"What do you have in mind?" Vargas asked.

"Using me as bait."

"Absolutely not," Hattie said, envisioning Maya becoming Baumann's next victim and being dragged to the dark basement, kicking and screaming.

Maya craned her head toward the back seat. "The decision isn't up to you, Hattie. My sister is missing. We have no other family, so I'll do everything possible to find her."

Hattie understood the burning need to protect her only sister. She had gone to great lengths to safeguard Olivia and her family. Putting herself in danger was one thing, but she could not sit still and let Maya do the same thing. "Let me go back there again. I'll find a way to get to the basement."

Maya shook her head vigorously. "I won't let you do that. Anna is my sister. If anyone is going to take a risk, it's me." She turned to Investigator Vargas. "I have an idea."

"Let's hear it," he said.

"Hattie can ask Baumann to the Halo Club under the guise of speaking to him about more singing lessons for his daughter. While he's there, I'll confront him with the photograph of him with Mrs. Moyer and tell him I plan to take the information to the newspaper. After last week's article about the women, it should make him angry. That's where you come in, Investigator Vargas."

He nodded. "When he abducts you, I swoop in and arrest him. The kidnapping and arrest will force my superiors' hands to search the plantation."

"Only if we notify the newspapers right away," Maya said.

"This is a crazy idea." Hattie's chest tingled when she envisioned Maya becoming Baumann's next victim. "So many things can go wrong."

Maya shifted on her bottom to look Hattie in the eye. "Vargas will be close by, keeping an eye on me. Catching Baumann in the act is the only way to get inside that compound without putting you in danger. I would never forgive myself if something happened to you." She narrowed her brow, her expression feeling like a soft caress.

"I wish we had more officers to back you up, Investigator Vargas," Hattie said. "The few times I've seen Baumann in town, he travels with one or two other men."

"The problem is that I don't know who to trust. If I enlist the wrong man, they could alert Silva or Baumann."

"I'll bring my gun." Maya turned her attention to Vargas. "I won't use it unless I have to."

Vargas scratched his chin. "That may not be wise. It would give Baumann access to another weapon."

"I don't like this," Hattie said.

Maya turned her gaze to Hattie. "This will work. It has to. The longer my sister remains missing, the less chance I have of finding her alive."

Hattie wasn't sure if Anna was still alive, but she had no argument other than her fear of Maya going missing or being killed. "When do you want to set this up?"

"The quicker, the better," Maya said.

Vargas stopped the car, surprising Hattie with the location. "How did you know Maya lives here?" she asked.

"I'm an investigator, Miss James." Vargas turned off the engine. "Let me know when you set up the meeting with Baumann." He jotted something onto a piece of paper and handed it to Maya. "Here is another number where you can reach me. Leave a message with the date and time if I'm not there. I'll call you to confirm."

Hattie and Maya exited his car.

Maya leaned in before closing the door and said, "Thank you for this. I don't know how to repay you."

"Thank me when this is over," Vargas said before driving off.

Once inside, Maya went straight to the kitchen and offered Hattie her phone. "Please, make the call."

Hattie folded her arms across her chest to make clear her concern. "Only if you promise to not take any unnecessary risks."

Maya made the cross sign across her chest. "I promise."

Hattie sighed and extended her hand. "All right."

"Thank you," Maya said. Instead of handing her the phone, she embraced Hattie and whispered, "Can you stay?"

Staying and sharing bodies with Maya again would be easy. Hattie could easily get lost in her kiss . . . her touch . . . her smell . . . her taste. But Agent Butler was expecting the pictures she and David took of Baumann's house yesterday, and Hattie needed to keep him off her back and clear the air with David. "I'd love to, but I have something important to do."

Maya pulled back. She said she understood, but her eyes revealed her disappointment. "Then let's make that call." She handed Hattie the phone.

Hattie sifted through her purse and asked the operator to connect her to the number on Baumann's business card. The call connected. Not since her childhood had Hattie hoped to God for anything, but right then, she hoped whatever God Maya believed in would watch over her once she set this in motion.

27

Heinz adjusted his tie while descending the stairs, with only minutes for breakfast. He rarely dedicated as much attention to his attire without planning a trip into town, but dressing respectfully to greet his superior was a must. The man seldom visited the plantation, so this morning's meeting meant he had something important to discuss. Heinz suspected the topic, leaving only the details of what solution his superior would make available.

He entered the kitchen and eyed the food trays Hilda had placed out. Elsa sat at the table, nibbling on bread and reading from a textbook. He kissed her on the forehead and spoke in German. "Good morning, Elsa. I understand you have a history test today."

"Good morning, Papa." She frowned. "Yes. I forgot to study last night."

"And why did you forget?" He sat in his chair, placing a cloth napkin over his lap.

"I was practicing my singing like Hattie told me to." Elsa sipped her juice. "When will I see her next week?"

"I doubt you will," he said.

"But she promised to get me ready for my recital."

"Miss James has other commitments."

Heinz had been curious about Hattie since reading last week's intelligence bulletin from Berlin about SS agents spotting her hopping on a plane in New York. And when his man reported seeing her arrive at the Rio airport, his curiosity turned into suspicion. Her arrival at the place of her father's disappearance was no coincidence and prompted him to have her followed. He was sure his visit to her mother's music studio and using his daughter's upcoming recital as a ruse to get close to either woman would shed some light on Karl's location. He just needed to remain patient.

"But—" Elsa started.

"But nothing." He eyed her as sternly as he did yesterday in the basement. "You will not speak of this again."

Elsa's lips trembled. He had taught her the consequences of defying him, so he was confident the questions would stop. Several tears tracked down her cheeks, but she remained silent, eating the rest of her breakfast. Upsetting her was the last thing he wanted, but he had little choice, especially in the face of today's visit.

"I don't mean to upset you, Elsa, but you must learn to obey and not talk back."

"Yes, Papa, but—"

"What did I just tell you about talking back? No playtime for you tomorrow. You will study all day."

Elsa crossed her arms in front of her chest and flopped back in her chair with a scowl. Perhaps he had gotten through to her this time.

Once he finished his food, Hilda met him in his office and set up a coffee carafe and fruit tray for his guest. "Will there be anything else, sir?" she asked.

"No, Hilda. Please escort my visitor back when he arrives."

"Of course, sir." Hilda excused herself, returning to her duties.

Heinz pulled from his desk drawer the logbook detailing the surveillance operations run out of the plantation for the last few months, the intelligence his men had gathered, and how they passed it along to Berlin. Everything was in order, and it showed how each man contributed. During his trip to São Paulo earlier in the week, his counterpart there had hinted change was coming but was reluctant to explain further. Heinz was prepared to use the logbook to defend the need for every man under his command.

Minutes later, Hilda announced his visitor. Heinz snapped to his feet and greeted Oberführer Ziegler in German. The man only went by his rank among trusted associates since it would otherwise compromise his position at the Swiss Embassy. Heinz suggested they sit in the tall leather chairs in the center of the room. "What brings you here today, Herr Ziegler?"

Ziegler was as tall as Heinz but was much thicker. He put little emphasis on physical fitness, while Heinz considered it a priority and put the quality of his work above all else. Conversely, Ziegler prioritized the relationships he'd built, earning him swift promotions. "Berlin is looking at expanding operations in Natal," Ziegler said. "We'll need to cut your staff by two-thirds."

"I understand the need," Heinz said, quietly seething. Cutting intelligence operations in Brazil's capital so dramatically was pure stupidity. When Himmler needed senior SS officers to help expand the Third Reich's reach and influence around the world, Heinz was the first to volunteer. He saw the importance Brazil would play in the control of the Atlantic. Whoever controlled the seas controlled the world, and Rio was the key. "Natal's strategic location is vital to securing our shipping routes through the Atlantic, but I question pulling resources from my sector. As the capital city, Rio is a hotbed of American and British activity. I'm happy to show you the numbers."

Ziegler waved him off. "Numbers won't change the priority of things. The navy is stretched thin after losing several U-boats to the British. Crippling the American and Canadian merchant shipping lanes supporting England in the north has required too many resources."

Heinz knew all too well the impact of the battle for control of the Atlantic. The day Karl James went missing, he had requested Berlin courier a photo of Karl James, but the dispatch was sunk in transit, necessitating a second request. He hoped the photo would make it to Rio soon so he would have more than a description of the man who had eluded him for weeks.

Ziegler continued. "Until we control the Suez Canal, bringing in material for the war effort through the shipping lanes is our top priority. The key is Natal. We must prevent the Americans from getting a foothold there if they enter the war."

"And my men brought you the information that American naval officers from Washington were seen at the embassy in Rio and traveled north to

Natal. Without us, you would have never known the Americans were interested in the location."

"And we recognize your good work. Besides losing track of Karl James and his lists, your production has been spotless. Unfortunately, your zealousness to locate him has been counterproductive. I received a call about it yesterday. Last week's newspaper article drew much attention, and people are asking questions. Your operation will be useless if the local authorities or the Americans learn of it."

"I will take care of it, Herr Ziegler. No one will ask questions after this weekend."

"I suggest you do. If the list of our agents gets into enemy hands, the war effort will be set back for years, and Berlin will not be forgiving." Ziegler didn't have to explain further. Heinz knew the consequences.

After escorting Ziegler to his car, Heinz returned to his office and closed the door. He sat in his desk chair and swung around to peer out the window to the compound, where the men tended to their plantation chores before performing their clandestine duties. The coffee farm wasn't his choice of a cover when he took over his new post, but within a year, he had turned it into the most productive intelligence-gathering operation in South America. He hated to think that his excessive zeal to correct his one mistake could end it, especially with his attack plan underway that may permanently tip the scales in Germany's favor. Ziegler had made it clear Heinz had blundered and had one chance to make it right. If Heinz failed, he would have to smuggle Elsa out of the country. And perhaps himself.

He opened his desk drawer and the small black address book inside and located the number he needed. He picked up the phone handset and asked the operator to connect the call.

"Investigações Policiais," the man answered.

"Can you talk?" Heinz spoke in English, which was their language in common.

"Yes."

"We have a problem," Heinz said. "Those two women we were concerned about are asking too many questions."

"They aren't asking the right people."

"But they're getting too close." Heinz gritted his teeth, thinking everything he'd built here was at risk if Miss James and her friend connected him to the missing women.

"What do you want me to do?"

Heinz detailed what he expected and ended the call. He flipped through the logbook, noting every entry connected to Karl James, including surveillance of his ex-wife since the night Mr. James failed to make it to the waiting U-boat. The surveillance had yielded nothing, no matter which man he assigned to watch Eva Machado. They had captured and interrogated several women who spent time with Machado or worked the cantinas at the docks following James's disappearance, but no one claimed to have seen him. Not even the one from the Halo Club knew anything. Karl James was a ghost. He didn't regret his tactics of abducting those women, but he was wholly disappointed in having yielded nothing but loose ends. However, while not helpful, they provided hours of entertainment for the men once Baumann introduced the hunt.

Instinct told him Hattie James was the key to correcting his one mistake and finding her father and the missing list. Encountering her in the basement yesterday could not have been as innocent as she had played it off. She had to evade Hilda's watchful eye by separating from Mr. Townsend and also convince Elsa to take her to the one place Heinz had set off limits. Though Fuller had found them and confirmed Miss James's story, Heinz didn't trust her. Considering the elusiveness of Mr. James, Heinz decided it was time to trust no one, especially the one vouching for Hattie's story. Beck had checked the backgrounds of every worker on the plantation, locals and Germans, and had vouched for everyone, including Fuller. Perhaps the man who did the checking needed checking as well.

He asked the operator to connect one more call to the German Embassy. He then requested the duty clerk for Section G, code for the intelligence wing. If the Americans or British paid operators to listen to phone calls, like Heinz had in theirs, they had to be careful and speak in code.

Another clerk answered and spoke in German. "How may I help you?"

"I had a German national applying for work and had needed to check his background to get a good picture of what he is like." That was code for the photograph he had asked for.

"Yes, I'm sorry it has taken so long to fulfill your request, but I expect the report to be ready tomorrow."

That was excellent news. Tomorrow, Heinz would finally have a picture of the elusive Mr. James and know the face of the man who had caused him so much grief. "I had two more men apply for work this week and would like the same information about them."

"Yes, I can help with that. How quickly do you need the information?"

"The quickest." Heinz looked up when motion caught his eye. Beck and Fuller were speaking outside his window, and he passed along their names to the clerk on the phone. He wondered how much he actually knew about these men. Beck had arrived with Heinz in Rio on the same ship from Spain four years ago, and Heinz knew nothing more about him than the day they met. Like Fuller, Beck only talked about work. While the others occasionally spoke of family in Germany or growing up in the city or countryside, both men were mysteries. Both had tireless work ethics, but the most he knew about Beck was his preference for long sleeves over short ones. Besides having a solid understanding of Cicero, he had learned nothing about Fuller during his time at the plantation.

"We should have everything prepared for you tomorrow around noon," the clerk said. "Can you send a courier?"

Trusting no one else, Heinz said, "I'll come myself." Until he was sure of both men, he would keep an eye on Hattie James himself.

After completing the call, Heinz locked his logbook in his desk and was about to check on Elsa when the phone rang. He picked it up. "Hallo."

"Hello, Mr. Baumann. This is Hattie James."

Heinz switched to English. "Yes, Miss James. What can I do for you?" Her call could not have come at a better time. Finding Karl James was his only way out of this mess, and instinct told him she was the key. She would either lead him to James, or he would use her as bait.

"I would like to discuss continuing Elsa's lessons."

"She broke the rules, Miss James, and must now suffer the consequences."

"I realize that, Mr. Baumann, but I hate to think she's being punished for something I did. She's quite nervous about the recital and needs more coaching to gain confidence. Considering her age and vulnerability, she may never overcome the embarrassment if she stumbles at the recital. Your daughter is talented. I would hate to see her abandon it."

Of course, he would not pass up an opportunity to pump Hattie for information, but she would see right through him if he agreed too quickly. He would hedge. "You make a convincing argument, but—"

"Hold that thought, Mr. Baumann. Come to the Halo Club tonight. Drinks and dinner are on me. I'll put on a performance showing you what your daughter could miss out on. If you're still not convinced, so be it. At least I'll know I tried my best."

Baumann laughed. "All right, Miss James. I'll come to your show tonight."

After completing the call, he went to the milling barn, where Beck was handing the men their assignments. Two were to relieve the men following Hattie James and Eva Machado. One would spend the rest of the day and evening at the docks, tracking the movement of cargo freighters. And another was to follow the American naval officers at the embassy and note who they met with.

Heinz pulled Beck aside before he doled out the final assignments. "I'll need to go to town tonight and tomorrow."

"Do you have a preference for a driver?"

Heinz looked around but could not locate the man he had in mind. "Fuller. Assign him to me until further notice. Where is he?"

"Feeding the animals."

Heinz left Beck to his work, descended the basement stairs through the exterior back door, and opened the first steel door. The lights were on, a sign someone was in the tunnels. Once through the second metal door, he walked silently so as to not alert Fuller to his presence. The closer he got to the holding cells, the more pungent the stench of human waste.

Fuller came into view. He dipped a ladle into the bucket of porridge, filled a bowl, added three drops of liquid from a vial, and slid it through the opening at the bottom of a bar door. He repeated the process for the four other occupied cells and looked up when he finished.

"Is there something I can do for you, Herr Baumann?" Fuller said in German.

"I'm going to town tonight and want you to drive," Baumann answered in German.

Fuller offered a polite nod.

"After you wash out the food pail, get rid of the smell. Dump the buckets in the outhouse and rinse out the pens. The gutters under the grates will drain to a collection bin."

Fuller nodded again and turned to walk out. The man never complained, always doing as he was told.

"Be showered and ready by seven," Heinz said.

"Of course," Fuller said. "Any particular attire tonight?"

Heinz raised his eyebrows at Fuller's first question. It was more clarifying than probing, a sign he wasn't fishing for information. "Any suit will do like last time."

"Very good. I'll be waiting with the car by seven," Fuller said before leaving Heinz alone with his prisoners.

He walked down the center aisle and stopped at the first door. The cell had two buckets on the stone floor—one with drinking water and the other for human waste. The woman huddled in the corner and used her fingers to eat the creamy porridge. She looked terrified and filthy with mussed hair, a smudged face, and dirty clothing. The second and third cells revealed the same scene. However, the third woman looked defiant. Her eyes bored at him like sabers, and she flung a dollop of porridge at him.

"Feisty," he said.

The woman stood with a slight wobble from the sedative in the food designed to keep them docile. This one, though, clearly needed a more potent dose to tame her. "We know nothing of the diplomat you're looking for."

"We will see." Heinz smiled. "One of you will tell me where he is, or you will die one by one."

28

Hattie parked the car in Eva's garage and walked inside the house, bracing herself for an interrogation. She'd been out all night and morning, arriving home before lunch. After slipping into the bedroom she shared with David, she found the bed empty and the shower running. She opened the bathroom door and saw the mirror and small window covered with steam.

"David?" she called out.

He slid the shower curtain open enough to stick his head out, his face pale from his hangover. She knew the feeling well enough to understand he had yet to get his bearings. "I'm surprised you stayed the night with Eva in the house," he said.

Hattie placed an index finger over his lips to shush him. He would be grumpy in his state, and she wasn't up for another argument. "Find me when you're done. We need to go to the cleaners."

He grunted and closed the curtain.

Hattie returned to the bedroom, pulled her Kodak from the dresser drawer, and slung the case strap over her shoulder. She carried it with her handbag containing the micro-cameras and the empty water pitcher to the kitchen. She filled the container with fresh water and turned to go back, discovering Eva in the doorway.

"I have no right to ask where you've been, but I've been worried about you. You were upset after seeing your father."

"Yes, I was. I'm sorry. I should have called, but I ended up driving around. When the sun came up, I checked on the club owner to see if she'd heard anything about her sister. I showed her the picture, and we took it to the police department." The partial truth was better than a complete lie, but her agitation grew. Every day meant another lie. Lies on top of lies.

"What did they say?"

"Nothing. They'll call us was all we got."

Eva shook her head. "That's a shame. You certainly care a lot about that missing woman."

"Yes, I do, and I would think you would too, considering you knew some of them." Hattie wanted to scream from the rooftop that she had pieced it together. That those women were taken because Baumann and the Nazis were looking for her father. Last night Karl had said to trust him and that his being a Nazi was only part of the truth, but his vague explanation only made things worse. She could neither believe nor distrust him, so she swallowed her guilt and silently renewed her determination to find those women.

"I do, and I'm worried sick about them," Eva said, "but as you're discovering, there's nothing I can do."

Hattie sighed, unable to reveal what she, Maya, and Investigator Vargas had planned without risking everything they had set in place. "I suppose you're right."

"I took a phone call for you this morning," Eva said. Her demeanor turned excited like she had flipped a switch. "The manager of the Golden Room at the Palace asked if you would be interested in performing there on a regular basis."

"Really?"

"Is that all you have to say?" Eva tossed her hands up like Hattie was completely bonkers. "Look, Hattie. No matter why you really came to Rio, the Palace is *the* place to perform in South America. Any singer would give their right arm to receive an invitation. And recurring? It's the opportunity of a lifetime."

Hattie reached out and cupped her mother's hands to calm her. "I realize that. I'm grateful, even if you had some influence over the matter." Eva's blush confirmed that Hattie's supposition was not far afield. "But I need to think about what I really want."

"I won't pretend to understand your hesitancy, but I will respect your need to think it over." Eva squeezed Hattie's hands.

Hattie couldn't think about committing to the Golden Room with so much looming. Between her father and the FBI breathing down her neck, the missing women and their being on the trail of Heinz Baumann, and Maya and their budding relationship, she had too many plates to keep spinning in the air. Letting even one drop would be disastrous. She wasn't even sure if she wanted to remain in Brazil once the FBI no longer blackmailed her into staying. The decision would hinge on whether she could clear her father's name in the eyes of the media, but after learning more about her father, she held little hope of doing so. The stain of being the daughter of a traitor while war waged in Europe would continue to define her, and she would never get back to the glittering lifestyle she once had in New York. Until that burden lifted, Hattie's choices were limited.

"Can you tell them I'll let them know by Monday?"

"I would be happy to." Eva squeezed harder. "I'm so delighted for you, sweetheart. Whether it's here or in New York, I know my little songbird will soar again."

David entered the room, looking much better, with fresh clothes and slicked-back hair. "There you are. Ready to go?"

"Yes," Hattie said, showing him the filled pitcher. "I need to return this to our room."

"I'll do that," Eva said. "You two go do whatever it is you have to do. I have several lessons to give this afternoon, so I likely won't see you until you return from the club."

"Thank you, Mother." Hattie handed her the water and, for the first time in years, kissed her mother on the cheek. She wanted Eva to remember the kiss, not their disagreements, if something went wrong tonight.

Once Eva disappeared into the kitchen, David grabbed the car keys in the bedroom and grumbled, "What the hell, Hattie? All night?"

"Not here," she shushed him. "She might hear." Hattie debated what to tell him. He was passed out for the most eventful night since their arrival in Rio. David guessed about Hattie and Maya consummating their undeniable attraction but knew nothing about her father showing up in the backyard last night, and she was inclined to keep it that way. In his current state, David might let it slip, unintentionally or not, if Agent Butler was unaware of her father's visit. She decided to keep it to herself until they left the dry cleaner's shop.

They drove to town, discussing her night with Maya in vague terms and the unfruitful visit to the police station early that morning. He parked the usual distance away, and they gained entry into the back area, where Agent Butler and Nala Cohen were waiting.

"It's about time," Butler groused. "You went to the plantation yesterday."

Hattie handed Nala both cameras. "I've been a little busy maintaining my cover."

"Right." Butler's sarcastic tone suggested he knew more about Hattie's night than he was letting on. She waited for the other shoe to drop about her father or Maya, but he said nothing. If Butler knew about her and Maya, he would likely hold that information in his hip pocket for future extortion. But since he said nothing about Karl, her father had apparently come and gone unnoticed, informing her he was trained to evade detection, another part of his life Karl hadn't told her about.

Nala left to develop the film.

"David had no luck upstairs with the nosey servant, and I didn't get very far into the basement before Baumann found me down there. I'm lucky his daughter was with me. Otherwise, I'm not sure what he would have done."

"What did you find?" Butler asked.

"No radio or codebook, but I saw crates with German markings. The basement had several corridors and locked rooms. It almost felt like a dungeon."

They waited until Nala returned and gave Hattie the cameras. "Each has a fresh roll of film." She laid out the developed pictures on the worktable.

Butler examined the photos. David had taken a few of the hallways inside the main house but they showed nothing of importance. Butler focused his attention on Hattie's pictures and pointed to the crates. "See those numbers here and here? Those are MP 40 submachine guns used by the SS and military-issued Model 39 hand grenades. They are armed for a small war. This is good, Hattie. Really good. Military-grade weapons mean we can bypass the Rio police and bring in the Brazilian military authority."

"Does that mean the military will raid his compound?" That was the best thing Hattie could have heard. If the military went in today or tomorrow, she could stop her other plan for Baumann, and Maya would not have to put herself in danger. Then again, what if her father was caught up in the raid? He would be arrested, and everything she'd done to protect him would have been for naught.

"Not yet. A raid won't tell us how Baumann is transferring intelligence to Berlin. He would have several minutes to destroy everything once the troops storm through the gate. I need you to go in again and get pictures or sneak out whatever you can."

David's mouth fell open. "You don't want her to snoop. You want her to steal." He slammed his fist on the table. "There's no way in hell she's stealing his secret papers. It's too risky."

"I'm not sure I'll return to the plantation," Hattie said. "Baumann put Elsa's singing lessons on hold after finding us in the basement, but I'll try to convince him otherwise if he comes to the club tonight."

"That's not good enough," Butler said. "Your sister's freedom depends on you getting into that place again."

"I can't control whether Baumann invites me to the plantation."

"Make sure he does. Baumann might store the codebook or other records in his office."

"There's no reasoning with him." David's words dripped with rage. He reached beneath the back flap of his suit coat, pulled out an automatic pistol, and shoved it under Butler's chin. "Maybe you'll listen to this. Hattie is no longer your pawn."

"David!" Hattie recoiled. This was getting out of hand. "Put that away. You're scaring me."

David raised the muzzle higher, angling Butler's chin upward. "Something has to be done."

Nala removed a gun from the waistband of her long skirt and moved directly behind David. "And I'll be the one to do it if you don't put that down."

David lowered his weapon and backed away slowly, returning the pistol to his waistband. "I don't care what you demand. You said you have enough to go after him, so do it. Stop putting the woman I love in danger."

Hattie jerked her head at his declaration. It could have been to shake the FBI off the scent of Hattie and Maya's relationship, but the emotion behind his words suggested his feelings were genuine.

Butler edged closer to David, standing toe to toe with him. A menacing look of rage was in his eyes. "The next time you pull a gun on me, you had better pull the trigger because I certainly will."

Mortified, Hattie tugged David's arm. "Let's go. We have a show to prepare for." She turned toward Butler and sneered. "I'll let you know what Baumann says."

Once in the car, Hattie slapped David on the shoulder. "What were you thinking, pulling a gun on an FBI agent?"

"It's clear you're unwilling to stand up for yourself, but I'm not."

"But a gun? Where did you get it?"

"It's Eva's. I went snooping and found it in the living room." David shifted in the seat and adjusted the gun until he was comfortable with that thing poking his back. "It's a good thing. This is getting too dangerous."

"I don't like it, David. We should leave the guns to the professionals."

"The professionals are sitting in that shop all comfy and safe while you risk everything by going to the plantation. Eva has a second gun. I'd feel better if you carried it to protect yourself if we get separated like last night." The subtle jab about her spending the night with Maya was slick, but it also made her think he was right.

"I don't know." Hattie thought about yesterday's events. If Elsa and her father hadn't been in the basement, Baumann could have easily shot her, and no one would have heard. A gun would have given her a fighting chance. "I don't know how to use one."

"I can teach you."

"Let me think about it."

Later that night, David parked in the lot two blocks from the Halo Club, grabbing one of the last spots. It was Friday night, and the streets were bustling in the Lapa district. Cars honked, and men whistled at Hattie as she passed. David puffed his chest and carefully looked over each offender —his way of protecting her. However, after what he said to Butler, she thought his territory marking was more real than not.

Hattie recognized a sedan across the street from the club. The man in the driver's seat had a hat on and partially hid his face, but she recognized Investigator Vargas and gave him a furtive nod. He wagged a finger, acknowledging her. His position had a view of the front door and side street exit for deliveries. If Baumann tried to take Maya against her will, he would be right on them, make an arrest, and have cause to search the plantation. Hattie and Maya setting the trap was the only step remaining.

Hattie and David entered the club thirty minutes before her first show. It was packed like the streets. The new bartender was holding her own, and Maya had dropped off a rack of fresh glasses. Hattie waved, getting Maya's attention, and gestured to meet them in the back. Maya signaled to give her a minute. Meanwhile, Hattie and David went to their dressing room.

"I need to talk to Maya," Hattie said. David was still hot from the visit with Butler, so she didn't want to discuss the night's plan in front of him. At the very least, he would lecture her, but he might also consider it too risky and purposely disrupt their ruse. "But I don't want her seen coming in here. Butler might have eyes inside the club. Can you send her to the ladies' room?" David mumbled his discontent but agreed to send her. "We need to have a serious talk sooner rather than later, David."

"Yes, we do."

Hattie reentered the dining room, walked down the hallway off the kitchen toward the club's delivery exit, and stepped into the women's restroom. The space had been updated recently with new fixtures, flooring, paint, and a countertop—more evidence Maya intended to transform the Halo Club into a classy establishment. She leaned against the wall near the sink and waited.

One woman occupied the first stall and flushed. Moments later, a server stepped out. "Evening, Miss James," she said while washing up.

"Evening, Monica. Please, call me Hattie."

Monica smiled, shaking her head. "Not after your appearance at the Palace. You are royalty now. The entire staff is speaking of it. We are proud to have you sing here."

Hattie laughed. "I'm just a performer who is equally proud to sing at the Halo Club."

"You'll have a hard time convincing the others." Monica threw the paper towel in the trashcan before opening the door. "Goodbye, Miss James." She giggled on her way out.

Maya appeared before the door closed and wagged her thumb toward the hallway. "What's with her?"

"Apparently, the staff considers me royalty now."

Maya laughed. "I should have warned you. They are in awe of anyone who appears at the Palace. It will take some time for the excitement to wear off." Her expression turned serious. "Why are we talking in here?"

"I haven't told David what's going on, and I want to keep it that way."

"You don't trust him?"

"He's becoming too protective. He might do something to stop this." Hattie lowered her gaze. "If I were honest, I'm tempted to do just that. My opinion hasn't changed. I think this is too dangerous."

"We'll be fine. Vargas said he would be right outside."

"He is. I passed him on the way in."

"Then we're set. We wait for Baumann to show."

Hattie locked the door, strode back to Maya, and searched her eyes. They held certainty, not doubt, and also love. Hattie didn't feel the urge to run and call it quits, which was frightening. She sensed the pull and didn't want to fight it, welcoming the intimacy of being completely vulnerable, and it felt liberating to be finally free of the past.

She drew Maya closer, kissing her briefly but deeply. Pulling back, she said, "When this is over, we need to have a serious talk."

Maya smiled. "Yes, we do."

29

At six thirty, Karl dressed in his only suit. He had bought it on his first day in Rio, using the cash he had lifted from the real Fuller's wallet. The suit was dark so as not to stand out in a crowd, and being off-the-rack, it didn't fit him as precisely as his collection of tailored suits in his Alexandria home before all of this mess. How he missed the feel of natural wool fabric and the look of a bold stripe pattern on him. All his suits at home were double-breasted like Baumann's, with a wide fit and peak lapel for its formal appearance. They were simply elegant. The dark suit he wore today had none of those features, but he had to fit in with the other men, so off-the-rack was the best he could do.

He finished his attire by placing the pistol he had checked out from the armory in a shoulder holster under his suit coat and strapping his knife sheath to the back of his belt. Baumann would know about the Luger but not about the Remington DuPont short hunting knife Karl had picked up in town. He wasn't sure of their destination tonight, but instinct told him they were returning to the Halo Club. If that were the case, the Remington might mean the difference between Hattie living or dying and the lists remaining in safe hands. He questioned the rationality of copying those lists in the first place to ensure he stayed alive long enough to find the Nazi mole in the War Department. All he accomplished was to put in danger the daughter he loved more than life itself.

At quarter to seven, Karl went to the garage. The plantation workday ended two hours ago, and all the vehicles not out for an intelligence-gathering mission were lined up. The stable of cars and trucks Baumann had assembled was impressive, rivaling that of any military or SS unit. While the trucks were employed on the plantation to move workers and materials, the sedans were used to travel to town to perform the true purpose of the coffee farm. Occasionally, the workers could check out a sedan for personal use if their trip did not interfere with official business, as Karl did several times to check on Hattie.

He grabbed the keys for Baumann's personal sedan from the pegboard housing all the vehicle keys and opened the rear passenger door to ensure the back compartment was clean and ready for Baumann to occupy. Being his driver meant catering to his predilections in food, drink, sexual partners, and anything else he might desire for the night. It was a duty Karl did not particularly care for after he learned what Baumann did with the last woman he seduced into his car with money and promises of a lavish evening. Another wave of guilt hit him, thinking how Baumann had picked several women, hoping to find the missing Karl James. He wanted no part in the man's sick games but had to play along to maintain his cover.

After checking the front compartment and the gas level, Karl replayed yesterday's conversation in the basement with Baumann when he first saw Hattie. He thought Baumann was suspicious of finding her and Elsa there, doubting her story of looking for an appropriate place to practice singing. Karl also got the impression Baumann suspected him of something after assigning him as his driver for tonight. This undercover business had taught Karl to keep his friends close but keep his enemies closer. He suspected Baumann was exercising that practice. If he were right, tonight's trip to town could be a trap for both him and Hattie, and he could not let that happen.

Karl circled to the back of the sedan, where the whitewall spare tire was mounted on a metal guard attached to the trunk lid. He removed the white cloth cover, unscrewed the valve stem cover, and let some air out. If needed, this could buy him time.

After securing the tire cover and pulling the car to the front of the main house five minutes before seven, Karl waited by the rear passenger door. Always prompt, Baumann stepped out the front door one minute before seven, wearing his signature double-breasted white suit and matching fedora. He was always dressed to impress when he went to town.

Karl opened the rear door on the passenger side and spoke in German. "Good evening, Herr Baumann."

"Good evening, Herr Fuller," Baumann said, sliding into the back seat.

Karl leaned in. "Where to, sir?"

"The Halo Club. Do you remember where it's at?"

Karl remained calm, forcing himself not to react. "Yes, it's close to the marina."

"Good. I want to make Miss James's first show at eight, so we best not dawdle."

"Of course, sir." Karl closed the door, cringing as he circled to the driver's side. The Halo Club meant Baumann had his sights set on Hattie, and buying time was Karl's only option.

He hopped in behind the wheel, drove down the access road, and slowed at the front gate. Max was working again, and he pressed the button, automatically opening the sliding solid metal panel. As they passed, the guard came to attention, and Baumann returned his salute.

Karl turned and drove down the road parallel to the plantation wall. Once on the two-lane main highway, he accelerated to a speed he thought would shave at least five minutes off the hour-long trip to the Halo Club to satisfy Baumann's instructions about not dawdling. Now, he had to choose when to fake car trouble. It couldn't be too close to town or the plantation, but farther away from town was better. Otherwise, they might get help too quickly, and Baumann might consider making Hattie's second show, a possibility Karl could not risk.

The fifty-mile stretch toward town was not lit well at night and had many hairpin turns descending the foothills into the Rio basin. Traffic was light but significant enough to make selecting the right spot to pull over tricky. However, Karl had traveled this route enough times to know several turnouts started appearing in about five miles. Taking the first would be too obvious, but the second or third should mask his ruse sufficiently. Those turnouts were narrower than the others, so he could pull over close enough to the vegetation on the roadside to keep Baumann in the car.

In the first few miles, Karl passed two slower vehicles on straightaways, maintaining the impression of hurrying to make Hattie's eight o'clock show. Glancing in the rearview mirror, Karl glimpsed Baumann in the back seat. He appeared unconcerned about their rate of travel.

Karl passed the first turnout, and no headlights were directly behind him. Now was the time to start his act. He gripped the steering wheel tighter, pretending to struggle with it, and acted surprised. After slowing, he steered more dramatically.

They spoke in German.

"Is something wrong, Herr Fuller?" Baumann asked.

"The car is pulling hard to the left. We might have a flat." Karl straightened the car and slowed more. "I'll pull over at the next turnout."

Baumann remained quiet.

Karl steered through two successive curves and slowed to a crawl at the turnout. The open space wasn't as wide as he remembered and was barely big enough to fit the Ford Deluxe. Once stopped, he craned his neck toward the back seat. "I'll check the tire. Stay here. There's not much room to work."

Karl glanced at the road behind him, ensuring no cars were approaching before opening the driver's door. After stepping out, he faced the car so Baumann couldn't see his back while closing the door. He then pulled his knife from the sheath attached to his belt, kneeled to inspect the tire, and stabbed it between the grooves on the tread, not the sidewall, to avoid leaving a visible puncture hole. The tire deflated, and Karl returned the knife to its home at his waist.

He stood and pressed against the fender when a car passed in his travel lane. The whoosh of wind meant the other car was too close for comfort. He opened the back door and slipped into the rear cabin beside Baumann. The moon and glow from their headlights provided enough illumination to see that Baumann was holding his Luger in his right hand and was aiming it at Karl.

"Either use it or put it away," Karl said. "I don't take kindly to having a gun pointed at me."

Baumann tilted his head as if sizing up Karl. After a long, tense moment, he lowered his weapon. "One can't be too careful."

"No, one can't. We have a flat. I'll get the spare. It should take about twenty minutes to change out, but I'm afraid you might miss the performance tonight."

"We shall see," Baumann said, sliding his pistol into his shoulder holster beneath his suit coat.

"I'll get to it, then." Karl stepped outside when it was safe and popped open the trunk for the jack and crowbar. He then removed the cover over the spare and squeezed the tire to test its pressure. It was mostly flat, as he had left it. After laying the tire on the ground, he returned to the back seat. "We have a slight problem. The spare isn't fully inflated. It should have enough air to get us back to the compound, but I wouldn't trust it all the way to town. There are too many sharp turns."

"Perhaps you're right," Baumann said. "Do what you can and nurse it home."

"Will do." Karl went around back, letting out a sigh of relief before placing his suit coat over the tire cage. If he stalled long enough, they would not make it to Hattie's second show once Karl cleaned up and changed cars.

He went to work lining up the jack on the undercarriage and raising it enough to know he had hit the plumb spot but insufficient to relieve the car's weight on the wheel to keep it stationary while he loosened the lug nuts. Karl put on an act, cursing and struggling with the crowbar to extend the repair time from twenty minutes to nearly forty. When he returned to the driver's seat, wiping the grease and grime from his hands with a rag, he said, "That wasn't my finest work. Two lug nuts were on tight and nearly stripped."

"It seems the mechanic maintaining our fleet of vehicles is not as talented as I was led to believe."

"It could be the tropical climate. Year-round humidity is tough on a car."

"Perhaps." Baumann's calm demeanor made him hard to read. However, when Karl glanced in the rearview mirror again, Baumann's eyes gave him away. He was leery of Karl and the flat tire.

Karl turned the car on the highway when it was safe and nursed it toward the plantation at a slow speed. Another half hour later, he pulled up to the gate, where Max was still at his post. He approached and scanned the interior of the car.

"Welcome back, sir," he said in German.

Baumann acknowledged him with a nod.

Karl crept the car to the front of the main house, parked, and opened Baumann's door to let him out. "Give me twenty minutes to clean up and change. Then I'll get another car."

Baumann checked the pocket watch in his front coat pocket. "I'm afraid we won't make it in time. Perhaps I'll go into town another night."

"As you wish," Karl said. "I'll return this to the garage." He spun on his heel to return to the driver's seat, but Baumann grabbed his arm, bringing him to a stop.

"That's quite the knife you have," Baumann said.

A sinking feeling took over, twisting Karl's stomach into knots. He cursed himself for forgetting to put his coat on and exposing the sheath at his waist. His mind was too focused on protecting Hattie while on the roadside, not the precautions he needed to take with Baumann in the back seat. Now that Baumann knew Karl had a knife, he might look into the flat tire and learn its actual cause. Karl had one chance to explain.

"Yes, I'm rarely without it."

"It must be handy."

"Yes. I've used it several times. A man should always have a means of defending himself wherever he goes."

"I cannot disagree," Baumann said, patting his Luger.

"Will that be all, Herr Baumann?"

"Yes, for now."

Karl returned the car to the garage, went to his room in the cabin, and flopped, seated, on the bed. He had stopped Baumann for the night but was unsure how long he could keep this up and keep Baumann away from Hattie. It was only a matter of time before Baumann abducted her to get information about him like he did with the other women. If things didn't change or he didn't devise a better plan, Karl might have to make use of his knife again.

30

Hattie belted out the final note of her second set to a packed crowd, roaring applause, and a cacophony of wolf whistles. The tourists and locals in Rio loved her performances, and she thrived on the synergy between her and the audience. Each fed on the other. The symbiotic relationship was impossible to recreate off the stage. She would not trade that feeling for a truckload of money because it already made her feel like a million bucks.

But as Hattie walked off the stage, she was disappointed . . . and a little relieved. She and Maya had exchanged glances during her two performances, ready to alert the other, but Baumann never showed. David's performance was spot on, so his hangover had passed, but he wasn't his usual playful self during each show. He was likely tired, but she suspected he was still upset over her dogged pursuit of the missing women and the escalating demands by the FBI. Perhaps it was a bit of both.

She went to the dressing room, changed out of her stage dress while David stayed in the dining room, and met up with him minutes later on a stool next to him at the bar after most of the crowd had left. She draped an arm over his shoulder and noted a cup of coffee in front of him, not a cocktail glass—an excellent sign.

"How are you feeling?" she asked.

"Better." He raised his mug.

"Glad to hear it." She patted him on the shoulder and went to the kitchen to look for Maya. The cooks were busy at the grill and stovetop cleaning up, and servers flowed in and out with the last of the dirty dishes. Each acknowledged Hattie with a polite smile and bowed like she was royalty.

Maya was near the sink, stacking trays of glasses on the drying rack with her back to the door. Hattie approached and waited until she had finished so as not to disturb her. "Do you have a minute?"

"Sure. I could use a break." Maya wiped her hands dry with the dish towel slung over her shoulder. The cashier was counting the night's receipts in her office, so Maya gestured her chin toward the swinging door. She guided Hattie out of the kitchen and down the corridor to the restrooms and side exit. She picked up a rock on the floor, opened the door, and ushered Hattie outside onto the side street, which was more like an alley. Instead of letting the door close, she laid the rock near the doorframe as a wedge. "Staff come out here for breaks. We'll be fine here."

They stepped ten feet further down the alley out of earshot of the door. One dim streetlight illuminated the area, highlighting crates, garbage cans, and a few stray cats. Hattie glanced toward the front of the building. A sedan resembling Vargas's was still parked across the street near the corner.

"What happened?" Maya asked. "I thought you said Baumann would show."

"That's what he said." Hattie shrugged. "I can stay until closing to see if he comes."

"No, go home like you usually do. We don't want to do anything out of the ordinary."

"You're right. Someone might be watching like Investigator Vargas." Hattie wagged her thumb in his direction.

"I'll let him know to pack things up for the night," Maya said. "Do you think Baumann would be suspicious if you called him again?"

"Yes. I think he would if I called right away."

Maya sighed deeply and lowered her head. "Another day lost. I'm starting to think I'll never find Anna."

Hattie gripped Maya by both arms before raising her chin with a finger. She wanted to take Maya into her arms and reassure her, but Vargas was at the corner. Until they could be alone again, really alone, the confidence behind Hattie's eyes would have to suffice. "We will find her. We won't stop looking until we know she's safe. Go tell Vargas we'll try again tomorrow. If Baumann doesn't come tomorrow night, I'll call again and again until he does."

Hattie was foolish to go to such lengths to find a woman she had only met once, but this wasn't about Anna or even Maya. It was about something much bigger. This was about regaining control of her life, and it was time she stopped keeping secrets and started trusting those close to her.

The door opened wider, and Hattie lowered her hands and stepped backward. An employee stepped out for a smoke break but stayed by the door.

Hattie lowered her voice to a whisper. "The next time we're alone, I need to tell you about my father."

~

Once in the car and the windows were rolled up, Hattie started a long, overdue talk with David. "I've been keeping secrets from you."

He started the engine. "If this is about Maya—"

She stopped him before he went down that road again and had him turn off the engine. Maya was a sore subject between them, but if Hattie was ever going to regain control of her life, the lies within her inner circle needed to stop, starting with David, the one person who had her back throughout this ordeal. "This isn't about her. This is about my father."

"What about him?"

Hattie took a deep breath. Once she spoke the truth in this dark parking lot, there was no going back. But David had been with her for two years, and she trusted him with her biggest secret—her love life. She needed to trust him and start working as a team again.

"I saw him yesterday at the plantation."

David snapped his head toward her. His expression was a mix of hurt and anger. "You saw him and didn't tell me?"

"I was in shock. We didn't speak to each other because Elsa was there. I didn't tell you because I needed time to think. You've been so moody about all of this, especially about me helping Maya find Anna. I thought you might tell Butler out of spite to get this over with."

"You think that little of me? That I would turn your father in?"

"Can you blame me? You've told me this was too dangerous at every turn, and we should call the FBI's bluff."

"I still think we should, but I would never do anything to hurt you."

"Because you're in love with me." Hattie watched his eyes carefully to measure his reaction, and they told her it was true. "David," she said softly, "I love you, but I can't love you in that way."

"I know." He visibly swallowed. "I would never ask you for anything you can't give."

"Why do you put yourself through this?"

He harrumphed. "I have no choice."

"What does that mean?"

"It means I would rather ensure you're safe than be alone."

"If it's any solace, I'm glad you came. I feel safer when we work together, not against one another."

"I do too."

"Then I need to tell you the rest of it."

"The rest of it?" He looked confused.

"When you were passed out . . ." Hattie explained about her father sneaking into Eva's backyard and what she learned about his Nazi association. "I was upset and couldn't talk to you, so—"

"So you went to her."

"Yes, but I didn't tell Maya anything about him or the FBI. Not when we think Baumann, who we know is a Nazi officer, kidnapped Anna and those women. I told her about the photograph, and we went to the police station this morning."

"I'm sure they were of no help."

"Not officially." Hattie went on to explain Investigator Vargas's offer to help after Inspector Silva had her and Maya thrown out of the station. "That's when he and Maya devised a plan to use her as bait." She explained the details, ending with David's look of disgust.

"You three are insane. The club has two exits, and Baumann travels in a pack. How does Vargas expect to arrest him without help?"

"He said he can handle him."

"Sure he can," David said in a snarky tone. "When is this supposed to happen?"

"It was supposed to tonight, but Baumann never showed."

"Tonight? It's a good thing he didn't. Your plan won't work if Baumann's men get the jump on Vargas."

"Well, we'll see again tomorrow night. If Baumann doesn't show up, I'll call him again. If he says no, I'll know I've blown my chance to find the women and get more intel for Butler."

"This is really important to you, isn't it?"

"Yes." Hattie swallowed the growing emotion in her throat. "This isn't only about Anna or the other missing women. It's about why they were taken—Baumann searching for my father. I'd never forgive myself if I didn't do everything I could to find them."

David leaned over and kissed Hattie on the forehead. "And that's why I love you. If you're going to do this, you need to do it right. Vargas will need help, so I'll be there with my gun."

"And mine," Hattie said. "I want you to teach me how to use it."

David started the engine. "Then we better get going."

31

The following morning

Last night's flat tire was too convenient, especially the part with the low spare. Heinz was sure Fuller intended to keep him from going into town to see Hattie James's show, but he didn't understand why. He knew of two instances when those two were in the same room—yesterday in the basement and eight days ago in the Halo Club. At the club, Fuller was quiet and remained in the shadows, but in the basement, he verified Hattie's story. Both encounters seemed benign, but now Heinz questioned that premise. He had to figure out what connection Fuller had with her and why she was important enough to keep him away.

That search would begin now.

Heinz swung open the door to the upstairs study, where his daughter worked on an extra math assignment. She looked up, gave him a hard, mean look, and returned to her studies. She was still angry with him for making her do schoolwork on a Saturday and not committing to more singing lessons with Hattie James, and she would likely remain so. After last night, he had no intention of resuming the lessons, even at the expense of getting closer to finding the woman's father. Fuller had become the priority.

Hilda sat in the corner, observing Elsa while she worked. She approached the door and spoke in German. "What can I do for you, sir?"

"Is she giving you any trouble?"

"Not at all. She's done every assignment."

"That's good to hear." Heinz took comfort in knowing her insolence extended only to him. "I'm heading into town this morning and should return before the end of her school day."

"School day?" Elsa groused.

"Your day of punishment for talking back at the breakfast table."

"I still don't understand why I can't see Hattie again."

"The only thing you must understand is that she won't return." Heinz twisted his neck to curb his temper. Her mother was much better suited for dealing with young girls. Still, five years after her death, he felt ill-equipped to handle Elsa lashing out without having her hate him. "It's now up to you to take what she taught you and prepare for the recital. I have faith you can do it."

Elsa folded her arms across her chest and harrumphed. He snickered and closed the door behind him, thinking her hard head would be her downfall. And his.

After descending the stairs, Heinz put on his double-breasted white suit jacket, grabbed his fedora, and exited through the front door. His secondary sedan was parked at the bottom of the steps. Fuller stood nearby and opened the rear passenger door, as he did last night. Heinz wouldn't let him stray far until he discovered the connection between him and Hattie James.

"I take it you have thoroughly inspected the vehicle this time," Heinz said. They conversed in German.

"Yes, even the spare."

"Good. Then I expect no trouble today." Heinz slid inside.

Fuller circled the car, sat behind the wheel, and craned his neck to better see Heinz in the back seat. "Where to, Herr Baumann?"

"The German Embassy."

"Very good, sir." Fuller was silent for the hourlong drive to town. However, the furtive glances in the rearview mirror were telling. He distrusted Heinz, and the feeling was mutual.

Traffic was thick this afternoon. The center of Rio was bustling with shoppers and fans attending the Saturday football games—amateur and professional. Football—soccer in the United States—was a religion in Rio, second only to Catholicism. Heinz understood the fanaticism of the sport, having grown up with it in Germany. But organized religion was more for his mother and dead wife. If not for a deathbed promise, he could do without the Sunday lectures.

Once in the Botafogo neighborhood and on São Clemente Road at the heart of embassy row, Fuller pulled up to the gate of the German Embassy. Like his plantation, the embassy was surrounded by a high wall with a guarded gate. While Heinz provided his own guards, uniformed Brazilian police protected the property and controlled entry.

Fuller rolled down his window and spoke to the guard, handing him his and Baumann's German passports. "Heinz Baumann hat eine termin."

Armed with a holstered pistol, the guard inspected both passports before checking the names on a clipboard. He then returned the documents to Fuller and gestured for the guard in the shack to open the gate.

Once the gate panels opened, Fuller proceeded, passing the substantial tropical garden and water fountain in the center of the curved driveway. Near the fountain was a tall flagpole with the Nazi flag flying at the top so it could be seen from the street. Fuller pulled in front of the white neoclassical building, topped by a prominent red roof. The vibrant color matched the flag flying proudly in the compound. The flag and roof projected power and strength—the essence of Germany, which made Heinz proud and a little homesick for the emerald-green lakes and breathtaking cliffs in the German Alps. But he would do his duty to remain in Rio for as long as the battle for the Atlantic shipping lanes waged.

Once parked, Fuller opened the passenger door.

"Wait with the car," Heinz said in German. "I won't be long."

While Fuller pulled the sedan into a parking spot inside the compound, Heinz entered the main door. The lobby was another ostentatious display of national pride with bright red fabrics, eagle statuaries, and framed pictures of the Führer and other high-ranking German officials. Several visitors and workers occupied the lobby in perfect rows and intervals—the image of efficiency.

Heinz walked up to the welcome desk, showed the receptionist his passport, and spoke German. "Heinz Baumann to see Benjamin Kemp in Section G."

The woman checked the logbook on her desk. "I'll tell him you've arrived." She dialed a number on her desk phone, spoke quietly, and hung up. "He'll meet you in the corridor." She pressed a buzzer on the desk, unlocking the door directly behind her.

"Thank you." Heinz entered the controlled area of the embassy and waited in the well-lit corridor. Six chairs lined both walls, but he chose to stand. People walked between offices, carrying files, and one pushed a cart with packages.

A small man in his thirties dressed in a dark suit approached at a fast pace. "Herr Baumann. I'm Benjamin Kemp. Please follow me," he said in German. His weak frame and thick glasses explained why he worked in an embassy six thousand miles from home and was not enlisted in the military or SS. He would not have lasted a week.

The little man guided Heinz to his office, where he closed the door and invited him to sit in the guest chair in front of his desk. He handed him a folder before sitting in his chair. "I've collected the material you requested, but without a diplomatic pouch, it should remain in the embassy."

Heinz waved him off. "That's fine. I'll read it right here."

"We had the other photos you requested on file here," Kemp said.

"Yes, yes." Heinz opened the folder. Several pages were fastened vertically at the top by a metal prong. The cover sheet signified the material was classified as secret by the German Embassy. He flipped the page, revealing a summary of the background material on Beck and Fuller. The file was meticulous, detailing where each man was born and lived, worked, and went to school throughout their life. It also listed similar information about their parents, siblings, wives, and children. Then came a section with a secondary classification cover, signifying the following information was classified as top secret by SS Intelligence. The next few pages summarized the intelligence operations they were involved in, including their assignments under Baumann. Nothing about Beck seemed out of the ordinary, but Fuller's operation involving the recovery and escort of Karl James was marked in red as a failure. Baumann surmised his file likely had a similar stain on an otherwise spotless record, and that angered him.

He then turned to the last pages containing the photographs. Beck's was on top and made Heinz snicker. Aren had more hair when this was taken. He flipped to the next photo, finding something not unexpected. The man who drove him to the embassy today was not Joseph Fuller, so who was he? Heinz turned to the photo he'd waited weeks for and got his answer.

~

After silently stewing in the back seat during the drive to the plantation about how to deal with the man behind the wheel, Heinz walked into the milling barn. Several workers were inside, stacking bags of beans onto a truck bound for an exporter and roasting. Aren Beck stood nearby carrying a clipboard, accounting for every bag the men had loaded.

Heinz approached. "We need to talk . . . privately."

Beck instructed the men to load the last bag and take the truck to the compound. Once they moved to the storage room and closed the door, he narrowed his brow at Heinz. "You look worried. Did something happen?"

"Joseph Fuller is really Karl James."

Beck jerked his head back. "You've confirmed?"

Heinz nodded. "Photos from the embassy. They look similar, but I'm sure."

"He drove you to town today. What did you do?"

"I phoned Oberführer Ziegler for guidance. Berlin ordered him shot following his escape in Rio. He's no longer a trusted asset, so Ziegler instructed me to deal with him how I see fit."

"And what have you decided?"

"I had him drive me back."

"So he's here. Shall I round him up?"

"No. I have something special planned for him, but I guarantee Karl James will not see another sunrise."

32

No matter what position Hattie tried in the front seat of Eva's Ford Deluxe, she could not get comfortable. The derringer pistol hidden in her garter belt kept digging into her inner thigh. The cold steel against her skin made her keenly aware of the danger looming tonight for Maya. Horrifying scenarios of her having to fire the gun to save Maya from Baumann or his men and her wildly missing her target swirled in her head. David had spent less than ten minutes instructing her on the derringer's operation and use, but she had yet to pull the trigger and was unsure if she could.

"That's it." She hiked her skirt up, exposing her legs and undergarments.

"What the hell are you doing?" David said, gripping the steering wheel tighter as he prepared to turn onto another street.

"This thing is making me too jittery. I gotta take it out." Hattie removed the pistol, slid her skirt down, and placed the gun in her handbag. "This will have to do. I'll keep my purse on stage with me during each set."

David laughed. "I always wondered how the ladies tolerated having a gun between their legs."

"I'm still wondering." Hattie laughed. "When we get there, I should let Investigator Vargas know you're in on the plan and can be his backup."

"Do you think it wise to talk to him while he's outside the club? Someone might be watching."

"I have an idea." Hattie sifted through the glove box, found a pen and paper, and jotted down the information.

Soon, David parked in the Lapa district lot as the last slivers of light retreated over the western mountains. Once they exited the parking lot on foot, she spotted Vargas parked across the street from the Halo Club. He had the driver's window down again and positioned his hat to obscure most of his face. Instead of walking on the same side of the street as the club, as they did most nights, Hattie and David crossed the street the instant they left the lot. She crumpled the note in her left hand, keeping it at the ready. They dodged the lively nightlife on the sidewalk, getting closer. When the traffic broke, Hattie crossed in front of Vargas's sedan, tossed the message inside the open window, and continued toward the club. She looked back. Vargas gave her a nod. He now knew she and David were armed and would be there to help.

David opened the door to the club to let Hattie enter first.

"He got it." She stepped inside.

"I hope *we* don't get it," David said, following Hattie. "Otherwise, Maya will be in big trouble." That was far from the reassurance Hattie needed at the moment.

The Halo Club was packed with a Saturday night crowd that was thicker than last night. The moment Hattie stepped into the dining room, someone yelled her name. Two hundred heads snapped toward her, and cheers broke out among several whistles. More people had come to see her perform and dine at the club. If this trend continued, the audience would outgrow the club's capacity, and Maya would have to control access like all the clubs Hattie performed at before her life crumbled.

Becoming popular in Rio so quickly had complicated her consideration of the Golden Room's offer. Performing there regularly would definitely kick-start her career again and possibly catapult it to greater heights internationally. Breaking into the Latin and European markets meant more money and stardom than she had dreamed of in her little New York apartment. Being a star in the United States was one thing, but worldwide fame was rare. Her mother had attained it, but it always seemed out of reach because Hattie never evoked her mother's name while building her career.

As customers greeted her politely, Hattie glimpsed Maya standing near a table speaking to a customer. A quandary built. The Golden Room had laid the possibility of fame and fortune greater than Hattie had imagined at her feet, but she couldn't be sure if she had earned it on her own by her performance with Maggie Moore or by her mother's string pulling. If she swallowed her pride and took the job, losing Maya would be a likely consequence. She feared Maya would become the one who got away, supplanting Helen as the one who broke her heart.

Maya looked up, locking gazes with Hattie. No one could deny Maya was attractive. Her athletic body and angular facial features caught the attention of anyone with a pulse, but Hattie measured her attraction by more intrinsic attributes defining how she carried herself—confidence, determination, and a steadfast refusal to take any guff. Hattie was always drawn to that type of woman, but Maya was the first who didn't fit Helen's mold of sultry curves and delicate arms. The change was refreshing.

Maya acknowledged her with a head wag toward the dressing room, signaling she wanted to talk. Hattie raised an index finger, telling her she would be one minute. Walking away from the customers waiting to see her would not help her reputation or Maya's business. She acknowledged each fan individually, shaking their hands, passing along her thanks, and telling them she hoped they enjoyed the show.

The gauntlet took longer than expected to clear, making Hattie think she should talk to Maya about arriving through the other door to avoid creating a commotion. Minutes later, she and David entered the private backstage corridor, walked past the storage room, and went into the dressing room.

Maya was inside and turned. Her expression was soft and sweet but transformed into disappointment when David appeared in the doorway. "Hello, David. We can talk later, Hattie." She started to walk out, but Hattie touched her arm, pulling her to a stop.

"It's okay, Maya," Hattie said. "I told David about tonight's plan, and he wants to help."

Maya pursed her lips tightly, and Hattie understood her skepticism. A willingness to help didn't equate to being pleased to do it. But Maya didn't know how loyal David was to Hattie, nor that he was in love with her. He would do anything to keep her happy and safe, and Hattie would do the same for him.

"I think you're wacky for doing this," David said.

Maya squinted in confusion at his use of slang.

Hattie twirled her index finger in a circle near her head. "Louca," she said, recalling her mother used the word often during her childhood when referring to her father.

"Ah." Maya nodded. "I can't disagree, but the police have left us no choice. Baumann is rich and powerful and has them in his pocket. Someone has to expose him. Otherwise, he'll take more women and do God knows what to them."

Maya's concern was correct, but Hattie knew the truth. Baumann would stop snatching up women once he found her father—all the more reason Hattie had to act. She needed to fix what her family had caused and save the women Baumann had captured.

"You need to play this smart, Maya," David said. "Vargas is set up right out front again, but don't go anywhere with Baumann unless you're sure Hattie and I have you in our sights. Scream if you have to, but don't let him take you without one of us giving you a signal. Ideally, he'll try getting to you while you're walking from the club to your car. When he does, Vargas or I will be right there." David pulled his pistol from his waistband. "Hattie and I are both armed tonight. That makes three guns against Baumann and whoever he brings with him."

"More like ten guns." Maya laughed. "Half the staff out there carry pistols, including me." She hiked up her skirt and raised her left leg bent at the knee atop a chair, exposing a strap securing a derringer around her thigh. "If there's any trouble in the club, we'll handle it."

"At least you're prepared," David said.

Maya cocked her head. David had clearly irked her. "I've been holding my own long before you arrived." She shook her head. "This is precisely why I don't hire men. Every one of you thinks we're helpless without you."

David turned sheepish. "Sorry. I didn't mean—"

"I know exactly what you meant. After your drunken episode the other night, don't you think it's time we air things out?"

"What do you mean?" David asked.

"I know you and Hattie have a protective partnership that's not romantic. But you don't like me because she's helping me find Anna, and I don't particularly like you because of your objections. If this is going to work, we need to get over our dislike for one another."

"That might be hard to do," David harrumphed. "Your seduction is holding her back."

"How am I holding her back?" Maya asked.

"Don't, David," Hattie said, thinking he must have heard her and Eva talking yesterday in the kitchen or Eva blabbed.

"No, Hattie." He put up his hand to shush her. "She needs to hear this." He shifted his attention to Maya. "She's been offered a job singing regularly at the Golden Club, but she hasn't given them an answer because she doesn't want to hurt your feelings. Singing at the Palace is exactly why she came to Rio."

Maya snapped her stare toward Hattie. "Is that true?"

Hattie had never felt angry enough to strangle someone, but that moment brought her pretty close. David had no right to tell Maya about the decision facing her. She sighed. "Yes, but—"

"No buts," Maya said. "You'd be crazy to turn down the Palace. You can't let an opportunity like this pass you by because you feel a certain loyalty to me."

"I haven't met with them yet to hear the terms of their offer, but I'm hoping to come up with a compromise where I can perform at both venues and continue bringing more business to the Halo Club. You have a wonderful place here, and I love the plan you have for it. I want to help make that dream come true for you and your sister."

"The staff will be impossible if you work at both places." Maya grinned.

"I guess I could get used to their bowing." Hattie laughed. "But we should rethink how I arrive for performances after tonight's crowd cornered me past the door."

"I think you're right." Maya dropped her smile and shook her head vigorously. "What am I thinking? The Palace will never let you work at both places. They'll want an exclusive contract."

"Then I won't accept. I had a similar contract with RCA. They not only controlled what I recorded but also where I performed. I won't do that again. I want the freedom to choose and control my schedule."

Maya's smile returned. "You would really do that for me?"

Hattie caressed Maya's cheek. "In a heartbeat."

"I hate to break this up," David said, "but we have a show to perform."

They had plenty of time until the show, so David's impatience was a sign that something bothered him. He'd seen Hattie show affection with women before, so his reaction was worrisome. Considering his true feelings, being in a cover relationship wasn't fair to him. Unless things changed, she would have to send him home after this was over.

Maya cleared her throat. "And a kidnapper to trap."

Dreading the thought of something going wrong, Hattie had to ask again, "You're sure about this?"

"I'm positive, and I feel better now that I know David is here," Maya said. "Another set of eyes makes it much safer."

"I guess men are good for something." He smirked.

~

Hattie sang her first show to another packed crowd, but Baumann didn't appear. As she ascended the stage for her second show of the night, she noticed a new set of people filling the room. Most tables were occupied, but one near the corridor leading to the restrooms was empty. A couple approached it to sit, but a man dressed in a dark suit standing nearby waved them off. He was saving it for someone, giving Hattie a sliver of hope that Baumann might still arrive.

Maya kept the house lights up so Hattie could easily see the audience.

Halfway through the set, she wasn't disappointed. Baumann arrived. He sat at the table the man had been saving, and a second man in a suit joined him. During a song, Hattie acknowledged Baumann with a nod, and David relayed his understanding that their target had arrived. She scanned the dining room but failed to locate Maya. What a time for her to be in the kitchen or restroom. Hattie turned up the energy in her performance and divided her attention between Baumann and looking for Maya until the crowd met her with applause and whistles at the end.

Stepping from the stage, Hattie finally located Maya behind the bar. A handful of fans gathered at the bottom of the steps, making it impossible for her to push toward Maya. She whispered to David, who was right behind her, "Make sure Maya knows Baumann is here. I'll change and go to his table in a few minutes. Tell her to give me at least five minutes with him before coming over."

David kissed her head, carrying his satchel of sheet music since they were done for the evening, and whispered back, "I'll be at the bar. Be careful."

Hattie kissed his cheek before he left. Two servers remained nearby while she greeted the fans, signed autographs, and took photographs with a few. Once the line died down, she rushed to her dressing room. She toweled off and changed into the blouse, long skirt, and comfortable flat shoes she arrived in, adding a light sweater to counter the chill the overhead dining room fans swirling the tropical air created.

A gut feeling told her she should not let the pistol out of her reach. She pulled the derringer from her handbag, hiked up her skirt, and slipped it securely into her garter belt. The cold steel against her skin again reminded her of the danger lurking. Knowing Maya was also armed gave her a sliver of reassurance that this could end well, but she could not shake the feeling that the odds were not in their favor.

As she searched for the doorknob, Hattie's hand shook. She paused to settle her nerves and gather the courage needed to fulfill the promise she had made to herself. She would not let those missing women be her family's legacy, nor stop until she found Anna. Releasing a long breath, she opened the door and walked down the empty hallway with its faded paint, passing the three bare hanging ceiling lights in succession. The door at the end of the corridor marked the point from which there would be no going back. She twisted the knob, putting the next part of their plan in motion.

Hattie weaved her way through the dining room. The crowd had thinned significantly, noted by the absence of conversation hum. The only sound was recorded music playing softly in the background. A few audience members acknowledged her, and others wanted to speak with her, but she apologized and pressed on to the back of the room.

When she approached the table, Baumann stood. He was alone. The man who had come in with him was no longer there. Her body tingled from a bubbling outrage as she remembered the man she was about to share a table with had kidnapped at least nine women. But Hattie capped her anger and put on a broad smile.

"Good evening, Miss James. That was quite the performance." He pulled out a chair for her.

"Thank you, Mr. Baumann." Hattie sat, placing her handbag on the table. A server came by and asked for her order. She requested ice water as she had immediately after every performance. "I wanted to give you an accurate picture of what could be in store for Elsa if you continue her singing lessons. When we first met, she told me she wanted to become a performer like me. I can help make her dream happen."

"Despite her hero worship, she must learn to obey," he said.

"Perhaps she and I are too close in age. She might be less distracted if my mother taught her."

"I thought your mother only teaches from her studio."

"I'm sure I can convince her otherwise, especially when I tell her how promising Elsa is."

The server dropped off the glass of water, and Hattie sipped.

He leaned back in his chair and studied Hattie for several beats. "Why is my daughter's future so important to you?"

"I won't insult you by saying that Elsa is so uniquely talented that success is guaranteed. She is talented, and with work and dedication, she can be very good. But I see a young girl without a mother or any friends. The truth is I feel sympathy for her. She has latched onto me and singing as her means of escape. I would like to foster her dream."

"You make a convincing argument, Miss James. I will consider it."

Hattie felt tired. Maybe it was the lack of sleep from tossing and turning most of the night, or perhaps the weight of everything since coming to Rio had finally set hold. Before she could yawn, Maya approached the table right on cue with rage in her eyes. It was something she didn't have to fake. Hattie also felt it the moment she sat at Baumann's table.

"Maya?" Hattie asked.

"How could you sit with this man after what I showed you?" Maya said, anger dripping from each word.

"It's all speculation, Maya. That picture could be completely innocent." Hattie's stomach tightened and cramped, causing her to wince. Perhaps it was nerves from setting the trap.

"Then let's settle this." Maya pulled the photograph of Baumann and Mrs. Moyer in the Golden Room from an envelope in her hand and slammed it on the table. "Explain this, Mr. Baumann. The woman you're sitting with disappeared the night this picture was taken. My sister disappeared after you walked out of this club with her. That's no coincidence. Where did you take her? Where did you take my sister?"

Baumann inspected the picture. "I don't owe you an explanation, but if I remember correctly, seating was limited that night, and the staff asked if I wouldn't mind sharing a table. As I recall, the woman was also agreeable, and we shared a pleasant conversation during dinner."

"Nonsense." Maya dismissed him with an insulting wave before snatching up the photo. "The police have been of no help with my sister's disappearance, so I'm taking this to the media. Perhaps more pressure will force them to do their job."

"I think I should leave," Baumann said.

Hattie grunted as her stomach twisted, and a wave of nausea washed over her.

"Hattie?" Maya turned, her voice suddenly soft and filled with worry. "What is it?"

"My stomach." Hattie looked up. The trap and Baumann had to wait. "Take me to the bathroom." She stood.

Maya threw an arm around Hattie's shoulder and guided her to the restroom corridor a few feet away. The back door was propped open, suggesting employees were outside for a smoke break. They were ten feet from the ladies' room. Hattie felt unsteady on her feet as the hallway wobbled. Her surroundings went out of focus.

Five feet away. Maya tightened her hold when Hattie's legs buckled, yanking her straighter. "Are you okay?"

"I don't know," Hattie slurred. As the room spun, she remembered

David's caution about the water at the plantation and questioned whether Baumann had put something into her water glass when she wasn't looking.

A voice behind them asked, "Can I help?"

"No, I have—" Maya said before someone pushed them farther down the hallway.

The door flew open to darkness. A man rushed in and snatched Hattie from Maya's grip. She struggled and tried to lift her arms and legs, but they flopped and wobbled weakly like Jell-O, making her feel like a rag doll. Hattie glanced over her shoulder, discovering the man who had reserved Baumann's table earlier had one hand over Maya's mouth and the other around her waist, forcing her toward the door.

The man who had Hattie dragged her to the side street where a delivery van was parked. He rushed her to the open back doors and threw her inside, thudding her shoulder onto the hard metal floor. It hurt, but she hadn't the strength to scream. She tried to focus through the spinning but could only catch brief glimpses. She couldn't be sure, but the van appeared void of cargo.

The sounds of struggling and muffled screams were close but stopped suddenly after a loud thwack. Then Maya was tossed in beside her, but she didn't move. *God no,* Hattie tried to scream as terror overtook her, but she still couldn't focus enough to raise her voice.

"Don't die," Hattie mumbled before passing out.

33

Heinz wiped the corners of his mouth with a cloth napkin before throwing enough cash on the table to cover the bill for his two drinks and a sizeable tip for the waitress. Things could not have gone better.

Getting up from his chair, he let a small grin form. It hadn't cost him much to get the two women precisely where he wanted them—unconscious inside the back of his delivery van. By now, the van was traveling north out of town, leaving only two loose ends to clean up before Heinz could head home. He briefly locked eyes with one at the bar before weaving through the tables and going to the main door. When he reached the entryway, someone placed a hand on his shoulder, stopping him.

"Not so fast, Baumann," David Townsend, Hattie's pet dog, slurred. "Where's Hattie?"

"Feeling disoriented? A little nauseous?" Heinz said as Townsend wobbled on his feet. "My guess is the room is spinning about now. You have about a minute or two before you pass out."

"What did you give me? How?" Townsend slammed a hand against the wall to keep steady.

"It's called scopolamine, an extract from the white angel trumpet growing wild on my plantation. After the show, the bartender who served you and Hattie water kindly added a drop to your glass at a price of only a thousand Brazilian reals. That's two hundred American dollars. That's how much Hattie James's life is worth to these people. They adore her on the stage and treat her like royalty. The next minute, they agree to drug her for pocket change."

"You son of a bitch." Townsend threw a punch but wildly missed and stumbled to the floor. He struggled more, but it was useless. The drug was working its way through his system, and it was only a matter of moments before he lost his fight.

"There is no use in fighting, Mr. Townsend. Don't worry. You won't die, at least not here." The main door opened, and Beck appeared. He waved the man over. "Take him."

"If you hurt her . . ." Townsend slurred.

"Mr. Townsend?" A server appeared in the entryway, looking concerned. "Is everything all right?" Townsend passed out, and the server caught him.

"Poor man can't hold his liquor," Heinz said, exiting quickly with Beck. Townsend was one lucky man, at least for now, and would require cleaning up once Heinz dealt with Hattie and her friend. If it was the last thing Heinz did, Townsend would not become another stain on his record.

He and Beck walked outside the Halo Club, crossed the street at the corner, and headed toward a parked sedan. The car was between streetlights, so its interior was dark—the perfect conditions. He opened the front passenger side door and slipped inside while Beck remained on the street.

The driver appeared surprised. "Mr. Baumann, did everything go as planned?" Vargas asked.

"Nearly," Heinz said. The only loose end was Townsend. "Thank you for keeping them in your sights the last few days, but I'm afraid you've outlived your usefulness."

Vargas narrowed his brow in confusion. "What do you mean? I've done everything you've asked."

Vargas had been an asset, but the man didn't know the meaning of discretion. He had been living well beyond his official salary for months and had drawn attention to himself by buying a new car and moving into an expensive apartment. "And I've paid you well for it. Too well, I'm afraid.

Now, our partnership must end." Heinz gestured toward the driver's window and nodded in the darkness when Beck approached.

Vargas turned his head left.

Beck raised his sharpened stiletto knife and slit Vargas's throat. Vargas reached up with both hands to stem the bleeding, but he was too late. He choked on his own blood. His coughing and spitting morphed into an amusing gurgle, signaling his time was almost over. He kicked frantically at the floorboard, fighting desperately to hold on to life.

His body slumped forward once his arms fell to his sides. Heinz caught him before he hit the car horn on the steering wheel, leaned Vargas back against the seat, and lowered his fedora over his face, making him appear asleep. The only obstacle was out of the way.

Heinz exited the car, joined Beck on the sidewalk, and walked toward their sedan. The stage was set. Now, he just needed to give Elsa the right amount of scopolamine, as he had done whenever he needed to ensure she slept through the night.

The hunt was on.

34

Hattie woke but kept her eyes closed. Opening them would have been unwise, if not impossible, until the wave of nausea passed. Her head pounded like a seven-margarita hangover, and her mouth was drier than her sister's Christmas fruitcake. She dreaded moving her tongue and the coming feeling of it being stripped raw from the roof of her mouth, but it had to be done if she hoped to speak again.

She peeled her tongue away like she was unzipping a woman's dress—slowly and tentatively, prolonging the anticipation and agony. However, this was out of fear, not lust. Once the last bit of flesh snapped away, she licked her parched lips without success. Every drop of moisture in her mouth had been sucked out by . . . By what? It disturbingly felt like a hangover.

Hattie tried to remember why she had tossed three years of sobriety down the drain. She had had enough of days like this and would never voluntarily return to this place, where every muscle was a limp noodle and her stomach was a sour volcano threatening to erupt. She couldn't even say mornings because, after most of her benders, she didn't wake until most kids had returned from school.

So why was she in this state? The last thing she remembered was . . . singing. Yes. She sang at the Halo Club and felt like a star surrounded by fans hounding her for an autograph and picture. Then she remembered

Maya looking ever so appealing in her blouse and skirt but also looking . . . angry. Yes, she was furious, and so was Hattie. They were at the table, and . . . Baumann.

Her eyes shot open at the realization they had been with Heinz Baumann, and Maya was the bait to trap him, but something went terribly wrong. Hattie remembered thinking she had been drugged as she was dragged outside, but the rest was blurry, and so were her dark surroundings. She reached between her legs to feel for her derringer, but it was gone. She frantically scanned the area and caught sight of the cinder block walls and a barred door resembling those in a jail cell. Enough scant light poured through the bars for her to spot something in the opposite back corner in the shadows.

Hattie maneuvered to stand, but her arms and legs were too wobbly to push herself up. She scooted along the cold, stone floor toward the silhouetted object and gasped when the outline came into view. "Maya."

Hattie moved faster than ever, sidling beside Maya's half-propped-up, slouched body and caressing her matted hair. "Maya, wake up." But she didn't stir. The dimness made it impossible to discern whether she was breathing, so Hattie had to check for signs of life. Her hand shook as it descended toward her chest and touched the soft cotton on Maya's blouse, but she still could not tell whether Maya was alive. There was only one way to discover the cold, hard truth. She pressed her hand firmly and waited for confirmation.

"Thank goodness." Hattie's hand rose and fell to Maya's shallow breathing. She summoned all her strength, settled Maya in a more comfortable position, and tried again to rouse her. "Maya, wake up," she whispered, caressing her cheek, but Maya refused to stir.

Nightmarish possibilities took form as more of her memory returned. Hattie remembered hearing a crack before one of Baumann's men threw Maya into the delivery van. She had no way of knowing how long they had been unconscious, but she had a feeling Maya should be awake unless she was hurt badly. Hattie removed her sweater, balled it, and placed it between Maya's head and the block wall as a cushion. She looked for signs of injury, but there wasn't enough light to be sure.

Hattie didn't own all the blame for the predicament, but enough for guilt to raise its ugly head. The plan was Maya's idea, but none of this—Maya being hurt and them being captured—would have happened if Hattie hadn't snooped around and found that picture from the Golden Room. She could have stood her ground and objected to Maya's idea. Could have insisted on leaving the investigation and capture of Baumann to the professionals. But she did neither. Now she had to live knowing she could have . . . should have done more.

Hattie leaned closer, kissed Maya on the forehead, and whispered, "I'm so sorry I failed you."

"You didn't fail me," Maya mumbled before lifting her hand to her head. She grimaced. "My head is killing me."

"Did they drug you or hit you over the head?" Hattie asked.

"Hit me, I think." Maya rubbed a spot on the back of her head. "I feel a knot."

"Let me see." Hattie placed her hand on Maya's head and explored with her fingers. She discovered a lump the size of a walnut but felt no dampness. "I don't think you're bleeding. How is your vision?" Hattie sat back and held up two fingers. "How many fingers am I holding up?

"Two." Maya blinked.

"Good. You still have your gun?"

Maya formed a sloppy grin. "Why don't you check for me?"

Hattie wagged her head, holding back a snicker. "You're loopy."

Maya felt between her legs. "Gone. How long was I out?"

"Don't know. Just woke up. Can you stand?"

"I think so. How about you? You were sick and dizzy in the club. Did Baumann drug you?"

"I think he did." Saying so was a relief. No matter how this situation turned out, at least Hattie hadn't thrown away her sobriety. Baumann had stolen it. If they didn't get out of this alive, she could die holding her head high. "But it's wearing off. I can probably stand now."

Hattie pushed herself up, realizing her shoes were missing. Her limbs were not as weak as when she first woke, so she helped Maya to her feet and steadied her, noting that her shoes were also gone. "Are you sure you're okay?"

"I'm far from okay, but I'm well enough to find a way out of here."

They stepped toward the metal bars, holding each other up. Hattie pushed on the door, but it was locked. Another cell with the same metal bars was visible across the cobblestone aisle about eight feet away. She craned her head left and right, discovering another two similar cells. A cinder block wall was on one end, and a solid metal door was on the other. If the pattern held for her side, this area had six built-in cages. This had to be where Baumann took the missing women.

Hattie talked in a soft voice so it would not carry beyond the metal door. "Is anyone else here?"

"Yes," a woman said in a meek voice.

"Yes," another said, and another, until she heard five distinct voices. The women across the aisle placed their faces between the bars, and Hattie assumed the others on the same side as her cell did as well.

"Anna?" Maya clutched the bars with both hands and pressed her face between an opening. "It's Maya."

Anna appeared at the bars one cell down and across from them. "My God, Maya."

"Thank God, I found you." Tears rolled down Maya's cheeks. And Hattie's. "You're alive." Maya slumped, and Hattie buoyed her with an arm.

"He took you too?" Anna asked.

"Who took you? Baumann?" Maya asked.

"I don't know," Anna said. "He said his name was Heinz."

"Yes, that's him." Maya gripped the bars tighter. "Heinz Baumann. He came to the club. Why the hell did you leave with him?"

"I'm not in any mood for one of your lectures, Maya," Anna groused.

"This isn't helping," Hattie whispered. "Ask her why he took her."

Maya nodded her understanding. "I'm sorry, Anna. What happened? Why did he take you?"

"He must have drugged me in the car because I woke up here. He keeps asking us about an American diplomat."

Hattie gasped, covering her mouth with her hand. Anna had confirmed her suspicion. Baumann had taken all those women in search of her father.

Maya turned to her. "Hattie? What's wrong? Do you know something about who Baumann is looking for?"

"Can we talk about this later?" Hattie said low enough so only Maya could hear.

"No." Maya's eyes narrowed. Her expression turned hard. "Tell me now. Who is this American diplomat?"

"Please, Maya. Not now," Hattie begged. If the others knew the truth, they would never trust her.

Maya grabbed her by both arms. Desperation and anger filled her eyes. "I said no. Tell me what you know. Now."

Maya's tone and aggressiveness frightened Hattie. Yet another person was forcing her to do something she didn't want. She expected it from the FBI and RCA executives but not from the woman she had made love to only two nights ago. She hoped for support and understanding, but this proved she didn't know the real Maya Reyes. Or maybe she did. Perhaps Maya was precisely like Hattie, willing to do anything to protect her family, even if it meant pushing away a lover.

More tears welled in Hattie's eyes. "His name is Karl James."

"James?" Maya squinted in confusion.

"Baumann is looking for my father."

Maya stepped back, stung by betrayal. "Your father?"

"Yes." Hattie briefly thought about concocting a lie to keep Maya from feeling more betrayed, but the lies had to stop. She explained about her father's arrest for giving secrets to the Nazis, his escape, the FBI coercing her to come to Rio, their suspicion that Baumann was a Nazi, and her suspicion that Baumann might think her father was here because of his connection to her mother. She ended by telling her about having already seen her father. Twice.

"My God, Hattie." Maya jerked her head back. "You knew why Baumann took Anna and said nothing?"

"I'm sorry, Maya." Hattie reached out to caress and reassure her, but Maya shrugged off her touch. "He's my father. I couldn't say anything until I was absolutely sure. Now we know why the women were taken. The ones who worked at the docks might have seen my father arrive on a ship. The others had connections to my mother or me. You have no idea how much this has eaten me up inside."

Maya looked at Hattie strangely, as if she was seeing her for the first time. "So, you helped me find Anna out of guilt, not for me."

"It was both." This was all going so badly. Even if by some miracle they survived, she had lost Maya. Hattie was sure of it, but this was no time to argue. "Debating this won't help things. We need to focus on getting out of here." Hattie leaned her head through the bars. "What can any of you tell us about this place? Who have you seen?"

Maya translated her question.

A woman further down spoke Portuguese, and Maya translated. "I don't know where we are, but I think I was drugged when they brought me here."

"I think they drug the food or water to make us sleep," Anna said, "which is why I only eat and drink what I must to live."

Another spoke in English. "There are five of us left. There were four others, but men took them two at a time. We never saw the women again."

Still another spoke Portuguese, and Maya translated. "I've seen four different men. Three are dressed like workers. Two brought me here, and another two give us food every day. The one who asks about the diplomat always wears a white suit."

"The man in the suit must be Baumann," Hattie said, but she omitted her suspicion that one man might have been her father. "We must be on his coffee plantation. It's an hour's drive north of Rio. I've been there twice."

Anna shook her head in disappointment. "That means we're far from anyone who can help us."

Hattie turned to Maya. "Maybe David and Vargas will."

"David, the piano player?" Anna asked.

"Yes, and Investigator Vargas from the police department," Hattie said. "He's been helpful." She explained Inspector Silva's reluctance to investigate and Vargas's help, including the plan to use Maya as bait to draw out Baumann. "By now, they must know we're missing and should be here anytime with help."

Maya sighed. "I hope so."

35

Darkness had fallen on the Plantação de Lobo, and Mr. Beck had issued strict orders for the night before leaving the plantation. If a man wasn't off performing an intelligence-gathering mission, he would remain in his quarters until called for duty. Karl heard knocks on other bedroom doors several times, followed by men leaving their hut, but no one had come for him. He kept vigil at the tiny window in his bedroom, watching the activity in the compound. Baumann and Beck left the compound five hours earlier in his personal vehicle. A plantation delivery van followed thirty minutes later. Then, in reverse order, the van returned two hours ago, and Baumann's car arrived a half hour later.

Activity at night and orders like Beck's were commonplace on the plantation, but something was up. Karl felt it in his bones. Movement in the compound picked up, making him too nervous to sit still much longer. Instinct told him that Hattie was in danger and he would not return to this hut once he left it.

Whatever was going on in the compound, Karl had to prepare to defend himself and Hattie. He opened the compartment in the baseboard, removed the money and fake identification papers, and stuffed them into a waist wallet secured around his belly. He fished out the hidden pistol and strapped it around his ankle above his boot. Finally, he pulled out a small vial of liquid and placed it in his canteen pouch. Beck had instructed Karl to add three drops of the liquid to the porridge when feeding the women. He suspected the container held an incapacitating drug to keep the women docile, so he snatched one bottle yesterday. Tonight, it might come in handy.

After snapping the knife sheath to his belt, he filled his canteen from the water jug in his room. Following several more minutes of movement in the compound, Karl lost his patience. After putting on his light jacket, he opened his bedroom door and walked toward the door at the end of the dark hallway, stopping when the door creaked open. Illumination from the compound floodlights poured into the doorway, silhouetting a stocky man. The figure was unmistakable and could cause trouble for him.

"Good evening, Herr Beck," Karl said in German.

"What are you doing out of your room?" Beck remained in the shadows. His tone sounded more like an accusation than a question.

"I needed to use the restroom." Karl raised his canteen. "And get more water."

"I ordered all men to remain in their rooms." Beck narrowed his eyes, clearly suspicious.

"Perhaps when you're my age, you'll understand that the body doesn't always listen to orders. Nature's urgencies often hit at inconvenient times, especially at night."

"Why are you wearing a jacket to go to the bathroom?"

"Mosquitos. I always cover up while I'm in there."

"Perhaps," Beck grunted. "Come with me. We are preparing for a hunt. You're riding with Herr Baumann again."

"May I get my hat in case it rains tonight?"

Beck gestured his chin down the hallway. "Make it quick."

Karl rushed down the hallway to his room, grabbed his fedora, and paused after glancing at the dresser. He had snagged two extra biscuits from dinner tonight to tide him over for what he had expected would be a long night's vigil, but he now had other plans for them. He shoved them into the deep front pockets of his pants.

Karl returned to the hallway and followed Beck to the milling barn, where men were loading a truck.

"Set up the torches with the men, then go with Jacobs to fetch the animals," Beck ordered.

"Yes, sir," Karl said.

He slung his canteen across his shoulder when Beck left and loaded the remaining torches and the barrel of kerosene on the truck's bed. Like last weekend, they drove on the access road to the compound's edge at the first rows of the coffee trees. Once they dipped and set up the torches, another man lit them, creating an ominous entrance into the fields. Into the darkness. Into death.

Karl and Jacobs descended the stairs to the basement while the other men went to the stables to gather the horses and rifles. They entered the juncture where Karl had seen Hattie and Elsa two days earlier, and Jacobs unlocked the steel door leading to the holding cells. They walked deep inside, and Jacobs opened the last door.

It creaked open.

As before, three overhead lights illuminated the three cell doors on each side of the aisle.

"Three tonight," Jacobs said. "Can you handle two?"

"I'm sure of it."

"We better use handcuffs just in case." Jacobs walked to the end, retrieved the key and restraints, and handed Karl two. "Center left," Jacobs said before stepping in front of the cell closest on the right.

Karl approached the center cell and ordered, "Hands through the bars."

Two women stepped from the shadows. Karl's heart nearly stopped when Hattie gasped. He could not say her name for fear of Jacobs overhearing, but he mouthed it, silently berating himself for failing to keep Baumann from her. Whether she told Baumann who Karl was, she was dead either way unless he stepped in, but the timing and circumstances had to be perfect, not in a dungeon with limited means of escape.

"Are you—" the other woman started to say before Hattie placed a hand over her mouth. Karl studied the woman's face and recognized her as the owner of the Halo Club, where Hattie performed.

Hattie whispered something to the woman, and they extended their hands through the bars to be cuffed. When he got to Hattie, he pretended she was struggling. "Don't fight it," he shouted, pulling her close and whispering, "Stay together. Strength in numbers. Find the Southern Cross. Head north and hide in the jungle. I'll find you before dawn."

Hattie scrunched her nose, a sign that she was confused.

"Go north. Stay together. Keep moving. I'll find you." Karl hoped he had given her the right advice. He knew the north end of the plantation had the most land to work with, and she could avoid being seen for hours, but so many other things could kill her. Her chance of survival was slim between the wolves in the fields and the jaguars and poisonous snakes in the jungle.

Putting those thoughts aside, he cuffed his daughter as Jacobs approached, holding his prisoner by the arm, and unlocked Hattie's cell. Karl opened the door and said, "Don't give us trouble. Otherwise, we'll come back and kill the others."

Hattie and the woman followed Jacobs through the door and down the corridor, with Karl bringing up the rear. When they reached the stairs, Karl had a decision to make. This was the perfect opportunity to pass Hattie the pistol hidden at his ankle. A gun might give her a fighting chance in the fields, but it might also ruin everything. She didn't know to wait until she and others were in the fields or camouflaged in the jungle and might use it too early while everyone was still in the compound. Hattie might get off one or two shots, and Karl might take out another two with his knife, but they would still be outnumbered.

No.

Time was Karl's friend. The other men were wranglers and knew only Baumann would take the kill shot. They would not want to face him afterward if they did otherwise, so that would give him more precious time. Karl couldn't trust the weapon Beck might issue him tonight, so his best bet was to keep the pistol for himself and take out the men one by one.

The group emerged at the top, and the women looked in every direction while they walked, getting their bearings. The torches were aglow, lighting the compound in warm amber colors. By now, Hattie likely recognized the plantation compound. The commotion of the women approaching set off the three German shepherd dogs into a barking frenzy. Their handlers quieted them and reformed a semicircle with their backs to the torches in front of the horses. Beck stood near the men. Baumann had yet to make an entrance.

Jacobs ushered the women to the center and threw out three pairs of sandals after uncuffing them. "Put these on. You'll need them."

Karl nodded to Hattie, sending the message to do as the man said.

The women donned the oversized sandals. Hattie stood alone, but the other two women embraced, shedding tears and speaking Portuguese.

"Quiet," Jacobs shouted.

The two women stopped speaking and held on to each other. They looked terrified. Hattie did as well. Karl tried to reassure her with his sympathetic eyes, but his gesture seemed to have been lost in the darkness or tense emotions swirling about.

Jacobs walked toward the other men and joined their talking and laughing. Karl veered toward the horses. Only one had saddlebags. The satchels likely contained the bags and rope needed to return the dead bodies to the compound after the hunt. Karl headed toward it since he was Baumann's protector and cleanup man for the night. He had ridden the mare before. She was the slowest and weakest in the barn. That was no coincidence. He suspected Baumann wanted him handicapped against the faster riders. A rifle was mounted on the saddle, but Karl trusted it would not work.

He counted four other men, excluding Baumann, who would be on the hunt tonight. Curiously, he was the only one without a sidearm. Baumann clearly had something in store for him, and he needed to even the odds while the others were occupied. He slipped between the horses in the shadows and tightened the flank cinch two notches on Jacobs's saddle. If he had loosened the strap, the saddle might slide when the rider mounted, which would have been quickly corrected. However, tightening the cinch ensured the horses could not take full breaths and would tire more easily.

Karl moved on to Jacobs's rifle. Though the weapon was reserved mainly to protect the rider from wildlife, not harm the prey, he could not chance Jacobs would not turn it on Hattie. He had field-stripped the Mauser Karabiner 98k enough times to know removing the firing pin was the most effective and least noticeable way to disable the weapon. However, he hadn't the time. He needed to better his odds and had to chance the dark would mask what he was about to do.

After placing the safety in the takedown position, he removed the bolt and returned the rifle to its leather sheath. He moved on to the next horse and to the next but heard the clopping of hooves and returned to his horse before sabotaging the fourth. After hiding the bolts in his saddlebag, he stepped to the front of his horse and petted her shoulder and long neck.

Moments later, Baumann appeared on horseback, dressed in the same hunting attire he wore last weekend. The man circled the huddled women, sizing up his prey.

Meanwhile, the dogs strained against the end of their leashes. The other horses rocked back and forth, offering an occasional snort. They were all eager to start the games. Baumann completed his second circle and stopped, leaning a forearm against the saddle horn. His horse remained still.

"It's a shame you won't be able to give my daughter more singing lessons, Miss James," Baumann said in English. "She is quite taken with you."

"You won't get away with this, Baumann," Hattie said, stiffening her posture and balling her fists.

"If you're expecting Investigator Vargas or your friend Mr. Townsend to come riding in on their white horses to save you, I'm afraid they won't make it."

"What did you do to them?" Hattie took one step forward in defiance. Fury was in her eyes.

"Sadly, Vargas outlived his usefulness, and Townsend was simply an annoyance. Neither will stop tonight's hunt."

Tears tracked down Hattie's cheek. News of David must have devastated her.

Baumann was heartless and continued. "I will give you a fifteen-minute head start. If you survive until sunrise, I will give you a choice."

"What choice is that?" the other woman from Hattie's cell asked.

"I will give you a gun with one bullet, or I will put you on the auction block and sell you to the highest bidder." Baumann turned to Hattie. "But you are special, Miss James. Tell me where your father is, and you may choose your fate. I won't force you through the hunt."

"I wouldn't tell you even if I knew where he was." Hattie wiped the tears from her face and straightened her posture again. The family fortitude had returned.

"Then tell me where his lists are, and I'll make sure you don't suffer before you die."

"What lists?"

That's right, Hattie, Karl thought. *You know nothing.*

"Come now, Miss James. Surely you know by now your father has something we want. He wouldn't safeguard the lists just anywhere or with just anyone. He had to have given them to someone he trusts, and Karl James trusts no one more than you."

"I still don't know what you're talking about, but I wouldn't tell you anything if I did. I'd rather die knowing I didn't help an evil man like you." Hattie scanned the area, looking at the men and giving Karl the impression that she was searching for him, but he stayed in the shadows so she wouldn't lock on him.

"That's a shame, Miss James," Baumann said. "The world will miss your talent."

Karl balled his fists, silently pleading for her to not focus on him and pressing so hard his nails likely drew blood. He wasn't afraid for himself but for her. He had done everything to shield his family from the life he led, but he clearly failed Hattie, just as he had failed Eva. Sometimes, he wished he had never chosen this path, but his recruiter had convinced him otherwise. The professor had said his German heritage, education, and the connections he'd made as a diplomat made him the only candidate to infiltrate the Nazi spy rings inside the United States. But now, the lists he'd collected against both sides as part of his cover and partly as insurance were hotter than lava and equally lethal. He had no choice but to hide them with Hattie. It was a decision he now regretted, one he was willing to die for in order to correct.

36

Hattie focused on Baumann, steady atop his steed, the image of power. He was also the definition of evil. He was about to hunt her, Maya, and Anna in some sadistic sport that would end in their deaths or being sold into sexual slavery. But most frightening, Hattie's father was familiar with the event. Baumann must have done this before with other women and with her father's help. One hostage had said four other women had been in the basement but were taken away, never to return. Baumann had likely hunted them, and her father had done nothing to stop it. The thought turned her stomach, but if Baumann had told the truth about Vargas and David, her father was their only ally. She had no other option but to trust him long enough to survive this ordeal.

Hattie swiveled her head toward the night sky. The glow from the torches masked much of the stars, but she knew the Southern Cross would stand out in the Brazilian sky. Remembering her father's instructions, she searched for the brightest stars—Alpha and Beta Centauri. Finally, over her shoulder, Hattie found them. They would point her toward the cross. The right red giant star Acrux, the farthest point south in the constellation and the bottom of the cross, stood out. From there, she trailed her gaze upward and located the giant red star Gacrux, the top of the cross. Mimosa and Imai, two bright white-blue stars, formed the crossbeam. She drew imaginary lines from the pointer and the cross, found the spot where they intersected, and depicted another line downward to the horizon. There. She found south. Her father had said to head north, so they should stay on course if she kept that point to her back.

Hattie moved closer to Maya and Anna, but Maya extended an arm to keep some distance. The smell of fear between them was strong, but Maya's cold, angry stare was overpowering. Maya had every right to be distrustful, but so far, she had heeded Hattie's warning that they would need her father's help to escape and to not turn him in.

Hattie pushed Maya's arm down and whispered in her ear, "I've been here. Trust me. I know where to go."

"Let the hunt begin." Baumann removed the Luger from his waist holster, raised it, and fired a single piercing shot. Hattie and the others flinched. The dogs barked and thrashed on their leashes while the horses neighed and shuffled in a startled jerk. "Fifteen minutes, ladies."

"Let's go." Hattie tugged Maya's hand. Her legs were still a little weak from the drugs but not so wobbly to keep her from taking advantage of their head start.

Maya grabbed Anna's sleeve, encouraging her to follow. "Come, Anna. Come."

The armed men laughed, forming a line and pushing the women toward the torches. Their ill-fitting sandals made taking full strides on the gravel road impossible. Hattie kept in mind the location of the Southern Cross in the sky and the general direction toward south. If her measurement was correct, the line of torches pointed northeast. She remembered Mr. Beck taking her to the edge of the fields to survey the lush trees during her tour. The access road bisected the field, ultimately curving toward the east. The rows to the right ran easterly, while the ones to the left ran more north-south.

Torches lined the access road, marking their initial route into the dark abyss, but it was deceiving. If they followed it too long, the road would take them in the wrong direction. According to Hattie's father, they would have to venture into the rows of trees to go north.

As soon as they cleared the fiery glow, Maya threw off Hattie's hand, firmed a hold around Anna, and continued running down the road, but their pace slowed dramatically. Both appeared weak as they stomped their way deep into the plantation. Maya likely had a concussion from the blow to her head, and Anna probably was fatigued from a week's worth of incapacitating drugs—all the more reason to stick together. Each had some impairment that would make them more vulnerable to Baumann and his men, but together, they could help each other.

Hattie felt like she could run faster but kept pace with the others, refusing to become separated. Their pace was a fast walk, but Maya and Anna were already breathing hard. Hattie felt taxed, but her energetic stage performances kept her legs and lungs in decent shape. She frequently glanced over her shoulder, orienting on the stars.

Hattie came to the bend in the access road and held her hands out, gesturing for the others to stop. "We need to cut through the fields and head north."

The others stopped, both with chests heaving from the exertion. "Why north?" Maya asked. "The road leads the other way."

"My father said to head north. The road goes east."

"And you believe him?" Maya snarled.

"Wait?" Anna blinked. "Your father is one of them?"

"It's a long story," Hattie said. "Before taking us out of the cell, he told me to head north, keep moving, and hide in the jungle."

"The one who has been feeding us . . . drugging us . . . is your father?" Anna recoiled. "I wouldn't believe a word he says."

"He would never do anything to hurt me," Hattie said. "We must stay together. He said he would find us."

"You, maybe, but what about us?" Anna sneered. "He'll kill us."

"He won't. I won't let that happen." Hattie squeezed Anna's forearm for emphasis.

"We're wasting time," Maya said. "We don't even know which way is north."

"It's that way." Hattie pointed at the trees to her left.

"How can you be sure?" Maya asked.

Hattie looked over her shoulder and pointed toward the sky. "The stars tell me so. If you draw lines from the Southern Cross and the pointer stars, their intersection is true south." Hattie pointed opposite the trees and toward the compound. "That's south. The other way is north. We need to go and stick together. You two are both weak, but we can help each other."

Maya and Anna glanced at each other but still looked unconvinced.

Hattie searched Maya's eyes in the darkness. The moon and stars provided enough illumination for her to see the battle raging behind them. Maya wanted to believe her, but convincing her to trust someone who had deceived them had to be done quickly. The clock was ticking.

"You can trust me, Maya." Hattie placed Maya's hand against her chest and pleaded with her eyes. "I promised to never stop until Anna was safe. I won't break a promise to you. Ever. Can you feel it? I'm telling the truth. If you want to live, come with me."

Tears threatened to fall down Maya's cheeks. She nodded. "Okay. Lead the way."

"Are you crazy?" Anna objected.

"I trust her, Anna. We need to go."

Anna looked back and forth between both women. "You two are sleeping together, aren't you?"

"It doesn't matter." Maya took Anna by the arm. "Let's go." Maya forced her along.

Hattie entered the orchard between two rows, and Maya and Anna followed. Wild birds in the trees hooted and croaked their uneasiness at someone disrupting their nesting grounds. The dirt was damp and muddy from recent overnight rains, so they would leave footprints. She had to hide their trail. "We need to cut through several times to hide the tracks we're making."

The trees on this side of the access road were shorter and less full than the ones on the eastern side, which made them easier to pass through but provided less concealment from Baumann and his men. They would have to reach the jungle before their fifteen-minute head start was up.

Hattie's sweater snagged on the branches as they slugged between the trees, but she was glad she had put it back on before being handcuffed since it protected her skin from the sharp ends. She looked back to check on Maya and Anna since they wore only a single layer of clothing. Anna held her upper arm like she had hurt it.

Hattie stopped and asked, "Are you okay?"

"It's only a scratch," Anna said, still appearing skeptical of Hattie. "Go on."

Hattie continued at a comfortable, steady pace. Maya and Anna helped each other through the shrubs and trees, leaving Hattie to plow through herself. Her route took extra time but was necessary to conceal their tracks and confuse the dogs.

They finally reached the end of the plantings and entered a twenty-yard-wide clearing. On the other side was the start of the thick jungle. The ground between the jungle and orchard was covered with trimmed wild grass and would not leave footprints. It was the perfect spot to cross into the rainforest. Hattie stopped to get her bearings, locating the Southern Cross and pointer stars in the night sky to determine true south. She then turned 180 degrees north.

"This way."

The dogs barked in the distance, followed by strange shouts, marking what Hattie feared was the real start of the hunt.

Maya slumped. "I need to rest."

"We can't stop," Hattie said. The night air had cooled from the day's heat to a comfortable level, but the humidity was still oppressive, making everyone sweaty and tired. She turned to Anna. "Can you continue?"

"I think so," Anna said.

"Good. Stay behind me." Hattie lifted Maya's left arm over her shoulder and wrapped her right arm around Maya's torso. "I have you. We need to keep moving." Buoying Maya, Hattie walked quickly toward the other end of the clearing, coming across a beaten path leading into the jungle.

They entered.

The dogs barked frequently while they followed the beaten trail deeper into the jungle among the palm and flowering trees. Veering off was too dangerous, with the possibility of snakes or jaguars looming in the brush. After passing a tall, barky jequitibá tree, Hattie stumbled over a sizeable depression in the trail, seemingly made by recent rain, taking Maya to the ground with her. Anna rushed forward, helping them to their feet.

"I'm so sorry, Maya," Hattie said, inspecting her from head to toe. "Are you okay?"

"I'm fine." Maya brushed debris from her skirt before looking at Hattie.

Her eyes narrowed with worry. "But you're hurt." She reached up to wipe something from her cheek when Hattie cupped her hand and gently squeezed it.

"I'm fine."

"You nearly broke your necks," Anna said.

"You're bleeding." Maya swiped her thumb against Hattie's cheek, slowly . . . deliberately.

Hattie's skin tingled beneath Maya's caress in a tender pause from the whirlwind that had swept them into this hellish nightmare. With the possibility of death swirling around them, Hattie leaned into Maya's loving gesture. She closed her eyes and swam in the memory of lying skin to skin in Maya's arms. The act of making love was erotic, but pressing their bodies together in the darkness without fear of being seen was pure intimacy. If she were to die tonight, she would carry that image through her final breath.

"Are you sure about this?" Maya asked, breaking Hattie from her trance.

Hattie opened her eyes. Her father had told her to keep moving, but their slow pace, impacted by the drugs and Maya's head injury, made it clear they could not outrun Baumann and his men. "My father said to go north and hide in the jungle."

Maya limped along, leaning her weight on Hattie. "If Baumann doesn't kill us, the wolves, jaguars, or snakes might."

"I was told the plantation is surrounded by a wall," Hattie said.

"That might be true, but I've seen a jaguar jump over five meters high."

"You could have left that part out. It's not very comforting," Hattie groaned.

"You mean like leaving the part about your father out."

"I said I was sorry. What else do you want from me?"

"Honesty," Maya said. "If we get out of this, no more lies between us."

"I promise to tell you everything." Hattie meant every word. She would tell Maya everything about her mother and Helen's betrayal and how she had closed herself off from falling in love since. Tell Maya she was the first woman with whom she wanted to feel vulnerable since that ordeal. Wanted to open her heart to the possibility of being broken again.

"I'll hold you to it," Maya said.

Hattie heard the dogs again. "They're going to catch up soon, but I have an idea. If we nearly broke our necks, the men on horseback might as well. What if we set a trap?"

"Like what?" Maya asked.

"We can make the hole bigger and cover it with leaves." Hattie inspected the area on either side of the depression. The location was perfect, containing minimal shrubs that could block their quick reaction. "We can hide behind the jequitibá tree and overtake the rider after he falls."

"Overtake him with what? Our sandals?" Anna scoffed. "What about the dogs?"

"We haven't heard barking since entering the jungle. We deal with the known enemy, the five men on horseback."

"Six, including your father." Anna nearly spat her words, but Hattie ignored them and scoured the area with her eyes. Hand-sized rocks were partially uncovered in the trail depression. She dug one out.

"We hit him with this." Hattie held up the stone. "A blow to the head will knock him out."

"That could work," Maya said.

Anna narrowed one eye in a sinister look. "Or several blows would kill him." She was hungry to exact revenge for her weeklong captivity.

"Exactly." Before Hattie knew the truth about her father, she never considered bludgeoning a man to death to be within her capability, but Baumann pulling her into his sick game made her willing to do anything to save them.

"Let's do it," Maya said. "I'll gather leaves."

"Anna and I will dig and collect rocks."

Hattie and Anna clawed desperately at the soft dirt to make a hole wide enough and deep enough to trip a rider. Hattie's arms quickly tired, and she cursed herself for not maintaining upper body strength. However, she willed herself not to stop and dug harder, sweat pouring from her brow.

Finally, after chipping most of their nails and embedding mud under them, Hattie and Anna completed the hole and Maya covered it with leaves. The trap was set, and the women hid behind the tall, thick tree where the brush was thin and the threat of snakes was low. They stood quietly with a rock the size of a baseball in each hand, ready to pounce.

Maya stood in the middle, closer to Hattie than Anna, a pleasant change from the beginning of the hunt. The rocks made it impossible to hold hands, but Hattie pressed their bodies together from shoulder to thigh, reliving the image of them in bed together over and over again. Her chest heaved at the memory of their lips touching, hands exploring, and tongues moving gracefully in an erotic dance.

Soon, someone or something rustled through the jungle brush. Maya's chest rose and fell more rapidly, matching Hattie's. Hattie settled her breathing to focus on the advancing danger. The sound became louder with each passing second, suggesting it could not have been a wild animal. A predator would have concealed its movements better.

Anna glanced over her shoulder and nodded at Maya and Hattie. They replied in kind.

A large, oddly shaped silhouette appeared on the path. A snort announced an approaching horse. The women remained still when the rider came into view. The men from the compound were dressed similarly, so it was impossible to tell from his clothing whether this man was her father. She prayed he wasn't, but it was a risk she had to take.

The horse kept a steady pace and passed the women's hiding position. They had gone undetected behind the tree. Three strides later, the horse stumbled and let out a loud squeal as it tumbled over, throwing off its rider. Hattie hadn't considered the danger to the horse and hoped it was unhurt.

The women sprang into action while the horse thrashed on the ground, groaning. They rushed the rider, who lay dazed, avoiding the horse's wildly moving legs. Maya pelted his chest. Anna went directly for the man's head and was relentless, striking him repeatedly. Hattie raised her rock but couldn't bring herself to attack the man who might be her father. She cringed when his body convulsed as blood spattered their clothing. Meanwhile, the horse turned upright and ran off.

"Stop, Anna," Maya said in a hushed voice. But she didn't stop.

Hattie gripped Anna's forearm, preventing it from delivering another blow. Anna turned, her eyes wild with rage. "He's dead, Anna. He's dead."

Anna panted and spat on the man before lowering her arm and turning her anger on Hattie. "No thanks to you."

Hattie finally summoned the courage to determine the man's identity, repeating in her head, *Please don't be Father*. The top and back of the man's head were a bloody, fleshy mess. Hattie slowly rotated the man's head toward her by the chin until she saw his face. She let out a long breath of relief. It was not her father.

Maya fumbled at the man's waist and unbuckled his utility belt, taking his gun and water canteen.

Hattie searched his pockets for anything else they could use and found a box of matches. The canteen was full, which they each took a small swig from, and the belt had extra ammunition for the pistol. They now had the means to fight back. "Let's drag him into the bushes and reset the trap."

"Okay, but I get this," Anna said, snatching the gun from Maya and sneering at Hattie. "I don't trust her to not shoot. She'll be thinking of her poor papa, the Nazi sympathizer."

Anna was right. Hattie was thinking of her father, hoping and praying he found them in time.

37

An hour earlier

Karl watched Hattie and the other women disappear into the darkness, silently promising, *I will find you, Hattie.*

The men released the dogs from their leashes and ordered them to stay so they could chat and laugh. Meanwhile, Beck approached Karl. The man was never pleasant to him, but tonight, he spoke with an extra sneer and spoke in German. "You're riding with Herr Baumann again. Stay close to him the entire night. Understand?"

Karl acknowledged with a nod before Beck headed to speak to Baumann. He went to his horse and pretended to check the saddle cinch and bag straps. When Karl was sure the others were occupied, he removed a biscuit from his front pocket and the vial from his canteen pouch. He wasn't sure how much liquid to add or if it would work on dogs. He aimed to make the dogs too sluggish to pursue Hattie and the others, not put them to sleep or worse. After breaking the biscuit into thirds, he did the math in his head and poured a single drop onto each piece. Now, it was a matter of timing to not give away that he'd drugged them.

Karl moved to his horse's head, stroked her neck, and spoke softly in English. "You're not the fastest, old gal, but I know you have some moves left. I can't make you any promises, but please do me this one favor. My daughter's life depends on whether you and I can outmaneuver your stablemates."

Karl gave his horse one more pat before moving toward the dogs. His internal clock told him he needed to drug the dogs within the next minute for his plan to work. When he came even with the men, Jacobs called him over, holding out a cigarette in one hand. "Feuerzeug?" he asked.

What type of man, especially one who smokes, doesn't carry a lighter? But there was no need to judge him. The man would be dead before sunrise. Karl reached into his front pocket, bypassing the other biscuit, and retrieved his lighter. He flipped open the lid, sparked it to life, and held it close for Jacobs.

"Danke," Jacobs said, gesturing with the lit cigarette, its tip glowing a dim orange.

"Genießen." Karl hoped he enjoyed it because it would be his last.

He continued toward the dogs and greeted the alpha first, letting her sniff the back of his hand. Once his tail wagged, the other two dogs let Karl pet them. Keeping his back to the men, he removed the biscuit pieces from his left shirt pocket and fed one to each dog, handing out a vigorous scratch behind the ear as he did. "Sorry, girls. I hope you'll forgive me."

"Wranglers, it's time," Baumann called out in German. "Herd them."

Jacobs whistled, and the dogs took off running. The men hollered as their horses galloped between the torches and disappeared into the coffee fields.

Karl climbed atop his horse and guided her toward Baumann and Beck. They stopped their conversation. Beck excused himself without acknowledging Karl and headed toward the milling barn.

Baumann sat higher in his saddle until he came eye to eye with Karl. His expression was strange, as if he was relishing the moment with Karl. The possibility was high that Baumann knew he wasn't Fuller, which meant tonight was as much a trap for Karl as it was for Hattie.

They spoke in German.

"Tonight should prove challenging with three prey," Baumann said.

"The greater the difficulty, the greater the glory."

"More Cicero."

"He was a wise man whose quotes hold true today," Karl said.

"The function of wisdom is to discriminate between good and evil." Baumann cocked his head. "Are you a wise man, Herr Fuller?"

"I like to think so."

"And what do you think of my hunt?"

"I suppose it serves a purpose. The men seem to enjoy it."

"But do you?" Baumann asked. "You dislike killing, no?"

"Killing doesn't bother me, but one should never take pleasure from it."

Baumann angled his head again. "Speaking truth is bold."

Karl looked him squarely in the eye. "To paraphrase Cicero, truth is the most sacred endowment of the human mind."

"So it is, Herr Fuller. So it is." Baumann pulled the reins and started his horse on a steady trot toward the torches.

Karl leaned forward in his saddle, patted his horse on the neck, and shortened the reins. "Show me what you got, old gal." With a flick of the straps and a squeeze of his legs, his mare took off in a trot, following Baumann down the access road and through the glowing gauntlet. When Karl caught up at the start of the coffee field, Baumann slowed to a walk.

The man's accuracy with a sniper's scope would limit opportunities for Karl to make his break, so choosing the right moment would be critical. Otherwise, he would be Baumann's next victim, and Hattie would follow.

Baumann had started the hunt in the same fashion as the previous one, suggesting he was a creature of habit. His rigid adherence would play to Karl's advantage. Like last week, Baumann took his time through the coffee fields, and Karl remained close, scanning for predators, animal and human alike, in the scant moonlight.

Logically, staying at Baumann's rear should make for an easy escape. He would only have to lag back and veer off at the right point. But Karl sensed a trap. He could not be sure because sounds echoed in the darkness, but he heard shouts from only three wranglers and thought he heard one behind him in the fields, a direction the women would not have gone. Karl had a gut feeling Baumann had assigned a wrangler for him, ordering him to shoot if Karl broke off. If that were the case, doing the expected would be a deathtrap, leaving only the unexpected as a viable option.

The end of the plantings came into view, which meant the clearing before the jungle was ahead—the juncture Karl had been waiting for. He slowed his horse to give her space for a running start when the time came. The aisle between the rows of coffee trees was wide enough for two people to walk, but not two horses. He would have to wait until Baumann had cleared the last tree to make his move, but that would not leave much time. If Baumann kept to his habit, as soon as he passed the trees, he would draw his sniper rifle from its sheath and ready it for his prey. Karl would have seconds to cross the clearing and travel deep enough into the jungle to escape Baumann's crosshairs.

Karl leaned forward in his saddle and stroked his mare's neck. "All right, old gal. It's do or die time." She was older but still had agility and could transition to a faster pace quicker than any nag in the barn. Her problem was that she could not sustain it.

His timing had to be perfect. After pushing his hat down on his head to secure it, he tightened the reins around his hand and squeezed his legs rapidly against her sides four times, urging her into an instant canter.

When Baumann's horse reached the last trees in the rows and Karl saw a sliver of an opening, he leaned well forward in his saddle, rising a few inches, and kicked hard. The old gal put it into gear and transitioned into a gallop like her life depended on it.

"That's it, girl," Karl whispered. She steered herself through the minute opening, bumping into Baumann's steed as she passed. He almost thought she did it on purpose. "Good, girl," he said. He nearly lost his hat but pushed it down and secured it.

Baumann jostled in his saddle. The time to settle and orient himself provided Karl with the extra seconds to make his getaway. The mare glided across the clearing. She aimed for the trailhead opening at the jungle's edge as if she knew where Karl planned to take her. She snorted and stretched her legs in perfect form without wasting energy.

The old gal still had it in her.

Karl kept a forward lean and controlled his bounce to help her. Within seconds, they reached the well-worn trail, but with Baumann's long reach with his scope, they weren't out of immediate danger yet. Karl continued to kick, telling her so. She gave another snort, and spit flew from her mouth, hitting Karl's hand. He crouched lower toward her ear and growled, "A little more, girl. A little more."

They scraped tree leaves, branches, and shrubs at top speed, but the mare wasn't deterred. She leaped over roots and rocks without breaking stride.

A shot rang out. The bullet whizzed past Karl's head, missing him and his mare. The trail turned, and his horse slowed a fraction, navigating the twist and escaping Baumann's view. Karl straightened in the saddle and gave his mare a steady squeeze, telling her she could slow. He eased her to a walk and veered off the main path onto a narrower, less traveled one that he thought would lead him north.

Karl gave her a vigorous pat on the neck. "You deserve a flush, open pasture for the rest of your life."

Now, he had to find Hattie and leverage his advantage. Unless they were forewarned, the wranglers considered him one of them, not a threat, especially on horseback. He let the mare set the pace as she navigated through the jungle but steered her when he wanted to take another path.

The whinny of another horse told Karl a wrangler was nearby. Saving his ankle pistol as a last resort, he unsnapped the tie securing his knife in its sheath, but he had to get close enough to the rider to use it.

He continued down the trail, stopped his mare at a spot wide enough for two horses to stand side by side, and waited. Moments later, a rider appeared on the trail. Schmidt held the saddle horn with one hand and a long whip in another. The rawhide was not for his horse but for the prey. A wrangler was not allowed to fire at the women, but he could entice them with the sting of a good lashing.

Schmidt lined up their horses side by side, facing opposite directions on the trail, and acknowledged Karl. "Herr Fuller."

"I have a note from Herr Baumann," Karl said in German.

Schmidt blinked in confusion but did not question Karl's claim.

Karl reached into his right shirt pocket with his left hand, where he typically stuffed receipts and notes. He wasn't sure what was in there, but any slip of paper would serve as a momentary distraction. Simultaneously, he pulled the first item he felt from his pocket and unsheathed his knife with his right hand. Karl extended his left arm so Schmidt would have to reach for the note, exposing his left flank. When Schmidt grabbed the paper, Karl clutched the man's wrist and thrust the knife deep into his side, pulling it upward and twisting it to maximize the damage.

Schmidt grunted and leaned into the attack but didn't have the strength to fight back. Karl kept him upright in his saddle while he gurgled his last breath. Once Schmidt slumped, Karl pushed him to the ground and snatched the canteen wrapped around the saddle horn. Karl dismounted, gathered Schmidt's Luger, searched him for anything else useful, and grabbed a flashlight attached to his belt.

He considered changing horses for the younger colt, but he valued agility over strength. Once he hid Schmidt's body in the brush, he tied the colt's reins to a rope from his saddlebag and secured it to the back of his saddle. Mounting his mare, Karl stroked her neck again. "We have some work ahead of us, girl."

The jungle canopy was too thick to read the stars, so Karl continued down a side trail he hoped would lead him north. Before confirming his heading, he heard another rider ahead and let the colt go for the moment. A similar scene played out as he disposed of him as he did with Schmidt. Once back on his horse after enticing the colt forward, he continued down the trail with the third horse following at will. He stopped where the treetops were thin. He saw enough of the stars to know he was going in the right direction and resumed his search.

A tall jequitibá tree was ahead. Few were along the trails, so it would serve as an excellent landmark once he located Hattie. The mare slowed dramatically, making Karl think she was finally starting to tire. Without warning, she stopped, and so did the other horses. Karl urged her forward, but she refused even when he squeezed her sides with his legs. Perhaps he had drained her.

Karl dismounted, pushed his hat back on his head to get a better look at her, and surmised she was thirsty. Schmidt's canteen had a cup at the bottom, so he poured water into it and stepped forward to let her drink. He whistled "Camptown Races" mindlessly as his mind drifted to his favorite times with his daughters when they were little. Before bed each night, he gave each girl a shoulder ride around the house, singing that ditty, ending the song by flopping them atop the bed to loud giggles.

"Father?" Hattie emerged from the bushes.

"Hattie? Thank God." Karl's knees nearly buckled in relief.

Hattie threw her arms around his torso and cried into his chest. "You found us."

Karl wrapped an arm around her, thankful he had found her alive and unhurt. "I always keep my promises to you." He looked at the others. They appeared distrustful of him, and one had pure hatred in her eyes. "Are you two all right?"

"We're unhurt," the one from Hattie's cell said.

"Father, this is Maya and her sister, Anna."

"I'm afraid we have no time for pleasantries. I've taken out only two of the riders. There are two more."

"One more," Anna said with a sneer, waving a Luger around. "We killed one."

"Resourceful and brave." Karl formed a lopsided grin briefly before turning serious. "We can scale the north wall using the horses and rope in my saddlebags, but we must hurry."

Once they mounted the horses, Hattie on the colt and the other two women on the third steed, Karl guided them to a fork in the trail and headed northeast. With one wrangler and Baumann still hunting them, they needed to make good time, so he maintained a robust pace. He stopped at the edge of a large clearing and oriented his location. His navigation was a little off from exploring this part of the plantation last week. The wall directly across from them was too high to scale even with the horses, but it was two feet shorter at a sudden rocky rise in the terrain somewhere around there. It might take some time to find, but he couldn't chance having Hattie and the others in the open for too long while he located the place to cross.

"Hide here. I need to find the right spot to escape. I'll scout and come back for you when I know it's safe. Use this if you have to." Karl handed Hattie a Luger he recovered from a dead rider and squeezed her hand.

Time was short, so there was no time for sentiments, but he could not imagine living another day without his sweet little songbird. She and her sister were why he sacrificed everything to do what he thought was right, but he had made a mess of things. Many women died because of him, a gut-wrenching fact he might never come to terms with, and Hattie and her friends were in grave danger. Compounding things, he had no clue whether the sheet music was safe. Everything he'd gone through for the last fifteen years would have been for nothing if those lists fell into the wrong hands. He could not rest until he fixed things.

"We'll be right here, Father." Hattie squeezed his hand in return and dismounted her horse. Maya and Anna also took to the ground.

Leaving her there was the hardest thing he ever had to do. He flicked the reins and squeezed his legs against his mare's sides. They took off toward the wall. "One more time, old gal. Let's find a way out."

They trotted across the field. Any faster might raise suspicion from the remaining rider. Reaching the wall, he went parallel to it, hoping to find the right spot to scale it.

"Halt!" a man shouted.

Karl removed the other Luger from his waistband before slowing the mare and stopping her. He scanned the area in the dark distance and spotted a man emerging from the jungle into the clearing. Once he was close enough, Karl recognized the last surviving wrangler as Jacobs.

Jacobs and his horse trotted up, and he stopped when he was even with Karl. They spoke in German.

"What are you doing here? I thought you were riding with Herr Baumann tonight."

"I was." Karl pivoted, angled his torso to better aim, and fired one shot into Jacobs's abdomen. His shocked expression lasted a few seconds before turning into anguish. Karl drew his pistol higher, aimed at his head, and fired again. A direct, lethal shot. Jacobs fell to the ground, making a loud thump. His horse bolted toward the jungle.

Four men down. Only Baumann remained.

A shot rang out.

Karl snapped his head toward the jungle's edge and his worst possible nightmare. His stomach instantly turned. "Hattie!"

38

Moments earlier

After tying the horses' reins to a bush, Hattie and Maya crouched shoulder to shoulder, clutching hands and watching from the edge of the jungle as Karl crossed the clearing and disappeared into the darkness. This nightmare would soon be over if they held tight and remained patient.

While the owls and toucans sang their nightly songs, Hattie fought an internal battle. She could not deny her father's part in the atrocities on the plantation nor dismiss what the FBI had accused him of. However, she had difficulty reconciling those awful things with the gentle, loving man who raised her. That man was not capable of violence, let alone betraying his country. However, the man risking his life to save her today seemed capable of those things and much more. Her father was a contradiction of an enormous magnitude.

Conversely, the woman holding her hand was an open book. Losing her parents had forged Maya Reyes into a strong woman, capable of anything she put her mind to. She valued family above all else, witnessed by the environment she had created at the Halo Club and her relentless pursuit to find Anna. Hattie did, too, but she hadn't included her mother until recently when she learned the real reason her parents' marriage dissolved.

Maya also appreciated honesty and considered anything less affronting. Before all this, Hattie thought her father was of the same mindset, but overnight events proved her wrong. Oddly, she trusted Maya, a woman she had known for ten days, more than her own father.

Hattie squeezed Maya's hand. They turned, looking at each other. Maya drew their hands to her lips and kissed Hattie's. Gratitude had replaced the earlier fear and anger in her eyes. "Thank you."

"For what?"

"For not stopping. No matter the reason, you helped find my sister."

"You're welcome." Hattie pulled Maya's chin closer and kissed her lips briefly, tenderly, before returning her attention to the clearing.

A gunshot pierced the night, causing Hattie and Maya to flinch. Hattie's heart thumped wildly at the possibility her father might be involved. Anna came closer and pointed toward the wall. "It came from that direction."

"I know." Hattie hated saying it, let alone thinking it, but Anna was right. The shot came from her father's direction.

A second shot came from the same area.

Hattie gasped.

"What should we do?" Maya asked.

"My father said to wait, so we wait."

"This is crazy," Anna said. "He could be lying dead somewhere for all we know. We need to make it to the wall."

"It's too dangerous to be out in the open," Hattie warned. "Baumann and the other rider could be close."

Anna gestured toward the clearing. "We at least need to know if he's alive."

"No, Anna. We wait here," Maya said.

"I can't just wait here. I won't go back into that cage." Anna kissed Maya's cheek. "I love you, sister."

"No, Anna." Maya gripped her hand, but Anna threw it off. "Stay."

Anna went to a horse, placed her left foot in the stirrup, and pulled herself into the saddle using a dangling strap. She turned to Hattie. "If I don't come back, get my sister out of here." She gently kicked the horse's sides and trotted from the concealment of the trees and shrubs.

"Anna! Anna!" Maya called out in a hushed voice. She stepped toward her, but Hattie pulled her back.

"It's too dangerous," Hattie whispered, holding Maya at the waist.

Before she was halfway across, another gunshot rang out. Anna seized and fell limp to the ground, and her horse ran off.

"Anna!" Maya let out a piercing scream as if her heart had been torn apart. She thrashed against Hattie's hold and broke free. Hattie reached out, but Maya darted across the field toward her sister.

Hattie rose to go after her but heard something approach from behind. She placed a hand on the gun she'd stuffed into the waistband of her skirt and turned as she drew it. Before she could level it, a man on foot emerged from the shadows, pointing a rifle toward the open field.

"I wouldn't do that, Miss James," Baumann said, "unless you want me to shoot the other Miss Reyes."

Hattie froze, but her heart pounded so hard it reverberated in her ears. He likely would have gotten off his shot by the time she twirled and aimed. It was a chance she couldn't take, so she lowered her weapon.

"It's good to see you're reasonable, Miss James. Now, throw it into the bushes." Once she did, he slung the rifle over his shoulder, across his chest, drew his sidearm on her, and took her by the arm. "As much as I want to see you dead, I want your father more."

Hattie gasped. Baumann knew her father's identity.

Maya wailed and moaned as if in physical pain. Her voice was hoarse and broken as she repeated her sister's name over and over in a mantra of despair. Hattie turned her head toward her. Maya had reached Anna and was clutching her limp body, rocking back and forth on her knees in a heartbreaking sight.

Baumann pulled Hattie tightly against his chest with her facing away from him and guided her to a few feet outside the tree line, holding the pistol to her temple. Smelling like sweat, vodka, and stale cigarette smoke from the Halo Club, he crouched so their heights were even and positioned them so Hattie was between Maya and him. He peeked around her head and shouted in English, "I have your sweet daughter, Karl James. Show your face, or I'll put a bullet in her head. You have one minute."

One minute wasn't enough time for her father to make his way across the clearing far enough away for Baumann to not see him and come close enough to get a clean shot at him. But if he gave himself up, Baumann would indeed shoot him and the rest of them. There was no way out.

Hattie squirmed in Baumann's grasp. "Don't, Father! Don't! We're dead either way. Save yourself!"

"Forty-five seconds, Mr. James."

Maya continued to weep over her sister ten yards away with no sign of letting up.

"Thirty seconds, Mr. James. Otherwise, your daughter dies first."

"I hope you rot in hell, Baumann." Hattie wriggled more, but her tormentor's hold was too strong for her to break free.

"Fifteen seconds, Mr. James." Baumann pressed the muzzle firmer against her temple.

"All right, Baumann," Karl said from the shadows. "You win."

"Show yourself," Baumann ordered.

"When did you figure things out, Herr Baumann?" Karl emerged from the jungle about twenty yards to the east, holding his hands up.

Baumann turned right, placing Hattie between him and her father.

Maya, now to their left, quieted. The screech of the toucan was the only sound.

Hattie sighed at her father's valiant effort. His location suggested he had tried to circle back and surprise Baumann on his flank but had run out of time.

"During our trip to the embassy. Now, throw out your guns." When Karl reached into his light jacket, Baumann jerked Hattie and pressed the gun harder. "Careful. Use only one finger."

Karl slowly removed his hand with a Luger dangling from an index finger via the trigger guard and tossed it several feet in front of him. "All right, what now?"

"Come now, Mr. James. I'm sure you have more than one."

Karl removed a second gun from his jacket and tossed it. "All right, Baumann. What do you want?"

"The lists. Berlin won't rest until we have them." Baumann stood straight without loosening his hold until his head towered over Hattie's.

Hattie could now turn her head completely but shifted enough to see that Maya held Anna in her lap.

"They are my insurance policy," her father said. "If I die, both lists will see the light of day. Is that what you want?"

"It would seem you have me over a barrel," Baumann said, "but are you willing to let your daughter die to save your own skin?" Sweat dripped from Baumann onto Hattie's neck. He was clearly anxious. "If you give me those lists, I will let her go."

"I learned a long time ago to trust no one but myself in this business," Karl said. "Let her and the other woman go. Once they are over the wall, you can have me."

"No, Father!" Hattie dreaded the thought of him sacrificing himself for her. "I won't let you." She squirmed and fought against Baumann's hold, but he was strong, so she stomped on his foot. He loosened his grip a fraction, allowing Hattie to kick out both legs and drop to her bottom, landing on the ground with a jolt and disorienting her.

A gunshot rang out. Hattie could not tell from which direction it came.

A second shot. Hattie flinched. Her heart pounded wildly, not knowing how to protect herself.

Baumann wobbled on his feet.

A third shot. Hattie lay flat and covered her head. Her breathing was so rapid and shallow she nearly passed out. Baumann fell to the ground next to her with a loud thud. She turned her head to peek, discovering Baumann wheeling his gun toward her. They locked gazes. Desperation filled his eyes as if he knew the end was coming.

Footsteps charged toward her from Karl's direction. A gunshot. Baumann's forehead split from the power of the bullet, sending blood and brain matter into the air. The evil man fell flat, and a wave of relief washed over Hattie.

Karl reached Hattie. "Are you all right?"

Hattie shook off the horrible sight she'd witnessed. "I'm fine. What about Maya and Anna?" She labored to her feet with her father's help, feeling a dull pain in her bottom. She would be bruised for days. She rushed toward Maya, discovering she was holding a Luger. Her hand was shaking. "Are you hurt?"

"She's dead." Maya's expression was blank when Hattie took the gun from her hand and handed it to her father. Her eyes were swollen from her weeping.

Hattie fell to her knees, wrapping an arm around Maya and drawing her to her chest. "I'm so sorry," she said repeatedly, rocking her in her arms. Hattie looked at her father. "What happened? How did you shoot him?"

"Maya shot first. Then me," Karl said. He turned and whistled.

Hattie snapped her stare to Maya. "You shot him?"

"We don't have much time," her father said. "I've killed all the riders. Other agents in the compound will look for them soon." A horse trotted up to Karl. He handed Hattie a length of rope from his saddlebag. "You and Maya escape over the wall while I take care of them. There's a section about a hundred yards east where you can climb over and ease yourselves down with the rope. Once over, head east toward the coast. Do you remember how to navigate during the day?"

"Yes. The sun rises in the east and sets in the west." Hattie tugged desperately on his mud-stained sleeve, taking in the warmth of his deep blue eyes. "But I'm not going without you, Father."

"I'll catch up." He squeezed her hand. "No matter what, be over that wall before dawn. The highway is five or six miles east." Karl handed her two guns. "Just in case, but you shouldn't need these." After loading Baumann's body onto the back of his horse, he kissed Hattie on the forehead and rode toward the compound.

Hattie returned to Maya. Anna's head was still in Maya's lap. Maya stroked Anna's hair, nuzzling back strands from her face. "She never liked it when her hair was messy," Maya said in a flat, numb voice.

"All beautiful women are a little vain." Hattie forced a laugh.

"I don't know what dress to bury her in. She never told me which was her favorite."

Hattie cleared the lump in her throat. "I'll help you pick one out. We'll make her look her prettiest, but we should leave now."

Maya shook her head, refusing to leave her sister's side.

Hattie's heart broke many times over the next hour, waiting for Maya to work through her grief and hoping for her father to return before going over the wall. She rubbed Maya's back when the first purple sliver appeared in the eastern sky. "It's almost daylight. My father said to escape over the wall. We need to go."

"I won't leave her." Maya shook her head but did not cry. Hattie didn't think she had any tears left.

Rustling in the jungle announced someone or something approaching. Hattie raised her gun, ready to fire, unsure if it was her father, one of Baumann's men, or a wild animal with its sights on breakfast. The noise got louder as the person or thing approached. The footsteps sounded heavy and leisurely, unlike a predator or someone with evil intent. Hattie shielded Maya, protecting her from the danger.

Moments later, the horse they had tied up appeared through the tree line, giving Hattie an idea. She clicked her tongue, encouraging the horse over. When it got close, she grabbed its reins and turned to Maya. "I know you won't leave Anna, but what if we took her with us?"

"We can't carry her five or six miles through the jungle."

Remaining in the open field was too dangerous, so they had to leave. "I know, but we can make Anna's death mean something. We can put her on the horse and return to the compound to free the other women."

Maya threw a hand over her mouth, whimpering into her palm.

"I know this is hard, but this is the only way to take her with us and save the others."

Maya agreed, and they worked together, loading and tying Anna to the back of the horse. Hattie oriented south from the fading stars in the predawn sky and chose a direction on foot through the jungle that she thought would take them back. Several times, she doubted herself and changed paths twice, but eventually, they emerged at the clearing at the end of the coffee fields.

The rapidly increasing light made it easy to navigate the rest of the way to the compound. They reached the access road and passed through the gauntlet of burned-out torches. Several saddled horses wandered about the yard between the buildings, and three dogs lay panting on the ground near a water bowl. The largest dog growled as Hattie walked the horse closer to the main house. She clutched the reins tighter.

"Nein! Bleib!" a man yelled from across the compound.

Hattie glanced toward the voice and gasped. Bodies hung upside down by their ankles from tree limbs and a wire strung between two ten-foot poles. Blood stained each corpse and dripped into puddles on the dirt beneath them. Her father had a hold of a rope and hoisted a body into the air until it hung from the wire. Once it was even with the others, he tied an end of the rope to a stake on the ground.

"You shouldn't have come," Karl said, wiping his hands on his bloody clothing.

Hattie gasped again, recognizing the body he'd hung next to Baumann. It was Hilda, the house servant who tended to the man's daughter. "Where is Elsa?"

"She's fine, still asleep from the drugs Baumann must have given her."

"And the other women?"

"Safe. I gave them fresh water and left the entry doors unlocked. The key to the cells is on the wall."

Hattie spun on her heels, surveying the gruesome bloodbath surrounding her. It was the work of someone savage. "What did you do, Father?"

"What I had to do in order to keep you safe. I couldn't be sure who else knew who I was, so I killed them all." When Hattie recoiled at the horror of his statement, Karl grabbed both her arms. "They would have come after you to get to me. Rest assured. I'll kill anyone who comes after you."

"But why are you hanging them like slaughtered animals?" The sight was sickening.

"To make it appear a favela gang did this. It's their trademark. When the police come, they will think they took revenge for taking and killing several of their women. This way, they won't ask you too many questions." He glanced at Maya, who was still in shock, guarding her sister's body several yards away. He spoke softly. "Is the Christmas present I gave you safe?"

Hattie peeled her stare from the horrible sight and narrowed her eyes at her father. She long suspected the sheet music held a secret meaning. "Yes. Why?"

"Keep it that way. Only turn it over to the professor if the United States enters the war. Understand?"

Hattie nodded. "Who is the professor?"

"A friend. Your mother can find her."

Sirens sounded in the distance, signaling the police were approaching. Karl handed Hattie a little black notebook from his back pocket, cupping his hands over hers. "This is your leverage if the FBI has backed you into a corner."

"What is it?" Hattie asked, surprised he knew the FBI had been using her as a pawn to get to him.

"Baumann's logbook. Safeguard it until you need it." Her father's carefully chosen words made Hattie think he was suspicious of everything. He kissed her forehead again. "I must go."

Hattie had never been more torn. She'd witnessed the father she once adored commit horrific acts, yet he was loving enough to save her and Maya. By his own admission hours ago, he traded in secrets at the expense of Germany and the United States. And by his question moments ago, Hattie suspected she held those secrets somehow hidden in the sheet music he gifted her. By any definition, he was a traitor, and the FBI would continue to hound her and Olivia until they had him in their clutches. If she let him go, she would give up any chance of ending this nightmare today.

"In Mother's backyard, you told me to trust you, that only part of the truth was known. Stay and clear yourself. I can take you to the FBI."

"Too much is at stake, sweetheart. I don't trust either side." Karl squeezed her hands. "I left pictures on Baumann's desk. They show all the women Baumann took. Their ashes are in the kiln in the milling barn. The police should find everything and release you." Karl mounted his horse.

Hattie removed the gun from her waistband, but when disappointment filled his eyes, she could not pull the trigger and lowered it. No matter what it cost her, she couldn't bring herself to turn in her father.

The sirens grew louder. The police were getting closer.

"Don't move, Mr. James," Maya said. Hattie turned, discovering she had her pistol aimed at her father. "You need to pay for what you've done."

"I did what I had to." Karl lowered and shook his head briefly. "I love you, Hattie." He flicked the reins, and the horse started to walk.

To Hattie's horror, Maya pulled the trigger, but the gun only clicked. She yanked it again and again, but still nothing happened. She grunted and threw the Luger at him.

Karl stopped his horse and twisted in his saddle to look at Maya. "You need bullets, Miss Reyes."

Hattie took several steps toward him and shouted, "How will I find you?"

"Signal me with my favorite flower in your lapel," Karl said. He kicked with his heels, the horse took off faster, and he disappeared into the coffee fields.

Maya tugged on Hattie's sleeve, nearly ripping the seam. "How could you let him go?"

"He's my father." Hattie gritted her teeth, biting back her anger for Maya. After everything her father had done for them, she had tried to kill him, and that was unforgivable. Only moments ago, she'd learned he was capable of the worst atrocities, but he was still her father. He trusted her with the logbook and sheet music containing some secret lists, so she had to return the show of faith. "If I meant anything to you, don't tell the police about him."

Minutes later, after Hattie hid the ledger in her waistband, eight police cars rolled into the compound, and the sirens quelled once they parked. Armed officers piled out, swarming the buildings. Two officers secured Hattie and Maya in their tattered clothes and tangled hair and brought them to a police car.

Inspector Silva stepped out. "What happened here last night?"

"Heinz Baumann happened." Hattie thought about what her father had said earlier about concocting a ruse. "He drugged us, took us here, and hunted us for sport. But a bunch of men from town stormed the compound and killed everyone. They left when they heard the sirens. I don't think they found the other women in the basement."

Silva instructed several officers to search the basement before returning his attention to Hattie. "It seems you were on the right track."

"No thanks to you." Hattie raised her nose at him.

The rear passenger door of Silva's police car opened. Hattie nearly fainted when David stepped out. They rushed to each other. "David!" She threw her arms around his neck, and he embraced her tightly. "I thought they killed you."

He loosened his hold but kept his hands firmly against her back. "They drugged me. When I came to this morning, the police had found Vargas dead in his car and questioned me for hours. Silva finally believed me about Baumann, and we rushed here." David held her at arm's length to inspect her. "Are you hurt?"

Hattie shook her head. "A few scratches." She glanced toward the horse in the compound's center and struggled to hold back her sorrow. "But Anna is dead. Baumann shot her."

David looked at Maya. "I'm so sorry, but I'm glad you two made it out alive. What happened after Baumann took you?"

Hattie held her breath, waiting to see if Maya would tell Silva about her father.

Maya locked eyes with Hattie for several tense moments before turning to David and Silva. "It's like Hattie said. Now, will someone please take my sister down from this horse so I can bury her?"

39

Inspector Silva had no sympathy for what Hattie and Maya had gone through. After releasing the other women from the basement and arranging for Elsa to be taken to the German Embassy, he questioned Hattie and Maya for hours at police headquarters in Rio. He had the decency to bring in a medic to tend to their minor wounds but not enough to take them to the hospital and have a doctor examine them thoroughly as he did for the other women.

Silva asked about Vargas's involvement in the trap she and Maya had set for Baumann. After explaining his role, Hattie added, "Baumann said he had outlived his usefulness."

Silva said, "That makes sense. Baumann was paying him off. We've had our eye on him and searched his home today. We found over twenty-five thousand reals hidden in his freezer."

Since the first time she and Maya had walked into the police station, Hattie had suspected Silva was on the take, but she was wrong. Silva was merely lazy or jaded but capable of actual police work when pressed by the public nature of events, and Vargas was the rotten egg. She shook her head at being so easily fooled.

"If you have nothing else to add," Silva said, "you ladies are free to go." He closed the file on his desk, signifying the case's closure.

"What?" Maya said. "No thanks for finding those women? No sympathies for my dead sister?" She stood and snubbed her chin at him. "You are a piece of work, Inspector Silva."

"I have one request, Inspector," Hattie said.

"What is that, Miss James?"

"Keep our names out of the media. We don't know who might have escaped, and they could come looking for us."

"Very well." Silva nodded.

"Let's go, Maya." Hattie placed a hand on her back and ushered her down the hallway.

When the elevator door closed and they were alone, Hattie dropped her arm, and Maya slid as far away as possible. Neither had forgiven the other —one for letting Karl go and the other for trying to kill him. Once they entered the lobby, David rose from his seat in the waiting area and escorted them to his car.

"I'd rather walk," Maya said, refusing to get in when David held the door open for her.

"Don't be so damn stubborn," Hattie said. "You're exhausted. Get in the car."

Maya stared daggers at Hattie before climbing into the back seat.

Once parked in front of Maya's house, Hattie asked David to wait in the car. "Maya and I need to talk."

He acknowledged with a nod, opened both passenger doors for the women, and returned to the driver's seat as Hattie and Maya walked silently to the front door.

Maya retrieved a key hidden under a loose wooden slat at the bottom of the frame, unlocked the door, and threw the key into a ceramic bowl a few feet inside.

As angry as Hattie was, the need to feel alive overpowered her. She spun Maya around, forced her against the wall, and kissed her with fervor . . . with anger . . . with sorrow . . . with relief that they were still alive. Maya deepened it and sent her hands sliding down Hattie's backside, ultimately pulling their centers firmly together. Their tongues fought for dominance, not in an erotic dance but in a desperate attempt to be in control. Every emotion they experienced in the jungle and on that plantation—from being hunted and fearing for their lives to Anna's death and the bloodbath her father caused—came pouring out. The soft caresses they shared when they first made love were replaced by aggressive squeezes and frenzied pawing at clothing until breasts were exposed and skirts were hiked. Hattie broke the kiss and crouched to take a breast into her mouth, but Maya pushed her away.

"Don't," Maya cried. Her chest heaved, and confusion was in her eyes. "I can't do this." She fixed her clothes and marched to her kitchen.

Hattie was frustrated but followed, returning her blouse and skirt to their proper positions. She'd never lost anyone close to her but knew enough about grieving to know emotions ran high and were often contradictory, requiring much patience.

Maya retrieved two tall glasses from the cupboard, filled them with ice and lemonade from the refrigerator, and handed one to Hattie.

"Thank you." Hattie took a long sip, enjoying the cool, sweet taste. At several points throughout the night, she didn't think they would survive, and this little indulgence was proof they were alive. "God, that tastes good."

Maya gulped half her drink. "Yes, it does." She placed her cup on the counter, turned her back to Hattie, and placed both hands on the surface, palms down. "I'm so lost, Hattie. Anna and I have been everything to each other since our parents died. I don't know what I'll do without her."

"I'm so sorry." Hattie's throat thickened. She stepped closer and touched Maya's back, but Maya shrugged her hand away.

"And I blame you. If you hadn't walked into my club last week, my sister would be alive today." Maya lowered her head and sobbed.

Hattie failed to hold back her tears. She could not deny what Maya had said. Anna died as part of Baumann's thirsty hunt for Hattie's father. It was that simple. Her anger over Maya trying to shoot her father drowned in her guilt. Hattie could not fault Maya for wanting to kill the underlying cause of her sister's death.

"Yes, she would be alive," Hattie said. "And I am profoundly sorry for that."

Maya spun around with fury in her eyes. "But not sorry enough to turn your father in."

And there it was—the wedge that had spread into a chasm between them. The FBI, holding her sister as a virtual hostage, could not make her turn on her father, and neither could Anna's death. Despite what he had done, Hattie's bond with him was too strong.

Hattie firmed her stance and summoned the strength to control her voice. "I'm sorry my presence put her in danger. I'm sorry I kept the truth from you, but I will not apologize for standing by my father after he risked his life to save us."

"Then I can't do this anymore, Hattie. It's too painful."

Hattie's lips trembled. She reached out her hand to caress away Maya's pain but quickly withdrew it. There was no denying the truth. Their end was inevitable. Only time could heal a wound this deep.

~

Relieved David didn't ask questions, Hattie accepted his hand during the drive to Eva's home when he wasn't shifting gears. She had received enough grilling from Inspector Silva and expected the same treatment from her mother. However, the drive wasn't peaceful. She replayed the events in Maya's home in her head, from their near tryst to Maya's last words over and over again. Her breath hitched at the start each time, reliving the feel of her fingertips stroking the woman's soft skin. By the end, her throat swelled at the realization she had lost Maya.

After pulling up to Eva's garage, David parked, explaining he would pull it in later, and helped Hattie out of the car. Once on her feet, she realized how much of a toll the night had taken. Her legs and arms were like lead from the drugs and hours of traipsing through the jungle, but she hadn't the time to rest yet. David forewarned Eva about Hattie's disappearance and subsequent recovery after they arrived at the police station, so Hattie expected an emotional reunion. She took his arm and leaned on him as he used his key to open the courtyard gate and led them across the garden.

The buzzer must have sounded when David unlocked the gate, because Eva opened the front door and rushed toward them. "Sweetheart." She flung her arms out, pulling Hattie into the tightest hug she had ever given her, and wept. "I almost lost you."

"I'm all right, Mother."

"David told me a bit of what you went through."

"Can we go inside? I'm quite tired."

"Of course. Of course." Eva slid an arm around Hattie's back and guided her to the living room. "What can I get you? Are you hungry? Thirsty?"

"Right now, I want a long, hot shower, but if you don't mind, would you fix some misto quente? I could use some of your home cooking."

"Of course, sweetheart. I'll have it ready when you get out."

Hattie turned to David. "Would you mind staying here? I need a few moments alone."

"Of course." He kissed her on the cheek.

Hattie trudged down the hallway to the room she shared with David, back to the lies and the trap she had set for herself—hiding who she was in exchange for acceptance. Once she closed the door, she located David's satchel, pulled out the stack of sheet music her father was so concerned about, and placed it next to Baumann's logbook on the bed.

Hattie reexamined a few pages of the sheet music. Her father was insistent about safeguarding the collection, and Hattie was sure the lists Baumann mentioned were there. She only had to find them.

She flipped through the ledger. It was written in German, but it had a treasure trove of information about the Nazi intelligence-gathering operations in Rio, precisely what Agent Butler was looking for. Otherwise, her father would not have given it to her. Hattie thumbed to the date the FBI said her father was seen disembarking a cargo ship and discovered his name and the word *Berlin*.

It was true.

Everything about her father being a spy was true. Hattie debated what to do. Both documents—the logbook and the sheet music—held secrets, and both sides would kill to get their hands on them. And both items would further implicate her father. Hattie was no traitor, and deep down, she believed neither was her father. No matter how cynical she had become about the FBI, she needed to do what was right and protect him. That meant safeguarding the sheet music and turning over information that could help the Americans, but she had to make it believable. She couldn't simply take photos of the book. Butler would never believe her captors had missed the micro-camera and that she later waltzed into his office and snapped a bunch of pictures without grabbing the book. She had to turn it over, but not before she created her leverage.

Hattie removed her Kodak from the dresser and took a picture of every logbook page, reloading the camera twice with rolls of film. After ripping out the page with her father's name, she flushed it down the toilet. She returned the sheet music to David's satchel, hid the rolls of film among her underwear, and stuffed the camera and notebook in her dresser drawer.

Once in the shower, Hattie stood under the stream, letting the hot water wash away the dirt and stink of last night. She cried for all that had happened. Five women Baumann kidnapped died because he was looking for her father, including Anna. Hattie could never deny that fact or wash away that blood. The guilt weighed heavy as she dressed and fixed her hair. She had to do something for the families to ease their suffering, though she didn't know what that was yet.

Hattie went to the kitchen, where her mother and David put the final touches on her food. "Thank you. This looks great." She devoured the sandwich and downed her drink in quick gulps.

"My, someone was hungry," Eva said.

"Being hunted will do that to a person," Hattie joked. "Did David fill you in on the details?"

"Yes, he told me about the trap you three laid to get the goods on that man, and I must say that was the height of stupidity. You and Miss Reyes were almost killed along with her sister."

"Can we dispense with the lecture, Mother? I already realize how dangerous it was."

Eva opened her mouth to say something but closed it without uttering a word.

"Thank you," Hattie said, going for a second sandwich and thinking of her next steps. Meeting with Butler could wait until tomorrow after she'd rested, but she needed to lay the groundwork for staying in Rio until she could find her father again.

After finishing the second misto quente, Hattie turned to Eva. "I've been thinking, Mother. Do you have the manager's number at the Palace? I want to accept their offer."

"Oh, sweetheart. That's wonderful. You won't regret working there."

Hattie already did. The Palace didn't have Maya Reyes.

40

The following morning

While David drove them through town, Hattie flipped open the morning newspaper. The headline "Plantation Massacre: Missing Women Found" was blazoned atop the front page. With Inspector Silva heading the case, she was surprised the story made the newspaper. He had done everything in his power to kill the story about the missing women, but Hattie supposed someone on his team leaked the information since it had become clear Vargas wasn't the source of the initial leak. Carnage of that magnitude could not have been held secret for long.

The story said that authorities suspected a gang from the Rio favelas had committed the murders in retaliation over the missing women, but it made no mention of Baumann's part in the kidnappings or the hunt. The article also reported that four missing women were found alive in the estate's basement, including Marta Moyer, and the investigation was ongoing. Hattie and Maya's involvement was thankfully omitted. Although it appeared Baumann's logbook contained dozens of names, any of whom might come after them to find out what they knew about the Nazi operation, she and Maya were safe for now.

David parked a block from the dry cleaners, and he and Hattie entered the shop. Nala Cohen ushered them to the secret office where Agent Butler awaited them. He stood from his chair. "Were you at the plantation when everything happened? We lost you at the Halo Club before Vargas was killed."

"Yes. Maya Reyes and I were almost two of his victims." Hattie reached into her purse and handed him the book. "I managed to get this before the police arrived. I believe this is what you've been looking for."

Butler examined several pages, his eyes lighting with excitement. "This is exactly it." He flipped more pages.

"Does this square us? Can I go home now?"

He looked up. "This is a goldmine, but it still doesn't square us with your father. You still need to flush him out. Besides, Baumann's superiors will be looking for this. Does anyone else know you were involved at the plantation?"

"Just the police."

"That could be a problem. Some are sympathetic toward the Nazis."

"What should I do?" Hattie imagined spies sneaking into her room in the middle of the night and slitting her throat to get to that logbook. But then she remembered her father's vow—*I'll kill anyone who comes after you*—and she felt safer.

"Act like it never happened."

Butler expected the impossible. So much had happened, and so much was lost, including Hattie's innocence. The realm of spies had been only in books and movies before Olivia's call saying her father had been arrested. Today, Hattie James was at the heart of that mysterious world. She would have to be careful about who she trusted and what she shared because one slip could spark another night like what happened at Baumann's plantation, and more innocent lives could be lost.

EPILOGUE

Five days later

Karl entered the busy delivery bay entrance confidently as if he worked there, to not draw attention by dawdling. Despite the evening hour, trucks and men unloading the goods occupied all four bays. He walked past them into the monochrome industrial area with concrete floors and cinder block walls, which was hectic with dozens of servers, housekeepers, porters, and valets scurrying about.

He followed the signs to the employee dressing area. Signage at the end of the corridor labeled one side "Homem" and the other "Senhoras." He peeled off toward the men's side and spotted an unattended busboy's jacket —just what he needed for the night. He snatched it, hanger and all, without breaking stride, and continued to the toilets in the back. Once inside a stall, he put on the jacket, leaving the hanger on the door hook. The uniform was a little snug around the shoulders, but he could button it over his white dress shirt and black tie.

Karl checked his watch. He had five minutes to make it to the kitchen. Otherwise, all this was for nothing. But he would move mountains to be there tonight. Before leaving the confines of the stall, he placed a single stem of edelweiss from Eva's plant room in the lapel of his jacket. The small white flower blended nicely with his uniform, only noticeable if someone was looking for it.

He followed the signs marked "Cozinha" and entered. The place was chaotic, with cooks and assistants shouting instructions and servers coming in and out for their orders. Two minutes before eight, he grabbed a busser's bucket and entered the dining room.

The packed space was awash with men and women dressed elegantly in tuxedos and formal gowns, eating from fine china, drinking from sparkling crystal glasses, and smoking expensive cigars and cigarettes. The chatter of hundreds of conversations created a loud hum. He scanned the room, focusing on the center near the stage, and found the one person he expected to see at tonight's table of honor. Eva had dressed up for a royal reception in a glittering black dress and had her long black hair styled and gathered above the neck, exposing her bare upper back.

He snickered and mumbled, "She can never be outdone."

The lights lowered, and the room quieted slowly. A male voice came over the loudspeaker and announced in Portuguese and English, "The Golden Room and Copacabana Palace are proud to present the American songbird, Hattie James." The audience roared with shouts and whistles and deafening applause.

The arched stage curtain retracted from the center, revealing a full band and David Townsend at the piano on the right. Hattie stepped out from the wings, dressed in a sophisticated white floor-length gown adorned tastefully in sequins to sparkle in the lighting. Karl laughed. He never thought anyone could outdress his ex-wife, but Hattie won that contest hands down. She had more beauty and gracefulness than Eva could ever hope to possess.

As she passed David, she gave his hand a tight squeeze. Karl had doubts about the man, as any father would, but Hattie seemed taken with him, so he would reserve his final judgment.

The crowd roared louder when the band began to play.

Hattie stepped up to the microphone stand center stage near the front and broke into her first song, and Karl could not have been prouder. His choices had stalled her career, ending her RCA contract and appearances in the United States. Though she might not have imagined Rio as the location for her comeback, he was sure she was destined for worldwide recognition and to outshine her mother in every respect.

Karl was in and out of the dining room for her performance, clearing tables near the back to keep Hattie and Eva from recognizing him. He'd missed several songs while dropping off dirty dishes in the kitchen, but of those he listened to, he sensed a little more sadness in her ballads than usual tonight. He was sure the horrific ordeal at Baumann's plantation and Anna's death still weighed heavy on her.

At the end of her performance, Hattie and David joined Eva. Three other men were at her table, but the table was spacious enough for all six. Eva greeted Hattie with an impassioned hug and gave David a much briefer embrace. The other men stood to welcome Hattie, and Karl finally got a good look at their faces. When the last one turned, his heart nearly stopped.

"Ziegler," he whispered.

Karl hadn't seen him in nearly two decades when his posting in Washington ended in 1923, but even then, Karl had had a bad feeling about the man. Ziegler was not the neutral diplomat the Swiss were known for. He quietly pursued his agenda outside official channels to get things done his way.

A thousand questions swirled in Karl's head, but most importantly, he needed to know what Ziegler was doing in Rio. It could not have been coincidental that Frederick Ziegler had weaved his way into Hattie's life. Not now.

A server passed by, but Karl grabbed his arm before he was out of reach. He handed the man the edelweiss from his lapel and asked him to give it to Hattie. The man nodded and went straight to her table. Hattie accepted the flower and instantly rose from her chair to scan the room.

"I'll protect you, Hattie, no matter the cost," Karl whispered, slipping out of the dining room but not out of Hattie's life.

THE RIO AFFAIR
Hattie James #2

When a disgraced singer is snared in the undercurrents of WWII espionage, she must learn to become a shadow in the limelight.

Still struggling with personal loss and haunted by the memories of her near-death experience at the hands of the Nazis, dazzling singer Hattie James desires to leave her past behind and focus on reviving her career and rising in the ranks of the glamorous Brazilian music scene.

But when she discovers that her mother's new suitor, Swiss diplomat Frederick Ziegler, is associated with SS leader Heinz Baumann, Hattie's suspicions ignite. Then, while performing for an exclusive gathering at Ziegler's residence, she overhears a chilling plan to assassinate a high government official and sabotage the Brazilian-American alliance by sinking a Rio-bound passenger ship—possibly the same one that Hattie's own sister is traveling on.

With this, Hattie is catapulted back into the delicate dance of espionage. But her fragile safety net suddenly evaporates when her agency contact goes dark. Forced to take matters into her own hands, Hattie uses her cover as a singer in a risky bid to gather crucial intelligence.

Alone in the field and with her family in danger, Hattie must cultivate unconventional contacts and trust uneasy alliances in order to protect her loved ones...and save hundreds of innocent lives.

ACKNOWLEDGMENTS

Thank you, Barbara Gould, my plotting partner in crime, for serving as the best sounding board I could ever ask for.

Thank you, Fran, Gaile, Lana, Kristianne, and Nancy, my incredible crew of beta readers, for slugging through my rough-as-sandpaper first draft and giving an unvarnished critique. Every comment whipped this story into shape.

Finally, to my family. Thank you for loving me...and the endless snacks.

ABOUT THE AUTHOR

A late bloomer, award-winning author Stacy Lynn Miller took up writing after retiring from the Air Force. Her twenty years of toting a gun and police badge, tinkering with computers, and sleuthing for clues as an investigator form the foundation of her Lexi Mills thriller series, as well as her Manhattan Sloane novels. She is visually impaired, a proud stroke survivor, mother of two, tech nerd, chocolate lover, and terrible golfer with a hole-in-one. When you can't find her writing, she'll be golfing or drinking wine (sometimes both) with friends and family in Northern California.

Sign up for Stacy Lynn Miller's reader list at severnriverbooks.com

Printed in the United States
by Baker & Taylor Publisher Services